THE DESPERADO

It wasn't Talbert Came.
sheriff's son, got in trouble with some Texas bluebellies, . ,
just naturally come after Tall as well. After all, Tall is a
known hothead who had clubbed a carpetbagger. Leaving
his girl behind, Tall and Ray take off for the hills and lay
low for a bit, until Ray decides to head back and face the
law. Now, Tall considers himself a peace-loving man, but
when he returns to find that Yankee soldiers have killed his
pa, he naturally has to even the score. But this score takes a
lot of evening, and pretty soon Tall is on the run. That's
when he meets Pappy Garrett, a veteran outlaw who takes
him under his wing and teaches him the tricks of shooting—
and staying alive. Tall's gun seems to take on a life of its own
as one score after another gets settled the hard way. Now,
like Pappy, Tall's a wanted man with a price on his head—
and the only peace to be found is the peace of the grave.

A NOOSE FOR THE DESPERADO

"It had been a long trail from Texas…" But now Tall
Cameron finds himself in Ocotillo near the Mexican border,
in a small town controlled by a gang of thieves. The fat man,
Basset, controls the set-up, but a corrupt Marshall named
Kreyler makes it all possible. The gang ambushes the
Mexican smugglers who come out of the hills laden with
silver. Basset wants Tall to join the gang and Tall reluctantly
agrees. But he runs into trouble before he even gets started
by attracting the unwanted attention of Black Joseph's girl,
Marta. Black Joseph is an Indian gun-slinger who'd just as
soon kill you as look at you. And Marta has got a helluva
temper herself. Tall has never been one to back down from a
fight. But this time he's fallen into a veritable snake pit, with
no one to trust but himself and his two 45s.

The Desperado

• • • • • • • • •

A Noose for the Desperado

Clifton Adams

Introduction by Bud Elder

Stark House Press • Eureka California

THE DESPERADO / A NOOSE FOR THE DESPERADO

Published by Stark House Press
1315 H Street
Eureka, CA 95501, USA
griffinskye3@sbcglobal.net
www.starkhousepress.com

THE DESPERADO
Originally published by Gold Medal Books, Fawcett Publications, Inc.,
New York, and copyright © 1950 by Clifton Adams.

A NOOSE FOR THE DESPERADO
Originally published by Gold Medal Books, Fawcett Publications, Inc.,
New York, and copyright © 1951 by Clifton Adams.

"Clifton Adams, Trailboss of Western Fiction"
copyright © 2017 by Bud Elder

ISBN-13: 978-1-944520-35-9

Cover art by Greg Shepard
Book design by Mark Shepard, SHEPGRAPHICS.COM

First Stark House Press Edition: November 2017

FIRST EDITION

Clifton Adams, Trailboss of Western Fiction

By Bud Elder

When once asked how he would describe himself, film director John Ford answered, "I make Westerns." So, ok, Clifton Adams wrote Westerns, a lot of them, over 50 novels and some 125 short stories. He wrote so many Westerns that he had to give himself a lot of names to avoid confusion. Ever see a Western written by Clay Randall? Jonathan Gant? Matt Kincaid? All were Clifton Adams.

An adapted quote from *Butch Cassidy and the Sundance Kid* seems appropriate:

"Clifton Adams had vision, while many of his peers wore bifocals."

American Western novels were, before the turn of the century, known as "penny dreadfuls" and, later, "dime novels." The first of these cheaply made page turners was published in 1860 with the unfortunate title *Malaeska: The Indian Wife of the White Hunter*. Also printed for mass consumption at this time were extremely fictionalized stories of derring do, featuring real life adventurers Billy the Kid, Buffalo Bill, Wyatt Earp and Jesse James. One imagines even now the young buckaroo reading in his bed by candlelight, under the covers so his parents don't know he's awake, his imagination wild with heroes and villains

From these yarn spinnings came the age of pulp magazines, sporting names like Cowboy Stories, Ranch Romances and Star Western and within those covers writers Max Brand practiced their craft while essential characters like Hopalong Cassidy cornered their first miscreants.

Throughout the decade of the 40s, readers saw the maturation of Western literature, with the publication of *The Ox-Bow Incident*, *The Big Sky*, and *The Way West*, all adapted into the movies.

Speaking of which, it was at the local bijou where Westerns peaked before sliding into mundane and unimaginative weekly television. On the silver screen in the 1950s a blur developed between the good guys and the bad guys in films like *The Naked Spur*, directed by Anthony Mann and starring James Stewart, the first of five Westerns made in partnership between the two, and *Seven Men From Now*, which would launch seven movies made with director Budd Boetticher and actor Randolph Scott.

It is within this so called "adult" era of Western fiction that Clifton Adams earned his spurs, writing an impossibly prolific 19 short stories in 1948 alone, beginning with "Empire of the Broken Gunmen," and then turning to novels in 1950.

Adams and others flourished in light of a rather new publishing phenomenon, the paperback novel, a concept which quickly took the place of pulp magazines.

This relatively new method of reading (paperbacks were originally printed overseas in the late 19th century) fit the lifestyle surrounding World War II: readership was vast, what with those in the military or shift workers on the home front, enjoying books that were inexpensive, portable and available everywhere, from bus and train stations to the local drug store and five and ten.

And, while the first incarnation of American paperbacks featured classic literature by Dickens and the like, it wasn't very long before paperback originals emerged, as pulp writers with their own predilections and talents switched to novel writing. Pick your poison, from science fiction to whodunnits and all in between. Want a dirty book? Make sure you have a brown paper bag. (How about this—literary giant Treska Torres published *Women's Barracks* in 1950, the first ever pulp lesbian novel.)

Founders of such paperback houses as Gold Medal or Ballantine or Ace (Clifton Adams wrote for all of these) were visionaries who knew to strike when the proverbial iron was hot. Gold Medal went from 35 titles in 1950 to 66 titles the next year.

Think of it this way: paperback originals were not unlike "B" pictures of the day, shorn of high mindedness and loaded with button pushing, spare plots, familiar characters and "see it coming down Broadway" endings. There were for sure unexceptional and dreadful paperbacks—the same with programmers—but when either resonated, when it all clicked, there was and is artistic expression arising from their modest intentions. There were few concerns by those responsible about making social statements or changing the world.

Heaven forbid that one espoused what Clifton Adams perceived as pretension or morality when the writer was within earshot—that same person usually received a verbal butt kicking.

Adams himself said this about the melding of creativity and commerce.

"There's only one way to approach the kind of writing I do," he once said, "and that's a business."

"I'm not selling art, I'm selling entertainment."

According to those who knew him, Clifton Adams was, well, a pistol. A character—persnickety and exacting.

Adams was an intellectual and a cultural beacon. He learned to cook while serving in the 2nd Armored Division across North Africa and Europe and, postwar, food and its preparation became a passion. He even wrote an article called "My Secret Sideline" for the *Roundup* magazine of the Western Writers of America where he described his culinary origins:

"The first Adams Rule of Cookery goes like this—whatever you do to C-ration stew can only be an improvement."

Our hero was born in Comanche, Oklahoma December 1, 1919, a piece of heaven in the southwestern portion of the Sooner state that was but a dirt clod's throw away from the city of Lawton, a town that fostered one Jim Thompson, master of fictional depravity. Did these two ever meet? Both were terrific in the genre swapping business, Adams wrote several thrillers while Thompson tried his hand at Westerns. One can only imagine that their paths must have crossed. (Personal privilege—we Oklahomans are rightly proud of the literary icons who strode down our almost mean streets. Aside from Thompson and Adams, we claim Ross Thomas, Carolyn Hart, Tony Hillerman and, yes, one who left here for the bright lights of Detroit, Elmore Leonard. Lou Berney, principal player in our next generation, won the Edgar Award last year for his Oklahoma City based novel *The Long and Faraway Gone*.)

After proudly serving his country and improving C-rations, Adams, who said "there wasn't much call for machine gunners in the post war world," decided to become a writer. He used the G.I. Bill to attend the University of Oklahoma, which was already gaining a reputation for its commercial approach to creative writing. It was at OU that he met his wife Gerry. In 1965, his alma mater named him the "Oklahoma Writer of the Year."

Adams lived in Oklahoma City until the late '60s, when he and Gerry loaded up the truck and moved to San Francisco. It was here that the writer thrived, haunting jazz clubs (he himself was a drummer sometime after the war), taking cooking classes and collecting first editions, another of his hobbies. And it was here that he died, tragically young at the age of 51 on October 7, 1971.

He was a proud member of the Western Writers of America and won their highly coveted Golden Spur award twice, for *Tragg's Choice* in 1969 and for *The Last Days of Wolf Garrett* in 1970.

If Clifton Adams was, indeed, a pistol, he also wrote about those weapons, as well as others of their sort, very well—from revolvers to automatics, repeaters to shotguns and derringers to Gatlin guns to a "Ball magazine carbine, with the magazine under the barrel holding eight .50 caliber cartridges, loaded from the rear." (Actually, one of Adams' characters harbors this opinion: "A six shooter is actually a six shooter only for fools and dime novels.")

Whatever the weapon, it is fired point blank in *The Desperado* and its follow-up, *A Noose for the Desperado*, originally published by Gold Medal in 1950 and 1951.

It's not the best of times in Texas after the Civil War. From 1870 to 1873, the state suffered under the carpetbag administration of reconstructionist Governor E. J. Davis and local communities were run roughshod with the chief executive's vile and corrupt state police.

"This was Texas after the war," says Talbert (Tall) Cameron, soon to become the books' title character, "Broke and hungry and if it tried to lift itself to its knees, it got kicked in the gut for its trouble."

While Tall comes from a decent ranching family outside of town, he has already been proven a hothead because he has "beaten the hell out of a carpetbagger with the butt end of a Winchester." When a young friend of the Camerons' rides into the ranch under the cover of darkness, after having leveled a corrupt lawman on his own, it is decided that both wanted boys should light out to the Brazos country until the political winds change.

As Tall rides away from home, he leaves behind any vestige of the respectability and domesticity of his youthful dreams.

For an example, Tall remembers his one room school house and its teacher:

"Professor Bigloe's Academy held classes three times a week in the smelly parlor of Ma Simpson's boarding house, but it was the only school in John's City so it was considered quite the thing."

"They said Old Man Bigloe had been a professor at the University of Virginia before the kicked him out for drunkenness. He always kept a bottle inside the breast pocket of his frock coat and he couldn't get through a spelling lesson without stepping back to Ma Simpson's kitchen three or four times to take a nip."

One doesn't have to be a literature major to understand what extraordinary talent Clifton Adams had for developing even minor characters.

Along the road, the two young men cross paths with an outlaw named Pappy Garret, known to them by reputation.

"Pappy Garret was one of those men that you hear about all your life but you never see. The stories they told about him were almost as wild as the ones about Pecos Bill or if you lived in the north country, Paul Bunyon. There wasn't a state in the southwest that hadn't put a price on his head."

It would have been within most authors' creative juices to make the character of Pappy a sentimental old cuss, with a secretly held heart of gold, admirably mentoring his new young, impressionistic charge, Tall Cameron. It is Adams' prerogative, and distinctive voice, to instead make Pappy an unrepentant, selfish villain who turns Tall into the vicious killer he will remain the rest of this life.

It's as though Shane had heeded young Joey's cries of "come back" and gave his charge brutal lessons in the ways of the west.

Credit Adams' masterful storytelling skills that, as Tall kills in either self-defense or revenge, little puffs of his soul are blasted out of the gun along with bullets. The reader begins to feel a sense of dread even as Pappy continues to encourage his young charge to perfect his shooting skills; all this isn't going to end well.

In the act of stealing Tall's horse Red, an outlaw named Creyton is the first character to feel the young man's wrath.

"Everything was so cut and dried that there wasn't any use thinking about it. I dropped to my knees with one of my new .44s in my hand. It all happened before Red could jump. I felt the pistol kick twice in my hand, the shots crowding right on top of Creyton's and something told me there was no use wasting anymore bullets."

After the shooting, Tall goes on:

"It had all happened too fast to make much of an impression on me at first. But now I was beginning to get it. I backed up and swallowed to keep my stomach out of my throat. I hadn't known that a man could die like that. Just a flick of a finger, enough to pull a trigger and he's dead. It's as easy as that."

By *A Noose for the Desperado*, Tall, a wanted man with a vile legend of his own, even at the tender age of 19, rides into the corrupted town of Ocotillo, Arizona, and uses his now unscrupulous wiles to become a sort of crime boss. This set up is not dissimilar from the Continental Op's Poisonville adventures in Dashiell Hammett's *Red Harvest*.

It's a paranoid, dysfunctional Tall who walks into an Ocotillo saloon after months on horseback. Here he meets a genteel juicehead named Bama, for his home state, who says this about the one dog town in which Tall Cameron's next adventures will be held:

"Welcome to Ocotillo," Bama said as if reading leisurely from a book, "the garden spot of hell, the last refuge of the damned, the sanctuary of killers and thieves and real badmen and would be badmen; the home of the money starved, the cruel, the brute and the kill crazy."

For this recitation, Tall thinks of Bama as a "queer galoot."

Neither *The Desperado* or *A Noose for the Desperado* have endings in which any character seems to be happy—call it "noir on the range."

How about this? Tall Cameron's character has a somewhat similar arc as does, believe it or not, Michael Corleone. Both began as wide eyed neophytes and then piece by piece turn into self-loathing killers who abide by no societal restrictions, pushing away all who care for them. (It should be noted that Mario Puzo admitted to close friends and peers that *The Godfather* was itself based on a Western—*Heritage of the Desert*, written in 1910 by Zane Gray.)

Donald E. Westlake, also known as Richard Stark, wrote a series of books featuring a hard bitten thief called "Parker" and these offer textbook examples of serious action and character and plot development in few words. Lean and mean. And he learned much from Clifton Adams.

"One of the early Gold Medals, a beautiful western by Clifton Adams called *The Desperado* was a novel with that same compact, understated and almost reluctant treatment of violence that first introduced me to the notion of the character adapting to his forced separation from normal society," he said.

Maybe Adams isn't better known to the American public because there seemed to be a disconnect between his work and Hollywood, although there was a movie based on *The Desperado* released in 1954 under the same name. The DVD is available as a made-on-demand disc from Warner Archive, who preserves and keeps this sort of thing.

Fans of the novel won't be too disappointed in the picture, a very low budget affair from Allied Artists—at least not at first. There's still those awful state policemen ordering everyone around and "Tom" not "Tall" Cameron and Ray Novak irk the boys in blue so much that they must leave town under the cover of darkness. Along the trail they meet "Sam" not "Pappy" Garrett and for another act or two the plot streamlines the book pretty well. Then things go to heck in a hand-basket and any similarities with the book ride out of town.

Wayne Morris, an old hand at "B" pictures like this, plays Garrett without too much menace and Jimmy Lydon looks about ten years too old for Cameron. There are familiar faces throughout like Beverly Garland and Lee Van Cleef and, come to think of it, there's enough authentic Western gibberish and clichés to keep the 80-minute movie watchable.

One hopes Adams took the Hollywood money and skedaddled out of town himself.

Students at the University of Oklahoma required to study Sooner state history from a longtime professor of the subject were asked to answer one question for the final exam.

"You're a rock on the ground in Oklahoma before the turn of the century—what do you see?"

Clifton Adams, as fast with his pen as his characters were on the draw, was that rock.

—July 2017
Purcell, Oklahoma

Bud Elder is the Minister of Culture for the state of Oklahoma. And an awful liar.

The Desperado
. . . .
Clifton Adams

Chapter 1

I awoke suddenly and lay there in the darkness, listening to the rapid, faraway thud of hoofbeats. The horse was traveling fast, and occasionally the rhythmic gait would falter and become uneven, then catch and come on again in the direction of the ranch house. It was a tired horse. It had been pushed hard and for too long. I could tell by the way it was running.

Pa had heard it too. I heard the bedsprings screech downstairs as he got up. Then the old wall clock began to clang monotonously. I didn't bother to count the strokes, but I knew it must be twelve o'clock. The hoofbeats were getting louder now.

I got up and pulled on my pants. I found my boots under the bed and stuffed my feet into them without bothering to light the lamp. Then, holding onto the banister, I felt my way downstairs and into the parlor.

Pa was standing at the front door, a slight breeze coming through the doorway and flapping the white cotton nightshirt against his bare legs. He was standing there peering into the darkness, holding a shotgun in the crook of his arm.

"Tall?" he said without looking around.

"Yes, sir."

"You better get that forty-four out of the bureau drawer. It's in there with my shirts somewhere. You can find it."

I said, "Yes, sir," and turned and felt my way into the downstairs bedroom that Pa and Ma used. Ma was sitting up in bed, her nightgown a white blob in the darkness and her nightcap a smaller blob above it. I went to the bureau and started feeling around in the drawer until I found the pistol.

"Talbert," Ma said anxiously, "what is it, son?"

"Just a rider, Ma. Nothing to worry about."

"What are you looking for there in the bureau?"

"Pa's pistol," I said. "Just in case."

She didn't say anything for a moment. But she was worried. She had been worried ever since I'd got into that scrape with the state police down at Garner's Store. But that had been a long time ago, almost six months. Anyway, I hadn't killed anybody; I'd just beaten hell out of a carpetbagger with the butt end of a Winchester. There had been a big stir about it for a while, but Pa had fixed it up with the bluebelly police for fifty head of three-year-old cattle. So I wasn't worried about that.

I said, "Rest easy, Ma. It's probably one of the neighbors. Maybe somebody's sick."

She still didn't say anything, so I went back into the parlor where Pa was. We heard the horse pull up and scamper nervously, and we knew the rider was swinging open the rail gate about two hundred yards south of the house.

Pa said, "Tall?" That's the way Pa would do when he was worrying something in his mind. He'd call your name and wait for you to answer before he'd come out and say what he was thinking.

"Yes, sir," I said.

"Tall, you haven't been up to anything, have you? You haven't got into any trouble that you haven't told us about?"

"No, sir," I said.

I could feel Pa relax. Then he reached over and roughed up my hair, the way he used to do when I was just a kid, when he was feeling good. Pa could stand just about anything but a liar, and he knew I'd tell him the truth, no matter what it was.

The rider was coming on now, and we could hear the horse blowing and grunting. The rider swung down at the hitching rack by our front porch and called out:

"Mr. Cameron! Tall!"

It was Ray Novak's voice. I would have known it anywhere. He was two or three years older than me, and his pa used to be town marshal in John's City, before the scalawags and turncoats came in and elected their own man. Ray was old enough to have fought a year for the Confederacy, and that set him apart from the rest of us who had been too young. Ordinarily, he was an easygoing, likable man, and the only thing I had against him was that he had been seeing a little too much of Laurin Bannerman. But that wasn't important. I knew how Laurin felt, and I knew I didn't have anything to be afraid of on that score. From Ray Novak or anybody else.

Pa pushed the screen door open and stepped out on the front porch. "Ray?" he said. "Ray Novak?"

"Yes, sir," Ray said.

"Well, come on in," Pa said. "Tall, light the table lamp, will you? And see if the kitchen stove's still warm. Pull the coffee pot up on the front lid if it is."

I lit the lamp and went back to the kitchen. The fire had gone out in the stove. When I came back to the parlor, Ray was saying, "I'm afraid

I can't stay, Mr. Cameron. The truth is I just stopped by to see if I could change my horse for a fresh mount. That animal of mine is about played out." He saw me then and we nodded to each other.

Ray Novak didn't look scared exactly, but he looked worried. He took off his hat and ran his fingers through thick, straw-colored hair. "I played the fool down in John's City this afternoon," he said. "I let myself get suckered into a scrape with the police. I guess I'll have to get out of the country for a while, until things cool off a little."

Pa looked at him sharply. "You ... didn't kill anybody, did you, Ray?"

Killing a state policeman in Texas, in 1869, was the same as buying a one-way ticket to a hanging. The bluebellies from the North had their own judges and juries, and their verdict was always the same.

But Ray shook his head. "It was just a fist fight," he said. "But they're pretty riled up. I was in the harness shop getting a splice made in a stirrup strap and this private cavalryman came in and started passing remarks about all the families around John's City—all the families that amounted to anything before the war. When he started on 'that goddamn Novak white trash that used to be town marshal,' I hit him. I busted a couple of teeth, I think. I expect a detachment of cavalry will be along pretty soon, looking for me. I don't aim to be around."

Pa nodded soberly. "It was a damn fool thing to do all right," he said. "And you won't be able to fix it with the police this time. First Tall, and now you. The Yankees'll feel bound to do something about it this time."

Ray looked down at his feet and shifted uncomfortably. "Yes, sir," he said. "That's about the way I figured it. That's one reason I came by your place. If they don't find me they might get to remembering Tall and start on him again." Then he looked up at me, his big bland face as serious as a preacher's. "I'm sorry, Tall, I didn't figure to get you mixed up in it."

"What the hell," I said. "The only thing I'm sorry about is that you didn't put a bullet in the bluebelly's gut."

"Tall?" Pa said.

"Yes, sir."

"Now just hold your head. Ray's right. This could be serious for both of you. We better take a little time and figure something out. Ray, have you figured on anything?"

"I thought maybe I'd go up to the Panhandle for a while, sir. I've got an older brother up there that has a little spread. I could work with him through the spring gathering season and come back in the summer. That ought to be time enough to let it blow over."

Pa thought about it, standing there in his nightshirt, still holding that shotgun in the crook of his arm. "Maybe," he said. "But the Panhandle isn't far enough. Tall's got an uncle down on the Brazos. You boys could stay there. I could write you a letter when it looks all right to come back."

Maybe I was still half asleep. Anyway, it was just coming to me what they were talking about. I said, "Just a minute, Pa. I don't aim to run. This isn't my scrape, it's Ray's."

"Tall?"

"Yes, sir," I said from force of habit.

"Now listen to me," Pa said soberly. "Pretty soon they'll be coming. When they don't find Ray they're going to be mad, and it won't take them long to remember that carpetbagger you clubbed with a rifle stock. You know what kind of a chance you'll have if the scalawags decide to bring it to court."

For a minute I didn't say anything. I knew Pa was right. If they didn't find Ray, they would be coming for me. The smart thing to do would be to get out of the country for a while. But knowing it didn't make me like it.

I liked things just the way they were. I liked it here on the ranch—being able to ride over to the Bannerman spread every day or so to see Laurin, going into John's City once a month when they held the dances in Community Hall. I liked it just fine right where I was, and I hated the idea of being chased away by a bunch of damned Yankee bluebellies and blacks who had been slaves only a few years ago. And pretty soon some of that hate began to direct itself at Ray Novak.

I looked at Ray and he knew how I was beginning to feel about it. He was sorry. But a hell of a lot of good that was going to do. He stood there shifting from one foot to the other, uncomfortably. He was a big man, and he couldn't have been more than twenty-one years old. But that didn't make him young. In this country a boy started being a man as soon as he could strap on a gun. And about the first thing a boy did, after he learned to walk and ride, was to strap on a gun.

Before I could say what I was thinking, before Ray Novak could put his discomfort into words, Ma came out of the bedroom and stood looking at us with worried eyes. Ma was a thin, work-weary woman, not really old, but looking old. There were deep lines around her pale eyes that came from worry and trying to gouge a living from this wild land. Ma had been pretty as a girl. There were faded pictures of her in an old album that gave you an idea how she must have looked when she married Pa. The pictures showed a young girl dressed in the rather daring fashion of the day—those low-cut dresses that all the great ladies of the Confederacy used to wear with such a casual air, as they sat queenlike, smiling and pouring tea from silver pots into delicate china cups. It was hard to believe that Ma had been one of those great ladies once. Her father had been a rich tobacco buyer in Virginia, but he lost everything in the war and died soon afterward.

I never saw Virginia myself. And those pictures in the album were just pictures to me, but I guess Pa still saw her as she had looked then, because something happened to him every time he looked at her. His wind-reddened face softened and his stern eyes became gentle—even as they did now as he saw her standing in the doorway.

She stood there, holding her cotton wrap-around together, smiling quickly at Ray.

"Good evening, Ray," she said.

"Good evening, Mrs. Cameron," Ray said uneasily.

"Mother," Pa said, "why don't you go back to bed? I'll be along in a few minutes."

But she shook her head. "I want to know what it's about. Tell me, Rodger, because I'll find out sooner or later."

"It's nothing serious," Pa said gently. "Ray just had some trouble in John's City with the state police. It's nothing to worry about."

"I don't understand," Ma said vaguely. "What has that to do with Talbert?"

"I just think it's best if they both go away for a while, until it blows over. There's been no killing. Just a fist fight. But there's no telling what the Yankee troopers will do while they're riled up. I'll send Ray and Tall down to my brother's place on the Brazos. You know how the police shift from one place to another. In a few months there won't be anybody around John's City to remember or hold a grudge, and then they can come back."

She considered it carefully, but I knew she wouldn't question Pa's word. That's the way it always had been.

"All right, Rodger," she said at last. "Whatever you say."

Her voice was heavy and edged with hopelessness. She had had great plans for me. Even before I was born she had started making plans to send me to the University of Virginia and make a lawyer out of me, or maybe a preacher. But the war had put an end to that. There wasn't anybody in Texas, except the scalawags and bureau agents, that had money enough to send their children off to places like Virginia. And I hadn't made things any easier for Ma. I had come into the world in the midst of great pain, almost killing her, and I had been a source of pain ever since. Like the time I cut Criss Bagley open with a pocketknife. She had tried to comfort me and to understand, and I had tried to explain to her. But I couldn't explain when I didn't know myself. I just knew that Criss had been coming at me with an elm club and I knew I had to get it away from him, one way or another. Criss was twelve and I was ten, and he outweighed me by thirty pounds or more, so the knife seemed the only way.

I remember the way he looked, standing there with his eyes wide in amazement—before the pain—staring down at his opened belly. We had been swimming down at Double-dare Hole, a muddy, deep hole in the arroyo that cut across our land, and in the spring and early summer it was almost always full. It was June, I remember, and four of us had stopped there on our way from school. And one of the kids—I don't know which one—tied knots in Criss's clothes, and that was the way it started. He thought I did it. He came out of the water yelling, "Goddamn you, Tall Cameron!" And I remember saying, "Don't goddamn me! I didn't tie knots in your dirty damn clothes!"

For a while we just stood there glaring at each other. Criss was naked and dripping, and fat around the belly and hips, like a girl. I had already dried myself in the sun and had my clothes on. The other two boys climbed up on the bank, grinning. Then one of them said, "What's the matter, Criss? You afraid of Tall? You just goin' to stand there and let him get away with tyin' knots in your clothes?"

Criss turned on the boy. "Keep your goddamn mouth shut. I guess I know how to take care of Tall Cameron ... unless he wants to untie my clothes, that is."

I know now that Criss really didn't want to fight. But I didn't know it then. I could have untied his clothes and that would have been the end of it. Instead, I said, "You can untie them yourself if you want them untied. I don't guess I'm bound to wait on you."

Criss was one of those people who never tanned in the summer, no matter how much he stayed out in the sun. His hair was kind of a dirty yellow, and so were his eyebrows; and his skin was as pink and soft as a baby's bottom. He stood there waiting for me to do something about his clothes. His pale little eyes shut down to angry slits.

"I'll count to ten," he said tightly. "If you don't have my clothes untied by then, it's goin' be too bad."

"You can count to ten thousand," I said. "I told you I didn't do it."

So he started counting. And I didn't move. And when he had finished he said, "All right, goddamn you!" and started toward me.

I had never fought Criss before. I'd never wanted to because of his size, but I wasn't afraid of him. And, after the first swing he took, I saw that it was going to be easy. He was big and fat and clumsy, and not very smart. I ducked under his fist and slammed him right in the middle of his pink, fat belly. He eyes flew open in surprise and he made a sound like a horse breaking wind. I hit him again in the face, and once more in the belly, and he sat down. He didn't fall or stumble. He just sat down. And when he got up again he had that stick in his hand.

I don't even remember getting the knife out of my pocket. I just remember Criss flailing away with that club, catching me once on the left shoulder and numbing it. Then he came in to hit me again, and that was when I cut him. Right across the belly. You could see layers of fat meat as the gash began to open. And at first little droplets of bright blood appeared like sweat on the raw edges of the cut. Then Criss sat down again, very carefully, and then he lay down and began to cry.

"Goddamn you, Tall! You killed me!"

For a minute I thought maybe I had. The blood was coming faster now, oozing out of the white gash and over his pink skin. I still wasn't scared, but I knew I'd have to get out of John's City if he died, and I would have to do it before the town marshal heard about it. That was when Ray Novak's pa was marshal, old Martin Novak, and he had a reputation for tracking killers. So I left Criss where he was, there on the ground, crying, and ran all the way to our ranch house.

I told Pa what had happened, and I remember him staring at me for a long, long time and not saying anything. He grew to be an old man in those few minutes. And he had been an old man ever since. At last he said, "Tall?"

"Yes, sir."

"You go to the house. You go to your room and stay there. Don't tell your ma anything about it until I get back. Give me your word."

I had to give him my word. And I had to stay with it, because that's the way it was between me and Pa. I went to the house, and from my room I watched Pa get the spring wagon hitched and head down toward the arroyo.

Criss didn't die, but there were some anxious days. Old man Bagley swore that he would kill me, and Pa too, if Criss died. But he didn't die. He stayed in bed for about two months and then he got up as well as anybody, except for an eight-inch scar across his belly, just below the navel.

I tried to explain to Ma the way it happened—the way Criss had come at me with that stick—but it wasn't any use. She would always end up by crying, "But son, why didn't you run from him? Why didn't you untie his clothes for him?" And I couldn't tell her. I didn't know myself.

So, for some reason, that was what I thought about as Ma stood there in the doorway holding her wrap-around together, and looking at Pa, and me, and Ray Novak. As she said:

"All right, Rodger. Whatever you say."

I said, "It's going to be all right, Ma. We'll just put in the spring working, and come home in the summer."

For a moment I forgot that I didn't want to leave the John's City country, that I didn't want to go away from Laurin, that I was mad at Ray Novak for bringing all this on. I wanted to see Ma smile more than anything else.

And she did, finally, but it was weak, not reaching her eyes. She said, "Of course, son. Will you be going ... right away?"

I looked at Pa and he nodded. "Yes," he said. "Right away."

Ma went into the kitchen and we heard her shaking the grate on the cookstove. Pa said, "Ray, did you come by your pa's place?"

"No, sir," Ray said. "I figured that would be the first place the posse would look for me."

Pa nodded soberly. "You did right. I'll go over and let him know that you're all right. I'll do it tomorrow."

"I'd be much obliged, sir."

Pa went into the bedroom and put on his pants and boots. He came out stuffing his nightshirt in his pants. Without saying anything, he handed me a cartridge belt with an open holster attached to it. I buckled the belt on and he slid the .44 into the holster, then I went upstairs to change my own nightshirt for a regular shirt and a mackinaw.

The whole thing struck me as something out of a dream. Only a few minutes ago I had been sound asleep, with not a worry in the world, unless maybe it was figuring out a way to see Laurin more often. And now I was getting ready to leave. Going down on the Brazos to a strange country that I had never seen before. Just because Ray Novak lost his fool head and hit a Yankee cavalryman.

I heard the front door open and close, and there was a thud of boots and a bright sound of spurs as Pa and Ray went out to the barn to get the horses ready. There was a familiar stirring sound downstairs,

wooden spoon against crock bowl, and I knew Ma was mixing a bat-
ter of some kind. Ma was like most women. In case of death or any
other disaster, her first thought was of food. The women themselves
never eat the food, but cooking gives them something to do. It takes
their minds off their troubles. Maybe it's the same as a man getting
drunk to forget his troubles. A woman cooks. Anyway, I knew Ray and
I wouldn't go hungry on our trip to the Brazos.

I went downstairs and outside, and the night was as clean and sharp
as a new knife. I stood out there for a few minutes, in the yard, looking to the west where the Bannerman spread was. I thought about Laurin. I let myself wonder if Laurin would miss me. If she would miss Ray
Novak—even a little bit. Goddamn Ray Novak, anyway.

Pa and Ray were working quietly in the barn, in the sickly orange light
of an oil lantern. Pa had cut out two horses from the holding corral,
and I saw immediately that one of them was the big copper-colored
gelding that was registered in the horse book as Red Hawk. But he was
just "Red" to me, and beautiful as only a purebred Morgan can be. Ray
was throwing a saddle up on a sturdy little black and Pa was taking
care of Red, patting him gently and crooning into his nervous pointed
little ears.

I came up and slapped Red on his smooth glossy rump and he
switched his fine head around and glared at me with a caustic eye. Red
was bigger than most Morgans; almost sixteen hands high and king
every inch of the way. The extra height was mostly in his hard-muscled
legs, which gave him speed. A barrel chest and a heart as big as Texas
gave him the stamina to do a hard day's work and not complain, although he had been bred as a show horse. An Eastern pilgrim had
brought him down from Vermont or Massachusetts or somewhere two
summers ago when the horse had been a two-year-old, and it had been
love at first sight between Red and Pa. Pa had bought him on the spot,
and Ma and me still didn't know what Red cost.

Pa looked up at me as he tightened the cinch under Red's belly. "I
guess Red will get you to Brazos country," he said, "and get you back
again."

I didn't know what to say. I knew how Pa felt about that blueblood,
and there were other horses on the place that would do just as well for
me. But I found the good sense to keep my mouth shut. Pa was giving
Red to me and he wanted to do it his own way.

After a while, Ma came out with some things for me done up in a
blanket roll, and she had a grub sack filled with coffee and bacon and

meal and salt and some fresh-cooked cornbread. And there was a small deep skillet done up in the blanket roll. I couldn't help grinning a little. It was more like getting ready for a picnic or a camp meeting than making a cross-country run with a posse on our tails.

I said, "Thanks, Ma. Now don't you worry." Then I kissed her cheek, and her skin was dry and rough against my lips. Her eyes were wide— a little too wide, and liquid-looking, but not a tear spilled out. She would wait until I was gone for that. I swung up on Red and Pa handed up a sealed white envelope.

"This is for your Uncle George Cameron," he said quietly. "Give it to him when you get to the ranch. It tells him who you are and asks him to give both of you a job of work through the spring season. It doesn't say anything about the police trouble. I don't figure there's any use worrying him about that."

He stopped and raked his fingers through his thinning hair. Pa had been a handsome man not many years before, and part of that handsomeness could still be seen. Men hold up better than women in this country. But he looked tired and old as he reached up to shake hands with me. Most of the age was in his eyes.

"Good-by, Tall. Be careful of yourself."

"Sure, Pa."

"Do you think you can find the place all right?"

"We can't miss the Brazos if we ride east," I said. "We'll head south and then ask questions if we have to."

He nodded. "I guess that's about right. Good-by, Ray. I'll let your pa know."

"Good-by, sir. Thank you."

We sat there for a minute, wondering if there was anything else to say. Then we all began to hear the noise of complex rattle and movement. For an instant I listened and looked at Ray Novak. He was thinking the same as I was. There was a rattle of loose steel and the aching screech of saddle leather, all muted and deadened by night and the distance. Then came the thudding of regimented horses, and we didn't have to be told that they were cavalry horses.

And still we sat there as the sound of horses and the rattle of cavalry sabers got closer. And I thought grimly, They sure as hell didn't waste time! Then I raked Red with the blunted rowels of my spurs, and we jumped out of the barn and into the darkness, with Ray Novak right behind.

The detachment of troopers saw us, or heard us. Somebody, an offi-

cer probably, bellowed out, "Halt! In the name of the United States
Army!"

I sank the steel into Red and we jumped out a full length in front of
Ray and the black. The cavalry recovered quickly and there were
more bellowed orders in the darkness. Then they were coming after us,
at full charge, from the way it sounded.

Chapter 2

It's fine to feel a horse like Red under you. I bent over his neck and
felt the long hard muscles along his shoulders as he began to stretch out
in a long, flowing, ground-eating stride. Then the cavalry started
shooting, but that didn't worry me much. They couldn't hit anything
in the darkness unless somebody got pretty lucky. And Ray and I had
one advantage over them. We knew the country.

We headed south first, toward some low rolling hills where the
mesquite and scrub oak was so thick that it was hard to get through,
even in the daytime, if you didn't know your way around. Red was running like a well-oiled machine now, and Ray's black horse was about
two jumps behind us. The black was a good horse, but he was used
mostly for cutting cattle and I knew he wouldn't hold up at the pace
we were going for more than a half a mile. So I turned in the saddle
and yelled back at Ray Novak.

"We'll head for the arroyo and take Daggert's Road!"

Ray yelled something, but the wind snatched the words away before
they got to me. Anyway, I figured he understood. It was the natural
thing to do if you knew the country, and Ray knew it as well as I did.
We went barreling across the flatland, pulling away from the cavalry
a little, but not enough to get lost. And then we blasted into the hills,
into the dagger-thorned chaparral and clawlike scrub oaks that grew
as thick as weeds. In the pale moonlight, we were able to look for familiar trails and find them, but I hated to think what Red's glossy coat
was going to look like when we came out of it.

The cavalry made up some lost time as we thrashed our way through
the brush. They were coming into shooting range again, they had their
carbines out now, pumping lead in our general direction, and I began
to be afraid that somebody was going to get lucky after all if they kept
that up for long.

But we blasted our way through the brush and went barreling down the slope again toward the ugly dark gash in the land below us, the arroyo. The spring rains hadn't come yet, so the sandy weed-grown bed was still dry as we slid our horses down the steep bank. The shooting had stopped again. I figured the cavalry had hit the brush and was having its hands full there. So we pounded on down the dry wash and finally we came to what we were looking for, a cutaway in the bank of the wash, only you had to know where it was to see it, especially at night. It was grown over with weeds and scrub trees, and it stayed that way the year around except for maybe two months in the spring when the rains up north set the wash to flowing.

That was Daggert's Road. If you knew where to look, there was room enough to squeeze a horse through the opening, through the hanging vines and scrubs, and you entered into a kind of a trail that wound up into the hill country. If you followed the trail far enough you'd find a little lean-to shack against a hillside, falling to pieces and rotten with years. Old-timers would tell you that shack used to be Sam Daggert's headquarters, that he used to hide out there after making one of his raids on the wagon trains crossing the Santa Fe Trail.

I don't know about the Sam Daggert part, but I know the cabin is there, and somebody must have made that trail for some reason. I used to ride out this way with Pa sometimes, looking for strays. And, kid-like, I would poke around the shack looking for buried treasure, or maybe skeletons or guns. But all I ever found was a few soggy, blackened bits of paper that might have been paper cartridges at one time.

Well, Sam Daggert or not, whoever made the trail, I was grateful to him. Ray Novak was first to go through the opening because his black was smaller than Red. Then I shoved Red through, and took a minute to rearrange the vines. We could hear the cavalry just beginning to jump their horses down the bank of the wash.

We waited where we were until they pounded past us, running south in the bend of the arroyo. And for a minute there I felt pretty good about it. I was pretty pleased with myself. I wasn't scared, for one thing, and hadn't been, through the whole business. And I don't think it had entered my mind that the cavalry would catch us, and even if they had caught us, they couldn't have done anything.

It wasn't cockiness exactly. It was training. One Texan was better than a whole goddamned regiment of bluebelly Yankees. I was as sure of that as I was sure the sun would come up the next morning. The War Between the States hadn't changed that. So that was the way I thought. Only it wasn't thinking, it was knowing, and for a few minutes there

I didn't hate Ray Novak for getting me into this mess, because I was enjoying myself.

But not Ray. His face was whiter than the pale moonlight that sifted through the brush. He wiped his face on his shirt sleeve and looked at me and Red, and then at his own black horse, as if he was surprised to see that we were still in one piece.

He said finally, "I guess I didn't bargain for a thing like this."

"For a thing like what?"

"I didn't figure they'd be so worked up. You'd think I'd killed somebody, from the way they came after us."

I couldn't figure Ray Novak out. He acted scared, but I knew he wasn't—or at least I'd never known him to be scared of anything before. He sat there, looking at me with those sober eyes of his, and wiping his face. "I don't like it at all."

"For God's sake," I said, "what don't you like about it? We got away from them, didn't we?"

He didn't say anything, so I pulled Red around and nudged him forward, heading north. I could almost feel Ray stiffen in surprise.

"Now where are you going? I had an idea we were headed east."

I said, "We're going away, aren't we? That's the time for saying goodby, isn't it?"

He knew I was headed for the Bannerman spread to see Laurin before starting the long ride to the Brazos. I half expected him to go on without me. At least, I expected an argument of some kind, but strangely enough he didn't offer any. He reined the black over and fell in beside me.

The Bannerman ranch house was dark when we got there, but it wasn't long before we saw somebody light a lamp and come out on the front porch. It was Joe Bannerman, Laurin's brother, holding a big hogleg six-shooter in one hand and the lamp in the other.

Before he decided to shoot first and ask questions later, I called, "It's me, Joe—Tall Cameron. Ray Novak's here with me."

I heard him grunt in surprise as Ray and I swung around the hitching rack in the front yard, making for the back of the house.

I said, "Blow the lamp out, Joe. The cavalry's after us. I don't think they're anywhere close, but there's no use taking chances."

"What the hell have you got yourself into now?" he said. He sounded half mad at being jarred out of bed at that time of night. But the lamp went out and he padded barefoot to the end of the porch, peering at us through the darkness. "Ray Novak, is that you?" Then we heard him spit in the darkness. "Has this young heller got you mixed up in some of his shenanigans?"

Joe never liked me much. He was a lot older than Laurin, and I knew he never liked it much when I came calling. But to hell with Joe Bannerman. Laurin was the one I'd come to say good-by to.

"It's me, all right, Joe," Ray Novak said, "but the trouble we're in is my fault. Tall didn't have anything to do with it."

For a moment, Joe didn't say anything. Then, "Well, I'll be damned...."

Ray started explaining about his fight with the bluebelly back in John's City, but I didn't stay to hear about it. Just then I saw her standing there at the back door. I dropped down from the saddle and gave Red a slap on the rump, sending him on around to the back of the house.

"Tall?"

She looked like a pale ghost, or an angel, standing there in the darkness. Her voice was anxious, touched with fear. Then she pushed the screen door open and came outside. She stood there on the top step, covered in one of those pale, shapeless wrap-arounds that all women seem to reach for when they get out of bed. I had never seen her like that before. In the pale moonlight, her face seemed even more beautiful than I had remembered it, and her dark hair was unbraided, falling around her shoulders as soft as a dark mist. I stood there at the bottom of the steps, looking up at her.

"Tall," she said urgently, "something's wrong. You wouldn't be here at this time of night unless ..."

"It's nothing," I said. "We're going down on the Brazos for a spell. I wanted to say good-by, that's all."

"We?" I don't think she had known there were two of us until then.

"Me and Ray Novak," I said. "He took a swing at a bluebelly and got the cavalry on him. Now they're after both of us."

She made a startled little sound, and I wanted to reach up and put my arms around her and tell her not to worry. I'd be back. All the bluebellys north of the Rio Grande couldn't keep me away from her.

But I didn't move. Joe Bannerman would have shot me in a minute if he had caught me laying a hand on his sister while she was still in her nightclothes. And probably that was just what Joe was expecting. He moved around to the corner of the house, still talking to Ray Novak, but careful not to let me out of his sight.

She lowered her voice, but the worry and urgency were still there.

"Tall, are you sure ... are you sure that you haven't ... done anything?"

That would have made me mad if it had been anybody else. Nobody seemed to believe me when I told them that Ray Novak was the one that started all the trouble. They seemed to think that Ray Novak was incapable of getting into any trouble, especially on the wrong side of the law. With Tall Cameron, that was the thing they expected.

But I couldn't get mad at Laurin. I said, "Don't worry about me. We'll put in a spell on the Brazos, until things settle down, and then I'll be coming back. Don't forget that. I'll be back."

At last she seemed to believe me. She smiled faintly and started to come down the steps, but a sullen grunt from her brother stopped her.

Damn Joe Bannerman, anyway. And Ray Novak. This was a hell of a way for a man to say good-by to his best girl. His only girl. I heard a rustling around inside the house, and then a match flared and lighted a lampwick. That would be Old Man Bannerman coming out to see what the fuss was about, and I didn't feel like I wanted to go through the whole rigmarole again, explaining that we were in trouble and it was Ray who started it and not me.

Ray Novak called, "We'd better be riding, Tall."

I knew he was right. There was no sense in staying here and letting the bluebellies finally stumble on us.

I was standing there, feeling helpless. One moment Laurin's face was quiet and composed, and the next moment it began to break up around her eyes. Then, somehow, she was in my arms.

"Laurin!" Joe Bannerman roared. "For God's sake, haven't you got any decency?"

The moment was over almost before I knew she was there. But I felt better. I had held her in my arms for that short moment, and that was something they couldn't take away from me. It was something I could remember for the month, or six months, or whatever length of time we had to be apart.

She had jumped back, startled at her brother's bellowing. Then the back door opened again and the old man came out, and the lamplight splashed around until it seemed to me that the cavalry couldn't miss seeing it, no matter where they were. I knew it was time to start riding.

I got Red and led him around to the corner of the house. Ray Novak was already in the saddle, waiting for me. So I swung up, too.

Laurin's face was cameo-soft and pale in the lamplight, and that was the way I remembered it.

"Take care of yourself, Tall. Don't ... let anything happen."

"Don't worry. There's nothing to worry about."

"Will I hear from you?"

"Sure. Anyway, I'll be back before you know it."

Ray Novak was sitting his horse impassively. Nothing showed on his face, but I could guess at what was happening inside him. All the time we had been here, Laurin hadn't even looked at him. Only when we reined our horses around to leave did she say:

"Good-by, Ray."

And he said, "Good-by, Laurin." And we rode out of the yard. I looked back once and she was still standing there by the steps, pale and beautiful in the flickering light from the oil lamp, and I realized what a lucky guy I really was. I could even afford to feel sorry for Ray Novak.

We rode east for what must have been two hours. I figured the Yankees would be so lost by now that they would be lucky to find their way home. And, as we put distance between us and John's City, I did some thinking about Ray Novak, trying to figure out what had got into him back there at Daggert's Road.

I added together all the things I knew about him and was a little surprised when it didn't come to much. The Novak ranch had been next to ours for as long as I could remember, and I had known him all that time, or thought I had known him. We had gone to Professor Bigloe's Academy together—a hell of a fancy name, I thought, for a school that held classes three times a week in the smelly parlor of Ma Simpson's boarding house, but it was the only school anywhere near John's City, and it was considered quite the thing. They said Old Man Bigloe had been a professor at the University of Virginia before they kicked him out for drunkenness. He always kept a bottle in the inside breast pocket of his frock coat, and he couldn't get through a spelling lesson without stepping back to Ma Simpson's kitchen three or four times to take a nip. Maybe he had had a good brain once, but it was fuzzy and booze-soaked by the time he opened the academy.

Anyway, he managed to get most of us through four steps of arithmetic and some spelling and history. The history and geography came together in the same class and it was the only class that Old Man Bigloe really liked. He would get to talking about Italy, and then Rome, and finally he'd get down to Caesar and he wouldn't give a damn if you threw spit balls or not. He was a thin man with a perpetual stoop to his shoulders, and sometimes he would go for two weeks without shaving. He always got a funny look in his eyes when he got to talking about Rome and those places, and it was generally agreed that he was crazy. During classes, Ma Simpson would always sit, fat and watchful, in one corner of the parlor, peeling potatoes or paring apples. She always arranged to have a murderous-looking butcher knife in her hands, just in case Old Man Bigloe had a "spell" and tried to kill somebody. But he never did.

So that was Professor Bigloe's Academy. Professor Bigloe's Academy for Learning and Culture, if you want the whole name. We went there three times a week, Mondays, Wednesdays, and Fridays, the boys riding in on horseback. There was a lot of hell raised, and a lot of fights; but now that I came to think of it, Ray Novak hadn't figured in any of them.

Maybe it was because of his size. He was a year or two older than most of us, and big for his age anyway. But then Criss Bagley had been bigger than any of us, and that hadn't kept him out of fights. I thought about that and finally had to admit that there was something about Ray Novak—but I didn't know what—that made you think twice before starting anything with him. He always had that quiet, sober look, even as a kid, and he didn't go in much for horseplay, as most of us did. He came to Old Man Bigloe's Academy for a curious reason, it seemed to the rest of us. To learn.

And, too, Ray's pa was the town marshal, and that made him something a little different. His pa had taught him everything there was to know about guns and shooting, and he was the only boy around John's City who could throw a tin can in the air and put two .44 bullets through it before it hit the ground. I only saw him do it once, but he did it so easily and perfectly that I knew it was no accident.

I don't think I ever liked Ray Novak much after that, although I had never thought about it until now. I remember practicing with Pa's old .44, the one I was wearing now, until my thumb was raw from pulling the hammer back, but one bullet in the can was the best I could do. I think that hit me harder than anything. I didn't mind it much when Ray would make one of his occasional rides over to the Bannerman ranch—trying to act as if he was just out looking for strays, and just happened to be on that part of the range. I knew that Laurin Bannerman was the real reason for his drifting off the home range. But I also knew that he was too bashful to do anything about it, except gawk. And, anyway, Laurin was mine.

Which was fine, but it didn't tell me the reason for that scared look on Ray Novak's face back there at the arroyo, while the cavalry was pounding by.

The sky in the east began to pale and we pulled our horses up to let them blow. Ray dropped down from his saddle and stretched, and I did the same. The morning was cool, and sharp with the early-spring smell of green things. I began to think of bacon, and coffee, and fresh-cooked cornbread.

"I figure we've got about another hour of riding time," Ray said. "We'll have to start looking for a place to bed down before long."

I said, "We'll ride until we find a place."

But Ray shook his head in that sober, solemn way of his. "I don't want to run into any more cavalry or police. Not in the daylight. We're in enough trouble as it is."

I asked a question then, one I had been remembering about: "Are you afraid of trouble?"

He looked at me and answered in one word: "Yes."

Then, after thinking a moment, he went on, "I don't like this running. If we run into the state police and they recognize us there'll be a fight, and almost always when there's a fight, somebody doesn't walk away from it. That's the kind of trouble I'm afraid of. We're on the wrong side of the law."

"What law?" I said. "The Davis police? The Yankee soldiers, and the carpetbaggers, and scalawags, and bureau agents? If that's the law, I'm just as glad to be on the other side."

But he kept shaking his head. "There has to be law."

He was a nut on the subject. The law was all he knew, I guess. He had lived it, talked it, breathed it, ever since he was old enough to know what a sheriff's star was. And he couldn't remember the time when his pa hadn't worn a star. Which was all right, as far as I was concerned—I'd never heard anything against Marshal Martin Novak. But all this talk of Reconstruction Law, as the turncoats called it, was beginning to disgust me.

I said, "Look, if you're so goddamned set on law and order, what are you running for? After you hit that cavalryman why didn't you go right on down to the jail and give yourself up? You seem to be forgetting one thing: Right now I'd be back on the ranch in my own bed if it hadn't been for you. If you hadn't come running like a wall-eyed coot and got me mixed up in it. Why did you run in the first place, that's what I want to know, if you're so damned set on the law being enforced?"

The more I talked the madder I got, and I said things that I wouldn't have said if I hadn't been so hot. It was as much my fault as his. If I hadn't clubbed that carpetbagger the Yankees wouldn't have been so worked up. Ray would have got off with a few days in jail and that would have been the end of it. But now it meant six months on the work gang, if they caught him. And me too. And I didn't intend to spend six months on the work gang, no matter whose fault it was.

For a long minute Ray Novak said nothing. In the first pale light of dawn, I could see his face getting hot and red, and I knew the smart thing to do would be to let him alone. But I was wound up and my mouth was running ahead of my thinking.

"Well," I said, "what are you going to do about it?"

He just stood there, getting hotter, and doing nothing. I guess Ray Novak wasn't used to being talked to like that. He was a lot like his pa— the quiet, serious kind, commanding respect but not making a show of it. He didn't know what to do now, with an eighteen-year-old standing up and the same as calling him yellow. For a minute I thought he might go for his gun, and at that point I didn't care one way or another.

He took a deep breath and let it out slowly, and I could almost see him taking hold of himself. He said softly, "I guess we both need some sleep. We'd better be riding on."

"Just a minute," I said. "I want to know what you're going to do. You'd better know now that if we run into any law I'm not giving myself up for a spell on the work gang. If you don't feel the same way about it, we'd better split up here and now."

He gave it careful thought before answering. "Tall," he said finally, "I told you once I was sorry for dragging you into this. That's all I can do. If I had been smart, I would have given myself up in John's City. But I wasn't smart. Now it looks like we'll have to hide out for a little while. I'll hide out but I don't intend to fight the law, if it comes to that. If you don't want to ride with me, we'll split up, and no hard feelings."

He was a hard guy to hate for a long stretch of time. He was so dead serious about everything. "Oh, hell," I said, "Let's go."

So we rode on, neither of us saying anything. For a while I amused myself by thinking of the cavalry, and how foolish they must look pounding up and down the arroyo and wondering what had happened to us. I enjoyed that. It was the same as a military victory, for the war was not over in Texas. It would never be over as long as Sheridan sent men like Throckmorton and his bluebelly generals to rule Texas with soldiers. Or men like Pease, who threw out all the judges and sheriffs and mayors who might have been able to keep some semblance of law and order and put in his own scalawags who didn't give a damn for anything except to bleed the ranchers and farmers and cotton growers, and fatten their own bank accounts back in New York or Ohio or Pennsylvania or wherever they came from. And even worse, men like E. J. Davis.

E. J. Davis, the "reconstruction governor." Colonel Davis, commanding officer of the First Texas Cavalry, U.S. Volunteers. But I'd heard him called other things, standing under the wooden awning of Garner's Store, listening to old men talk. Old men with angry faces and outraged eyes, some of them with Minie balls of the war still lodged in their lank, hungry bodies. "That bastard, Davis," was the way they usually put it. "Commanding officer of the First Texas Traitors, Cowards, and Sonsofbitches." Around the time war broke out, Davis rounded up all the scum in Texas—or that's the way I always heard it, anyway—called them the First Texas Cavalry, and offered its services to the North. And, as reward for this thoughtfulness and foresight, Sheridan, in his fine office in New Orleans, from behind a blue cloud of fifty-cent-cigar smoke, had decided that E. J. Davis was just the man for the governor's office in Texas.

Oh, there was an election. General Philip Sheridan was a man to do things right. When the people of Texas began to get restless and complained that their livestock was all dying and the children weren't getting enough to eat because the Northern army was taking everything, the General began to give it some thought. By God, if the people of Texas didn't like the army, then he would give them a governor. There would be an election and they could choose anybody they wanted.

The only trouble was, if you wanted to vote, you had to take the "Ironclad Oath," and that weeded everybody out except the newly freed slaves, and some white trash, and maybe the veterans of the First Texas Cavalry, U.S. Volunteers. Davis won in a walk. "The people's choice!" the scalawag newspapers said.

While the war was going on, I wasn't old enough to understand everything about it. But I understood the bitterness as the ranchers' big herds dwindled down to a few mangy-looking old mossyhorns, and I remembered trying to eat meat without salt because ships couldn't get through the Northern blockade. And, somehow, I knew it was all the Yankees' fault.

Hating came as natural as breathing, in those days, in Texas. I remember overhearing a conversation in front of the hardware store in

John's City, where some men were laughing over the old joke of "You know what I just heard? A feller back there claims 'damn Yankee' is two words instead of one!" I laughed, but it wasn't until a couple of years later that I found out what it was about. Even Professor Bigloe said "damnyankee" and I figured he ought to know.

That was Texas, after the war. Broke and hungry, and if it tried to lift itself to its knees it got a kick in the gut for its trouble. Pa got off easier than most ranchers, because he had been too old to go to war and was able to stay on the ranch and look after his herd. Most of the ranchers weren't so lucky. After they got back, they found that their cattle had scattered from hell to Georgia—what was left of them after the Union soldiers took what they wanted. And the Confederate soldiers too, for that matter. And the calves were unbranded and wild and belonged legally to anybody who could catch them and burn them with his own iron. Most of the cattlemen had to start all over again, and if they got their beef back it was usually with a gun. The best guarantee of ownership was a fast draw and a sure aim.

After Davis came the Davis police, or state police, and the governor was burned in effigy so often that the smell of smoke would automatically bring out a squad of soldiers with bayoneted rifles. The police were supposed to take the place of the soldiers who were being gradually drawn out of the South. But they weren't any better. They were worse, if anything.

Thinking of the Davis police brought me back to Ray Novak. Old Martin Novak was hit hardest of all by the police, because he had to sit back and watch white trash and hired gunmen take over his marshal's job and run it to suit themselves. There was no law in John's City, if you wanted to side in with the turncoats. And if you didn't, there was a law against everything. A rancher could be fined a hundred dollars for elbowing his way to a saloon bar, and, if he didn't have the money to pay, it would be taken out in beef cattle, with a dozen or so of the police going along to see that the collection was made. And all Martin Novak could do was watch. And wait. And hope that someday things would change and he could bring another kind of law back to John's City.

And Ray ... Maybe that was what he was afraid of—of hurting his pa's chances of getting back into office. Maybe that was the reason he was so anxious to avoid any kind of brush with the law.

I was tired thinking about it. Maybe he was just plain yellow and had a streak up his back that you couldn't cover with both hands. I decided that when we started riding the next night Ray could go his way and I'd go mine. To hell with him.

It was just beginning to get light when we came to the creek, so we didn't have to argue about whether or not we were going to ride in the daylight. It was just a little stream, with the banks pretty well grown up in brush and salt cedars, and here and there a big green cottonwood. We rode along the bank for a while, looking for a place to stop. It looked like a good place for snakes, but not much of a spot for pitching camp. Finally we saw what we were looking for, a wide bend in the creek where the bank sloped down to the water, and the ground was brilliant green with new shoots of grass that was just beginning to come up. I didn't notice the horse until it was too late. It was a big black, with a white diamond in the middle of his forehead, grazing a big circle in the new green grass from the end of a picket rope. As we rounded the bend, the horse was the first thing we saw. But it didn't hold our attention long. The next thing we saw was the muzzle of a carbine.

I don't know how long I sat there looking at that gun before I realized that somebody had to be holding the thing. I don't suppose it was more than a small part of a second, but it seemed like a long time. By the time I was through looking at it, I knew everything about it.

It was a Ball magazine carbine, with the magazine under the barrel holding eight .50-caliber cartridges, loading from the rear. I had seen one or two of them before in cavalry officers' saddle boots. But guns like that didn't come easy, not even to cavalry officers. It was a beautiful piece of killing equipment. You could almost imagine that a man would be glad to get shot with a gun like that, if he cared anything for firearms. It had a tricky ramrod that pulled out the magazine spring to make loading fast and easy. Rim fire. It was a Yankee gun, but they hadn't brought it out in time to use it in the war, and I was glad of that. If they had, there would have been a lot more graves and a lot more boys sleeping under faded red flags with blue St. Andrew's crosses on them. I could almost tell, by looking at that carbine, what kind of man would be holding it.

The gun looked deadly, but quietly so. I figured the man would be the same. The gun didn't have an angry look or a belligerent look, but at the same time you knew it wouldn't stand for any foolishness. I wondered where the hell the owner had managed to get it, because I knew he wasn't a soldier, even before I looked at him.

And I was right. He was a long, hungry-looking man with faded gray eyes and a curious twist to his mouth that at first seemed like a smile, but after a second look you knew it wasn't. He had a face as long as a nightmare. His long, sharp nose drifted off to one side of his face, and there was a scar across the bridge, and a dent that you could lay the barrel of a .44 into. A week's growth of dirty gray beard didn't help his appearance any.

For clothes, he wore a hickory shirt with two buttons missing, a dirty bandanna around his scrawny neck, and a pair of serge pants slick from saddle wear. His hat had been black once, a long time ago, but it wasn't much of any color now.

I knew, before looking, that he would be wearing two side guns. I was right again. Two Colt .44's, the regular "Army" percussion model, but they had been altered to use metallic cartridges and looked like different guns. The ramrods and lever were gone, and new blued ejectors were molded to the sides of the barrels, and the new cylinders had loading gates. They were clean and cold and deadly-looking, and the gunsmith who had done the altering had been a man who loved his work.

I saw all this while maybe a tick of a second went by, while Red was rearing up just a little because of the jerk I had given on the reins. And by the time Red's forefeet hit the ground again I had the feeling that the stranger and I were old friends—or rather, old acquaintances, because he didn't look like the kind of man who would have many friends. I didn't know what Ray Novak was thinking, but I noticed that he didn't do anything foolish, like going for his own .44 or trying to ride the man down. There was something about the stranger that told you instinctively that a trick like that would only get you a sudden burial.

It crossed my mind quickly that maybe the stranger was a bounty hunter. The Yankees had plenty of such men working for them, freelance killers who hunted fugitives from carpetbag law at so much a head. But I discarded that thought before it had time to form. This man wasn't working for the carpetbag law, or any other kind of law, for that matter. I don't know how I was so sure of that. He just wasn't the type.

"Ain't it kind of early in the morning," the man said softly, "to be taking a ride?"

"Or late at night," I said.

The stranger's mouth twitched slightly in what was almost a nervous tic, and he made an almost silent grunting sound that came all the way up from his belly. It was like no sound I had ever heard before, but I was to find out later that it was laughter—or the closest thing to laughter that he ever came to. He hadn't asked us to raise our hands or drop our guns, so I figured that he didn't have anything against us in particular, except for the fact that we were strangers riding at an unusual hour.

I said, "We figured to make camp here on the bend, but I guess we can move on to another spot...."

He made a negligent little motion with his shoulders. He had sized us up quickly as men not too friendly with the law. Why else would we be riding by night and sleeping by day? But he studied us for a while longer with that gray gaze of his. He regarded Red appreciatively, and the grub sack thoughtfully. I think it was the grub sack that made up his mind.

"I don't mind a bit of company ... once in a while." That, I knew, was all the invitation we were going to get. He lowered his carbine, holding it in the crook of his arm, and I started to swing down from the saddle.

Then Ray Novak spoke for the first time. "We'll just move on," he said. "I reckon there are other places."

Ray hadn't taken to the stranger. Disapproval was stamped all over his face as he sat slouched in his saddle, his forehead screwed up in thought. Ray Novak had lived on law for so long that he recognized and hated outlaws instinctively. He was a special breed of man. Breeding, and blood lines, and training made his hackles rise at the sight of an outlaw, just as naturally as a long-eared Kentucky hound gets his back up at the sight of a badger. The fact that he was now an outlaw himself had nothing to do with it. He was still the son of Martin Novak.

I could see Ray thumbing back in his memory, going through all the dodgers on outlaws that had come through his pa's office, trying to place the stranger. He hadn't placed him yet. But sooner or later that plodding mind of his would come across the right dodger, and the right photograph or drawing, and the stranger would be pegged.

In the meantime, I didn't give a damn. I'd rather bed down with an outlaw than pull a stretch on the work gang. Anyway, I was tired of riding, and I was tired of Ray Novak. I dropped down from the saddle.

"If you want to ride on," I said, "you can ride. I'm stopping."

He didn't like that much. But he thought it over for a minute and didn't argue. Maybe he wanted to study the stranger some more. Or maybe he figured that all this was his fault in the first place and that made him bound to stay with me. I didn't know or care.

The stranger watched us carelessly as we unsaddled our horses and staked them around the bend near his big black. When we came back, he had a small fire going down near the water. He worked easily, almost lazily, selecting just the right kind of dry twigs. It was an expert fire, big enough to cook on, but practically no smoke came from it. He looked up and smiled that half-smile of his as I got the skillet out of the blanket roll and brought it and a bacon slab down to the fire. We were all friends, it seemed. But I noticed that he never let himself be maneuvered into a position that would show his back.

Before long, the sharp air of early morning was heavy with the rich smell of frying bacon. We propped the skillet over the fire on two rocks and once in a while I would turn the meaty slabs with a pocketknife. There is nothing like the smell of bacon in the early morning, but I was the only one that seemed to be interested. The stranger, I knew, was half starved, but he regarded the food only passively, hunkering down on his heels, with his back against the solid trunk of a cottonwood. Ray Novak hadn't said anything since we had unsaddled the horses, but I could see that he was still poking at the back of his mind, trying to get the man placed. I think the stranger saw it too. But he didn't seem to care.

We ate the bacon with Ma's cornbread, spearing the dripping slices with our pocketknives, chewing and swallowing without a word. The stranger helped himself only after Ray and I had what we wanted. After we had finished, I went down to the creek and rinsed the skillet and filled it with fresh water. When I got back, the two of them were still sitting there on the ground, without saying a thing, staring thoughtfully at each other.

We boiled coffee in the skillet and I found two tin cups that Ma had packed in the blanket roll. I poured for Ray and myself, and still not a sound from anybody. I began to wonder what Ray Novak would do after he finally dug the stranger out of his memory. The stranger must have been wondering the same thing. And I had a crazy kind of feeling that the stranger was feeling sorry for Ray.

The coffee was black and strong and coated with a thin film of bacon grease. Like the bacon, the stranger had his coffee after Ray and I had finished. The silence was beginning to work on me. It magnified faraway sounds and brought my nerves out on top of my skin and rubbed them raw.

At last the stranger got slowly to his feet. "I'm much obliged for the grub," he said. "I guess I'll stretch out for a while. It's been a long night."

I said, "Sure." Ray Novak said nothing. The stranger walked up the slope a way, still not showing us his back, and stretched out under a rattling big cottonwood where his saddle was. He seemed to go to sleep, but there was no way of being sure about that. He pulled his hat partly over his face and lay down with his head on his saddle, but I had an uneasy feeling that he was just waiting.

I rinsed out the skillet and cups and put them back in the blanket roll. Ray had moved over to another cottonwood, still studying the stranger. Without looking at me, he said, "You'd better get some sleep, Tall."

"How about you?"

"I can stay awake for a while. I've got a feeling that one of us had better keep his eyes open."

The way he said it made me burn. It was in that offhand sort of way— the way you'd tell a kid to go on to bed, you had important things to do. Maybe he thought my eighteen years made me a kid. Maybe, I thought, Ray Novak could go to hell.

But I didn't try to make anything of it. Beginning tonight, I didn't intend to ride with him any more. I spread my saddle blanket and sat leaning back against my saddle. I wasn't particularly sleepy, and, anyway, I wanted to see what Ray would do when he finally figured out who the stranger was.

Maybe fifteen minutes went by without either of us making a sound. Then, suddenly, Ray Novak made a little grunting noise and started to shove himself away from the cottonwood.

"All right," I said.

"All right what?"

"Who is our gun-loving friend? You've been working on it ever since he first stuck that carbine in our faces."

That took the wind out of him. "How did you know that?"

I shrugged. What difference did it make?

"Well, you were right," Ray said softly. "I should have figured it out a long time ago, but the beard and broken nose were things the government dodger on him didn't show. But I pegged him finally. He's Garret. Pappy Garret."

I didn't believe it at first. Pappy Garret was one of those men that you hear about all your life, but never see. The stories they told about him were almost as wild as the ones about Pecos Bill, or if you live in the north country, Paul Bunyan. He was wanted by both North and South during the war for leading plundering guerilla bands into the Kansas Free State. There wasn't a state in the Southwest that hadn't put a price on his head. Pappy Garret had the distinction of being probably the only thing in the world that the North and South saw alike on. They were out to get him.

Twenty notches was Pappy's record, as well as records of men like that could be kept. Some put the number of men who had gone down under Pappy's guns as high as thirty. But most claimed it was twenty, more or less, with some few claiming that he was overrated as a bad man and had never killed more than fifteen men in his life. No one, but Pappy Garret, would know for sure about that. And maybe Pappy didn't even know. The story was that he had a hideout up in the Indian Territory where he lived like a king by robbing the westbound wagon trains. Some people said that he lived with an Indian princess, the youngest daughter of the head chief of the Cheyennes. Others had it that he had been killed during the war fighting for the Confederacy—or the Union, depending on who was telling the story—and the real killer was Pappy Garret's son, a child of his by the Indian princess.

But most people didn't put much stock in that story. They figured that such a child couldn't be more than five or six years old, and a boy that age wasn't apt to be doing much killing. Not even a son of Pappy Garret's.

Still others had it that Pappy had gone to South America shortly after the war and was settled down there on a big plantation as respectable as you please, and all the killings that were laid to him were done by men who just happened to look a little like Pappy. Many such stories sprang up from time to time. Nobody really believed them, but it gave them something to talk about. The peace officers probably had the best idea of what Pappy was really like. He had killed two marshals on the Mexican border, and one up in the Panhandle country not long before, when they tried to arrest him. They saw Pappy Garret as a killer, without any fancy trimmings.

It was hard to believe that the lank, hungry-looking man not twenty yards away could be Pappy Garret, but Ray Novak didn't make mistakes about things like that. I knew one thing, however: Pappy hadn't been living like a king up in the Indian Territory, or anywhere else. He looked like he hadn't had a full belly since he was a child. Lying there with his eyes closed, with his head on the saddle, he looked more like a tired old man than a killer.

And maybe that was the reason I wasn't afraid of him. If I felt anything at all for Pappy Garret, it was sympathy. I'd had one night of running from the law, and that was plenty for me. I wondered how Pappy must feel after running for four or five years.

In the back of my mind, I realized that ten thousand dollars in bounty money was mine if I wanted it. All I had to do was dry my gun and empty it into Pappy Garret's skinny body and it was mine. There wouldn't even be any trouble when I rode back to John's City. The carpetbag law would be so glad to see Pappy's lifeless body dangling across that big black horse of his that they would forget the grudge they had against me. I'd be a hero, and a rich one at that. With ten thousand dollars, I could buy a piece of free range and have the beginnings of a ranch of my own. I could even marry Laurin Bannerman, which was what I wanted more than anything else.

But I didn't think I would be able to sleep at night without seeing that ugly, tired face of Pappy's; so the thought of killing him never really got to be an idea.

Ray Novak had ideas of his own. He stood up quietly, his hand unconsciously going down to his hip and feeling of the butt of his gun. I said, "Just what do you aim to do?"

There had never been a doubt in Ray's mind about what to do, after he had figured out who Pappy was. I don't think it was the bounty that set his mind for him. He probably never even thought of that. He just had too much law in him to let a killer like Pappy Garret lie there and do nothing about it. He glanced at me briefly, without saying anything. I guess he figured that my question wasn't worth answering.

I said, "Let him alone. He hasn't done anything to us."

Ray had his gun out now. He glanced at me curiously, and there were two small clicks as he pulled the hammer hack. "Are you crazy?"

"We can saddle up and go our own way," I said. "Let the law catch him if they want him. What has the law ever done for us?"

"You *must* be crazy," Ray Novak said softly, not bothering to keep the scorn out of his voice. "Didn't you hear me? That man's Pappy Garret. He's killed twenty men. He'll kill that many more if somebody doesn't stop him. Stopping a man like that isn't just a job for the law. It's a job for every man who wants to live in peace, for every man who wants to see law and order come back to Texas."

I don't think I would have done anything if he hadn't made that speech, but when he got to talking about the right of law, and the wrong of outlaws, he got a holier-than-thou glint in his eyes like a camp-meeting preacher. Anyway, I was tired of Ray Novak. I was tired of his reverential respect for a tin sheriff's badge. I said, "Oh, hell, stop being so goddamn self-righteous!"

He looked as if I had kicked him in the gut while he wasn't expecting it. Over beneath the cottonwood, Pappy Garret stirred uneasily, and it occurred to me to wonder why a man like that would go to sleep in the company of two strangers. Because he was asleep. There was no mistake about it now. Ray threw one quick angry glance in my direction—a glance that said that he was through with me, that from now on we could ride our separate ways.

"Very well, Tall," he said tightly. "I'll take care of it myself. You don't have anything to do with it."

"You're going to shoot him while he's asleep?"

"I'll take him any way I can. You don't give a mad dog a chance to protect itself, do you?"

All the talk had been in low whispers, but it was over now. Ray stepped out quietly, his gun at the ready. I could see what was going to happen. Ray would say something to wake Pappy—I knew he didn't have it in him to shoot a sleeping man. He would wake Pappy and Pappy would see how it was and try to get his guns. That would be the last move he would ever make. I had seen Ray handle guns and I knew Pappy Garret didn't have a chance.

I watched the sleeping gunman as those thoughts went through my mind. Pappy's face was relaxed now and I could see the deep lines of incredible weariness around his eyes and mouth. He looked as if he hadn't slept for days. I knew that he hadn't slept for years. Not real sleep. But now he lay like a log, numbed with weariness and comforted with hot food in his belly. He didn't look like a killer to me. He looked like an old man—very old and very tired—who couldn't hold his eyes open any longer.

Ray was coming up on Pappy's left, moving silently. In just a minute it would be over, if Pappy made a move for his guns. He would be able to sleep then—the long sleep that lasted forever.

The shout, when it came, startled me as much as anybody. It came high-pitched and loud and I hardly recognized it as my own.

"Pappy, look out!"

I lurched up to my feet. I don't know what I thought I was going to do then. It was too late to do anything but to stand there, half-crouched, and watch.

If I hadn't seen it I wouldn't have believed it. I never could entirely believe it when I watched Pappy handle guns. And you wouldn't believe that a man like Pappy could come awake as quick as he did, or that a man could move as fast. It all happened so fast that you couldn't be sure where the movement started and where it ended. He flipped over on his stomach and rolled on his right side, and his right hand started plunging down to his holster before my first word was out. Ray was almost on top of him. His .44 was already out and cocked, and Ray was the man who could put two holes in a tossed-up can before it hit the ground. But by the time he got his second shot off this time, it was too late.

Ray Novak's first bullet slammed into Pappy's saddle, where his head had been only an instant before. Before he could thumb the hammer and press the trigger again, Pappy's own deadly .44 had bellowed. Pappy lay on his side, firing across his body. He must have drawn the gun and cocked it while he was flopping over, but it looked as if it had been in his hand all the time. One bullet was all he used.

I still hadn't moved. I stood there in that frozen half-crouch waiting for Ray Novak to go down. When Pappy fired only once, I knew it was over. He got to his knees and slowly lifted himself to his feet, darting a glance in my direction.

He said mildly, "Just unbuckle your pistol, son, and kick it over here."

I slipped the buckle on my cartridge belt and dropped it. Then I kicked it toward Pappy. But the thing that held me fascinated was Ray Novak. He was still standing. He wasn't even swaying. Then I saw that his gun hand was empty and I began to understand what had happened.

It hadn't been anything as fancy as shooting a man's gun out of his hand. Not even Pappy Garret could have done that, shooting as fast as he had, from the position he had been in. He had shot to kill, but the bullet had nicked Ray's forearm, making him drop the gun.

I lost any suspicion I had about Ray Novak's guts. He had plenty. There was nothing he could do now but stand there and wait for Pappy to finish him off. But he didn't flinch, or beg, or anything else. He just stood there, staring into those pale gray eyes of Pappy Garret's, while bright red blood dripped from his fingers and splashed in a little pool at his feet.

"What are you waiting on, Garret?" he said. "Why don't you go ahead and finish it?"

Pappy smiled that tired half-smile of his. He said softly, "I wouldn't waste another bullet on you. If I decide to kill you, I'll beat your brains out with a pistol butt. Now get the hell out of here before I do it."

Ray Novak's face burned a bright red. For a moment he didn't move. Then Pappy started toward him, slowly, holding his .44 like a club.

Ray said, "I'll get you, Garret. There won't always be carpetbag law in this country. And then I'll get you, if it's the last thing I do."

Pappy kept coming, half-smiling, with his pistol raised.

Ray turned then, and walked off, leaving a little trail of crimson in the tender green shoots of young grass. He didn't look at me. He walked on by. Around the bend he got his horse saddled, and pretty soon we heard him ride away.

I started to go myself. There was no explaining the reason I had yelled the way I had. Probably it had been because of a lot of things. Ray Novak and his everlasting talk of law. Ray Novak being able to put two bullets in a tin can. Even those rides of his over to Laurin's might have had something to do with it. All that, and Pappy lying there under the cottonwood, looking like a tired, helpless old man.

Anyway, I had done it. Ray Novak and I were through for good now, but I didn't give a damn about that. I turned and started up toward the bend in the creek to get Red saddled up.

But Pappy said, "Just a minute, son. I'd like to talk to you."

Chapter 3

I turned around. Pappy looked at me as he punched the empty cartridge out of his pistol and replaced it with a live round. After a moment he said:

"Thanks."

"Forget it. I wasn't trying to buy anything."

"You called me Pappy," he said. "How did you know who I was?"

"The other fellow figured it out. His old man used to be a town marshal and he saw your picture on one of the dodgers that came through the office."

Pappy shook his head, puzzled. "I know a man on the run when I see one. And he was on the run, the same as you. He didn't look like a marshal's son to me."

"His pa was marshal before the carpetbaggers took over."

Pappy began to understand. He rubbed a hand thoughtfully over his bushy chin. He moved back up the slope a few steps and sat down, leaning back with his elbows on his saddle. After a moment he untied the dirty bandanna and mopped his face and the back of his neck.

There was something about him that fascinated me. Only a minute ago he had come within a hair's breadth of getting a bullet in his brain, and all the emotion he showed was to wipe his face with a dirty handkerchief.

"Well," he asked, "what are you staring at?"

"You," I said. "I was just wondering how you came to go to sleep at a time like that."

He thought about that for a moment, and at last he sighed. "I was tired," he said simply. "I haven't slept for more than two days."

I should have saddled Red right then and rode away from there. There was trouble in the air. You could feel it all around, and you got the idea that trouble flocked to Pappy like iron filings to a lodestone. But I didn't move.

I said, "Ray Novak will be on your trail again. Sooner or later he'll be riding behind a marshal's badge, and when that happens he'll hunt you down. You should have killed him while you had the chance."

I half expected Pappy to laugh. The idea of Pappy having anything to fear from a youngster like Ray Novak would have been funny to most people. But Pappy didn't laugh. He studied me carefully with those pale gray eyes.

"A man does his own killing, son, and that's enough," he said. "I reckon if you want this Novak fellow dead, you'll have to see to it yourself."

I flared up at that.

"I don't care if he's dead or alive. Ray Novak doesn't mean anything to me."

Something changed in Pappy's eyes. I had an idea that way down deep he was smiling, but it didn't show on that ugly face.

"Maybe I spoke out of turn," he said finally. "I guess you're right. I should have killed him ... while I had the chance."

There didn't seem to be any more to say. I turned and headed around the bend to where Red was picketed, and Pappy didn't make any move to stop me. But I could almost feel those eyes on me as I threw the double-rigged saddle up on Red's broad neck and began to tighten the cinches. I got my blanket roll and tied it on behind and I was ready to go. I was ready to leave this creek and Pappy Garret behind. I had enough trouble as it was, and if I got caught, I didn't want it to be with a man like Pappy. I swung up to the saddle and pulled Red around to where the outlaw was still standing.

"I guess this is where I cut out," I said. "So long, Pappy."

"So long, son."

He looked a hundred years old right then. His heavy-lidded, red-

rimmed eyes were watery with fatigue, and once in a while little nervous tics of sheer weariness would jerk at the corner of his mouth.

"Well," I said, "take care of yourself."

"The same to you, son," Pappy said. I started to pull Red around
again and head downstream, when Pappy added, "Just a minute before you go."

He moved over a couple of steps to where his saddlebags were. He
opened one of them and took out a pair of pistols, almost exactly like
the ones he was wearing. Gleaming, deadly weapons, with rubbed wal-
nut butts. He came over and handed them up to me.

"Bad pistols are like bad friends," he said. "They let you down when
you need them most. You'd better take these."

I didn't know what to say. I looked at Pappy and then at the guns.

"Go on, take them," he said. "A fellow down on the border let me
have them." And he smiled that sad half-smile of his. "He wasn't in any
condition to object."

I took the guns dumbly, feeling their deadly weight as I balanced them
in my hands. I had never held weapons like them before. They had almost perfect balance. I flipped them over with my fingers in the trigger guards, and the butts smacked solidly in my palms, as if they had
been carved by an artist specially to fit my hands.

I took a deep breath and let it out slowly. "All right, Pappy," I said
finally. "You win."

He looked surprised. "I win what?"

"I'll keep watch while you catch some sleep. That's what you wanted,
wasn't it?"

Then I saw something that few people ever saw. Pappy Garret smiled.
Not that sad half-smile of his, but a real honest-to-God, face-splitting
smile that reached all the way to his gray eyes.

"I think we'll get along, son," he said.

So that's the way it was. I unsaddled Red again and staked him out,
then I took my position up on the creek bank while Pappy stretched
out again with his head on the saddle. He raised up once to look at me,
still slightly amused.

"My hide is worth ten thousand dollars at the nearest marshal's office," he said. "How do I know you won't try to shoot me while I'm
asleep?"

"If I'd wanted ten thousand dollars that bad," I said, "I'd have
killed you the first time you went to sleep. And I wouldn't have been

polite enough to wake you up first. I don't let my conscience bother me, the way Novak does."

Pappy's mouth twitched, and there was that almost silent grunting sound, and I knew that he was laughing. He was dead asleep before his head hit the saddle again.

I had time to do some thinking while Pappy slept. I decided that maybe it wouldn't be a bad idea, after all, to stick with Pappy until we reached the Brazos. If anybody would know all the outtrails to miss the cavalry and police, Pappy Garret was the man. And avoiding cavalry and police was about the most important thing I could think of right now.

I didn't think much about Ray Novak. We had never been anything in particular to each other, and now that we were separated for good, I was satisfied. I didn't give a damn where he went or what he did.

But I thought of Laurin Bannerman. Laurin, with eyes a little too large for her small face, and her small mouth that always looked slightly berry-stained, and her laugh that was as fresh as spring rain. I thought about her plenty now that I had time on my hands and there was nothing else to do. It was a funny thing, but I had never paid any attention to her until a couple of years ago. I guess that's the way boys are around that age. One minute girls mean nothing, and the next minute they're everything.

That was Laurin for me. Just about everything.

It was late in the afternoon when Pappy woke up. I was sitting under a cottonwood up on the creek bank, flipping my new pistols over and over to get the feel of them. Pappy sat up lazily, stretching, yawning, and scratching the mangy patches of beard on his face.

"That's better," he said. "Much better." He got up on his feet and hobbled around experimentally. "You handle those guns pretty good, son," he said. "Do you think you can shoot them as well?"

"Well enough, I guess."

Pappy shook his head soberly and beat some of the dust from his battered hat. "That's one thing no man ever does—shoot well enough. Sooner or later, if you keep looking, you'll find some bird that can slap leather faster."

"How about you?" I asked.

Pappy grinned slightly. "Maybe I haven't looked long enough," he said. "But I don't expect to live forever."

He began getting his stuff together, a ragged gray blanket that still had C.S.A. stenciled on it in faded black letters, a change of clothing, and

that was about all. He did have some tobacco, though. He took the sack
out of his shirt pocket and poured some of the powdery stuff into a little square of corn shuck, Mexican style, and tossed the makings up to
me.

"You figure to ride east tonight?" he asked casually.

"That's what I had in mind."

"Alone?"

He was holding a match up to his cigarette and I couldn't see his face.
"I guess that's up to you," I said.

He got that surprised look again. "How do you mean, son?"

He came up the slope and held a match while I got my cigarette to
going. "Isn't that what you had in mind all along?" I said. "You look
like a man that's just about played out. I don't know what you're running from, or how long you've been at it, but I know a man can't stay
on the alert twenty-four hours a day, the way you must have been doing. I'm on my way to the Brazos country. If you want to ride along
and keep clear of the bluebellies, that's all right with me. We'll take turns
sleeping and watching, and split up when we get to the river."

He tried to look all innocence, but he didn't have the face for it. "Do
you think I'd let a mere boy tie up with a wanted man like me?"

"I think that's what you've been figuring on all along," I said.

I thought for a minute that he was going to break down and have a
real laugh. But he didn't. He only said, "I guess we'd better get ready
to ride. The sun will be down before long."

We made about twenty-five miles that night, and I knew before we
had covered a hundred yards that I had picked the right man to get me
through hostile country. Pappy knew every trick there was to learn
about covering a trail. When a hard shale outcropping appeared, we
followed it. When we crossed a stream we never came out near the place
we went in. We even picked up the tracks of some wild cattle and followed them for two or three miles, mingling our own horses' hoof-
marks with the dozens of others.

Pappy didn't ask me, but I told him about myself as we rode. I even
told him about Laurin, and Ray Novak, and how we came to be on
the run, but there was no way of knowing what he thought about it.
He would grunt once in a while, and that was all.

The next day, when we started to ride again, Pappy found a holster
for me in one of those saddlebags of his. "Some people will tell you that
a good shot doesn't need but one gun," he said, "but that's a lot of foolishness. Two of anything is better than one."

I felt foolish at first. It seemed like a lot of hardware—a lot more than an ordinary man needed to pack. But then, Pappy Garret wasn't an ordinary man, and when you were with Pappy you did as he did.

The day after that he said we didn't have to ride at night any more. He knew the country and there was nothing to worry about between us and the Brazos. Pappy, I gathered, was figuring on tying up with a trail herd headed for Kansas, but he never said so. He never said anything much after we got to riding, except for things like: "Loosen your cartridge belt, son. Let your pistols hang where your palms can brush the butts. Boothills are full of men that had to reach that extra inch to get their guns." Or, at the end of a day maybe, when we were sitting around doing nothing: "Clean your pistols, son. Guns are like women; if you don't treat them right, and they turn against you, you've got nobody to blame but yourself."

It was almost sundown of the fourth day when we raised the wooded high ground with a sagging little log shack partly dug into the side of a hill. A thin little whisper of smoke was curling up from a rock chimney.

"It looks like they're expecting us," Pappy said, squinting across the distance.

I looked at him, and he saw the question before I could ask it. "*They,*" he said "could be almost anybody. Anybody but the law, that is. The shack was built a long time ago by a sheepherder, but the cattlemen chased him out of Texas before he had time to get settled good. Some of the boys I know use it once in a while. I use it myself when I'm in this part of the country."

Well, I figured Pappy ought to know. We rode up toward the shack, and before long a man came out of it and stood there by the front door—the only door the cabin had—nursing what looked like a short-barreled buffalo gun. A Sharps maybe, about a .50 caliber, I guessed, when we got closer.

The man himself wasn't much to look at. About twenty-three or so, with a blunted, bulldog face, and long hair that hung down almost to his shoulders. His clothes were in about the same shape as Pappy's, and that wasn't saying much.

Pappy grunted as we pulled up near the crest of the hill. "It looks like one of the Creyton boys," he said.

I had a closer look at the man. The Creyton boys had hard names in Texas. They were supposed to have been in on a bank robbery or two down on the border. There were three of them: Buck, and Ralph, and

a younger one called Paul. I figured the one at the shack was Paul Creyton, because he looked too young to have done the things that Buck
and Ralph had to their credit.

The man recognized Pappy as we drew up into the thicket that
passed for a front yard. I saw there was a lean-to shed on the side of
the shack—a place for keeping horses, I supposed—but there was no
horse stabled there. The man lowered his gun and came forward.

"Pappy Garret," he said flatly, "I had an idea you was up in Kansas."

Pappy grinned slightly and leaned across his big black's neck to
shake hands. "A Texan likes to see the old home place once in a while.
How are you, Paul?"

The man glanced sideways at me, and Pappy said quickly, "This is
Tall Cameron, a friend of mine. He's riding as far as the Brazos with
me."

We nodded at each other. Paul Creyton said, "You haven't seen
Buck, have you?"

"Not for about two years," Pappy said.

"We split up down on the Black River," Creyton went on flatly, as if
he had gone over the story a hundred times in his mind. "A Morgan
County sheriff's posse jumped us just south of the river. Ralph's dead.
A sonofabitch gave him a double load of buckshot. My horse played
out about four miles off, down in the flats, and I had to leave him in
a gully."

I watched Pappy stiffen, just a little, then relax. "That's too bad about
Ralph," he said softly.

"A double load of buckshot the sonofabitch gave him," Paul Creyton said again. "Right in the face. I wouldn't of known him, my own
brother, if I hadn't been standing right next to him and seen him get it."
His little eyes were dark with anger, but I couldn't see any particular
grief on his face. He jerked his head toward the shack. "It ain't much,
Pappy, but you and your friend are welcome to stay with me. I was just
going out to see if I couldn't shoot myself some grub."

Pappy looked at me. We had been riding a long way and our horses
needed a rest, but he was leaving the decision up to me.

"I've got some side bacon and corn meal," I said. "I guess that will
see us through supper."

We cooked the bacon at a small rock fireplace in one corner of the
shack, then we fried some hoecake bread in the grease, and finally made
some coffee. Pappy and Paul Creyton talked a little, but not much.
Somehow I gathered that Pappy wasn't such a great friend of the Crey-

tons as I had thought at first.

After supper, it was almost dark, and the only light in the shack came from the little jumping flames in the fireplace. Talk finally slacked off to nothing, and Paul Creyton sat staring into the fire, anger written into every line of his face. Whatever his plans were, he wasn't letting us in on them. Whatever was in his mind, he was keeping it to himself.

Pappy got up silently and went outside to look at his horse. I followed him.

"What do you think about that posse?" I said. "Do you think they'll follow Creyton up to this place?"

Pappy shook his head, lifting his horse's hoofs and inspecting them. "Not tonight. This place is hard to find if you don't know where to look, and Paul can cover a trail as well as the next one."

I rubbed Red down and gave him some water out of a rain barrel at the edge of the shack. His ribs were beginning to show through his glossy hide, and there were several briar scratches across his chest. But there wasn't anything wrong with him that a sack of oats or corn wouldn't fix.

I heard Pappy grunt, and I looked up. He had his horse's left forefoot between his knees, gouging around the shoe with a pocketknife. "A stone bruise," he said. "He's been walking off center since noon, but I figured it was because he was tired." He got the rock that was caught under the rim of the shoe and flipped it out. "Well, there won't be any riding for a day or so, until that hoof is sound again."

"That means staying here tomorrow?"

"It means *me* staying here. You don't have to. Another day's ride will put you on the Brazos."

For a minute I didn't say anything. I hadn't figured that it would be any problem to pack up and leave Pappy any time I felt like it. But there was something about that ugly face that a man could get to like. He didn't have many friends. Maybe I was the closest thing to a friend that he had ever had. I made up my mind.

"I'll wait," I said. "We'll ride in together."

I imagined that I saw Pappy smile, but it was too dark now really to see his face. Then, without looking up, he said, "In that case, you'd better keep an eye on that red horse of yours."

"What is that supposed to mean?"

"If you were on foot," Pappy said, "and in no position to get yourself a horse, what would you do?"

"Like Paul Creyton."

"We'll say like Paul Creyton."

I began to get mad just thinking about it. "If he lays a hand on Red," I said, "I'll kill him."

Pappy turned, and stretched, and yawned, as if it were no concern of his. "Maybe I'm wrong," he said, "but I doubt it. He's got to have a horse, and that animal of yours is the closest one around."

He started back toward the shack, toward the doorway faintly jumping in orange firelight. "Just a minute," I said. "How are you so sure that he won't try to steal that black of yours?"

Pappy smiled. He was in the dark, but I knew he was smiling.

"Paul Creyton knows better than to steal an animal of mine," he said.

When I got back to the shack I decided that Pappy had the whole thing figured wrong. Creyton had his blanket roll undone and was stretched out in front of the fireplace when I came in. He didn't look like a man ready to make a quick getaway on a stolen horse. Pappy was sitting on the other side of the room with his back to the wall, smoking one of his corn-shuck cigarettes.

"It seems like Paul just came from your part of the country," he said.

"John's City?"

Creyton sat up and worked with the makings of a cigarette. "That's the place," he said. "Me and Ralph and Buck came through there a few days back. About the day after you pulled out, according to what Pappy tells me."

I looked at Pappy, but his face told me nothing.

"Well, what about it?"

"Nothing about it," Creyton said bluntly. "We just came through it, that's all. The carpetbag law was raisin' hell. Stoppin' all travelers, police makin' raids on the local ranchers. All because some white punk took a swing at a cavalryman, they said."

I hadn't been ready for that. I had figured, like Ray Novak, that if the two of us got out of the country for a while it would all blow over. But here the police were raiding the ranches, because of us. Our own place, maybe. Or the Bannerman place, where Laurin was.

If one of the pigs so much as laid a hand on Laurin ... The thought of it made me weak and a little sick. I wheeled and started for the door.

"Where do you think you're going?" Pappy said.

"Back to John's City."

"Do you plan to go on foot? I don't care what you do with yourself, but I hate to see you kill a good horse out of damn foolishness. Wait till tomorrow. You'll make better time in the long run by giving your horse a rest."

Pappy was right. I knew that, but it wasn't easy staying here and wondering what might be happening to Laurin, or Ma and Pa, and doing nothing about it. Creyton got slowly to his feet, standing there in front of the fireplace, looking at me.

"You'd better listen to Pappy, kid," he said. "When you need a horse you need him bad. I ought to know."

I didn't want Creyton's advice. For all I knew, he just wanted me to stick around a while longer to give him a better chance to steal my horse. But I knew they were both right. Red had been pushed hard for the past few days, and if I tried to push him again tonight he might break down for good.

So I stayed. When the fire burned out, we made blanket pallets on the dirt floor, and before long Pappy's heavy breathing told me that he was asleep. He didn't snore. From time to time the rhythm of his breathing would break, he would rouse himself, look around, and then go back to sleep again. That was the way Pappy was. He never slept sound enough to snore. You had a feeling that he never let his mind be completely blanked out, that he always kept some little corner of it open. Being on the run had done that. He was afraid to allow himself the luxury of real sleep. A man like Pappy never knew when he would have to be wide awake and ready to shoot.

I lay awake for a long while, listening to a night wind moan and fling gravel and dust against the shack. Creyton seemed to be asleep. His breathing was regular, and once in a while he would snort a little and roll over on the hard ground. I lay there, with my eyes wide open, not taking any chances.

The night crawled by slowly. How many hours, I don't know. My eyes burned from keeping them open, and every so often I'd feel myself dropping off and I'd have to start thinking about something. I wanted a cigarette, but I didn't dare light one. I was asleep, as far as Paul Creyton was concerned, and I wanted to keep it that way in case he had ideas about that red horse of mine. I started thinking about Laurin.

I was dreaming of Laurin when something woke me. I didn't remember going to sleep, but I had. I sat up immediately, looking around the room, but it was too dark to see anything. I could hear Pappy's breathing. But not Paul Creyton's.

Sickness hit in my stomach, and then anger. Then, outside the shack, I heard Red whinny, and I knew that was the thing that had wakened me.

I went to the door, and in the pale moonlight I could see Paul Creyton throwing a saddle up on Red's back. So Pappy had been right all
along. I found my cartridge belt on the floor, swung it around my middle and buckled it. Pappy didn't move. Didn't make a sound.

I didn't feel angry now, or in any particular hurry. I knew Creyton
wasn't going to get away with stealing my horse, the same as that time,
years ago, when I had known that Criss Bagley wouldn't hurt me with
that club. I didn't know just how I would stop him; but I would stop
him, and that was the important thing.

The night was quiet, and the sudden little scamper of Red's hoofs was
the only thing to disturb it as I stepped out of the shack. Creyton had
the horse all saddled and ready to ride by the time I got out to the shed.
He was standing in the shadows, on the other side of Red, and I could-
n't see him very well. But he could see me.

I never heard of a man talking his way out of horse stealing, and I
guess Creyton never had either. Anyway, he didn't try it this time. He
moved fast, jerking Red in front of him. Everything was so cut and dried
that there wasn't any use thinking about it, even if there had been time.
I dropped to my knees, with one of my new .44's in my hand. For just
a moment I wondered how I was going to get Creyton without hitting
Red. Then I made out the figure of Creyton kneeling under the horse's
belly, and his gun blazed.

It all happened before Red could jump. I felt the .44 kick twice in my
hand, the shots crowding right on top of Creyton's, and something told
me there was no use wasting any more bullets. Red reared suddenly
and, as he came crashing down with those ironshod hoofs, there was
a soft, mushy sound, like dumping a big rock into a mud hole.

I thought for a minute that I was going to be sick. But that passed. I
ran forward and caught hold of the reins and stroked the big horse's
neck until he began to quiet down. There were nervous little ripples running up and down his legs and shoulders, but he got over his wild spell.
I petted him some more, then led him away from the place and hitched
him to a blackjack tree near the shack.

Paul Creyton was dead. I dragged him out into the moonlight and had
a look at him: His face was a mess of meat and gristle and bone where
Red's hoof had caught him, but that wasn't the thing that had done it.
He had a bullet hole in the hollow of his throat, just below his Adam's
apple, and another one about six inches up from his belt buckle. The
one in the throat went all the way through, breaking his neck and leaving a hole about the size of a half dollar where the bullet came out. His

head flopped around like something that didn't even belong to the rest of the body, when I tried to pick him up.

It had all happened too fast to make much of an impression on me at first. But now I was beginning to get it. I backed up and swallowed to keep my stomach out of my throat. I hadn't known that a man could die like that. Just a flick of the finger, enough to pull a trigger, and he's dead. As easy as that. The night was cool, almost cold, but I felt sweat on my face, and on the back of my neck. Sweat plastered my shirt to my back. I walked away from the place and headed back toward the shack.

It occurred to me to wonder what had happened to Pappy. He must have heard the shooting. The way he slept.

As I stepped through the doorway, a match flared and Pappy's face jumped out at me as he lit a cigarette. He put the match out and I couldn't see his face any more, just the glowing end of that corn-shuck tube, with little sparks falling every once in a while and dying before they hit the floor.

He said at last, "Creyton?"

"He's dead."

I could see the fire race almost halfway down the cigarette as he dragged deeply. I was still too numb to put things together. I only knew that Pappy had been awake at the time of the shooting and he had made no move to help me. He hadn't even bothered to come out and see if I was dead or not. He took one more drag on the cigarette and flipped it away.

"Well," he said, "it's just as well. Maybe I could have stopped it, but I doubt it. Sometimes it's best to let things run until they come out the way they're bound to in the end, anyway."

"Were you awake," I asked, "while he was trying to steal my horse?"

"I was awake."

"A hell of a friend you are! What was the idea of laying there and not even bothering to wake me up?"

"You woke up," Pappy said mildly. "Anyway, it wasn't any of my business. I did my part when I warned you about Paul Creyton. What if I had walked into the quarrel and shot Paul for you? What difference would it have made? He's dead anyway."

"But what if he had shot me?" I wanted to know.

I could almost see Pappy shrug. "That's the way it goes sometimes. By the way, you handle guns pretty well, at that. Paul Creyton wasn't the worst gunman in Texas, not by a long sight."

It took me a while to get it. But I had a good hold now.

All the time I had been thinking that Pappy was my friend. He didn't even know what the word meant. Bite-dog-bite-bear, every man for himself, that was the way men like Pappy Garret lived. Unless, of course, some dumb kid came along who might be of some use to him for a few days. I'd played the fool all right, thinking that you could ever be friends with a man like that.

"Buck Creyton," I said. "You were afraid to take a hand with his kid brother because you knew you'd have Buck Creyton on your tail."

"I'll admit I gave Buck some thought in the matter," Pappy said.

I found that I still had the pistol in my hand. I flipped it over and shoved it in my holster. It's surprising how fast the shock of killing a man wears off. I wasn't thinking of Paul Creyton now. I was just thinking of how big a fool I had been, and getting madder all the time.

"This finishes us, Pappy. From now on you take your trail and I'll take mine. This is as far as we go together."

There was another flare of a match as Pappy lit a fresh cigarette. "Of course, son," he said easily. "Isn't that the way you wanted it all along?"

I left Pappy in the shack. I'd had enough of him. I went outside and gentled Red some more and wondered vaguely what to do with Paul Creyton. I didn't have any feeling for him one way or the other, but it didn't seem right just to leave him there.

What I finally did was to drag him down to the bottom of the slope and roll up boulders to build a tomb around him. That was the best I could do since I didn't have anything to dig a grave with. It was hard work and took a long time, but I stuck with it and did a good job. Anyway, it had a permanent look, and it would keep away the coyotes and buzzards.

When I finished, the sky in the east was beginning to pale, and it was about time to start riding back toward John's City. I stood there for a while, beside the tomb, half wishing I could work up some feeling for the dead man. A feeling of regret, or remorse, or something. But I didn't feel anything at all. I looked at the pile of rocks that I had rolled up, and it was hard to believe that a man was under them. A man I had killed.

When I started up toward the shack again, I saw that Pappy had come outside and had been watching the whole thing. There was a curious twist to his mouth, and a strange, faraway look in his eyes, as I walked past him. But he didn't speak, and neither did I.

I got Red saddled again, and, as I finished tying on the blanket roll, Pappy came over.

"You probably don't want any advice," he said, "but I'm going to give you some anyway. Go on down to your uncle's place on the Brazos, like your old man wanted. You'll just get into trouble if you go back home and try bucking the police."

I swung up to the saddle without saying anything.

Pappy sighed. "Well ... so long, son."

I had forgotten that I was still wearing the guns that he had given me, or I would have given them back to him. As it was, I just pulled Red around and rode west.

Chapter 4

Around the second day, on the trail back to John's City, I began to think straight again. I began to wonder if maybe Pappy hadn't been right again and I was acting like a damn fool by going back and asking for more trouble from the police. Maybe—but I had a feeling that wouldn't be wiped away by straight thinking. It was a feeling of something stretching and snapping my nerves like too-tight banjo strings. I couldn't place it then, but I found out later what the feeling was. It was fear.

Up until now it was just a word that people talked about sometimes. I always thought it was something a man felt when a gun was pointed at him and the hammer was falling forward, or when a condemned man stood on the gallows scaffold waiting for the trap to spring. But then I remembered that I hadn't felt it when Paul Creyton had taken a shot at me a few nights back. This was something new. And I couldn't explain it. When I felt it, I just pushed Red a little harder in the direction of John's City.

We made the return trip in three days, because I wasn't as careful as Pappy had been about covering my trail. We came onto the John's City range from the north, and I made for the Bannerman ranch first because it was closer than our own place, and I wanted to see if Laurin was all right. I remember riding across the flat in the brilliant afternoon, wondering what I would do if the cavalry or police happened to be waiting for me there at the Bannermans'. I had been around Ray Novak and his pa enough to be familiar with the law man's saying: "If you want to catch a fugitive, watch his woman."

But I didn't see anything. I raised the chimney of the Bannerman ranch house first, sticking clear-cut against the ice-blue sky. And pretty soon I could make out the whole house and the corrals and outbuildings, and that feeling in my stomach came back again and told me that something was wrong.

It was too quiet, for one thing. There are sounds peculiar to cattle outfits—the sound of blacksmith hammers, the rattle of wagons, or clop of horses—sounds you don't notice particularly until they are missing. There were none of those sounds as I rode into the ranch yard.

And there were other things. There were no horses in the holding corrals, and the barn doors flapped forlornly in the prairie wind, and the bunkhouse, where the ranch hands were supposed to be, was empty. The well-tended outfit I had seen a few days before looked like a ghost ranch now. And, somehow, I knew it all tied up with that feeling I had been carrying.

I rode Red right up to the back door and yelled in. "Laurin! Joe! Is anybody home?"

It was like shouting into a well just to hear your voice go round and round the naked walls, knowing that nobody was going to answer.

"Laurin, are you in there?"

Joe, the old man, the ranch hands, they didn't mean a damn to me. But Laurin ...

I didn't dare think any further than that. She was all right. She had gone away somewhere, visiting maybe. She *had* to be all right.

I dropped down from the saddle, took the back steps in one jump, and rattled the back door.

"Laurin!"

I hadn't expected anything to happen. It was just that I didn't know what else to do. I was about to turn away and ride as fast as I could to some place where somebody would tell me what was going on here. Something was crazy. Something was all wrong. I could sense it the way a horse senses that he's about to step on a snake, and I wanted to shy away, just the way a horse would do. I took the first step back from the door, when I heard something inside the house.

It moved slowly, whatever it was. Not with stealth, not as if it was trying to creep up on something. More as if it was being dragged, or as if it was dragging itself. Whatever it was, it was coming into the kitchen, toward the back door where I still stood. Then I saw what it was.

"Joe," I heard myself saying, "my God, what happened to you?"

He was hardly recognizable as a man. His face had been beaten in, his eyes were purplish blue and swollen almost shut. His mouth was split open and dried blood clung to his chin. Blood was caked on his face and in his hair and smeared all over the front of his shirt.

"What are you doing here?" he asked dully. I noticed then that his front teeth were missing. But I only noted it in passing. In the back of my mind. I could think of only one thing then—Laurin.

I jerked the screen door open and went inside. "Joe, where's Laurin? Is she all right?"

He looked at me stupidly and I grabbed the front of his shirt and shook him.

"Answer me, goddamn you! Where's Laurin?"

He shook his head dumbly and began to sag. I held him up and pulled a kitchen chair over with my foot and let him sit down.

"So help me God," I said, "if you don't tell me what happened to Laurin I'll finish what somebody else started."

He worked his mouth. I couldn't tell if he understood me or not. It took him a long time to get a sound out. He worked his mouth, rubbed his bloody face, licked his split lips.

Then, "Laurin ..." he said finally. "She's ... all right."

I realized that I had been holding my breath all the time it had taken him to get those words out. Now I let it out. It whistled between my teeth, and my heart began to beat and blood began to flow. Relief washed over me like cool water on a hot day.

"Where is she, Joe? Tell me that."

He started to get up, then sat down again. He made meaningless motions with his hands. Whoever had worked on him had done a hell of a good job. I wondered if maybe there wasn't a hole in the back of his head where all his brains had leaked out.

"Answer me, Joe! Where is she? Where is Laurin?"

"Your place," he managed at last. "Your place ... with your ma."

I didn't stop to wonder what Laurin would be doing at our ranch. I was too relieved to wonder about anything then. Joe started to stand up again and I pushed him down.

"Stay where you are," I said. "I'll get you some water."

I found a bucket of water and a dipper and a crock bowl on the kitchen washstand. Then I got some dish towels out of the cupboard and brought the whole business over and put it on the kitchen table. I wet the towel and wiped some of the blood off his face. I squeezed some water over his head and cleaned a deep scalp wound behind his ear.

That was about all I could do for him. He didn't look much better after I had finished, but he seemed to feel better.

I gave him a drink out of the dipper and said, "Can you talk now?"

He touched his mouth gently, then his eyes and nose. "Yes," he said.
"I guess I can talk."

"What happened to you?" I asked. "What happened out there?" I
motioned toward the empty corrals and barns and bunkhouse out in
the ranch yard.

"The police," he said. "The goddamned state police. They came here
yesterday morning wanting to know where you were. When we did-
n't tell them, they ran off all the livestock—that's where the hands are,
looking for the cattle. They threatened to burn the place if we didn't
tell them. They're mad. Crazy mad. That bluebelly that Ray gave the
beating to was the governor's nephew, or cousin, or something, and all
hell's broke loose in John's City. They're out to get every man that ever
said a word against the carpetbag rule. They want you especially bad,
I guess."

"Why do they want me so bad? Hell, I wasn't the one that hit the governor's kinfolks."

"Because you're the only one that got away from them," Joe Bannerman said. "Ray Novak came back and gave himself up. But they're
not satisfied. They got to thinking about that fight you had a while
back. They won't be satisfied until they've got you on the work gang,
right alongside of Ray Novak."

So Ray Novak had come back. Gave himself up to carpetbag law. It
didn't surprise me the way it should have. Maybe I knew all along that
sooner or later all of that law-and-order his old man had pounded into
him would come to the top. Well, that was all right with me. He could
put in his time on the work gang if he wanted to, but not me. Not while
I had two guns to fight with.

Joe Bannerman was studying me quietly, through those purple slits
of eyes. Something was going on in that mind of his, but I couldn't make
it out at first. There was something about it that made me uneasy.

"The police," I said, "they came back today to have another go at
finding out where I'd gone. Is that how you got that face?"

He nodded and looked away. It hit me then, and I knew what it was
about his eyes that worried me. For some crazy reason, Joe Bannerman
was feeling sorry for me. That wasn't like him. Refusing to give information to the bluebellies was different—any honest rancher would have
done the same thing—but that look of sympathy—I hadn't been ready

for that. Not from Joe Bannerman.

He said, "Tall, have you been home yet?"

"Not yet," I said. "I wanted to make sure that Laurin was all right."

He looked at his hands as if there was something very special about them. As if he had never seen another pair just like them before.

"I thought maybe you knew," he said. "I figured maybe that was the reason you came back."

I looked at him. "You thought I knew what?"

"About your pa."

"Goddammit, Joe, can't you come out and tell something straight, without breaking it into a hundred pieces? What about Pa?"

Then he lifted his head and he must have looked at me for a full minute before he finally answered. "Tall, your pa's dead."

I don't know how long I stood wanting to curse him for a lousy liar, and all the time knowing that he was telling the truth. That was the answer to the feeling I'd had. It all made sense now. Pa, a part of me, had died.

Somehow I got out of the house. I remember Joe Bannerman saying, "Tall, be careful. There's cavalry and police everywhere."

I punished Red unmercifully going across the open range southeast toward our place. I rode like a crazy man. The sensible part of my brain told me that there was no use taking it out on Red. It wasn't his fault. If it was anybody's fault, it was my own. But the burning part of my brain wanted to hit back and hurt something, as Pa had been hurt, and Red was the only thing at hand.

But all the wildness went away the minute our ranch house came into sight, and there was nothing left but emptiness and ache. There were several buggies and hacks of one kind or another sitting in front of the house, and solemn, silent men stood around in little clusters near the front porch. I swung Red around to come in the back way, and the men didn't see me.

I didn't see any police. All the men were ranchers, friends of Pa's. The womenfolk, I knew, would be inside with Ma. As I pulled Red into the ranch yard, Bucky Stow, one of our hands, came out of the bunkhouse. When he saw who it was, he hurried toward me in that rolling, awkward gait that horsemen always have when they're on the ground.

"Tall, for Christ's sake," he said, "you oughtn't to come here. The damn bluebellies are riled up enough as it is."

I dropped heavily from the saddle and put the reins in his hands. I noticed then that I had brought blood along Red's glossy ribs where I had raked him hard with my spur rowels, and for some crazy reason that made me almost as sick as finding out about Pa. Pa had loved that horse.

But I slapped him gently on the rump and he seemed to understand. I said, "Give him some grain, Bucky. All he wants."

"Tall, you're not going to stay here, are you?"

I left him standing there and headed toward the house. I went into the kitchen where two ranch wives were rattling pots and pans on the kitchen stove. They looked up startled, as I came in. I didn't notice who they were. I went straight on through the room and into the parlor where the others were.

The minute I stepped into the room everything got dead quiet. Ma was sitting dry-eyed in a rocker, staring at nothing in particular. Laurin was standing beside her with a coffee pot in one hand, holding it out from her as if she was about to pour, but there was no cup. She stared at me for a moment. Then, without a word, she began getting the other women out of the room.

In a minute the room was empty, except for just me and Ma. I don't believe it was until then that she realized that I was there. I walked over to her, not knowing what to do or say. When at last she looked up and saw me, I dropped down and put my head in her lap the way I used to do when I was a small boy. And I think I cried.

One of us must have said something after that, but I don't remember. After a while one of the ranch wives, well meaning, came in from the kitchen and said timidly:

"Tall, hadn't you better eat something?"

It was so typical of ranch wives. If there's nothing that can possibly be done, they want to feed you. Ma would have done the same thing if she had been in the woman's place.

I got to my feet and said, "Later, not now, thank you." The words sounded ridiculous, like somebody turning down a second piece of cake at a tea party. And out there somewhere Pa was dead.

The woman disappeared again, and I touched Ma's head, her thin, gray hair. "Ma ..." But I didn't know how to go on. I wasn't any good at comforting people. And besides, she was still too numb with shock to understand anything I could say to her.

As I stood there looking at her, the ache and emptiness in my belly began to turn to quiet anger. Slowly, I began to put things together that I had been too numb to think about before. Instinctively, I knew that Pa hadn't died in any of the thousand and one ways a man could die around a ranch. He had been killed. I didn't know by whom, but I would find out. And when I did ...

Ma must have sensed what I was thinking. She looked up at me with those wide, dry eyes of hers. She noticed the two .44's that I had buckled on, and I saw a sudden stark fear looking out at me.

"Tall ... no! There's nothing you can do now. There's nothing you can do to bring him back."

But that anger that had started so quietly was now a hot, blazing thing. I heard myself saying:

"He won't get away with it, Ma. Whoever it was, I'll find him. Texas isn't big enough for him to hide where I can't find him. The world isn't that big. And when I do find him ..."

That helplessness and terror in her eyes stopped me. She looked at me, and kept looking at me, as if she had never seen me before. I should have kept my thoughts to myself, but it was too late to change that now.

"Ma," I said, "don't worry about me."

But she didn't say anything. She just kept looking at me.

I went back to the kitchen and motioned to one of the ranch wives. "Would you mind looking after Ma for a while?" I asked. "I want to go outside for a minute, where the men are."

"Of course, Tall." She was a tremendous, big-bosomed woman, holding a steaming coffee pot in her hand. She had that same look of sympathy in her eyes that I had noticed with Joe Bannerman, and I hated it.

I went out the back way instead of the front, where I would have to pass through the parlor again and face that look of Ma's. Jed Homer was the first man I saw, a small rancher to the south, down below the arroyo. He and Cy Clanton were talking quietly near the end of the front porch. Neither of them seemed especially surprised to see me. They came forward solemnly to shake hands, something they never would have bothered about if Pa had been alive.

"We guessed that you'd be comin' back, Tall," Jed Horner said soberly, "as soon as you got the word."

"I guess you know all about it, don't you?" Cy Clanton asked.

"I don't know anything," I said, the words coming out tight. "But I'd like to know."

The two men nodded together, both of them glancing curiously at my two pistols. Then I noticed something strange for a gathering like this. All the men were armed, not only with the usual side guns, but some of them with shotguns and rifles.

"It was the police," Homer said. "Some damned white trash from down below Hooker's Bend somewhere. It seems like all the Davis police in Texas have congregated here at John's City. They claim they're goin' to teach us ranchers to be Christians if they have to kill half of us doin' it." Then he patted the old long-barreled Sharps that he held in the crook of his arm. "But we've got some idea about that ourselves."

"About Pa," I said. "I want to know how it happened."

"The police, like I said," Horner shrugged. "There must have been about a dozen of them, according to your ma. They started pushin' your pa around, tryin' to make him tell where you'd gone, and one of them hit him with the barrel of his pistol. That, I guess, was the way it happened."

"The funeral was yesterday," Cy Clanton said. "We buried him in the family plot, in the churchyard at John's City. There wasn't a better man than your pa, Tall. If the police want a war, that's what they're goin' to get."

The anger was like a knife in my chest. The other men drifted over one and two at a time until I was completely surrounded now. Their eyes regarded me soberly.

I said, "Does anybody know the one that did it? The one that swung the pistol?"

Pat Roark, a thin, sharp-eyed man about my own age, said, "I heard it was the captain of the Hooker outfit. It seemed like he was a friend of that carpetbagger you gun-whipped a while back. Name of Thornton, I think."

I knew what to do then. I turned to Bucky Stow, who had sidled in with the group of men. "Bucky, cut out a fresh horse for me, will you? I guess I'll be riding into John's City."

There was a murmur among the men. A sound of uneasiness. "Don't get us wrong, Tall," Jed Horner said. "We're behind you in whatever you decide to do about this. Like I said, there wasn't a better man than your pa. But I think you ought to know it would be taking an awful chance riding right into town that way. Police are thick as lice on a dog's back."

I turned on him. "You don't have to go with me. It's my job and I can take care of it myself."

"Tall, you know we don't mean it that way. If that's what you want, why, I guess you can count on us to be with you."

The other men made sounds of agreement, but a bit reluctantly. Then a man I hadn't noticed before pushed his way to the front. He was a small man with a ridiculously large mustache, and dark, intelligent little eyes peering out from under bushy gray eyebrows. He was Martin Novak, Ray Novak's father.

"Don't you think you ought to think this over, Tall?" he asked quietly. "Is it going to settle anything if you and the other ranchers go riding into town, looking for a war?"

"I'm not asking anybody to go with me," I said.

He regarded my two pistols, and I wondered if Ray had told him about Pappy Garret. But those eyes of his didn't tell me a thing. Then he seemed to forget me and turned slowly in a small circle, looking at the other men.

"Why don't you break it up?" he asked quietly. "Go on home and give things a chance to straighten out by themselves. It'll just make things worse—somebody else will get killed—if you all go into town looking for trouble." Then he turned back to me. "Tall, you're wanted in these parts by the law. These other men will be breaking the law, too, if they tie up with you in this thing. Sooner or later there'll be real law in Texas. When that happens, this man Thornton will get what's coming to him. I'll give you my word on that."

He actually meant every word of what he was saying. He had lived law for so long that anything that walked behind a tin badge got to be a god to him.

"Do you expect me to do like your son?" I asked tightly. "Would you want me to give myself up to the bluebellies, after what they have just done here?"

He started to say something, and then changed his mind. He looked at me for a long moment, then, "I guess it wouldn't do any good to tell you what I think, Tall. You'd go on and do things your own way."

He turned and walked through the circle of ranchers. I heard Pat Roark saying, "Well, I'll be damned. I never figured the marshal would back down on his own people when it came to a fight with the bluebellies."

Then Bucky Stow came out of the barn leading a saddled bay over to where we were. Slowly, the circle began to break up and the men went, one and two at a time, to get their horses.

I said, "Thanks, Bucky," as I took the bay's reins. "Take good care of Red. I'll want him when I get back."

Bucky shuffled uncomfortably. He was a quiet man who never said much, and I'd never known him to carry a gun, much less use one. He said, "Tall, I guess you know how I felt about your pa. I'd be glad to ..."

"You stay here, Bucky. You look after the womenfolks."

His eyes looked relieved. I led the bay over toward the corral where the ranchers were getting their horses cinched up. I hadn't taken more than a dozen steps when Laurin came out on the front porch.

"Tall?"

I wasn't sure that I wanted to talk to Laurin now. There was only one thing in my mind—a man by the name of Thornton. But she called again, I paused, and then I went over to the end of the porch. Her eyes had that wide, frightened look that I had seen in Ma's eyes a few minutes before.

"Tall," she said tightly, "don't do it. They'll kill you in a minute if you go into town looking for trouble."

I tried to keep my voice even. "Nothing's going to happen to me. You just stay here and take care of Ma. There's nothing to worry about."

She made a helpless little gesture with her hands. Even through all the bitterness that was in me, I thought how beautiful she was and how much I loved her.

"Tall, please, for my sake, for your mother's sake, don't do anything now."

"I have to do something," I said. "Don't you see that?"

"I just know that there's going to be more trouble, and more killing. It will be the start of a war if you go into town bent on revenge."

I tried to be patient, but there was something inside me that kept urging me to strike out and hurt. I said, "What do you want me to do, turn yellow like Ray Novak, and turn myself over to the bluebellies?"

"It wouldn't be turning yellow, Tall." Her voice was breathless, the words coming out fast, stumbling over each other in their haste. "Tall, can't you see what you'll be starting? If you can't think of yourself, think of others. Of me, and your mother."

The ranchers were waiting. They had their horses saddled, and the only thing holding them up was myself. I started backing away. "This is man's business," I said. "Women just don't understand things like this." Then I added, "Don't worry. Everything's going to be all right." But the words sounded flat and stale in my own ears.

We rode away from the ranch house with me in the van, and Pat Roark riding beside me. There was about a dozen of us, and we rode silently, nobody saying a word. I concentrated on the thud of the bay's hoofs, and the little squirts of powdery red dust that rose up, and a lazily circling chicken hawk up above, cutting clean wide swaths against a glass sky. I didn't dare to think of Pa. There would be time enough for that.

We traveled south on the wagon road that we always used going to Garner's Store, across the arroyo and onto the flats. We reached Garner's Store, a squat boxlike affair made of cottonwood logs and 'dobe bricks, about an hour after leaving the ranch house. It set in the V of the road, where the wagon tracks leading from the Bannerman and the Novak ranches came together. As we sighted the store, we saw two Negro police leave in a cloud of dust, heading south toward John's City.

There was no use going after them. A dozen armed men couldn't very well ride into town and expect to surprise anybody. We pulled our horses up at the store and let them drink at the watering trough. After a while Old Man Garner came out looking vaguely worried.

I said, "Those were Davis police, weren't they, the ones that fogged out of your place a few minutes back?"

The old man nodded. "I guess they was kind of expectin' something out of your pa's friends, Tall. Anyway, they stayed here until they saw you comin', and then they lit out for town."

Pat Roark said, "Did they mention what outfit they was out of?"

The old man thought. "They mentioned Hooker's Bend. I reckon they come from around there."

Pat looked at me. "You ready to ride, Tall?"

"I'm ready."

Chapter 5

As we rode, Pat Roark seemed to be the only man in the whole group who was completely at ease. He rode slouched over to one side of his saddle, grinning slightly, as if he was looking forward to the excitement. He's just a kid, I thought. Nothing but a damned green kid who doesn't know what he's getting into. But then I realized that he was as old as I was. Maybe a few months older. I'd never thought of him before as being a kid.

"Cavalry," Pat Roark said, as if he had been giving it considerable thought. "They're the ones we've got to watch out for. The police don't amount to a damn."

"How much cavalry is there?" I asked.

He shrugged. "There's a detail up north somewhere, about a half a troop, I think. They come and go in John's City, but they've got too much territory to cover to stay there all the time."

"But the police will be there," I said.

He looked at me. "They'll be there. This Thornton I mentioned—Jake Thornton, I think his name is—probably we'll find him in the City Bar. It's the only place in town that caters friendly to carpetbaggers."

I kept my voice level. "Do you know this Thornton when you see him?"

"I know him. I'll point him out to you when the time comes. It'll be a pleasure."

I knew then that Pat Roark was the only one I could really depend on when things got down to shooting. The others, mostly, were just coming along because they didn't have the guts to stay back. They were all good men, and I didn't have anything against them, but this was my fight, not theirs, and they knew it better than anybody.

When we sighted the town, Pat took out his pistol to check the loading. I said, "Do you mind if I look at that?" He grinned and handed it over.

It wasn't much of a weapon—an old .36-caliber Cofer revolver. It was mounted on a brass frame and had a naked trigger without any guard. I recognized it as one of the guns that the Confederacy had bought from some outlaw arms dealers before the war, probably because the Yankees were afraid to shoot them and they were cheap. Across the top of the frame and barrel there was the mark: T. W. Cofer's Patent, Portsmouth, Va. I figured it was about an even bet that the cylinder would explode before you could get off the third shot.

I handed the pistol back to him. Then, on impulse, I drew one of those new deadly .44's that Pappy had given me and handed that over too.

"You'd better take this," I said, "in case you need a pistol."

He took it, admiring its velvety finish and fine balance. Then he grinned again and shoved it into his waistband. "Thanks, Tall. I guess with a pair of these between us, we haven't got anything to worry about."

In Pat Roark, I knew that I had one good man on my side. And one good man was all I needed.

We rode into Main Street in no particular formation, Pat and myself still in the van, and the others strung out in the rear. The town was ready for us. Everything that a bullet could hurt had been taken off the plank walk and dragged inside. The street was almost deserted, with only two or three horses standing at the block-long hitching rack. The last buckboard was just pulling out of the far end of the street as we came into town.

"We hit it right," Pat Roark said out of the side of his mouth. "The cavalry's not in town." He was moving his head slowly from side to side, not missing a thing. The thumb of his right hand, I noticed, was hooked in his cartridge belt, close to the butt of that new .44. When his head turned in my direction again he said, "You want to try the City Bar first?"

I nodded. The bar was a two-story frame building standing on the corner, at the end of the block. When we reached it, I motioned for Pat to pull in, and I waited for the others to come up.

"Look," I said, as they grouped up around me, "I know this is none of your fight. I'm not asking you to come in with me, but I'll appreciate it if you keep watch outside here and see that nobody has a chance to get me and Pat in the back."

The men looked as if they wanted to object and join in on the fight, but nobody did. Jed Homer was the only one to say anything.

"Tall, we don't want you to get the idea that we're not with you. It's just like I said ..."

I left him talking and looped the bay's reins over the hitching rack. Pat was waiting for me on the plank walk, his back against the building.

"I guess we might as well go in," I said.

"I guess so."

We kicked both batwings open at the same time and stepped inside. I was ready to draw from the first. I half expected a rifle, or maybe a shotgun, to be looking at us from over the bar. But there was nothing out of the way. Business was going on as usual. A couple of Davis policemen were having beer at the bar, a handful of turncoats and scalawags were in the back of the place where the gambling tables were. A roulette ball rattled like dry bones as the wheel spun, then the rattling stopped abruptly as the ball went into a slot. "Black, twenty-three," I heard somebody say.

"He isn't here," Pat said under his breath.

The bartender and two policemen were watching us carefully, but nobody made a move. There was something about the whole setup that I didn't like. I knew the bartender recognized me, and probably the two policemen as well. Then why didn't they do something? I was the one they wanted.

I went over every inch of the place with my eyes. There were nine men in the place, counting the bartender, a croupier, and a blackjack dealer. In the back of the place there were some stairs leading up to a small

gallery jutting out over the gambling area, but there was nobody up
there that I could see.

Without turning his head, Pat said, "You want to try the marshal's
office?"

That would be the logical thing to do, but there was still something
about this place that I didn't like. I walked over to the bar, and Pat
stayed where he was, by the door. The roulette ball didn't rattle any
more. The blackjack dealer paid off, raked his cards in, and waited.
Everybody seemed to be waiting for something.

The bartender moved away from his two police customers and came
down to the end of the bar where I was.

"What'll you have, Tall?" he asked easily. Maybe a little too easily.

"Information," I said. "I'm looking for a man. A man by the name
of Thornton."

He thought it over carefully. "You ought to try the marshal's office,"
he said finally. "That's his headquarters, not here."

He started to reach under the bar for something. A bar rag maybe,
or some fresh glasses. But it could have been a shotgun.

I said, "Just keep your hands where I can see them." The two policemen were watching us, but so far they hadn't made any move toward their guns. One was short and big around the belly and hips. The
other was big all over, maybe six feet tall and weighing around two hundred pounds. I called down the bar.

"You down there, where's your captain?"

The big one set his glass down. He looked at the short, fat one, and
they both grinned quietly, as if they were enjoying a secret little joke just
between the two of them.

"Down at the marshal's office, I reckon," the big one said.

He was lying. I was sure of that without knowing how I was sure. I
could have killed him right there, both of them, with no regrets, no feeling at all. It could just as easily have been one of them, I thought. I'd
never be able to look at a policeman again without thinking that, without feeling that sick anger blaze up and burn again.

And the two of them stood there grinning. The bartender and the others didn't do anything.

I heard myself saying, "Do you know who I am?"

The big man shrugged. The short one had another go at his drink.

"The name is Cameron," I said. "Tall Cameron. I hear you Davis police are looking for me."

They didn't even blink. I was hoping that they would make a move for their guns, but they didn't move at all. The big man spoke mildly. "You must of heard wrong, kid. We don't want you."

"You're a goddamned liar," I said.

That jarred them for a minute. I watched the grins flicker and fade. They looked like they might go for their guns after all, and I was hoping they would. I was praying that they would give me an excuse to put a bullet ... But that was as far as the thought went. Pat Roark stopped all thinking, all action that might have taken place, with:

"Tall, look out!"

I wheeled instinctively. I vaguely noticed that the bartender's hands had darted under the bar again and I caught the glint of a brutish sawed-off shotgun. And I was aware of the two police clawing for their own side guns—but all that was in the back of my mind. It was the gallery that held my attention.

The man up there had a rifle pointed at my chest. I didn't know how he got up there. Probably he had been up there all the time, waiting for me to turn my back. I knew, with the same instinct that told me the big policeman was lying, that the rifleman was Thornton. Before I had half whirled about I heard Pat Roark's .44 crash and saw the bartender sliding down behind the bar, the shotgun dropping from his limp fingers. Somehow my own gun was in my hand.

At a time like that you don't stop to think. Your mind seizes all the facts in a bunch and there is no time to separate them and decide where to act first. The two policemen were still clawing for their pistols, awkwardly. But the man on the gallery didn't have to draw. The rifle was ready, aimed, and I imagined that I could see the hammer falling. I forgot about the two policemen. The .44 bucked twice in my hand and the room jarred with the roaring. Two shots, I knew, would have to do it. I couldn't wait to see if the man would fall. The two policemen were awkward with pistols, but they weren't that awkward.

By the time I swung on them again, the big man's gun was just clearing his holster. I shot him in the belly and he slammed back against the bar, clawing at the neat black hole just above his belt buckle. The fat one didn't have a chance. He shouldn't have been allowed to carry a gun. He didn't know what to do with one. He was still fumbling with the hammer as my bullet buried itself in the flabby folds of fat under his chin. He reeled back and blood began to come out of his mouth.

It all happened in a second. Two seconds at the most. I stood there watching the fat man die. He sagged, clutching at the bar to hold himself up. But his fingers missed and he hit the floor with his back, kicked once or twice, and lay still.

Pat Roark shouted, "The door, Tall. I'll keep them covered while you back out."

But it wasn't over yet. Thornton, the man on the gallery, was still alive. He was on his knees clutching his middle, and bright red blood oozed between his fingers. I counted my shots in my mind. Two at Thornton, one at the big man, and one at the fat one. That was four. I had one bullet left. A six-shooter is actually a six-shooter only for fools and dime novels. There's always an empty chamber to rest the hammer on when the pistol is in the holster. I leveled the pistol at Thornton and fired my last bullet. I thought, This one's for you, Pa. It's too late to do you any good, but it's the only thing I know to do.

Thornton came crashing down from the gallery, falling across a poker table like a rag doll, then dumping into a shapeless heap on the floor.

I stood there breathing hard, the empty pistol still in my hand.

Pat said, "Tall, for God's sake, come on!"

But I waited a few more seconds, almost hoping that Thornton would move again so I could go over and beat the life out of him, the way he had done with Pa. But he didn't move. His eyes had that fixed glassy stare that always means the same thing. I had done all I could do.

The spectators—the carpetbaggers, and white trash, and scalawags— still hadn't moved. Their faces were pale with shock as they stared at the lifeless figures on the floor. That wasn't the way they had expected it to work out. They had been confident that their man could kill me easily from his place on the gallery, but now that it hadn't worked out that way, they weren't sure what they ought to do.

My pistol was empty, but they didn't realize that, so I kept it trained on them.

I said tightly, "Take a good look at the man that killed my father. Being a member of the Davis police didn't save his dirty hide; that's something the rest of you might remember."

"Tall," Pat Roark said again. I started backing out, keeping them covered with my empty pistol.

Outside, we hit the saddles and our horses lit out for the far end of the street in one startled jump. The other ranchers fell in behind us, fogging it out of John's City.

We traveled north toward Garner's Store for maybe two miles, and then the ranchers started splitting up, cutting out from the main body and heading toward their own outfits. They were nervous men for the most part, and I could see by their faces that they thought they had been suckered into something that they hadn't bargained for. Well, I thought, to hell with them. If they were afraid to fight for their own kind, there was nothing I could do for them.

By the time we reached the store, Pat Roark was the only one still with me. As we let our horses drink at the trough, Pat stood up in his stirrups, looking back along the road.

"The police don't seem so damned anxious to follow us," he said, still with that thin grin of his.

I wasn't worrying about the police. It was the cavalry that was going to give us trouble when they heard about it. We hitched our horses and went inside the store.

Old Man Garner wasn't glad to see us. Things had a way of happening to people who helped fugitives. A man's store could burn down, or he could get robbed blind. All kinds of things could happen.

He came slowly out of the dark interior of the store. He could smell trouble and he didn't like it.

"Tall, you get out of here," he said gruffly. "I know the police are after you; so don't tell me different."

"I'm not going to tell you different, Mr. Garner. But they won't be along for a while. Is my credit still good?"

He grunted. "I reckon. If it'll get you out of here."

We got a dozen boxes of .44 cartridges, some meal, salt, and a slab of bacon. "If you don't see me for a while," I said, "you can get the money from Ma."

"Money won't do me no good," he said peevishly, "if the police catch me helpin' you out this way. Now scat, both of you." Then on impulse, he went behind the counter and came out with a small tin skillet and a bag of ground coffee. "You might as well take these too, as long as you're gettin' everything else you want."

I took the things and wrapped them up in newspapers. Old Man Garner didn't like turncoats any better than most people, and he wasn't as put out about helping us as he tried to make us believe. As we started back for our horses, I said, "When the bluebellies come along you might just mention that you saw us heading east, toward Indian Ridge."

At last his curiosity got the best of him. "Did you ... kind of get things settled up, Tall?"

"As well as it can be settled," I said. "Remember, east, toward Indian Ridge."

"I won't forget. Now go on, get out of here."

We headed northwest along the road to the Bannerman ranch for a mile or more, and then cut due west on some hard shale that would be difficult to trail us on. We moved on up to some low rolling hills and finally reached the arroyo. I looked at Pat Roark.

He was a funny guy. And, as we headed toward Daggert's Road, I began to wonder just why he was sticking his neck out this way. The Roarks had a small one-horse outfit over east of John's City—that is, the old man had the outfit. Pat, I remembered, was the youngest of five sons, and the others had drifted off to other parts of Texas before the war and hadn't been heard from since. Pat's old man had never amounted to much. What little money he made by brush popping went mostly for whiskey. Pat had never had the money to attend old Professor Bigloe's Academy like the rest of us.

So maybe he was just looking for a chance to get away from John's City, and he figured this was it. Whatever the reason, I was glad to have him along.

We rode down the arroyo until we came to the cutaway that Ray Novak and I had ducked into before. Pat had never seen the place. I held some of the vines and scrub trees back and motioned him to go on in, and he said, "Well, I'll be damned." He looked around appreciatively as I covered the entrance again. "So this is Daggert's Road," he said. "Well, it'll be nearly hell for anybody to find us in a place like this."

I said, "It'll do for tonight. We'll go on up to the old cabin and stay there. If things look all right I'll ride over to our place. There's that red horse of mine. I sure would hate to leave him behind."

It was clear that we weren't going to be able to stay around John's City for long. Pretty soon the cavalry would be cutting tracks all over northern Texas looking for us, and it wouldn't be the work gang if they caught us this time. It would be a hanging.

Then, for the first time, I thought of those dead men back there in the saloon. I didn't feel anything for them, not even hate, because most of the hate had burned itself out the minute I emptied my pistol. There was just the faint feeling of satisfaction, that kind of feeling that comes to a man after he has paid off a big debt, and that was all. I didn't experience those few hard minutes, the way I had after killing Paul Creyton.

Four men I had killed in as many days—but even that didn't bother me. They had all needed killing. Nobody held it against you for killing a horse thief like Creyton. And Thornton and the other two policemen weren't any different. I would have to hide out for a while, until the carpetbaggers were out of Texas. A year, maybe. Two at the most, because Texans wouldn't stand for that kind of treatment for long. Then I could come back and stand trial. No jury of John's City ranchers would convict me for what I had done.

There were only two things that bothered me. How would Ma get along without me or Pa to look after her? And Laurin—it was going to be a hard year, or two years, being away from her.

"Is that the place?" Pat Roark pointed toward the sagging shack at the end of the trail.

I nodded. "I guess that'll hold us for a few hours. We can fill our bellies and rest our horses, and figure out where to go."

Pat laughed. "While the bluebellies cut tracks all over Indian Ridge."

Nothing seemed to bother him. If he regretted having to pull out like this, without even a chance to say good-by to his old man, it didn't show on that grinning face of his. He seemed to have completely forgotten the fact that he had killed a man a short time back.

We picketed our horses behind the shack where there was plenty of new green grass. By the time we got our saddles off and lugged our supplies inside it was almost dark. I wondered about making a fire, then decided we might as well have a hot meal while we had a chance.

Later, as we sat on the dirt floor eating dripping pieces of bacon and hoecake, Pat said, "I know it's none of my business, and don't get the idea I'm complaining, but don't you think it's a little dangerous staying this close to John's City? We could cover some ground tonight without punishing our horses."

"I told you I didn't want to leave that red horse behind," I said. "Hell, the cavalry won't find us here. They'll be cutting tracks on Indian Ridge, like you said."

Pat shrugged. "All right. I was just thinking."

Probably he knew the real reason I didn't want to pull out right away. It was Laurin, not that red horse. But he didn't say any more about it.

As night came on, we put the fire out, and my ears seemed to grow sharper as darkness closed in. The moan of the wind and the rattle of grass made startling sounds in the night. Once I got up abruptly and went outside with my gun in my hand when I heard a movement in the brush. But it turned out to be a swamp rabbit making his bed for the night under a clump of mesquite.

Pat said, "You'd better go see about that horse, if you're so almighty anxious about him."

He didn't say I was getting the jumps, but that was what he meant. All the things that had happened today began to grow and magnify in the darkness. I wouldn't let myself think about Pa. I had done all I could. He would understand that, wherever he was.

But Laurin was something else. She hadn't wanted me to go to town in the first place. What was she going to say about those bluebellies that I hoped were burning in hell by now? Somehow, I had to explain that to her before I went away. And I wasn't sure how I was going to do it.

I said, "Maybe you're right, Pat. I'll see about the horse. Then maybe we'll cover some ground before daybreak."

"Whatever you say." He had torn off a piece of his shirttail and was using it to clean that new .44 I had given him.

"You'll be all right here," I said. "The cavalry won't get around tonight."

"Don't worry about me." He looked up. "You're the one that better watch out the bluebellies don't get you."

It was completely dark now. I went outside and got the bay saddled, and Pat came to the door and watched as I rode off.

It wasn't a smart thing to do, I knew that. Pappy Garret would have skinned me alive for pulling a fool stunt like that ... but it was one of those things that I had to see all the way through. Before long—if I didn't set things straight with Laurin—I'd be snapping at Pat, and we'd end up the same as me and Ray Novak, riding our own separate trails. And I needed Pat. One man wasn't any good on the run. Pappy had been proof of that. It occurred to me that I had already learned to think the way Pappy Garret thought. I didn't really give a damn for Pat Roark, but I could use him, and that was what I meant to do.

That shocked me for a moment. A few days ago I had never even thought of killing a man, and now I had four to my credit, a longer string than a lot of well-known badmen could boast. I felt nothing for them. They could have been calf-killing coyotes, and not human beings.

I tried to work back in my mind and find the beginning of it. Paul Creyton—there was nothing I could have done about that. He had been trying to steal my horse, and that was reason enough for killing anybody in this country. And Thornton—nobody could blame me for that. And the other two—they had been pulling on me, and if I hadn't killed them they would have killed me. I hadn't started any of it. They had all brought it on themselves.

But still I could taste the uneasy tang of doubt, and I wondered if it all would seem so clear-cut and inevitable to Laurin as it did to me.

Coming out of the hills, I rode straight east, heading for our place. I would have a hard time explaining it to Pat, if I came back without that red horse, and, besides, for some strange reason, I wanted to put off seeing Laurin until the very last.

There was no sign of cavalry or police as I crossed the open range. Probably, I thought, the Cameron ranch would be the last place they would look for me, especially if Old Man Garner had told them we were headed for Indian Ridge.

The ranch house was dark when I got there. The only light I could see was in the bunkhouse. When we reached the rear of the ranch yard, I got down and led the bay toward the barn where I figured Red would be.

"Tall."

It was just a whisper, but there in the darkness it came at me like a bullet. I dropped the reins and wheeled.

"It's me, Tall! My God, be careful with that gun!"

It was Bucky Stow, coming from the far side of the barn. I didn't remember pulling my pistol, but there it was, in my hand, the hammer pulled back and ready to fall. I heard somebody breathing hard, breath whistling through his teeth. After a moment I realized it was me.

"You want to be careful how you slip up on people," I said weakly. Bucky would never know how close he came to being number five on my string. I shoved the pistol back in my holster.

"Tall, what in hell are you doin' here, anyway? There's cavalry and police all over this part of Texas."

"I came after that red horse," I said. "Is he ready to go?"

Bucky screwed up his face. "I reckon," he said. "But he could stand fattening up. A horse like Red ain't supposed to take that kind of treatment."

"Never mind about Red, he can take it. Is Ma doing all right?"

"She's over at the Novak place now," he said, rubbing his chin sadly. "She kind of figured that maybe you'd come back here. She wanted me to tell you to come to Virginia as soon as you get a chance."

I looked at him. "Virginia?"

"She's selling the ranch and moving back there with her people. Runnin' a ranch is too big a job for a woman. And since your pa ..."

His voice trailed off, but I knew what he was thinking. Now that Pa was gone, and I couldn't stay here to help her, there was nothing else for her to do. It hurt me at first, thinking about giving up this ranch that Pa had worked so hard for. But Ma had never really liked it. She only wanted to be where Pa was. It was the best thing, I thought, for her to move back with her own people until I could clear myself with the Texas courts.

I said, "Tell her I'm all right, Bucky. Tell her not to worry about me, and I'll see her in Virginia as soon as this thing blows over."

Bucky said, "Sure, Tall. Now I'll get that horse for you."

He went in the barn and in a few minutes he came back with Red, all saddled and ready to go. I slapped the horse's glossy rump. "You ready to travel, boy? You got your belly full of corn?"

Red switched his head around and nuzzled the front of my shirt. I thought wryly, That's the first sincere gesture of welcome I've had since I got back.

Chapter 6

I didn't try to go to the Novaks' and say good-by to Ma. That would be pushing my luck too far. I got on Red and we headed west again, crossing the Bannerman wagon road just in case the cavalry was up in that direction, then we went north, cross-country, until the big ranch house and barns loomed up in the darkness. I didn't have any guarantee that there weren't any soldiers in one of those barns just waiting for me to pull a fool stunt like this, but that was a chance I had to take. As I got closer, I saw that there was a light in the back of the house, in the kitchen.

I left Red at the side of the house, and the back door opened.

"Joe, is that you?"

Then I stepped into the light, and Laurin gasped. Her hands and arms were white with flour, and there was a pale powdery smudge on the side of her nose. She was just beginning to bake the week's supply of bread.

"Tall!" Her voice was frightened. "Tall, you can't come here. The cavalry left only an hour ago, looking for you."

"The cavalry can't keep me away from you," I said. "Nothing can."

Quickly, she dusted her hands and arms on her apron and came down the steps. I put my hands on her shoulders and I could feel her shiver as I drew her close and held her tight. "Oh, Tall," she cried, "it's no good. Meeting this way, in darkness, afraid to be seen together."

I kissed her lightly and we stood there clinging to each other. I pressed her head to my shoulder and the clean smell of her hair worked on me like fever. "I'll come back," I said. "It won't always be like this." Then I asked the question that I was half afraid to ask. "Laurin, will you wait for me? Will you trust me to straighten things out in my own way?"

For a moment she didn't say anything. Her body was rigid against me and I knew that she was crying.

"You know I'll wait," she said at last. "Forever, I suppose, if I have to. It's just that I'm afraid ... something awful and wrong is happening to us."

I knew she was thinking about those three men.... She didn't know about the fourth. "Can't you see, I had to do it?" I said. "I couldn't just stand by and let them get away with it—doing what they did. You see that, don't you?"

"I don't know," she breathed. "I just don't know."

"I'm not going to get into any more trouble," I said. "Don't be afraid of that. I'll join a trail herd and go up to Kansas until the bluebellies are out of Texas courts. Then I'll come back and stand trial."

She raised her head and looked at me for a long time. And at last she began to believe it.

"I'll wait," she said quietly. "If you'll do that, I'll wait as long as I need to. It won't be too long."

That was the way I remembered her, the way she looked as she said, "I'll wait." And then her face softened, and for a moment it seemed that she was almost happy. "I'll get you some bacon," she said, "and some fresh bread. You'll need something to eat while you're traveling."

"We'll get supplies," I said. I didn't want to go, but the time had come and I couldn't put it off any longer. Then I kissed her—hard enough to last as long as it had to last. "Don't you worry," I said. "I'll come back." It seemed that I was saying that more often than was necessary to convince her. Maybe I was trying to convince myself.

I looked back once as I rode away, and she was still standing there with the lamplight streaming out the door and falling over her like a veil of fine silk. She half lifted her hand, as if to wave, and then let it drop. After a while, she went back into the house and that was the last I saw of her.

It was a quiet trip riding back to the shack. There was no sign of soldiers or police anywhere, and I made up my mind to get out of this part of Texas as soon as I got back to where Pat Roark was. I was afraid that we had stretched our luck about as far as it would go.

I judged that it was about midnight by the time we reached the hills.

I nudged Red down into the gully that was Daggert's Road and stopped for a moment to listen, but there was still no sound except the faint night wind and the faraway bark of a coyote. We had almost reached the cabin when Red started shying away from something in the darkness.

I pulled up again and listened. There still wasn't anything that I could see or hear, but that didn't mean that there was nothing out there in the darkness. I felt of Red's ears. They were pricked up, stiff, his head cocked to one side. I reached far over and felt of his muzzle. It was hot and dry.

That worried me. Normally a horse's nose is cool and moist; it's only when he senses danger that it gets that hot, dry feel. Then I felt little ripples of nervousness in the long muscles of his neck. I knew something was wrong. But before I could do anything about it, a voice shouted:

"Throw up your hands, Cameron. We've got you surrounded!"

Instinctively, I drove the steel in Red's ribs and he jumped forward with a startled snort. I didn't know who was doing the shouting, but I could guess. I dumped out of the saddle as we neared the cabin, and Red spurted on like a scared ghost, heading for higher ground. I hit the ground hard, rolled, and scrambled for the door of the shack. If I had stayed on Red, they would have cut me down before he could have taken a dozen jumps, and besides, that gully of a road led to a dead end about a hundred rods up in the hills.

A rifle bellowed in the darkness, another one answered it, and then the whole night seemed to explode to life. Carbines, I thought as I crawled the last few yards to the doorway on my hands and knees. Cavalry carbines. Why the hell doesn't Pat shoot back?

Then my foot hit something soft and wet and sticky, and I had my answer. Pat Roark was dead. I didn't have to make an inspection to know that. I tried hurriedly to roll him over and it was like rolling a limp sack of wet grain. I let him stay where he was, got the door closed, and fumbled in the darkness for the window.

The shooting had stopped now. They saw that they had missed me on the first try, and now they were ready to think up something else. I wondered why they hadn't placed a man in the shack to shoot me as I came in—but I got my answer to that, too, as I was fumbling around looking for an extra box of cartridges. There was a man in here.

But he was dead, the same as Pat. The hard-visored forage cap on the floor told me that he was a soldier, probably a cavalryman. I felt for his head and jerked my hand back as I touched the clammy sticky mess that had leaked out of the hole in his skull. Well, they had done a good job on each other, I thought grimly.

I went back to the window and tried to see something. They hadn't started to move in yet. Probably, they were in positions on high ground overlooking the cabin, but I hadn't had time to notice that much when the shooting was going on. There was a little clearing all around the shack and I could watch three sides from the windows and door. But the rear was blind.

I took another look to make sure that they hadn't decided to rush me, then I went to the rear wall and began to knock out the 'dobe plaster between the logs. In a minute I had a porthole cleaned out big enough to shoot through and see through. But I wasn't sure how much good that was going to do me. I couldn't be in four places at once.

"Come out with your hands up, Cameron," the same voice shouted, "and we'll see you get a fair trial in court!"

I could imagine what kind of a trial I'd get in a carpetbag court, after killing three state policemen. I went back to the west window and looked out carefully. The voice, I judged, was coming from behind a rock up above the gully. An officer, probably.

"This is your last chance, Cameron!"

"Go to hell," I shouted. "If you want me, come and get me."

Nothing happened, and I began to wonder what they were waiting on. They had me surrounded. I wasn't questioning their word about that. Then why didn't they close in and begin shooting me to pieces? That's what I would have done if I had been in their place. Or maybe burn the cabin down. That would make a clean job of it.

But they were still waiting on something. I felt my way across the shack again and got my other pistol out of Pat Roark's dead hand. I rolled the soldier over against the wall to get him out of the way, and, as I was giving him the last nudge with my boot, the answer came to me.

The reason they were reluctant to start any wild shooting or burning was that they thought their man was still alive. I went back and inspected Pat Roark a little closer this time. Sure enough, he was still warm, lying there in the doorway with a bullet in his gut. It all began to make sense now. I could almost see it, the way it must have worked.

Pat had been out of the cabin for some reason when the ambush had been set, and when he came back, there was the soldier waiting to take him. I could imagine the way Pat Roark's face must have looked. He probably never even lost his grin as he jerked that .44 and shot the

trooper's brains out. But not before he got a carbine slug in the gut for
his trouble.

The others must have been wondering where I was and had set themselves to catch me when I came back—if I came back. Anyway, there
was the dead cavalryman, and Pat, who must have lived two or three
hours with a hot lead slug in his belly, waiting for me to come back and
save him. But I hadn't got back in time. And I couldn't have saved him
anyway. I couldn't even save myself now.

The best I could do was to try to keep things going the way Pat had
started it, by making the cavalry believe that their man was still alive.

"All right," the voice behind the rock called. "We gave you your
chance, Cameron. Now, we're coming after you."

I shouted, "Try it and this trooper of yours gets a bullet in his brain."
I had guessed right. That had them worried.

"How do we know he's not already dead?" the voice wanted to know.

"Why don't you come in and see for yourself?"

But they didn't accept the invitation. They were going to think it over
a while longer, and in the meantime I had some time for thinking myself. I wondered how they found this shack so quick. Probably some
turncoat had told them about it. I kept forgetting that Texas was full
of traitors. I remembered Pappy Garret saying once, "One mistake is
all a man is allowed when he's on the run." It looked like I had made
mine early.

I kept moving from window to window, from the door to the rear of
the shack, but I still couldn't see anything to shoot at. The waiting began to get on my nerves. I couldn't very well make a deal with them.
I couldn't get away without a horse, and from the way Red was going
the last time I saw him I guessed he must be close to Kansas by now.

So we waited some more. From time to time the voice would yell for
me to come out or they were coming after me. But they kept holding
off. Then, as the first pale light began to show in the east, I knew they
had finally made up their minds. I could hear them moving around out
there, and the officer giving orders in a low, hushed voice. They had decided their man was dead. There was no use for them to wait any
longer.

I could hear them spreading out, circling the cabin. It was light
enough to see by now, but they were behind rocks or brush, waiting
for the signal to rush. I waited by the west window, thinking, So this
is the way it's going to end—when the shooting and yelling started at
the rear of the cabin. I jumped over to the rear wall and got a pistol

through the crack. I shot twice before I saw that there was nothing to shoot at.

It was a trick. They had planted two or three men back there to draw my attention while the others started rushing from the front and two sides. I wheeled and headed back for one of the windows, but I could already see that it was too late. They were almost on me before I could get a shot off. I remember thinking coolly all the time, I'll have time to get one of them, maybe two. They'll have to pay for me if they get me. And I fired point blank into a cavalryman's face. The man running beside him fell away to one side, hit the ground and scrambled for the cabin. Behind me, I heard the others closing in on my blind sides.

I wheeled away from the window and took a shot out of the door. Then I saw a crazy thing. One of them stumbled, grabbed his belly and fell—not the one I was shooting at, but another one. Then I saw another one fall, and another one.

I didn't try to understand what was happening. For a moment I stood there dumb with surprise, and, by that time, panic had taken hold of the cavalry and they scrambled again for cover, what was left of them. I circled the inside of the cabin, counting the soldiers that hadn't made it back to cover. There were six of them. That stunned me. I had accounted for only one of them. I was sure of that. Then who had killed the other five?

Probably the cavalry was wondering the same thing. I could hear the officer shouting angrily, trying to get his men grouped for another rush. And after a minute they came again. Their force was cut to half this time, but they came running and yelling from all sides. Before I could raise my pistols, one went down. Then another one.

I didn't even bother to shoot again. The cavalry had had enough. They turned and scattered like scared rabbits, and there wasn't any officer to pull them together this time. The officer, a lieutenant, lay outside my window with a rifle bullet in his brain.

It had happened too fast to try to understand it. I only knew that there were eight dead men outside the shack, and I had killed only one of them. I heard the cavalry detail—what was left of it—scrambling down in the gully, and pretty soon there was the clatter of hoofs and the rattle of chain and metal as they lit out for the south. By this time they probably figured that the cabin was haunted, that there was a devil in there instead of an eighteen-year-old kid. And I wasn't so sure that they were so far wrong.

I should have known, I suppose, with that kind of shooting—but

Pappy Garret never entered my mind until I saw him coming down from the high ground, astride that big black horse with the white diamond in the center of its forehead. He was riding slouched in the saddle, looking more like a circuit-riding preacher than anything else, except for that deadly new rifle, still cradled in the crook of his arm. In one hand he held a pair of reins, and that big red horse of mine was coming along behind.

Pappy rode up in the clearing in front of the cabin, looking at me mildly, with that half-grin of his. Then he snapped the leaf sight down on his rifle, and sighed. Like a woodsman putting away his ax after a good day's work.

"Son," he said soberly, "you sure as hell have got a lot to learn."

"Where did you come from?" I blurted. "How did you know I was here?"

"Now don't start asking a lot of damnfool questions," he said. "You'd better just climb on this horse, because we've got ourselves some hard riding to do."

It was incredible that Pappy would stick his neck out like this to help a kid like me. But there he was. And if I wanted to be smart, I'd just be thankful and let it go at that.

I managed to say, "Thanks, Pappy. If you ever need a favor ... well, I owe you one."

I went in the cabin and gathered up the extra cartridges and grub and rolled it all up in a blanket. In a few minutes I had it all tied behind the saddle and was ready to go.

Pappy looked at me, and then at Red. He said, "We'll see now if that red horse was worth killing for." Then he added, "He'd better be."

For the next four days, I learned what hard riding really was. Pappy had it worked out to a science. Walk, canter, gallop. Walk, canter, gallop. Rest your horse five minutes every hour. Water him every chance you got, but be careful not to let him have too much at once. Steal grain for him. Raid cornfields or homestead barns. Take wild chances— chances that a man wouldn't dare take for money—just to get a few ears of corn for your horse.

We didn't have time to eat, ourselves. The horses were the important things. I wanted to stop and cook some bacon, but Pappy said no. He had some jerky that he saved for times like this, so we chewed that while we rode. We traveled cross-country, never touching the stage roads except to cross them. Skirting all towns and settlements. Avoiding communities where we saw telegraph wires strung up.

Then, on the fourth day, we saw red dust boiling up ahead of us like low-hanging clouds. And as we got closer we could hear the bawling of cattle and the hoarse cursing of trail hands. At last we pulled up on a small rise and looked down on the constant stream of animals and men. It didn't look like an easy way to get to Kansas, but it was the best way for us. The law didn't bother trail herds. The big ranchers and cattle buyers saw to that. Their job was to get cattle to the railheads in Kansas, and they weren't particular about the men they hired, as long as they got the job done.

"Well, Pappy?" I said.

Pappy shook his head. "This is still dangerous country. Probably those cattle were gathered around Uvalde. They'll travel along the eastern line of army posts until they get to Red River Station. We'll push on east and catch a herd coming up the Brazos."

So we headed east and north, skirting the main trails until we got to Red River Station. The Station was a wild, restless place, milling with bawling cattle, and wild-eyed trail bosses trying to keep their herds in check until their time came to make the crossing. Herds from all over Texas gathered here to make their push through Indian Territory— shaggy brush cattle from along the Nueces, as wild and murderous as grizzlies; scrawny, hungry-looking steers all the way from Christi; fat, well-fed ones from the Brazos. Wild cattle and the near-wild men that drove them, all took advantage of the Station's limited facilities to break the monotonous, fatiguing routine of trail life.

The only building there was a long, cigar-box-shaped log hut along the river bank, and Pappy and I made for it. There was no sign of police or cavalry, and, when I mentioned it to Pappy, he laughed dryly.

"They wouldn't do any good here. In the first place, it would take a regiment of cavalry and the whole damn state police force to make an impression on a bunch of drovers. Anyway, all a man has to do is jump across the river and he's in Indian Territory where the police couldn't follow him."

There was a long bar inside the Station's one building, where men stood two deep waiting for their wildcat whiskey at two bits a drink. There was gambling in the back of the place, and half-breed saloon girls moving among the customers, promoting one kind of deal or another. Pappy and I waited at the bar until the bartender got around to us.

"Well, son, what do you think of it?"

"I'm not sure," I said. "I never saw anything like it before."

Pappy grinned slightly. "Wait until you see Abilene." He picked up a bottle and we went to a table in the back of the place. It felt good to sit down in a chair for a change, instead of a saddle. I didn't feel sleepy. You got the idea that nobody ever slept in a place like this. There was too much excitement for that.

I said, "Do you think we'll be safe here?"

"As safe as we'd be anywhere," Pappy said. "As long as we don't overdo it. I'll look around and pick out a herd to hook up with before long. Abilene beats this place. Besides, the marshal there is a friend of mine."

For the past four days, I hadn't had time to think. And now I was too tired to think. The fight with the cavalry seemed a long way in the past. It was hard to believe that it had happened.

We stayed at Red River Station that night, spreading our blanket rolls on the ground, the way the drovers did, and the next day Pappy went to see about a job for us.

That was the day I met Bat Steuber, a wiry little remuda man from an outfit down on the Brazos. A remuda man, I figured, might be able to rustle up some grain for Red and that big black of Pappy's, if he was handled right.

The way to handle him, it turned out, was with whiskey. I bought him three drinks of wildcat with Pappy's money and he couldn't do enough for me. He took me down to where the outfit was camped and got some shelled corn out of the forage wagon. Or rather, he was about to get the corn, when a man came up behind the wagon and cut it short.

"The boss says look after the horses," the man said.

He was a big man, his shoulders and chest bulging his faded blue shirt. His eyes were red-rimmed from riding long days in the drag, and his mouth was tight, looking as if he hadn't smiled for a long time.

Bat Steuber said, "Hell, Buck, I finished my shift. It's your..."

The man cut him off again. "I said see about the horses."

The voice cracked and Steuber jumped to his feet. "Sure, Buck, if you say so."

The man watched vacantly as Steuber went back to the rear where the remuda was ringed in; then he turned to me. I had a crazy idea that I had seen the man before, but at the same time I knew I hadn't. There was something about him that was familiar. His eyes maybe. I had seen eyes like those somewhere, clear, and blue, and deadly. He wore matched .44's converted, the same as mine, and I didn't have to be told that he knew how to use them. There are some things you know without having it proved to you.

"What's your name, kid?" he asked flatly.

"Cameron," I said. "Talbert Cameron. I don't think I caught yours."

He looked as if he hadn't heard me. "You're the kid that rode in with Pappy Garret yesterday, ain't you?"

He was asking a lot of questions, in a country where it wasn't polite to ask a stranger too many questions. But I said, "That's right."

I thought something happened to those eyes of his. He said flatly, "When you see Pappy, tell him I'm looking for him to kill him."

For a moment, I just stood there with my back against the wagon wheel. He said it so quietly and matter-of-factly that you wondered afterward if he had spoken at all.

I tried to keep my voice as level as his. "Don't you think that'll be kind of a job? Men have tried it before, I hear."

His voice took an edge. "You just tell him what I said, kid. That way maybe you'll live to be a man someday." He turned abruptly and started to walk away. Then he turned again. "Just tell him Buck Creyton is ready any time he wants to show his guts. If there is any question as to why I want to kill him, you might ask if he remembers my brother Paul."

He was gone before I could think of anything to say. Buck Creyton—a name as deadly as a soft-nosed bullet. A name as well known as Pappy Garret's, when the talk got around to gun-fighters.

I thought, Have you lost your guts? Why didn't you tell him that you were the one that killed his brother, and not Pappy?

I didn't know. I just thought of those deadly blue eyes and felt my insides turn over. He would kill me without batting an eye. Then I thought, Just like I killed his brother, and the three policemen, and the cavalryman.

I walked over to Red and swung up to the saddle. "Come on, boy," I said. "Let's get out of here."

Chapter 7

I waited for Pappy at the camp we had made, up the river from the herds. I wasn't sure whether I wanted to run or to stay with Pappy and see the thing through with Creyton. Maybe I would have the decision made for me, if Pappy ran into Creyton before he got back to camp.

Then—out of nowhere—I heard the words: Don't worry about me. I'm not going to get into any more trouble. They sounded well worn and bitter. They were words I had said to Laurin, and a few hours later I had killed another man, a soldier.

Now I had the government officers on my tail as well as the state police. Laurin ... I'd hardly had time to think about her until now. I could close my eyes and see her. I could almost touch her. But not quite.

I picked up a rock and flung it viciously out of sheer helplessness and anger.

I hadn't asked to get into trouble. It was like playing a house game with the deck stacked against you. The longer you played, the harder you tried to get even, and the more you lost. Where would it stop? Could it be stopped at all?

I realized what I was doing, and changed my thinking. You'd go crazy thinking that way. Or lose your guts maybe, and get yourself killed. And I wasn't planning on getting killed, by Buck Creyton, or the police, or anybody else. I had to keep living and get back to John's City. I had to get back to Laurin.

They didn't really have anything against me—except, of course, that one trooper that I had shot up at Daggert's cabin. But a jury of ranchers wouldn't hang me for shooting a bluebelly. Just lay quiet, I told myself, and wait for the right time.

But there was still Buck Creyton to think about. My mind kept coming back to him. I wondered vaguely if Paul Creyton had any more kinfolks that would be bent on avenging him. Or the policemen, or the trooper.

At last, when I finally went back to the beginning of the trouble, there was Ray Novak. He was the one who had started it all. I realized then that I hated Ray Novak more than anybody else, and sooner or later ...

But caution tugged again in the back of my mind. Lie quiet, it said. Don't ask for more trouble.

Pappy came in a little before sundown, covered with trail dust and looking dog tired. I didn't know how to break it to him about Buck Creyton. I wasn't sure what he would do when he found out that Creyton was after him for something he hadn't done.

"I got us fixed up with a job of work," he said, wetting his bandanna from his saddle canteen and wiping it over his dirty face. "The Box-A outfit needs a pair of swing riders to see them through the Territory. Forty dollars a month if we use our own horses. That all right with you?"

"I guess so," I said.

He wrung his bandanna out and tied it around his neck again. "You don't sound very proud of it," he said. But he grinned as he said it. I could see that Pappy was in good spirits. "It seemed like I rode halfway to the Rio Grande looking for that outfit," he went on. "But it's what we want. The trail boss is a friend of mine and he don't allow anybody to cut his help for strays. Cavalry included." He patted his belly. "Say, is there any of that bacon left?"

"Sure," I said. I got the slab and cut it up while Pappy made the fire. I decided I'd better let him eat first before saying anything.

It was almost dark by the time we finished eating. Pappy sat under a cottonwood as I wiped the skillet, staring mildly across the wide, sandy stretch of land that was Red River. There was almost no river to it, just a little stream in the middle of that wide, dusty bed. Quicksand, not water, was what made it dangerous to cross.

I put the skillet with the blanket roll and decided that now was as good a time as any.

"Pappy," I said abruptly, "we're in trouble."

He made one of those sounds of his that passed for laughter. "We were in trouble," he said. "Not any more. We've got clear sailing now, all the way to Kansas."

"I don't mean with the police. With Buck Creyton."

I saw him stiffen for a moment. Slowly, he began to relax. "Just what do you mean by that?" he asked. Some people, when they get suddenly mad, they yell, or curse, or maybe hit the closest thing they can find. But not Pappy. His voice took on a soft, velvety quality, almost like the purring of a big cat. That's the way his voice was now.

But I had gone too far to back down. I said, "I saw him today. He's working with one of the outfits getting ready to make the crossing. He's looking for you, Pappy. He says he's going to kill you."

Pappy sat very still. Then he said, "You yellow little bastard."

The words hit like a slap in the face. I wheeled on him, my hands about to jump for my guns, but then I remembered what Pappy had done to Ray Novak, and dropped them to my side.

"Look, Pappy," I said tightly, "you've got this figured all wrong."

He didn't even hear me. "You told him I was the one that killed Paul, didn't you?"

"I didn't tell him a thing," I said.

"I'll bet! You didn't tell him that *you* did it." Slowly he got to his feet, his hands never moving more than an inch or so from the butts of his pistols.

I suppose I was scared at first, but, surprisingly, that went away. I began to breathe normally again. If he was determined to think that I had crossed him, there was nothing I could do about it. If he was determined to force a shoot-out, there was nothing I could do about that, either. He was standing in a half crouch, like a lean, hungry cat about to spring.

"You yellow little bastard," he said again.

I said, "Don't say that any more, Pappy. I'm warning you, don't use that word again."

I think that surprised him. He thought I was afraid of him, and now it kind of jarred him to find out I wasn't. Pappy was good with a gun. I'd seen him draw and I knew. Maybe he was better than me—a hundred times better, maybe—but he hadn't proved it yet.

He said, "I picked you up. I went to the trouble to save your lousy hide, and this is what I get. This tears it wide open, son. This finishes us."

"If you're not going to listen to reason," I said, "then go ahead and make your move. You've got a big name as a gun-slinger. Let's see how good you really are."

He laughed silently. "I wouldn't want to take advantage of a kid."

I was mad now. He hadn't given me a chance to explain because he thought he could ride his reputation over me. I said, "Don't worry about the advantage. If you think you've got me scared, if you think I'm going to beg out of a shooting, then you're crazy as hell."

He still didn't move. "You think you're something, don't you, son? Because you got lucky with Paul Creyton, because you killed a couple of state policemen who didn't rightly know which end of a gun to hold, you think you're a gunman. You've got a lot to learn, son."

"Draw, then," I almost shouted. "If you think you're so goddamned good and I'm so bad. Draw and get it over with. You're the one that got your back up."

For a moment I thought he was going to do it. I could see the smoky haze of anger lying far back in those pale eyes of his. I felt muscles and nerves tightening in my arms and shoulders, waiting for Pappy to make a move.

Suddenly he began to relax. The haze went out of his eyes and he sat slowly down by the cottonwood.

"What the hell got into us anyway?" he asked, shaking his head in amazement. "Hell, I don't want to kill you. I don't think you want to kill me. Sit down, son, until the heat wears off."

It took me a long time to relax, but I didn't feel very big because I had made Pappy Garret back down. I knew it wasn't because he was afraid of me.

"Go on," Pappy said softly, "sit down and let's think this thing over."

The anger that had been burning so hot only a minute ago had now burned itself out. Me and Pappy getting ready to kill each other—the thought of that left me cold and empty. Pappy had saved my life, he had given me a chance to live so someday I could go back to Laurin.

"It's just as well we got that out of our systems," Pappy said at last. "I'm sorry about the things I said. I didn't mean them."

That was probably the first time Pappy had ever apologized to anybody for anything. And he was right. It was just as well that we got it out of our systems. Sooner or later, when two men live by their guns, they are bound to come together. But there was slight chance of it happening again. You don't usually buck a man if you know he isn't afraid of you.

Pappy got out his tobacco and corn-shuck papers, giving all his attention to building a cigarette. After he had finished, he tossed the makings to me.

I said, "Hell, I guess I was just hot-headed, Pappy. I'm ready to forget it if you are. We're too good a team to break up by shooting each other."

Then Pappy smiled—that complete, face-splitting smile that he used so seldom. "Forgotten," he said.

After it was all over, I felt closer to Pappy than I had ever felt before. We sat for a good while, as darkness came on, smoking those corn-shuck cigarettes of his, and not saying anything. But I guess we both had Buck Creyton in our minds. I had already decided that I would hunt Creyton down the next day and tell him just the way it happened; then if he was still set on killing somebody, he could try it on me. I couldn't guess what Pappy was thinking until he said:

"This is as good a time as any to push across the river. You get that red horse of yours, son, and we'll be moving as soon as it's a little darker."

I got the wrong idea at first. I thought Pappy was running because he was afraid of a shoot-out with Buck Creyton. But then I realized that he wouldn't admit it that way if he was. At least he would make up some kind of excuse for pulling out.

But he didn't say anything, and then I began to get it. He was moving out on my account. He was ready to cross the Territory without the protection of a trail herd so that Buck Creyton wouldn't have a chance to find out that I was the one who had killed his brother. He was protecting me, not himself.

I didn't see the sense in it. It seemed like it was just putting off a fight that was bound to come sooner or later, and why not get it over with now? But I didn't want to argue. I didn't want another flare-up with Pappy like I'd just had. So I went after Red.

We crossed the river about a mile above the Station, keeping well east of the main trail, and pushed into Indian Territory. We rode without saying anything much. I didn't know how Pappy felt about it, but I didn't like the idea of running away from a fight that was bound to come sometime anyway. I figured he must have his reasons, so I let him have his way.

By daybreak, Pappy said we were almost to the Washita, and it was as good a place as any to pitch camp. The next day we pushed on across the Canadian, into some low, rolling hills, and that was where I began to see Pappy's reason for running.

First, we picked a place to camp near a dry creek bed; then Pappy insisted on scouting the surrounding country before telling me what he had in mind. Fort Gibson was on our right, Pappy said, over on the Arkansas line, but he didn't think it was close enough to bother us. The Fort Sill Indian Reservation was on our left, on the other side of the cattle trail, but the soldiers there were busy with the Indians and wouldn't be looking for us. The thing we had to worry about now, he went on, was government marshals making raids out of the Arkansas country. But we would have to take our chances with them.

"I've told you before," Pappy said, "that you've got a lot to learn." He led the way down to the dry creek bed and pointed to a log about forty yards down from us. "Pull as fast as you can and see how many bullets you can put in it."

SHOOTING
LESSON

It sounded foolish to me. And dangerous. What if soldiers heard the shooting? But I looked at Pappy, and his face was set and dead serious. I shrugged. "All right, if you say so."

I jerked at my righthand gun, but before I could clear leather the morning came to life with one explosion crowding on top of another. Pappy had emptied his own pistols into the log before I had started to shoot.

Pappy looked at me mildly and began punching the empties out of his two .44's. I didn't even bother to draw my own guns. My insides turned over and got cold as I thought of what Pappy could have done to me the other night, if he had wanted to. I breathed deeply a few times before I tried to speak.

At last I said, "All right, Pappy. Where do I start to learn?"

He grinned faintly. "With the holsters first," he said. "If you don't get your pistols out of your holsters, it doesn't make a damn how good a shot you are." He made me unbuckle my cartridge belts and he examined the leather carefully. "See here?" he said, working one of the .44's gently in and out of the holster. "It binds near the top where it's looped on the belt."

We went up to where the blanket rolls were, and Pappy got some saddle soap out of his bags. "You don't develop a fast draw all at once," he said, rubbing the saddle soap into the leather with his hands. "You cut away a piece of a second here, a piece of a second there, until you've got rid of every bit of motion and friction that's not absolutely necessary. All men aren't made to draw alike. Some like a cross-arm draw, or a waistband draw. Or a shoulder holster under the arm is the best for some men. You've got to find out what comes easiest and then work on it until it's perfect."

He stood back for a moment, looking at me as if I was a horse that he had just bought and he wasn't sure yet what kind of a deal he'd got.

Finally he shook his head. "Your arms are too long for the cross-arm or border draw. That goes the same for the waistband. At the side is the best place, low on your thighs, where your hands cup near the butts when you stand natural. You can't work out any certain way to stand, you've got to be able to shoot from any position."

He handed the belts and holsters back and I buckled them on again like he said. He looked at me critically.

"Unload your pistols and try drawing."

I punched the live rounds out and shoved the guns back in my holsters. Then I grabbed for them and snapped a few times at a spot in front of me.

"Again," Pappy said.

I did it all over again, but Pappy wasn't satisfied. He went over to where his saddle rig was and cut a pair of narrow leather thongs from his own bridle reins. Then he made me stand still, with my legs apart, while he put the thongs through the bottom of my holsters and tied them down to my thighs. "Arms too long, that makes the holsters too low," he said briefly. "They'll flap when you walk if you don't tie them down. Now try it again."

I pulled two more times and snapped on empty chambers so Pappy could get the right perspective.

"I guess they'll do," he said reluctantly. "Now we'll get to the shooting. The drawing can come later."

The dozen boxes of cartridges that I'd got from Old Man Garner went that afternoon. And most of Pappy's extra ammunition went the next day.

"Hell, no!" Pappy would shout when I tried to shoot from the hip. "Aim. That's the reason they put front and rear sights on a pistol, to aim with."

Then I would try it again, holding the pistol straight in front of me, like a girl, aiming and shooting at whatever target Pappy happened to pick. Once in a while Pappy would nod. Once in a great while he would grunt his approval.

"Now aim without drawing your gun," Pappy said finally. "Imagine that you've got your pistol out in front of you, aiming carefully over the sights!" He threw an empty cartridge box about thirty yards down the draw. "Aim at that," he said.

I stood with my arms at my sides, trying to imagine that I was aiming at the box.

"Now draw your pistol and fire. One time. Slow."

I drew and fired, surprised to see the box jump crazily as the bullet slammed into it.

"Now with the other hand," Pappy said.

I tried it again with the left hand and the box jumped again.

I turned around and Pappy was looking at me strangely. "That'll do for today," he said. He rubbed the ragged beard on his chin, glaring down the draw at the cartridge box. "You've still got a lot to learn," he said gruffly, "but I guess you'll do. It took me two years to learn to shoot like that."

I thought I had been doing something big when, as a kid, I had managed to put a bullet in a tossed-up tin can. But I knew that hadn't been shooting. Not shooting as an exact, deadly science, the way Pappy had worked it out.

The next day we worked on my draw, starting with empty pistols, drawing in carefully studied movements. It was agonizingly slow at first. Arms, and hands, and position of the body had to be correct to the hundredth of an inch. Only after everything was as perfect as it could possibly be did Pappy let me try for speed.

I watched Pappy do it slowly and it seemed so easy. His hands cupping around the butts, starting the upward pull. Thumbs bringing the hammers back as the pistols began to slide out of the holsters, forefingers slipping into the trigger guard. Then firing both pistols, not at the same time, as it seemed, but working in rhythm, taking the kick on one side and then on the other.

"All right, try it," Pappy said.

He pitched out another cartridge box, and I drew slowly, carefully, for the first few times to get the feel of it. Then, as I holstered the pistols again, Pappy shouted:

"Hit it!"

I wheeled instinctively, catching a glimpse of the small cardboard box that Pappy had tossed in the air. The pistols seemed to jump in my hands. The right one roared. Then the left one crowded on top of it. The cartridge box jerked crazily in the air, then fluttered in pieces to the ground.

I stood panting as the last piece of ragged cardboard hit the earth. I could feel myself grinning. I thought, Ray Novak and his two bullets in a tin can! I wondered what Ray Novak would say to shooting like this. I was pleased with myself, and I expected Pappy to be pleased with the job of teaching he had done. But when I turned, he was frowning.

"Take that silly grin off your face," he said roughly. "Sure you can shoot, but there's nothing so damned wonderful about that. I could teach the dumbest state policeman in Texas to shoot the same way, if I had the time. You just learn faster than others, that's all."

I didn't know what was wrong with him. He had worked from sunup to sundown for two days teaching me to shoot, and now that I had finally caught the knack of it, it made him mad.

Then his face softened a little and he looked at me soberly. "Now don't get your back up, son. I'm just trying to tell you that knowing how to shoot and draw isn't enough. Boothills are full of men who could outdraw and outshoot both of us. Shooting a man who's as good as you are, and shooting a pasteboard box, are two different things. Look...."

He drew his pistols and held them out to me butts first.

"What do you want me to do?" I asked.

"Is this the way you'd disarm a man? Make him hand over his pistols butts first?"

"Sure," I said.

"Then take them."

I reached for them. The pistols whirled almost too fast to see, with no warning, no twist of the hand. With his fingers in the trigger guards, Pappy had flipped the pistols over, forward, cocking the hammers as they went around. In a split second—as long as it takes a man to die—he had whirled the .44's all the way around, cocked them, and snapped, with both muzzles against my chest.

The pistols were empty. Pappy had seen to that beforehand. If they had been loaded I would have died without ever knowing how. My mouth had suddenly gone dry. I swallowed to get my stomach out of my throat.

Pappy holstered one pistol and casually began to load the other. "I said it once before," he said. "When it comes to guns, a man is never good enough. Now get your blanket roll together. We've stayed in one place too long already."

That night it rained, but we moved anyway, because Pappy said we had already used more luck than Indian Territory allowed. That night it caught up with us.

First, we almost rode into a detail of cavalry and, later, a hunting party of Cheyennes that had strayed off the reservation. We pulled up in a thicket of scrub oak and waited for the Indians to pass. I looked at Pappy and his face was just a blur in the rain and darkness, and I swore at myself for not bringing a slicker when I left John's City.

Pappy said, "I don't like it. With Indians off the reservation, there's bound to be cavalry all over this part of the Territory. Two stray riders wouldn't have much of a chance getting to Kansas."

I said, "The cattle trail can't be far from here. We can move in that direction, and if the cavalry sees us we can tell them we're drovers, looking for strays."

Pappy gave a sudden shrug. He didn't think much of the idea, but, with cavalry and Indians on the other side of us, there wasn't anything else to do. Pappy didn't mention Buck Creyton, and neither did I. After the Indians had passed on in the darkness, behind a slanting gray sheet of rain, we began moving to the west.

I think I smelled coffee even before I heard the nervous bawling of the cattle. Steaming, soothing coffee to warm a man's insides, and Pappy and I both needed it. We pulled up on a rise and looked down at the flatland below that some outfit was using for bedground. A herd of what seemed to be a thousand or more cattle was milling restlessly, and above the beat of the rain we could hear the night watch crooning profanely.

But the thing that caught our attention was the coffee. We could see a fire going under a slant of canvas that we took to be the chuck wagon, and that was where the smell was coming from.

Pappy looked at me. "You ever see that outfit before?"

"I don't know. I can't see enough of it to tell."

We were both thinking how good a hot cup of coffee would taste. We sat for a moment with rain in our face, rain plastering our clothing, rain running off our hats and slithering down our backs and filling our boots. Without a word, we started riding toward the fire.

As we circled the herd I heard one of the night herders croon, "Get on it there, you no-account sonofabitch," to the tune of "The Girl I Left Behind Me." There were three or four men standing under the canvas where the coffee smell was coming from. Pappy and I left our horses beside the chuck wagon and ducked in under the canvas sheet.

"Can you spare a couple of cups of that?" Pappy said to the cook, nodding at the big tin coffee pot.

The cook, a grizzled old man half asleep, grunted and got two tin cups and poured. The other men looked at us curiously, probably wondering where the hell we came from and where we left our slickers. I took a swallow of the scalding coffee, and another man ducked in under the canvas, cursing and shaking water from his oilskin rain hat. He looked at me and said:

"Well, I'll be damned."

For a minute, I stopped breathing. The man was Bat Steuber, the remuda man I had met back at Red River Station. We had run onto the same outfit that Buck Creyton was working for.

Chapter 8

Bat Steuber looked at us for a long minute, but I couldn't tell what he was thinking. Finally he turned to the other men and said, "The boss says, every man in the saddle that's supposed to be on night watch."

Cursing, the men left one at a time, got on their horses, and rode toward the herd again. Bat got his coffee and came over to the edge of the canvas where Pappy and I had moved.

"Is this Pappy Garret?" he said to me.

"That's right."

For a moment, he looked at Pappy with a mixture of awe and admiration. "I'm glad to know you, Pappy. I've heard about you." Then he laughed abruptly. "As who hasn't?"

Pappy nodded, looking at me. Steuber's voice went down almost to a whisper as he turned to me again. "Kid, it looks like I got you in a mess of trouble without meaning to. He's after you now instead of Pappy. Me and my goddamned big mouth."

"Who's after me?" I said.

"Buck Creyton." Steuber wiped his face nervously. "Hell, kid, I wasn't trying to get you into trouble. I was just trying to get Buck cooled down. He wasn't worth a damn on the herd as long as that temper of his was boiling. Anyway, after you left that day Buck was hellbent on a shoot-out with Pappy here. And I said, 'Hell, Buck, what makes you think Pappy Garret killed your brother? It don't stand to reason. He wouldn't have no call to shoot Paul for nothing—and you know damn good and well that your brother wasn't going to pick a fight with a man like Pappy.' "

Steuber wiped his face again. "That was all I said," he went on. "I remember Buck didn't say a word for a long time, and I could see him thinking about it, way at the back of those eyes of his. And finally he said, 'That goddamned punk kid.' "

I felt my insides freeze as I remembered those kill-crazy eyes of Buck Creyton's. Pappy didn't say anything. He didn't move.

I said, "Where's Creyton now?"

"Out with the herd somewhere." Steuber made a helpless gesture. "Hell, kid, I'm sorry...."

"Forget it," I said. "If you see him, tell him the punk kid is down at the chuck wagon. Tell him if he wants to shoot off his mouth to do it to my face."

I could feel Pappy stiffen. Bat Steuber's eyes flew wide and he searched around for something to say, but the words wouldn't come. After a minute he made that same helpless gesture again. "All right, kid, if that's the way you want it." He ducked out into the rain.

Pappy said flatly, "Now that was a damn-fool thing to do."

I said, "Maybe. But a showdown has got to come sometime, and it might as well be now. I should have told him that first day when he was gunning for you, but I guess I lost my guts for a minute."

"You're not ready for a man like Creyton," Pappy said. "Now get that red horse of yours and we'll ride toward Kansas."

"And get taken by the cavalry?"

I looked at Pappy and his eyes were sober and sad. I said, "It's no good like this, Pappy. I appreciate what you've done for me, but you can't fight my fights for me. Remember what you said: 'A man does his own killing, and that's enough'? Well, this is between me and Buck Creyton. I don't want to go along for a month, or six months, or a year, looking over my shoulder every time I hear a sound and expecting Buck Creyton to be there. And sooner or later he *would* be there, and maybe by that time I'd have lost my guts again."

For a long moment Pappy didn't move, didn't say anything. Then, at last, he got out a soggy sack of tobacco and his corn-shuck papers and began rolling a cigarette. After he had finished, he handed the makings to me.

"If that's the way it has to be," he said, "then I can't help you. It'll be between just you and Buck."

We stood there watching the rain, listening to the crooning of the night watch, and the nervous bawling of the cattle. After a while, I got a rag from the cook, wiped my guns dry, and put in fresh cartridges. After that there was nothing to do but wait.

Pappy didn't try to change my mind again. I guess he knew what it was like to be hunted, not only by the law, but by other killers like himself. And he knew it was better to get it over with now before the slow rot of time ate your guts away.

There was no way of knowing how long it would take the word to get to Creyton, but it would get to him. All I had to do was stand here, and before long he would be coming after me. I couldn't tell if I was scared or not. I wasn't very curious about it. There was an emptiness in my belly, and a dull ache ... and maybe I was scared, after all. But not so much of Buck Creyton. My mind kept going back to better days and better lands, and, no matter how I fought it, I couldn't keep my thoughts away from Laurin.

That was what I was afraid of, not of getting killed, but of leaving Laurin.

In the darkness, we heard the hurried sucking sound of soggy boots coming toward the chuck wagon. I turned quickly. Beside me, Pappy jerked out of the weary slouch that he had fallen into.

"Watch it, son," he said quietly. "Don't frame yourself against the firelight."

The boots came on. A blurred figure began to take shape in the rain, walking quickly and making sloshing sounds in the gummy mud. But it wasn't Buck Creyton. It was a man I had never seen before, in dripping, rattling oilskins. He ducked under the shelter and stood glaring angrily at us.

"Get the hell out of here," he said abruptly. "I don't know who you are, but you're not goin' to start a shootin' scrape and stampede a thousand head of steers. Not if I can help it."

Pappy said softly, "Now wait a minute. We're not starting anything. We just dropped in for a hot cup of coffee."

The man spat. "Like hell," he said. "You ride up and in ten minutes the whole camp's in an uproar." He looked at Pappy. "You ever hear of Buck Creyton?"

"I heard of him," Pappy said.

"He's comin' after you," the man said, grinning suddenly. He looked as if he expected Pappy to turn pale and start running at the mention of Buck Creyton. When Pappy didn't move, his eyes were suddenly angry again.

Pappy began rolling another cigarette. "It's not me he's after," he said. Then he nodded at me. "It's him."

The man stared. He was a short, round, hard little Irishman, with a baby-pink face and a blue-red nose. The herd's trail boss, I guessed. He didn't believe that an eighteen-year-old kid would stand still when he knew that a man like Creyton was gunning for him. He wheeled back on Pappy, about to call him a liar, when there was the sound of boots again, coming out of the darkness.

"The firelight, son," Pappy said softly. "Don't frame yourself."

I moved away, to the edge of the canvas shelter.

"Further," Pappy said.

I moved out into the rain. The rain hit my face like slender silver spikes driving out of a black nothingness. I felt empty and all alone out there, away from the fire's warmth, the canvas's shelter, Pappy's friendliness.

There was just me and the night and the rain, and the sound of boots coming toward me. I thought: This is the way it had to be, Laurin. You understand that, don't you?

There was little comfort in the night's answer. The boots were getting closer. From the corner of my eye I could see Pappy standing there under the shelter, looking into the darkness. And the pink-faced little trail boss, with his mouth working angrily, but no sound coming out. The sound of the boots stopped. A voice came out of the night.

"Pappy, I want to see that killing little bastard you ride with."

I thought I could see Pappy smile. A sad, forlorn smile. "I reckon you'll see him, Buck, if you just keep walking."

"Where is he? Hid out to shoot me in the back, the way he did Paul?"

I heard myself saying, "I'm not hid out. I'm here in the rain, just like you are. And I didn't shoot your brother in the back. But I shot him."

I heard him swearing. "You won't shoot anybody else, punk. Not after tonight."

He started walking forward again, slowly now, carefully. I suppose I should have stayed where I was, stood still, with my pistols out. That way I could have followed the sound, and that would have cut down Creyton's advantages. But suddenly I didn't want any advantage. Pappy never asked for one. All he ever asked for was an even break, and I could get that here in the darkness. I started walking toward the sound.

I heard Pappy give a grunt of dismay. The trail boss said hoarsely, "My God, stop it! This is crazy!"

But we didn't stop. It couldn't be stopped now. With every step we got closer together and I expected to see him. My eyes began to jump from peering so hard into the darkness. I didn't dare close them for an instant, even to blink away the water that was caught on my lashes. An instant was all it took with a man like Buck Creyton.

Pappy, and the trail boss, and the flickering firelight seemed to fade off into the distance and disappear completely. There was just me and a sound out there in the night. I wondered if Creyton had drawn yet. I wondered if that sighting-before-shooting technique of Pappy's worked in the rain. Would anything work in the rain? This was a hell of a place for a gun fight, in the rain and darkness where you couldn't see anything. I thought: If you don't stop thinking about it, Buck Creyton's going to spill your guts in the mud. And then I saw him looming out of the darkness.

He looked as big as a mountain. He had his slicker pulled back behind the butts of his pistols and water was pouring in a sheer veil off the brim of his hat. His face shone faintly over the shapeless bulk of his body, as cold and distant as the moon. I imagined that I could see those icy eyes of his. But that was only imagination. Everything happened too fast, and it was too dark, to make out details.

His hands were just a blur going after his pistols, and thought: He's fast. He's fast, all right. Pappy himself, on the best day he ever saw, was never any faster than that. Then everything in my mind became crystal clear and painfully sharp. It was that instant in a lifetime that a few people experience once, and most not at all—that instant of walking the razor-sharp edge of time and space, knowing that if you fall there is nothing but disaster all around you. Even my hearing was tuned sharper than the best-bred hunting dog's. I imagined that I could hear every raindrop hit. I could hear the double clicks as the hammers of Creyton's pistols were jerked back. And I thought: So this is the way it is. It's almost worth getting killed just to be a part of the excitement of dying. And then the night exploded into sound and fire.

I was vaguely aware of the pistols in my hands, and the roaring in my ears drowning all other sound. It was almost like being drunk, but no man had ever been drunk the way I was for that instant. Not on anything that came out of a bottle. For that moment I wasn't afraid of Buck Creyton, nor of any man on earth. I just held my guns and they did the rest, one crash crowding another until the night was crazy with sound. And after a time there were hollow, empty clicks as hammers fell on empty chambers, and I looked up ahead and there was only a shapeless hulk on the ground where Buck Creyton had been standing. I stood there gasping for breath, as if I had been running hard until my lungs couldn't take it any longer. And over the monotonous beat of the rain, I could hear the trail boss saying, "My God! My God!" over and over, as if he had to say something and those were the only two words he knew.

From far away, it seemed, I heard the sound of alarm and the crazy bawling and the pound of hoofs. And a voice in the darkness shouted, "Stampede!" and the running boots headed for the chuck wagon suddenly stopped, wheeled, and ran toward the remuda pen for the horses. Over it all, the trail boss was bellowing wildly, but it all seemed far away and no concern of mine.

Pappy came out from under the shelter, looking at me strangely. Then he went over to what was left of Buck Creyton.

"Jesus Christ, son," Pappy said, "did you have to shoot him all to pieces?"

"I couldn't stop," I said. "I started shooting and something got ahold of me, and I couldn't stop."

Pappy looked at me again in that strange way. I couldn't tell what was behind those gray expressionless eyes of his. I couldn't tell if he was glad or sorry that it had worked out the way it had. For a moment, as he looked at me, I thought there was fear in those eyes. But I must have been mistaken about that.

"Do you feel like riding?" Pappy said at last.

"Sure," I said. "But why should we ride anywhere?"

He jerked his head toward the bedground where all the noise and commotion was going on. All hell was breaking loose, but I was just beginning to become conscious of it. It was almost like returning suddenly from a long visit in a strange place, and it took a while to get used to things as you used to know them. The cattle had broken toward the north, running blind and wild with fear. The riders, some of them just in the underwear they had been sleeping in, were riding hard on the flanks, trying to turn them.

"After starting this ruckus," Pappy said, "the least we can do is help them turn the herd."

Pappy started in an awkward half-lope toward his horse beside the chuck wagon. In a moment I came out of it. I ran toward Red, and on the way I passed the bloody, shapeless form that had been Buck Creyton a few minutes before. He lay twisted, in the mud, looking straight up, with the rain in his face. There were bright, shimmering puddles forming all around him.

I hit the saddle hard, and Red switched his head in angry protest. He didn't want to move. He had lulled himself into a kind of stupor there in the rain, and he just wanted to be let alone. I drove the iron to him and he reared sharply. Finally I pulled him around and he fell into a quick, ground-eating run to the north.

We caught Pappy on the herd's flank just as the break began to settle down to a real stampede. There wasn't time to be scared, the way they say you always are after a fight. There was just the blind race along the flanks of the herd, and once in a while I could feel Red slide and fight for his footing again in the mud, and I tried not to think what would happen if he put a hoof down on a loose rock or into a prairie-dog hole. Red and Pappy's big black spurted ahead of most of the other riders. Up ahead, I could hear the trail boss yelling and cursing.

He was trying to turn them by himself as Pappy and I came up alongside him. He drove his rugged little paint into the van of the stampede. Leaning far over his pony he shoved the muzzle of his pistol behind the shoulders of the lead steer and fired.

The big animal thundered down, rolling and churning the mud, slowing the herd's rush. Without looking back to see who we were, he roared, "Turn 'em, goddammit!"

I thought I could make out that faint grin of Pappy's as he drove his big black into the point of the herd. I shoved Red in after him, and the trail boss came in on our heels. The startled cattle began to slow down their crazy rush for nowhere. The point began to give, began to edge to the left as Pappy and the trail boss pushed in, yelling and firing their pistols over the animals' heads.

There wasn't much to it after the point began to give. We cut them over and headed them back until we had two columns of cattle going in opposite directions; then the riders came up and milled them in a wide circle.

After the riders got the mill going, there was nothing for me and Pappy to do. We pulled up the slope a way to let our horses blow after the hard run. I noticed then, for the first time, that it had stopped raining.

"One steer lost," I said. "It could have been worse."

Pappy looked at me. "One steer and one rider," he said dryly. He nodded toward the bottom of the slope to where a rider was coming toward us. It was the trail boss.

Surprisingly, he didn't seem mad this time. He just looked relieved to get his herd under control with the loss of only one steer. He pulled up in front of us, mopping his face with a rain-soaked bandanna.

"By God," he said wearily, "I ought to turn the two of you over to the bluebellies."

Pappy straightened in the saddle. "What makes you think the bluebellies want us?"

The little Irishman laughed roughly. "You're Pappy Garret, the boys tell me. And this kid's name's Cameron, ain't it?" Without waiting for an answer, he took a folded, soggy square of paper from his hip pocket. It was too dark to read, but a sinking feeling in my stomach told me what it was.

"Reward," the trail boss said pleasantly. "For killin' off some bluebelly cavalry down in northern Texas. Ten thousand for Garret, five for the kid. Here, read it for yourself."

Pappy made no move to take the paper. "Are you aiming to make a try for that reward money?" he asked softly,

The trail boss laughed abruptly. "Hell, no." Then his voice got serious. "It's no concern of mine if the army wants to take you in. I'm short of hands and good horses. From the way you two jumped in and turned that herd, it looks like my problem is taken care of. That is, if you want a job."

Pappy looked at me. He was thinking the same thing I was. "I kind of figured," he said, "that you'd be sore because the boy killed off one of your riders."

The trail boss snorted. "It was small loss. Creyton was trouble from the first day I signed him on. He thought he was Godamighty with them two pistols of his ... and I guess he had everybody else thinking it until tonight." He looked at me with much the same expression that I had seen in Pappy's eyes. "I'll tell you the truth," he said. "I never expected you to beat Buck Creyton, son. I was expecting we'd he burying a kid of a boy in the morning." He shrugged. "But I guess you never know."

He pulled his paint around and studied the herd for a minute. "Think it over," he said. "If you want to sign up, I'll see you at the chuck wagon for breakfast."

He rode down the slope again and into the darkness. I looked at Pappy and he was shaking his head slowly from side to side. "I guess it's like the man says," he said soberly. "You never know."

It was too good a thing to pass up. With fifteen thousand dollars on our heads, every soldier in the Territory was a potential bounty hunter. The next morning we were at the chuck wagon and Bass Hagan, the hard pink-faced little trail boss, signed us on. Somebody must have buried Buck Creyton, but there was no mention of it at breakfast. There was no talk of any kind, for that matter. The riders regarded Pappy with a kind of dumb awe, and me ... I couldn't be sure just what they were thinking about me. I could feel their eyes on me when they didn't think I was looking. Curious eyes, mixed with a kind of fear, I thought. They ate their breakfast quickly and silently as a cold sun began to come up in the east. Then, with elaborate casualness, they sauntered down to the remuda pen to get their horses.

It took a while to get used to that kind of treatment, but I finally did, as one long, weary, dust-filled day dragged into another. The men let me and Pappy strictly alone. And I began to appreciate how Pappy had lived all these years with that reputation of his. It was like being by yourself on the moon. You couldn't have been more alone. In every man you looked at, you saw that same mixture of curiosity and fear—like men partially hypnotized by a caged and especially deadly breed of snake. They couldn't take their eyes off it. But they knew better than to get into the cage with it.

That was the way it was after getting a reputation by killing a man like Buck Creyton.

Bass Hagan, the trail boss, was the only man who didn't seem to be afraid of us, but he spent most of his time up in the van, and Pappy and I ate dust back in the drag. And it wasn't long before I learned to hate the nights, when time came for sleeping. I learned to sleep the way Pappy did, always keeping a corner of my mind open, never letting myself slip into complete unconsciousness. I learned to sleep—if you could call it sleeping—on my back, with a cocked pistol in my hand. I kept thinking of that reward money. I wondered how long it would be before somebody tried to collect.

I learned a lot of things in those days as we pushed from the Canadian up to North Cottonwood in Kansas. Pappy was my teacher. A little at a time, every day, he showed me the little tricks that men like us had to know to stay alive. The first rule, the most important rule of all, was to trust no one. Accept it as truth that every man you met was scheming to kill you, that every footstep behind you was a man ready to shoot you in the back. Never get caught off guard. Never relax. Never take more than two or three drinks, and let women alone. Never let anyone do you a favor without paying for it, never become obligated to anybody.

And that was only the beginning. He coached me on how to enter a door, any door. First you listened; if it sounded all right, then you stepped inside fast, with a quick step to the side so as to get your back against a wall and not frame yourself against the light. There was a certain toe-heel way to walk when you didn't want to be heard, and a way to block your spur rowels to keep them from jangling. Little things, all of them. Things that ordinary men would pay no attention to, but with Pappy they were matters of life and death.

I learned to value my pistols above all other possessions, and to take care of them before seeing to anything else. My horse came next, almost as important as the pistols. I learned that my own comfort was almost of no importance at all. A thousand things came ahead of that, if I wanted to keep living.

What Pappy had to teach me, I learned fast, the way I learned to shoot. Already, among the trail hands, there was talk of Davis being removed from the governor's chair in Austin, and that meant that military rule and the Davis police would go with him. It was important that I learn everything that Pappy could teach me, because I had to stay alive, to go back to Texas.

North Cottonwood was the settling-up place for the cattlemen before going the last thirty-five miles to Abilene. It was there that the riders were paid off and discharged, unless they happened to belong to the drover's own outfit, and then they went on to the railhead with the herd. It was there that all the scrawny and sickly cattle were cut out of the herd and left to fatten before going to market. It was a crazy patchwork of wagons, and dust, and bawling cattle, and cow camps. Punchers who hadn't had a drop to drink and hadn't seen a woman for more than two months began peeling off their filthy trail clothing, bathing, shaving, and putting on their one clean pair of serge pants that they had brought in their saddlebags all the way from the Rio Grande, maybe.

I could see Pappy's eyes take on new life after we finally got the herd rounded up on a bedground that suited Bass Hagan.

"This is the place, son," he said. "You haven't seen a town until you've seen Abilene."

He even found a clean pair of pants and a shirt with all the buttons on it, and put them on to celebrate the occasion. But Pappy got a jolt that afternoon as the riders were being paid off. Bass Hagan called us over to one of the supply wagons where they had set up headquarters.

"Now, what the hell?" Pappy said.

I said, "Maybe we're so good he wants to hire us for another trail drive."

Pappy grunted. Trail driving was work, and he had had enough of that to last him for a while. What money Pappy needed he could usually get over a poker table.

But we went over anyway. Hagan was slicked and duded up in a fancy outfit that he had been saving for the end of the trail. He was just cinching up a big bay, the best horse in the remuda, when Pappy and I got there.

"I want you boys to stay with the herd," Hagan said without looking around. "It'll mean extra pay for a couple of days. I've got to ride into town on business."

Pappy said, "We don't need the extra pay. We just signed up as far as North Cottonwood."

The trail boss turned slowly, frowning. "I figured I done you boys a favor by hiring you on and getting you through Indian Territory. But if you figure it's too damn much to ask, staying over a couple of days ..."

Pappy glanced at me. Sure, Hagan had done us a favor, but we had earned our money on that trail drive. I could see Pappy's face grow longer. "Never let anyone do you a favor without paying for it," he had said. "Never become obligated to anyone."

Pappy shrugged. "All right, Bass. I guess we can stay here a couple of days. What do you want us to do?"

Hagan brightened. "Nothing special, just help my other riders take care of the herd till I get back." He swung up on the bay, grinning quietly. As we watched him put his spurs to the bay and lope off to the north, an idea got stuck in my mind and I couldn't get it out.

I said, "Something just occurred to me. Do you think Hagan would think enough of fifteen thousand dollars to try to get us arrested?"

Pappy took a long time rolling one of his corn-shuck cigarettes. He held a match to it thoughtfully, handing the makings to me. At last he smiled that sad half-smile that I had come to expect. "I think I've said it before, son," he said. "You learn fast."

But we stayed on with the herd, and, if Pappy was worried, it didn't show on that long face of his. We didn't mention Hagan again that day, but when night came we fell automatically into a routine that we had worked out, of one sleeping and one watching.

Once Pappy said, "Money is a funny thing. The root of all evil, they say. Men steal for it, kill for it, lie for it ..." He inhaled deeply on a cigarette. "Money," he said again. "I never had much of it myself. I could have hooked up with the Bassett gang once when they was robbing the Confederate payrolls. If I'd done it, maybe I'd have been a rich man now."

He laughed abruptly, without humor. "My ma always taught me that it was a sin to steal. I never stole a dime in my life ..."

Pappy's voice trailed off. He didn't know how to say it, but I thought I knew what was going on in his mind. I had thought about it too, since I saw that reward poster with my name on it. Most men got something out of their crimes—maybe not much, when they stood on the gallows thinking about it, waiting for the floor to drop out from under them, but something. Men like me and Pappy, we didn't get anything. All the money we had was the thirty-odd dollars that Hagan had paid us for the trail job. All the satisfaction we had was that of knowing that we were faster with guns that most men, and that wasn't much of a satisfaction when you thought of what other men had. Security, homes, wives. Things that Pappy could never have. And—I had to face it now—things that I would never have if I didn't somehow fight my way out of the crazy whirl of killing that seemed to have no beginning and no end.

The thought of that scared me. It made me sick all the way down to the bottom of my stomach when I thought of ending up the way Pappy was bound to end. Without Laurin. Without anything. Until now, I had been telling myself that there really wasn't anything to worry about, all I had to do was hold out until I could get a free trial in Texas. But now I wasn't sure. Paul Creyton, the policemen, the cavalryman, Buck Creyton—after each one I had told myself that there wouldn't be any more killing. I could still say it, but I couldn't believe the words any more.

"I never stole a dime in my life," Pappy said again, as if just thinking about that particular clean part of his life made him feel better.

I found myself hoping desperately that Bass Hagan would let well enough alone and just tend to his cattle business in Abilene. I thought bitterly: If they would just let us alone ... If Paul Creyton hadn't tried to steal my horse, if the bluebelly hadn't killed Pa ...

But it was too late for tears. We couldn't change the past—nor the future either, for that matter. If Hagan had it in his head to try for the reward money, nothing would stop him. If it wasn't now, it would be later.

Chapter 9

The next morning was hot and hazy with dust from ten thousand stamping cattle scattering as far as you could see in any direction. There wasn't anything for Pappy and me to do. Hagan's regular riders were taking care of the herd and remuda, and guarding the wagons. I thought: It seems crazy as hell for Hagan to pay good money for riders he doesn't need. Unless, of course, he was figuring to get his money back, and some more with it. I watched Pappy plundering around in one of the supply wagons, and after a while he climbed down with a towel over his shoulder and a bar of soap in his hand.

"I figure we might as well wash up," he said with a thin grin, "as long as there doesn't seem to be any work for us to do."

I said, "Don't you think one of us better keep watch?" We still hadn't mentioned Hagan, but he was never far out of our minds.

Pappy shrugged. "We can watch from the creek. Maybe we've just got a case of the jumps. Anyway, we need a bath. We can't ride into Abilene looking like a pair of saddle tramps."

Pappy was the careful one; if he thought it was all right, then it was all right. We went down to the remuda herd and cut out Red and Pappy's big black and got them saddled. The creek was only about a hundred yards back of our wagons, but a horseman never walks anywhere if he can ride.

We left the horses down by the water, and I took my place under a rattling cottonwood while Pappy bathed first. Nothing happened that I could see. I had a clear view of the herd and wagons, and everything was going on as usual. Behind me, I could hear Pappy splashing around and grunting at the shock of cold water. After a while he climbed up the bank where I was, wearing his new serge pants and clean shirt. But he didn't look much different, with that scraggly crop of whiskers still on his face.

"No sign of Hagan yet?" he asked.

I shook my head.

"Go on and take your bath," he said, handing me the wet bar of yellow lye soap. "I'll let you know if we've got company."

I peeled off my clothes and waded out knee deep in the bitter cold water. I didn't have a change of clothes. That was something else I forgot to bring from John's City, along with a slicker. Well, I had over thirty dollars in my pocket. That would buy me some clothes in Abilene — providing nobody got too set on keeping us out of Abilene.

In the meantime, I washed the clothes I had, lathering them with the lye soap, then weighting them down to the bottom of the stream with a rock while I washed myself. I was grimy from top to bottom, not just my hands and feet and face, like it used to be on Saturday nights when Ma put the big wooden washtub in the kitchen and filled it for me and Pa. I scrubbed hard, using sand on my elbows and knees when the soap wouldn't do the job. I didn't feel naked until I got all the dirt off. After I had finished, I felt like I must have polluted the stream for ten miles down.

After I had sloshed my clothes around to get the soap out, wrung them out and hung them on a bush to dry, I went downstream to take care of Red. He wasn't as dirty as I had been, but I rinsed off some caked mud on his legs and rubbed him down and he looked better.

"You about finished down there, son?" Pappy called.

"Sure," I said. "I was just sprucing Red up a little."

"You better get your clothes on," Pappy said with a mildness that still deceived me sometimes. "It looks like we're going to have company, after all."

I stiffened in the cold water. Then I splashed over to the edge and went over to the bush where my clothes were. They weren't dry, but they weren't as wet as they had been the night of the rain—the night I had killed Buck Creyton. I put them on the way they were, stuffed my feet in my boots, and buckled on the .44's.

As I went clawing my way up the bank, Pappy said, "Keep down, son. We don't want to tell them anything they don't already know."

I raised my head carefully over the edge of the bank, the way Pappy was doing. Sure enough, it was Hagan and four other men that I'd never seen before. All of them were heeled up with guns. Hagan was the only one not carrying a rifle in his saddle boot.

"Who are they?" I said.

"Jim Langly's men."

I shot Pappy a glance. Langly was the marshal of Abilene.

I said, "I thought the marshal was a friend of yours."

Pappy smiled that smile of his, but this time it seemed sadder than usual. "That was a mistake I made," he said quietly. "You never know who your friends are until you get a price on your head."

"What are you going to do?"

"I don't know," Pappy said slowly. "I haven't decided yet."

We lay there for a long moment watching Hagan call one of the herders over. The man pointed toward the creek, evidently in answer to a question. The man went away, and Hagan called the four Langly men together and talked for a minute. Then the men fanned out, taking up positions inside the covered supply wagons.

"Well, that's about as clear as a man could want it," Pappy said.

I felt myself tightening up. The rattle of the cottonwood seemed louder than it had a few minutes before. Smells were sharper. Even my eyes were keener.

"That bastard," I said. "That lousy bastard."

"Hagan?"

"Who else?"

Pappy seemed to think it over carefully. "I guess we really can't blame Hagan much," he said. "Fifteen thousand is a lot of money for a few minutes' work—especially if you don't have any idea how dangerous work like that can be." He paused for a minute. "But Jim Langly ... We've been good friends for years. This is a hell of a thing for Jim to do."

He still didn't sound mad, but more hurt than anything. "What are you going to do?" I asked again.

After a long wait, Pappy said, "I think maybe we'll ride up the creek a way, and then make for Abilene and talk to Jim."

"You're not going to let Hagan get away with this, are you?" I was suddenly hot inside. I had forgotten that last night I had promised myself no more trouble.

"We can't buck four saddle guns," Pappy said.

I knew he was right, but my hands ached to get at Hagan's throat. I wanted to see that pink face of his turn red, and then blue, and then purple. But I choked the feeling down and the effort left me empty. It always has to be somebody, I thought. Now it's Hagan, and Langly. Why can't they just let us alone?

Slowly, Pappy began sliding down the bank. His eyes looked tired and very old.

We went upstream as quietly as we could, scattering drinking cattle and horses, and once in a while coming upon a naked man lathering himself with soap. We rode for maybe a mile in the creek bed, until we were pretty sure that nobody in the Hagan camp could see us; then we pulled out in open country and headed north.

Pappy rode stiffly in the saddle, not looking one way or the other. After a while the hurt look went out of his eyes, and a kind of smoky anger banked up like sullen thunderheads.

We left North Cottonwood behind; and I wondered vaguely how long it would be before Hagan and his law-dogs would get tired of waiting in those covered wagons and send somebody down to the creek to see what had happened to us. Maybe they already had.

I tried to keep my mind blank. I tried to push Hagan and Langly out of my brain, but they hung on and ate away at me like a rotting disease. As we rode, the morning got to be afternoon and a dazzling Kansas sun moved over to the west and beat at us like a blowtorch. Gradually the monotony of silent march lulled me into a stupor, and I found myself counting every thud as Red put a hoof down, and cussing Bass Hagan with every breath.

Actually, it wasn't Hagan in particular that I was cursing, but mankind in general. The thousands of greedy, money-loving bastards like Hagan who were never satisfied to take care of their own business and let it go at that. They were like a flock of vultures feeding on other people's misery. They were like miserable coyotes sniffing around a sick cow, waiting until the animal was too weak to fight back and then pouncing and killing. I had enough hate for all the Hagans. The thousands of them. All the bastards who wouldn't let us alone, who insisted on getting themselves killed. And every time they insisted, it put a bigger price on our heads.

I remember looking over at Pappy once and wondering if he had ever thought of it that way. Pappy, who had never stolen a dime in his life, who had never wanted to hurt anybody except when it was a matter of life or death for himself—I wondered if he felt trapped the way I did, if he could feel the net drawing a little tighter every time some damned fool forced him to kill. If Pappy ever felt that way, he had never talked about it. He wasn't much of a man with words. And then it occurred to me that maybe that was the reason he was the kind of man he was. Being unable to depend on words, maybe he had been forced to let his guns do the talking.

Then, out of nowhere, Laurin came into my brain and cooled the heat of anger and helpless frustration, the way it happened so many times. When everything seemed lost, then Laurin would enter into my thoughts and everything was all right again. I'll be coming back, I promised. And I could almost see that hopeful, wide-eyed smile of hers. They can't keep me away from you, I said silently. You're the only important thing in my life. The only real thing. Everything's going to be all right. You'll see.

I looked up suddenly and Pappy was giving me that curious look. I felt my face warm. I had been speaking my thoughts out loud.

"Well?" I said.

"Nothing, son," Pappy said soberly. "Not a thing."

It was late in the afternoon when we finally sighted Abilene. The noise, the bawling of cattle, the shrill screams of locomotive whistles around the cattle pens, the fitful cloud of dust that surged over the place like a restless shroud gave you an idea of what the town was like long before you got close enough to be part of it. Over to the west we could see new herds coming up from North Cottonwood, heading for the dozens of giant cattle pens on the edge of town. Pappy and I circled the cattle pens, and the combined noise of prodded steers and locomotives and hoarsely shouting punchers was like something out of another world. It was worse than a trail drive. It was like nothing I had ever seen before. I had never seen a train before, and I kept looking back long after we had passed the pens, watching the giant black engine with white steam spurting in all directions, and the punchers jabbing the frightened cattle with poles, forcing them through the loading gates and into the slatted cattle cars.

Then we came into the town itself, which was mostly one long street—Texas Street, they called it—of saloons and barbershops and gambling parlors and dance halls. Some of the places were all four wrapped in one, with extra facilities upstairs for the fancy women who leaned out of the windows shouting at us as we rode by. The street was a mill of humanity and animals and wagons and hacks of every kind I ever saw, and a lot I had never seen before. Every man seemed to be cursing, and every jackass braying, every wagon squeaking, and every horse stomping. The whole place was a restless, surging pool of sound and excitement that got hold of you like a fever.

So this was Pappy's town. I didn't know if I liked it or not, but I didn't think I did. I didn't think the town would ever quiet down long enough to let a person draw an easy breath and be a part of it.

I couldn't help wondering what Pappy was going to do, now that he was here. Would he be crazy enough to walk up and kill the marshal of a town like this? I couldn't believe that Pappy would try a thing like that, not unless he knew he had some backing from somewhere. More backing than I would be able to give him.

But his face didn't tell me anything. A few curious eyes watched us as we pushed our way up the street, but most of the men were too intent on their own personal brand of hell-raising to pay any attention to us. At last Pappy pulled his big black in at the hitching rack near the middle of the block. I pulled Red in, pushing to make room between a bay and a roan.

We hitched and stepped up to the plank walk, but before we went into the bar that Pappy was headed for, I said, "Pappy, don't you think this is damn foolishness, trying to take the marshal of a place like this?"

He looked at me flatly. "You don't have to go with me, son. This is just between Jim and me."

"I'm not trying to get out of anything," I said. "It just looks crazy to me, that's all."

Some men had stopped on the plank walk to look at us. Perhaps they recognized Pappy, for they didn't loiter after Pappy had raked them with that flat gaze of his.

"You go buy yourself some clothes," Pappy said quietly. "I can take care of this."

He seemed to forget that I was there. He turned and pushed through the batwings of a place called the Mule's Head Bar, going in quick in that special way of his, and then stepping over with his back to the wall.

I didn't think about it, I just went in after him. Somehow, Pappy's fights had got to be my fights. I hadn't forgotten the way he had taken care of the cavalry for me that time at Daggert's cabin.

We stood there on either side of the door, Pappy sweeping the place in one quick glance, taking in everything, missing nothing. "Well, son," he said, "as long as you've dealt yourself in, you might as well watch my back for me."

I said, "Sure, Pappy." But it looked like it was going to be a job. The saloon was a big place with long double bars, one on each side of the building. There were trail hands two and three deep along the bars seeing how fast they could spend their hard-earned cash, and the tables in the middle of the floor were crowded with more trail hands, and saloon girls, and slickers, and pimps, and just plain hardcases with guns on both hips and maybe derringers in their vest pockets.

Down at the end of the bars there was a fish-eyed young man with rubber fingers playing a tinny-sounding piano. The tune was "Dixie," and a dozen or so cowhands were ganged around singing: "Oh, have you heard the latest news, Of Lincoln and his Kangaroos ..." One of the million versions of the tune born in the South during the war.

The gambling tables—faro, stud, draw, chuck-a-luck, seven-up, every device ever dreamed up to get money without working for it—were back in the rear of the place. That was what Pappy made for. I hung close to the doors as Pappy wormed his way between the tables and chairs, trying to keep my eyes on the gallery—I didn't intend to let a gallery fool me again—and on the men with the most guns. Before Pappy had taken a dozen steps, you could feel a change in the place. It wasn't much at first. Maybe a man would be talking or laughing, then he'd look up and see those awful, deadly eyes of Pappy's, and the talking or laughing would suddenly be left hanging on the rafters. One after another was affected that way, suddenly stricken with silence as Pappy moved by. By the time he had reached the gambling part of the saloon, the place was almost quiet.

I moved over to the bar on my left, keeping one eye on Pappy and the other on the big bar mirror to see what was going on behind me. Most of the men had turned away from the bar now, watching Pappy with puzzled expressions on their faces, as if they couldn't understand how a scrawny, haggard-looking man like that could draw so much attention. Then mouths began to move and you could almost feel the electricity in the place as the word passed along.

Somebody spoke to the man beside me. Automatically, the man

turned to me and hissed, "It's Pappy Garret! He's after somebody, sure's hell!"

The men around the piano sang: "Our silken banners wave on high; For Southern homes, we'll fight and die." Still to the tune of "Dixie." Their voices died out on the last word. The piano went on for a few bars, but pretty soon it died out, too. All eyes seemed to be on Pappy.

I didn't have any trouble picking Jim Langly out of the crowd. His eyes were wider, and his face was whiter, and he was having a harder time of breathing than anybody else in the place. When he had looked up from his poker hand and had seen Pappy coming toward him, he'd looked as if he was seeing a ghost. And maybe he was, as far as he was concerned. Maybe he'd figured that Pappy would be dead on a creek bank by now, and all he had to do was wait for the reward money to come in and think up ways to beat Hagan out of his share.

He started to get up, then thought better of it, and sat down again. You could almost see him take hold of himself, force himself to be calm. He laid his cards face down on the table, fanning them carefully.

"Why, hello, Pappy," he said pleasantly.

He was a big, slack-faced man wearing the gambler's uniform of black broadcloth and white ruffled shirt. He wasn't wearing side guns, but there was a bulge under his left arm that looked about right for a .38 and a shoulder holster.

"Hello, Jim," Pappy said quietly. "I guess you didn't expect to see me coming in like this, did you?"

I thought I saw the marshal's face get a little whiter. "Nobody ever knows when to expect Pappy Garret," he smiled. One of his poker partners wiped his face uncomfortably, gathered in his chips, and eased away from the table. Langly pushed the empty chair out with his boot. "Sit down, Pappy. It's been a long time."

Pappy shook his head soberly. Carefully, I moved down the bar, looking for a place where I could do the impossible of covering the saloon with two guns. I saw that Langly was having trouble again getting his words out.

"What can I do for you, Pappy? Is there any trouble?"

"Maybe, Jim," Pappy murmured.

Marshal Langly wiped his face with a neat, clean handkerchief. "What is it, Pappy? What do you want?"

"I came to kill you," Pappy said softly.

The words were soft, but they hit Langly like a sledge. You could hear the wind go out of him, see his guts leak out. He groped for words, but there weren't any there.

"That's the way it goes with men like us, Jim. You tried to kill me and failed. A man only gets one chance in this business."

"Pappy, what the hell's wrong with you? I don't know what you're talking about!"

"Sure you do, Jim," Pappy went on in that velvety voice of his. "Hagan, our trail boss, came to you yesterday with a proposition. A profitable proposition for you, Jim—maybe fifteen thousand dollars, if you could figure out a way to keep Hagan from getting his split of the reward."

"How could I do anything to you, Pappy? Hell, I've been here all day playing draw."

"But not your deputies," Pappy said. "They're right on the job. The job you put them on."

The saloon seemed to be holding its breath. I glanced at faces around me. There were quizzical half-smiles on most of them, as if they thought it was all some kind of a big joke. I turned back to Pappy. I couldn't take my eyes off of him.

For a long moment he was silent, motionless. Langly was frozen. Then Pappy said, "You might as well draw, Jim."

The marshal's mouth worked. "Pappy, for God's sake!"

"I'll give you time to clear leather," Pappy went on, "before I make a move. That ought to make it about even."

"Pappy, listen to me!" The marshal was begging now, begging for his life. "Pappy, for God's sake, I had nothing to do with it!"

"I'll count to three," Pappy went on, as if he hadn't heard. Then something hard jabbed me in the small of the back.

I jumped, grunted instinctively. Pappy stiffened, but he didn't turn around. "What's the matter, son?" he asked quietly.

I had to tell him.

"Somebody's got a gun in my back," I said. "I'm sorry, Pappy. I guess I'll never learn."

Chapter 10

I couldn't see who was holding the gun, and I didn't turn around to look. The slightest movement, I knew, would only get me a sudden trip to Boothill.

Marshal Langly started to breathe again. He stopped sweating and shaking, and his face began to get some color. Suddenly he sat back and laughed out of pure relief.

"Pappy Garret," he chuckled after he caught his breath. "The notorious gunman!" Then his voice barked. "Unbuckle your cartridge belts and drop your pistols to the floor!"

Or I would get a bullet in the back, his eyes said.

For an instant I wondered if Pappy really cared what happened to me, as long as he could take his revenge out on Langly. But I didn't have to wonder long. Wearily, he unbuckled the belts and the pistols dropped at his feet.

"All right, Jim," he said tiredly. "I guess you've got it going your way now."

Langly had his own .38 out now. "You bet I have, Pappy. I've got it going my way and that's the way it's going to stay." He sat back, looking pleased with himself. "You didn't think your old friend Jim Langly would be the one to bring you to your knees, did you? Well, you were wrong, Pappy. You haven't got any friends—not even that kill-crazy kid you've been riding with. Sooner or later he would have turned on you, because he's just the same as you are."

He was enjoying himself now. Him with a pistol in his hand and Pappy's .44's on the floor. And me with a gun in my back. He wasn't afraid of anything now. He was a hero and enjoying every minute of it. But the crowd in the saloon was still too stunned to be sure that is wasn't a joke.

"You know what you are, Pappy?" the marshal smiled. "You're a mad dog. You kill by instinct, the way a mad dog does. I'll be doing the whole country a favor by locking you up and turning you over to the Texas authorities."

My stomach sank. I might as well die here as on a carpetbag gallows.

But Pappy didn't move. He said, "I don't suppose the price on my head had anything to do with it."

Langly went on smiling. He could afford to smile now. He got up from the table and said, "All right, Bass, take the kid's guns and we'll lock them up."

The man behind moved around in front. When he got around to face me I was too startled to guess what was going on in Pappy's mind. The man was Bass Hagan.

He must have come into Abilene right behind me and Pappy, but he hadn't used the same trail we had. He stood there with the pistol in my belly, grinning that wide grin of his.

"The pistols," he said. "Hand them over, kid."

And then I began to get it. Pappy still had his back turned to me, but I knew what he must be thinking. I reached very carefully for my right-hand pistol, slid it out of the holster.

"Butts first," Hagan grinned. He was the careful kind. He was stand-ing back far enough so that I couldn't rush him, even if I was crazy enough to rush a man with a cocked pistol in his hand. "Just hand them over, kid," he said.

If he had known more about guns and gunmen he would have done as Langly had done, ordered me to unbuckle my belts. But he didn't know. I took the pistol by the barrel, slipping my finger into the trig-ger guard, and held it out. It had been a beautiful maneuver when Pappy had done it. But this time it wasn't Pappy. And the gun in my belly was loaded and cocked.

Maybe I would have handed the gun over if he hadn't been grinning. But he kept on grinning and I thought, There never would have been this trouble if it hadn't been for you. And my hand did the rest.

The pistol was just a blur as it whirled forward. The hammer snapped back as it hit my thumb on top of the turn, and fell forward.

I think Bass Hagan began to die before the bullet ever reached him. I could see death in his eyes even before the muzzle blast jarred the room, before the bullet slammed into his chest and he reeled back with-out ever pulling the trigger.

The shot affected the saloon customers like a stunning blow of a pole ax on a steer. They stood dumb, watching Hagan go to his knees and die, then fall on his face. Even Langly couldn't seem to move.

But Pappy could. He sliced across with the edge of his hand and sent the marshal's little .38 clattering to the floor. A split second was all it took. I wheeled instinctively to turn my pistol on Langly, but Pappy said sharply:

"No, son!"

For some reason, I held my fire. Nobody but Pappy could have stopped me then. But Pappy's voice did it. I held the hammer back and my finger relaxed a little on the trigger.

Pappy said, "He's not worth wasting a bullet on." But his eyes, not his voice, put the real bitterness into the words. "Come along, son," he said, picking up his guns. "I guess Abilene's not our town after all."

Well, if that was the way Pappy wanted it ... I started toward the doors, moving sideways, trying to keep my eyes on both sides of me and on the bar mirror on the opposite wall. Then Pappy said:

"Just a minute, son. The marshal will be going with us."

I began to get it then. With the marshal dead, our chances of getting out of Abilene would be cut down to nothing. But with the marshal going with us, under the threat of sudden death if anybody tried to stop us, then maybe we could do it.

I waited, covering Pappy's retreat. Langly's mouth was working again. He looked as if he was going to be sick on the floor.

"Pappy, for God's sake, can't you take a joke?" he said quickly. "You don't really think I'd turn you over to the Texas police, do you?"

Pappy's face didn't show a thing. He reached out with a clawlike hand, grabbed the front of the marshal's ruffled shirt, and gave him a shove toward the door. Then he paused for just a moment to address our stunned audience.

"I don't guess it will take a lot of figuring," he said, "to guess what will happen to the marshal if anybody tries to follow us out of town." He waited another moment to make sure that they had it clear. Then he said, "All right, son, let's be moving."

I waited at the doors, keeping the crowd covered, while Pappy got our horses in the street. He said something under his breath and Langly got on a gray mare that had been hitched beside Red. It was funny, in a way. Men with guns on both hips, pushing and shoving in both directions on the plank walk, and none of them bothering to give us a second look. I slammed the batwings then, turned and vaulted up to Red's back.

We fogged it down Texas Street in a wedge formation, Langley in the point and me and Pappy on both sides. Pappy let out an ear-splitting yell like a crazy man, then drew one pistol and emptied it in the air. But Pappy wasn't so crazy. The crowd in the street, thinking we were drunk trail hands, scattered for the plank walks, and we had a clear road to travel out of Abilene.

"Make for the dust!" Pappy yelled, pointing toward the low-hanging red clouds rising up from a herd coming in for shipment. I crowded Langly on my side, turning him to the west. I looked back once as we went into the dust, but nobody was coming after us yet.

I didn't like the idea of making a getaway along the trail of incoming herds. Too many people could see us. But pretty soon night came on and we didn't have to depend on the dust for concealment. Then we swung to the west, Langly still in the middle.

At last we came to a creek, and we stopped there to let our horses blow. Pappy seemed to be in good spirits again. He kept looking at the marshal with that half-grin of his.

"Jim," he said, "it looks like your friends in Abilene are going to take our advice and look after your health." Then he added with mock soberness, "They sure must love you, Jim. But you always did have a way with people, I remember."

The marshal had got over his scare. I guess he already saw himself as good as dead, and there wasn't anything to be afraid of after that.

He said, "You'll never get away with it, Pappy. They'll get you. No matter where you go, they'll get you."

"Maybe," Pappy said mildly, "but I doubt it. I hear law dogs don't go snooping around much in No Man's Land, down in the Oklahoma country."

Langly spat. "No Man's Land is a long way off."

I could almost see Pappy grinning in the darkness. I caught a glimpse of steel as he drew his right-hand pistol, and I thought, without any emotion at all, This will be one more to add to Pappy's score.

But he didn't shoot. There was a blue blur in the night, and then a sodden thud as the pistol barrel crashed the marshal's skull. Langly dropped leadenly out of the saddle and hit the ground. Casually, Pappy holstered his .44.

"Now why the hell did you do that?" I said. "You're not going to leave him alive, are you?"

Pappy said, "Jim will do us more good alive than dead. When he gets back to Abilene, maybe he'll send a posse down to No Man's Land. But he'll have a hell of a time finding us there." He looked over to the east. "The Osage country," he said, "down in Indian Territory. That's where we'll make for. The Osages like the cavalry about as well as we do, and white man's law even less." He nodded. "That's the place to make for."

It was a long ride—half the width of Kansas—from Abilene to the northeastern border of the Oklahoma country. But Pappy had traveled it before and he knew every foot of the trail, even at night. We left Langly on the creek bank with a knot on his head and without any pants. Taking the marshal's pants had been something that Pappy had thought of on the spur of the moment, and he still grinned as he thought about it. "Losing his pants," Pappy chuckled, "will be almost as bad on Jim as getting killed. Besides, he won't get back to Abilene in such a hurry if he has to scout around for a horse and another pair of pants."

By this time, doing the impossible, crossing half of Kansas when every law officer in the territory was out to get us, didn't surprise me. I had come to expect the impossible from Pappy. I began to suspect that he would live forever, even with the net drawing tighter and tighter around him all the time, because he knew instinctively what to do at exactly the right time. While Langly, and maybe the army, were cutting tracks all over southeastern Kansas and No Man's Land, we were heading for Indian Territory.

And we made it, in that walk-canter-gallop system of march that Pappy had developed, traveling only at night and going to elaborate pains to cover our trail. We came to the wild-looking hill country, bristling with pine and spruce and hostile Indians—a place where not even the government agents dared to go without military escort. And not often then.

We found a natural cave about ten miles from the border, and Pappy said that was good enough. There was plenty of wild game to keep us eating, and water in a small stream for us and the horses.

I remember the day we rode into the place. Pappy stood in the mouth of the cave, grinning pleasantly, not bothered at all at the possibility of having to stay here for months before we dared venture out into civilization again.

"Well, son," he said, "this is going to be our home for a spell. We might as well settle down to getting comfortable."

I felt an emptiness inside me. A kind of hopelessness. I felt as if I had cut away the very last remaining tie to the kind of life I had known before. This was living like an animal, killing instinctively like an animal.

I tried to keep the sickness out of my voice as I said: "Sure, Pappy. This is our home."

That was spring, in June, and it wasn't so bad at first. We made friends with some of the Osages. They were on our side the minute they learned that we were enemies of the white man's government. Sometimes they would bring us pieces of government issue beef, but not often, because the government didn't give them enough to stay their own hunger. Mostly, Pappy and I lived on rabbits that we trapped, or sometimes shot. Occasionally the Osages would bring us a handful of corn, and we would parch it over a fire and then grind it up and make a kind of coffee. Once in a great while, an Indian would overhear snatches of conversation about the white man's world and would relay the information to us.

It was in August, I remember, when we first heard that Davis was no longer the governor of Texas. But that didn't solve all my problems as cleanly as I had once thought it would.

Pappy said, "Now don't try to rush things, son. It's going to take time to get the army out of Texas, even if Davis isn't governor any longer. And don't forget the Texas Rangers; they'll be taking the army's place. And the United States marshals ..." Then he looked at me with those sad, sober eyes of his, and I knew the worst was yet to come.

He said slowly, "It won't ever be the same as it was before, son. They won't be forgetting that bluebelly cavalryman you killed, especially the government marshals."

I felt that old familiar sickness in the pit of my stomach.

Pappy said, "Forget about this John's City place, son. You won't ever be able to go back there again. We'll head for the New Mexico country, or maybe Arizona, where nobody knows us." He laughed abruptly. "Who knows, maybe we'll turn out to be honest, hard-working citizens."

But he knew what I was thinking. And he said, "Forget about the girl, too, son. It will be the best for both of you."

I knew Pappy was right. I could look ahead and see how things would be from now on. But I couldn't forget Laurin. She was a part of me that I couldn't put away. Then Pappy's words hit me and I saw a new hope. We'll head for the New Mexico country, Pappy had said. Why couldn't Laurin go with us? If she loved me, if she believed in me, she would do that. I'd change my name and we could homestead a place in New Mexico. We could live like other people there....

Pappy was looking at me with those eyes that seemed to know everything. "Forget about her, son. Women just don't take men like us."

For a moment, I wondered if Pappy was speaking from experience. But that thought soon passed from my mind. The idea of Pappy ever being in love was too ridiculous to consider seriously. Besides, I couldn't forget Laurin any more than I could forget that I had a right arm. She was a part of me. She would always be a part of me.

And I suppose that Pappy saw how it was, and he didn't try to change my mind again.

But he insisted that we stay in our cave until the last of the cattle drives were made in the fall. By then, he said, the army should be out of Texas. If I was bound to go back to John's City, he said, winter would be the best time.

Chapter 11

So that was the way it was, because I had learned by this time that it didn't pay to act against Pappy's judgment. We watched August and September crawl by with painful slowness. Then came October with its sudden frosts and red leaves and sharp smells, and I think that was the hardest month of all.

And at last November came and Pappy went out to scout the country to the west, and when he came back he said we could try it, if I was still bound to go. It was a bitter cold night when at last we rode out of the hills and headed south, and we still had on the same clothes that we had worn for months. We were still without slickers, or coats of any kind. But I didn't mind the cold because I was going back to Texas again, to Laurin.

We crossed the Red River far west of Red River Station, on my nineteenth birthday, and Pappy said maybe that was a good sign. Maybe we would make it to John's City and everything would work out after all. But he only said it with his voice, and not with his eyes.

Nineteen years old. I could just as well have been ninety. Or nine hundred. I didn't feel any particular age, in this country where age didn't mean much anyway. Men like Pappy, and Buck Creyton, could have notched their guns long before they were nineteen, if they had been the kind of men to make a show about it.

I was on familiar ground when we crossed the river and got into Texas again. I half expected Pappy to leave me there and go his own way toward New Mexico, but he only said, "We've been together now for a pretty good spell. I guess I wouldn't rest good without knowing how you made out."

It didn't occur to me to wonder what I was going to do or say when the time came to face Laurin. I didn't know how I was going to explain away the reputation I'd got as a gunman, and it didn't worry me until we had come all the way and sighted the Bannerman ranch house in the distance.

And Pappy said, "Well, son, from here on in, I guess it's up to you."

Pappy knew what he was, the things he stood for. And he knew that he wouldn't do my cause any good if Laurin saw us together. And, for the first time, I saw Pappy as Laurin would have seen him—a hard, dirty old man with ratty gray hair hanging almost to his shoulders. A man in pitiful rags and tired to death of running, but not knowing what else to do. A man with no pride and no strength except in his guns.

Laurin would see only death in those pale gray eyes of Pappy's, missing the shy kindness that I knew was there, too. Laurin would look at Pappy and see me as I would be in a few more years.

I said, "Is this good-by, Pappy?"

He smiled faintly. "Maybe, son. Or maybe I'll see you again. You never know."

I said reluctantly, and Pappy could see the reluctance in my eyes and it made me ashamed, "You might as well come with me, Pappy. The Bannermans set a good table, and we both could use some grub."

But he shook his head. "You go on, son." We shook hands very briefly. "And good luck with that girl of yours." He jerked his big black around abruptly, and without a good-by, without a wave of his hand or a backward look, he rode back to the north.

I watched him until he disappeared behind a rise in the land, and I felt alone, and unsure, and a little afraid. Doubt began to gnaw at my insides.

Good-by, Pappy.... Good luck.

I nudged Red gently and began riding over the flatland that I knew so well, toward the ranch house. Toward Laurin. As I got closer the uneasiness inside me got worse. For the first time in months, I was conscious of the way I looked—my own ragged clothes, my own shaggy hair hanging almost to my shoulders. And in contrast, my shining, well-cared-for pistols, tied down at my thighs. No pride and no strength except in his guns. That was the thought I had used in my mind to describe Pappy ... and all along I had been describing myself.

For a moment, I was tempted to turn and ride as hard as I could until I caught Pappy. Pappy was my kind. We understood each other.... But the thought went away. Clothes didn't make a gentleman. Long hair didn't make a killer. Laurin would understand that.

The thought of turning back went away, but not the feeling of uneasiness, as I got closer to the ranch house. I came in the back way, around by the barns and corrals, and a couple of punchers in the shooing corral looked up and watched for a moment, and then went on about their work. They didn't even recognize me. More than likely they pegged me for a saddle tramp looking for a few days' work, and, knowing that Joe Bannerman never hired saddle tramps, lost interest.

Then, as I rode on through the ranch back yard, I saw a man come out of a barn with a saddle thrown over his shoulder, heading for a smaller corral near the house where the colts were kept for breaking.

He glanced at me once without slowing his walk. Suddenly he stopped, looking at me. He waited until I pulled up alongside him, and then he said:

"My God, Tall!"

The man was Laurin's brother, Joe Bannerman. He looked at me as if he wasn't entirely sure that his eyes weren't playing tricks on him. He looked at Red, who had been a glossy, well-cared-for show horse the last time he saw him, but whose coat was now shaggy and scarred in a thousand places where thorns and brush had raked his royal hide.

I tried to keep my voice light, but I knew that the change in me was even more shocking than the change in Red. I said. "How are you, Joe? I guess you might say the prodigal has returned."

But Joe Bannerman had no smile of welcome. He shifted the saddle down to the crook of his arm. "Tall, you're crazy! What do you mean, coming back to John's City like this?"

But he knew before I had time to answer. Laurin. Something happened to his face. He said, "Look, Tall, if you know what's good for you, you'll get out of here in a hurry. There's nothing in John's City for you any more." Then he added, "Nothing at all."

"Don't you think that's up for somebody else to decide, Joe?"

"She's already decided," Joe Bannerman said roughly. "Next week she's getting married."

I stiffened. At first the words had no meaning, and then I thought: Joe never liked me. This is just his way of trying to get rid of me. I even managed a smile when I said, "I guess I won't put much stock in that, Joe, until I hear Laurin say it herself."

He glanced once at the house and then jerked his head toward the barn that he had come out of. "For God's sake, Tall, be sensible. Get that red horse in the barn before somebody sees you."

There was something in his voice that made me rein Red over. I followed him, not quite knowing why, as he walked quickly to the other side of the barn, where the house was blocked from view. I dropped down from the saddle and said, "Now maybe you'll tell me what this is all about."

Joe Bannerman dropped his saddle to the ground and seemed to search for the right words. He said, "I don't want you to get the idea that I'm doing this for your benefit, because I don't give a good round damn what happens to you. But I don't want any trouble around here if I can help it." Then his voice got almost gentle. And I didn't understand that. "You ought to realize better than anybody else," he went on, "that things have changed since ... since you went away from John's City. You're a hunted man, Tall, with a price on your head."

I said, "You wouldn't be having any ideas about that reward money, would you, Joe?"

"Don't be a damned fool!" he said angrily. "I just want to keep you from getting killed on my doorstep. Like I told you, there's nothing here for you. Why don't you just ride off and let us alone?"

"I'd still like to hear it from Laurin," I said, "before I do any riding." I started to turn toward the house again, but an urgency in Joe Bannerman's voice cut off the movement.

"Goddammit, Tall, listen to me! I'm trying to tell you that it's all over between you and Laurin." Then he sighed wearily. "I guess you've got a lot of catching up to do. I'll try to give it to you as straight as I know how. Ray Novak's in that house, and he has orders from the federal government to get you. Ray was made a deputy United States marshal after the bluebellies were pulled out of Texas. I told you that things changed...."

I think I knew what was coming next. I tried to brace myself for it, but it didn't do any good when Joe Bannerman said, "It's Ray Novak that Laurin is in love with, Tall. Not you. She's afraid of you. You've got to be just a name on wanted posters, like this Pappy Garret that you've been riding with. You've got to be a killer, just like him." He shook his head. "I don't know, maybe you had a right to kill that policeman on account of your father. But all those others ... What is it, Tall, a disease of some kind? Can't you ever turn your back on a fight? Don't you know any way to settle an argument except with guns?"

Then he looked at me for what seemed a long time. "I guess you don't even know what I'm talking about," he said. "That's the way you always were, never turning your back on a fight. And you never lost one before, did you, Tall? But you're losing one now. It's Ray Novak that Laurin's going to marry. Not you."

I stood dumbly for a moment before the anger started to work inside me. I still didn't believe the part about Laurin. A thing like ours couldn't just end like that. But Ray Novak—at the very beginning of the trouble it had been Ray Novak, and now at the end it was the same way. I started for the house again, but Joe Bannerman stepped in my path.

"Tall, you can't go in there. Ray has been sworn in to get you."

I said tightly, "Get out of my way."

He didn't move.

I said, "This is my problem and I'll settle it my own way. If you try to stop me, Joe, I'll kill you."

His face paled. Then I thought I saw that look in his eyes that I had seen once before—just before he told me that Pa was dead. For some reason that I didn't understand, he was feeling sorry for me, and I hated him for it.

Slowly, he stepped back out of my way. He said quietly, "I believe you would. Killing me wouldn't mean any more to you than stepping on an ant. It wouldn't mean a thing to you."

"Don't be a damned fool," I said. But he had already stepped back, watching me with that curious mixture of awe and fear that I had come to expect from men like him. He didn't try to stop me as I went around the side of the barn and headed for the back steps of the house. Maybe he didn't feel it was necessary, because it was too late to stop anything now. Ray Novak was waiting for me at the back door.

If he had made the slightest move I would have killed him right there. I realized that I had never really hated anybody but him. It would have been a pleasure to kill him, and I knew I could do it, no matter how much training his pa had given him with guns. But he didn't make a move. He didn't give me the excuse, and I'd never killed a man yet who hadn't made the first move.

He said mildly, "I guess you better come in, Tall."

He was just a blurred figure behind the screen door and I couldn't see what his eyes were saying. Then another figure appeared behind him. It was Laurin.

Woodenly, I went up the steps, opened the screen door, and stepped into the kitchen. Laurin was standing rigidly behind Ray, and I thought: She's grown older, the same as I have. Those large eyes of hers were no longer the eyes of a girl, but of a woman who had known worry and trouble and—at last I placed it—fear. She had changed in her own way almost as much as I had changed. Only Ray Novak seemed the same.

Ray said, "We don't want any trouble, Tall. Not here. Maybe it's best that you came back this way and we can get things settled once and for all."

Laurin said nothing. She didn't move. She looked at me as if she had never seen me before, and in my mind I heard Joe Bannerman saying: There's nothing for you here in John's City. Nothing at all. But I fought back the sickness inside me. Laurin had loved me once, that was all that mattered. She still loved me. Nothing could change that.

Ray Novak moved his head toward the parlor. "Do you want to come in here, Tall? We've got a lot to say and not much time to say it in. My pa is coming in from town in a few minutes to pick me up in the buck-board. We'll have to get everything settled before then."

I said, "I can settle with you later. This is just between me and Laurin."

I looked at her and still she didn't move. I couldn't tell what she was thinking. At last she said, "It's Ray's affair as much as ours, Tall. You see, we're going to be married."

I guess a part of me must have died then. Joe Bannerman had said it and I hadn't believed it. Now it was Laurin herself, telling me as soberly as she knew how that it was all over between us, and I knew that this time it was the truth. I wasn't sure what I felt, or what I wanted to do about it. I suppose I wanted to go to her, to take hold of her with my hands and shake some sense into her. Or hold her close and make her see that it wasn't over with us, that it never would be. But her eyes stopped me. Perhaps she had expected something like that, and I saw that look of fear come out and look at me. She started backing away. She was afraid of me.

Ray Novak said, "I wanted you to know about me and Laurin before I went out looking for you. I didn't want you to think that I was going around behind your back...."

I shoved him aside with the flat of my hand and took Laurin's arm before she could back away. She tried to twist out of my grasp, but I held on and jerked her toward me. Anger like I've never known before was swelling my throat. I said, "Tell him to get out of here! If he does-n't, so help me God, I'll kill him where he stands!"

Ray Novak started to step forward. Instinctively, his hand started to move toward his gun, and I was praying that he would follow through with the motion. But Laurin said:

"Ray!"

And he stopped. Then something strange happened to Laurin. A moment before her eyes were bright and shiny with fear, but now they showed nothing.

She said, "Ray, do as he says."

Ray Novak's face darkened. "I'm not leaving you alone with him. He's crazy. There's something wrong and mixed up and rotten in that head of his."

"Ray, please!"

He hesitated for another moment. Then he relaxed. "All right, Laurin. Whatever you say. But I'll be outside if ..."

He left the rest unsaid. He turned and went out the back door, taking up a position a few paces away from the back steps.

I heard myself laugh abruptly. "So that's the man you're going to marry! A man with a yellow streak up his back that shows all the way through his shirt!"

But I stopped. That wasn't what I wanted to say at all. Anyway, I knew that Ray Novak wasn't yellow. He might be a lot of things, but a coward wasn't one of them.

Laurin said, "Tall, please. You're hurting me."

I turned loose her arm. My thoughts were all mixed up in my mind and I couldn't get the words arranged to tell her what I wanted to say. I found myself standing there dumbly, rubbing my face with my hands and wondering how I was going to explain it to her. If I could only explain it in a way she could understand, then everything would be all right again. But she didn't give me a chance to get my thoughts arranged.

She said flatly, "Why don't you go away, Tall? Go far away so that we'll never see you or hear from you again. Ray will give you that chance, because he knows what you meant to me once. He has been sworn in as a special deputy to get you. He's working for the government, Tall, a United States marshal—but he'll give you a chance if you'll only take it."

I said, "I don't need any favors from Ray Novak!" But that wasn't what I wanted to say, either. "Laurin, Laurin, what's wrong? What have they said ... what have they done to turn you against me like this?"

She shook her head, a bewildered look in her eyes. "You actually believe that your trouble is caused by other people, don't you?"

Think? I *knew* there wouldn't have been any trouble if it hadn't been for the Creytons, and Thorntons, and Hagans, and Novaks. But how could I explain that to her? Women didn't understand things like that. I remembered what my ma had said, long ago, about my fight with Criss Bagley: But, Tall, why didn't you run?

I said quickly, "Laurin, listen to me. This isn't the end of us. It's only the beginning. It won't be the same as we planned, but we can make it good. We can be together." I took her arm, gently this time, and she didn't try to pull away. "They'll never catch me," I said. "The army, Ray Novak, nobody else. We'll go away. Pappy knows a place in New Mexico. We can go there. We'll be together, that's the only thing that counts. You don't mean it about marrying Ray Novak, it's just because you've heard wrong things about me. You love me, not him."

The words came rushing out in senseless confusion, and they stopped as abruptly as they had begun. The look of bewilderment went out of Laurin's eyes, and amazement took its place.

"Love you?" she said strangely. "I don't even know you. I don't suppose I ever knew you. Not really, the way you get to know people and understand them, and be a part of them. You're ..." She shook her head helplessly. "You're nobody I ever saw before. You're some wild animal driven crazy—by the smell of blood."

Her voice was suddenly and painfully gentle, cutting worse than curses. She dropped her head.

"I'm sorry I said that, Tall."

But she meant it. She didn't try to get out of that. I turned loose of her and walked woodenly to the door. I pushed the door open, went down the steps and into the yard.

Ray Novak said, "Tall."

I went on toward the barn where I had left Red. I don't know where I thought I was going from there. To catch up with Pappy, maybe, and try to make it to New Mexico with him. Maybe I wasn't going anywhere. It didn't make any difference.

Ray Novak caught up with me as I was about to climb back into the saddle. "I'd better tell you the way things are," he said. "I'm giving you a day's start to get out of John's City country. Then I'll be coming after you, Tall."

I said flatly, "Don't be a goddamned fool all your life. I don't want any favors from you. I'm right here. Take me now if you think you can."

He shook his head. "That's the way Laurin wants it." He hesitated for a moment, then added, "Don't underrate me, Tall. I've learned things about guns and gunmen since you saw me last. I won't be as easy as Hagan, and Paul Creyton, and some of the others. Don't think that I will, Tall."

"You and your goddamned two bullets in a tin can," I said. "You don't even know what shooting is. But I'll teach you. You come after me and I'll teach you good, Ray."

I got up to the saddle and rode south, without looking back. Without thinking, or wanting to think. I didn't know where I was going and I didn't care. I just knew that I had to get away and I had to keep from thinking about Laurin. I should have hated her, I suppose. But I couldn't. And I suppose I should have killed Ray Novak while I had the chance, but, somehow, I couldn't do that either. Not with Laurin looking. I felt a hundred years old. As old as Pappy Garret, and as tired. But, like Pappy, I had to keep running.

I didn't see the buckboard until it was too late. And by that time, I didn't care one way or another. It was old Martin Novak coming up the wagon road from Garner's Store, and I vaguely remembered Ray saying that his pa was coming by the Bannermans' to pick him up. I had forgotten all the rules that Pappy had gone to so much trouble to teach me. I let him get within fifty yards of me before I even noticed him, and by that time things had boiled down to where there was only one way out.

It's the same thing all over again, I thought dumbly. But they never understand that.

Nobody could understand it, unless maybe it was Pappy, or others like him. The monotonous regularity with which it happened would almost have been funny, if it hadn't been so deadly serious. It was like dreaming the same bad dream over and over again until it no longer frightened you or surprised you—you merely braced yourself as well as you could, because you knew what was going to happen next.

Martin Novak had the buckboard pulled across the road. I could just see the top of his head and the rifle he had pointed at me, as he stood on the other side, using the hack for a breastwork.

"Just keep your hands away from your pistols, Tall," he called, "and ride this way, slow and easy."

I didn't have a chance against the rifle, not at that range. But I felt a strange calm. I never doubted what would happen next. I didn't even wonder how it would end this time, because this time I knew.

But I played it straight, the way Pappy would have done. I said, "What's this all about? What's that rifle for, anyway?"

"I think you know, Tall," he called. "Now just do as I say. Ride in slow and easy, and keep your hands away from your guns."

I nudged Red forward, keeping my hands on the saddle horn. If it had been Pappy, he would have been wearing his pistols for a saddle draw, high up on the waist, with the butts forward. I had forgotten to make the switch, but even that didn't bother me now. I looked at Martin Novak and thought: There's only one way, I guess, to teach men like you to leave us alone.

When I got within about twenty yards of the buckboard, he motioned me to stop. He was wondering how he was going to disarm me, and probably remembering stories he had heard about what had happened to Bass Hagan.

He said, "I don't want to have to kill you, Tall, but I will if you don't do exactly as I say. Now just reach with one hand, where I can see, and unbuckle your cartridge belts."

I said, "Just a minute, Mr. Novak. Hell, I never did anything to you."

He raised up from behind the buckboard and I could see the star pinned to his vest. The Novaks and their goddamned tin stars, I thought.

"It's more than that, Tall," he said solemnly. "You're wanted by the law. It's my job to arrest you, and that's what I intend to do." He studied my hands, which still hadn't moved toward my belt buckles. But he still had that rifle aimed at the center of my chest, and he wasn't too worried.

He said, "You've ... been to the Bannermans', I guess."

I said, "Yes. I've been there."

He nodded soberly. "Ray shouldn't of done it," he said thoughtfully, almost to himself. "He should of took you in himself. But," he added, "I guess Laurin wanted you to have one more chance."

I said, "I guess she did." I didn't particularly want to kill him. I didn't have anything against him except that he insisted on making my business his business. And if I killed him I knew I wouldn't get that day's start that Ray Novak had promised. But that didn't bother me. Ray Novak could come after me any time he felt like it. I was ready for him.

For a moment, I thought I'd try to talk the old man out of it, but I knew that it wouldn't do any good. Like Pappy, I had grown tired to trying to talk to people in a language that they didn't understand. It was easier to let my guns speak for me.

"There's no use holding off, Tall," the old man said soberly. "Just go on and drop your guns."

I looked for a brief moment behind my shoulder. I could still see the Bannerman ranch house. A shot would be heard there, if I was forced to shoot. Maybe they were even watching us. It was possible that Ray Novak was already getting a horse saddled to come after us and try to stop it.

I didn't care one way or another. I had stopped caring about anything when Laurin cut herself away from me. What was there to care about?

I said, "All right, Mr. Novak. I guess you win."

I could see relief in his eyes as I began to unbuckle my left-hand gun. He was slightly surprised and, because of my reputation, maybe a little disappointed because I gave up so easy. But he was relieved. And the relieved are apt to be careless.

I unslung the cartridge belt, but instead of dropping it, I handed it down to him. Instinctively, he reached for it, pulling his rifle out of line.

Marshal Martin Novak was a smart man. He caught his mistake almost immediately. But by that time it was already too late. He was off balance, in no good position to use either pistol or rifle. He knew that he was going to die before I ever made a move toward my other .44. I saw death in those dark, solemn little eyes of his. I thought, You've got all the time in the world. Take your time and do a good job of it. And then I shot him.

The bullet went in just above his shirt pocket on the left side, and he slammed back against the buckboard. The team scampered nervously for a moment, but I pulled Red over in front of them and quieted them down. Martin Novak went to his knees, held himself up for an instant with his hands, then fell with his face in the dust. He didn't move after that.

I sat there for a moment looking at him. Red was nervous and wanted to pitch, but I reined him down roughly with a heavy hand. I heard myself saying:

"I didn't want to kill you, Mr. Novak, but, goddamn you, why couldn't you let me alone?"

Then I realized that he couldn't hear me. And I knew that before long somebody would start wondering about that pistol shot. I pulled Red around and headed toward the hills.

Chapter 12

Instinct, I suppose, made me head for the place that had given me protection before, Daggert's Road. It was a fool thing to do probably, because that would be the first place Ray Novak would look for me, but I couldn't think of anything else. I raked Red's ribs cruelly with the rowels of my spurs, even though he was already running as fast as he could.

I looked back once and saw little feathers of dust rising up around the Bannerman ranch yard, and I knew that would be Ray Novak and some ranch hands pulling out to see what the shooting was about. Well, they would find out soon enough, but by that time I would be in the hills...

Suddenly, all thoughts jarred out of me. The world became a whirling, crazy thing, and I crashed to the ground and the wind went out of me. For a moment I lay stunned, gasping for breath. I shook my head, trying to clear it. After a while I tried moving my arms and legs. They were all right. I just had the breath knocked out of me. Finally, I pulled myself to my knees and looked around. And then I saw Red.

He lay quietly behind me, looking at me with big liquid eyes, full of hurt. "Red, boy! What's the matter?"

I dragged myself to my feet and limped over to him. His right foreleg was twisted under him. His blood was staining the ground, and I glimpsed the awful whiteness of bone that had broken through the hide. Then I saw what had happened. Because of that crazy run I had forced him to over this rough ground, he hadn't been able to judge the distance correctly. He had been thrown off balance at a small gully jump that ordinarily he would have taken in stride. His leg had snapped as he went down.

For that moment I didn't wonder how I was going to get away from the posse that was sure to be coming. I knelt beside Red, taking his head in my arms and rubbing my hands along his satiny neck and shoulders. "It's all right, boy. Everything's going to be all right." But those hurt eyes knew I was lying. I loved that horse more than I loved most people. Red was all I had left. And now I didn't even have him.

I think I would have cried—sitting there on the ground, holding Red's head in my lap—like some small child who had broken its best-loved toy in a moment of anger, not realizing what the loss would mean until it was too late. But then I looked down on the flatland and I could see Ray Novak and the others ganged around the buckboard. They were the ones responsible, I thought bitterly. Not me.

I stood up slowly, anger making a red haze of everything. I could see them wheeling now, not much more than specks in the distance, and heading in my direction. I thought, Let them come! It all started with Ray Novak—let it end with him. I was ready to meet him where I stood. I was *eager*.

Then a voice said: "You'd better come along, son. There's not much time."

I wasn't particularly surprised. I had come to expect the impossible of Pappy. I turned and looked up the slope, and there he was, sitting that big black of his, mildly rolling one of those corn-shuck cigarettes. He nudged his horse gently and rode on down to where I was, seeming entirely unconcerned with the posse charging across the flatland toward us. He glanced once at Red, and then looked away.

"I'm sorry, son," he said gently. "He was a good horse."

"Pappy, for God's sake, what are you doing here?"

He shrugged slightly. "It's a long trail to travel by yourself."

It was the closest thing to sentiment, or regret, or fear, that I had ever heard in Pappy's voice. From the very first, I figured that Pappy had picked me up because he needed a kind of personal bodyguard, but I knew now that it wasn't that. It had never occurred to me before that a man like Pappy could be lonesome. That he needed friends like other people.

I said, "Pappy, get out of here! Go on to New Mexico, or wherever you were going. You can't help me now."

But he only smiled that sad half-smile of his. Then he shook a boot out of a stirrup and held it out. "Just step up here," he said. "I guess this black horse won't mind riding double for a little piece."

"Pappy, you're crazy. You can't expect to outrun a posse by riding double."

He shrugged again. "But we can find a better place than this to fight from. Come on, son. There isn't much time."

Pappy's word was law. I knew that he wouldn't budge until I did as he said. Dumbly, I put my foot in the stirrup and swung up behind him.

I glanced at the posse. They were already in rifle range, but they were holding their fire until they had us cold. Then I looked at Red, knowing what I had to do, but not knowing if I had the guts for it.

"Just look away, son," Pappy said softly.

There was one pistol shot, and Red lay still.

Good-by, Red. Good-by to the last thing I ever gave a damn about, except Pappy. And I wasn't even sure that I cared a damn about Pappy. Maybe he was just something to hold to, a device that men like us used in order to live a little while longer. I felt empty and angry and there wasn't much sense to anything.

The big black took us as far as the top of the ridge, and that was the end of the line. We could hear the hoofs pounding now as Ray Novak pushed his posse of ranch hands on up into the hills after us. The black was a good horse—as good as Red, maybe—but he couldn't carry two men and be expected to outrun the sturdy range horses chasing us. When we hit the crest of the rise Pappy dumped out of the saddle, clawing that fancy rifle of his out of the saddle boot. I came off after him and the black went on down to the bottom of the slope.

"Over here, son!" Pappy yelled. And when I stopped rolling I saw that he already had a private fortress picked out for us. Three big rocks gave us cover on three sides and we could sweep the hill with fire in all directions. As I crawled up beside him, Pappy already had that rifle in action. He fired twice and two of the posse dumped out of their saddles and lay still. That cut the original five down to three, and I thought maybe we would get out of this after all, if we could catch one of the loose horses, and get rid of Ray Novak.

But Novak and the two ranch hands began to scatter before Pappy could cut any more of them down. They scrambled for rocks near the base of the hill and for a few moments it was quiet. Those two dead riders gave them something to think about before trying anything foolish.

Pappy looked at me, grinning slightly. "Well," he said, "we've been in worse places. That's always some consolation, they say."

I said nothing. I searched the land below us, but nobody was moving. It was quiet—deadly quiet. I wondered what Ray Novak was thinking down there. The Novaks and their tin badges! After looking at his pa, he would know that tin badges didn't make a man immune from bullets.

Pappy stacked his rifle against the rock, got out his makings, and began to roll a cigarette. Like a man knocking off work for a few minutes to take a breather. There was no way of knowing what he was thinking. For a moment he stared flatly down the side of the slope; then he looked at me.

"It didn't work out, did it, son?" he said. "I didn't think it would, but I was hoping...."

I knew he was talking about Laurin. And I didn't want to talk about Laurin. I didn't want to think about her.

Nodding his head toward the bottom of the hill, he said, "He got her, didn't he?" meaning Ray Novak. "I think maybe I knew from the first that he would. It was just a feeling, I guess, after you told me how things were."

"Cut it off, will you, Pappy?" I said angrily.

"Sure, son, I didn't mean to butt in." He sat back against the rock, with that cigarette dangling between his lips. "He's a good man, though," he said thoughtfully. "He damn near put a bullet in me that day. Probably he's learned some things since then. I don't think I'd be in any hurry to stand up to him now."

"He's a goddamned tin soldier riding behind a tin badge," I said. "His pa was the same, but he died just as easy as anybody else."

Pappy's eyes widened. "You killed his old man?"

"Sure I did. He tried to arrest me."

Pappy shook his head sadly from side to side. "Maybe we're going to have trouble," he said heavily. "Maybe we're going to have more trouble than we ever saw before."

It was still quiet down on the slope. I said, "This is no good. We can't run, and we can't fight if they don't come out from behind those rocks. But we can't just sit here. By now, somebody from the ranch will be headed toward John's City for more help. We've got to get away from here before that comes."

Pappy nodded and spat out his cigarette. Then a horse nickered back behind us and I could almost see Pappy's ears prick up. "Just a minute," he said. "I'd better look after that black of mine."

He crawled on his hands and knees to the naked side of the hill and peered down below. Suddenly, something jabbed me in the back of the brain. Intuition, they call it. Or hunch. Some men have it and some don't. Sometimes, when it hits you, it tells you to put your stack on the red and all you have to do is watch the roulette ball drop in. Or it may tell you that around the next corner is sudden death. When I felt it, I whirled and yelled:

"Pappy, look out!"

But the moment had passed. It had come and gone and I hadn't got my bet down in time. I heard a rifle crack in the afternoon, and I turned just in time to see Pappy go down.

"Pappy!" I yelled again.

But I knew it was too late. I ran over to where he was, silhouetting myself against the sky, but not caring now. Then I saw the rifleman— that sober, stone-cold face that was past anger, or grief, or any emotion at all. It was Ray Novak.

I didn't stop to wonder how he had slipped around to the naked side of the hill. He had done it, and that was enough. Dumbly, he was looking at me now. Probably, he had figured it out cold and clear in his mind what he was going to do to me when he caught me, but suddenly finding himself face to face with me startled him. And that was Ray Novak's mistake. I shot before he could swing the rifle around.

I watched as the bullet slammed into his shoulder, jerking him around. He went to his knees and began tumbling down the side of the hill.

Instinct told me that he wasn't dead. There was only a bullet in his shoulder and that wouldn't stop him for long. But before I could do anything about it, the two ranch hands were drawn around to the naked side of the hill by the shooting. I aimed very carefully at one of them. I could see horror in his eyes as he started backing away, too scared to use the gun in his hand. I pulled the trigger and he fell away somewhere out of my line of vision. I forgot about him.

I didn't bother about the other posse member. Like a damned fool, he forgot that I was in perfect position to kill him and went running across the open ground to where Ray Novak was stretched out unconscious. For a moment I watched as he pulled Novak out of the line of fire and I thought: Let him go, there's no use killing him. I knew he would get Ray back to the ranch house as soon as he could, and that would take care of the last of the posse. And, anyway, there had been so much killing, maybe I had lost the stomach for it. Then I remembered Pappy.

He was crumpled at my feet as limp and lifeless as a discarded bundle of dirty clothing. I turned him over gently and straightened his long legs. "Pappy!"

But he didn't move. And a sick feeling inside told me that Pappy wasn't going to move. The bullet had gone right through the middle, about three inches above his belt buckle, but there was only a little blood staining his dirty blue shirt. All the bleeding, I knew, would be on the inside. I felt his throat for a pulse and it was so faint that I imagined that it wasn't there at all. After a moment the glassiness that was beginning to crowd his eyes receded just a little, and that was my only way of knowing that he wasn't dead.

I didn't know what to do. There was nothing I could do, except to stay there beside him and not let him die all alone, the way he had lived. I didn't even have a drink of water to give him. I couldn't think of anything to say that might make it any easier. Down at the base of the hill, I could hear a horse scampering and I knew that would be the ranch hand taking Ray Novak back to the ranch house. Soon it was quiet again, except for the dirgelike mourning of the wind and the rattle of dry grass.

I knelt there watching the glassiness returning to Pappy's eyes. Vaguely, I wondered what his last thoughts were, if there were any thoughts. I wondered if I was a part of them. Was there any sorrow, or regret, or dismay at the way he had used his life? Would he use it any differently if he had the chance to live it all over again?

I got my answer when, for just an instant, his eyes cleared. He looked at me, smiling that sad half-smile. Then he spoke quietly, precisely, as if he had thought the matter over for a long time.

"You were right, son. I should have killed him that day ... when I had the chance."

So that was the way Pappy died—with no dismay and only one regret—sorry only that he had made the mistake of leaving a man alive. I stood up slowly, looking up at the endless sky. I think maybe I wanted to pray for Pappy—but what was there to say? Who was there to listen?

Good-by, Pappy. That was all I could think of. The wind moaned, cutting through my thin clothing, and I realized that winter had at last come to Texas. Winter was the time for dying. I bent down and closed Pappy's staring eyes. Sleep, Pappy. You can rest now, for there will be no more running for you. And Pappy's quiet face said that he was not sorry.

I left Pappy there on the hilltop with the wind and the sound of the grass. I took his rifle and went down to the bottom of the slope and found his big black horse trembling like a whipped kid down in the bottom of a gully. I said, "Easy, boy," and stroked his sleek neck until he quieted down, and then I swung up to the saddle.

I headed west again, higher into the hills, and not looking back at the hill where Pappy lay. Pappy was gone. Nothing could be done about that. First my pa, then Laurin, and now Pappy. I had lost them all, as surely as if they were all dead, and in the back of my mind one name kept burning my brain. Ray Novak.

I didn't bother to cover my tracks. I purposely left a trail that a blind pilgrim could have followed, because I knew that before long Ray Novak would be coming after me. It would be only a matter of hours before he got his shoulder patched up, and I knew him well enough to know that he wouldn't allow a posse to track me down. He would do it himself. That was the kind of man he was. And that was the way I wanted it—just me and Ray Novak.

I found the place I wanted, a ragged bluff overlooking the lowland trail that I had been following, but I traveled on past it for a mile or more and then circled around to approach the bluff from the rear.

It was perfect for what I wanted to use it for. I could see all approaches to the bluff, and anybody passing along the trail I had taken would have to come within easy rifle range. That was the important thing. All I had to do was wait.

And think.

I tried to keep my mind blank except for the job I had to do, but I couldn't keep the thoughts dammed up any longer. I couldn't go on shutting Laurin out of my mind and pretending that she never existed.

She had existed, but she didn't any more. Not for me. I had lost her, and where she had once been there was only emptiness and bitterness. I had to admit it sometime, and it might as well be now.

The hours were lonesome dragging things up there on the bluff, and the wind was cold. The wind died as night came on, but the chill was worse and I didn't dare risk a fire. There was nothing to do but wait.

The night became bitter cold, and a frost-white moon came out and looked down upon the bluff. That night I learned what it was to be alone. And I learned something else—that fear grows in lonely places. I hadn't let myself think about it before, but now I began to wonder why I had chosen this way to take out my hate on Ray Novak. Why didn't I wait for him on the trail and face it out with him, the way I had done with Buck Creyton?

The night and the moon, I suppose, had the answer. I was alone. And nobody really gave a damn whether I lived, but a great many people were wishing me dead. There was no comfort in anything except perhaps the feel of my guns, but that wasn't much help. I could hear Pappy saying: Maybe we're going to have more trouble than we ever saw before. Pappy was dead, and Ray Novak was still alive. He damned near put a bullet in me that day, Pappy had said, and probably he's learned some things since then.

Then Ray himself saying: I won't be easy, Tall....

I was scared. Worse than that, I was scared and I wouldn't admit it.

Somehow the long night wore itself out, and dawn came at last, cold and gray in the east. I got through the night without running, and that was something. I wondered how many more nights there would be like that one, and cold sweat broke out on the back of my neck.

But with the daylight it was better. The sun warmed me, and Pappy's rifle had a comforting feel in my hands again. And, instinctively, I knew that I wouldn't have much longer to wait.

But it was almost noon when I finally saw him. He came riding out of the south, along the trail I had left for him, and suddenly I realized that it would be so easy that I was amazed at the worrying I had done the night before. The distance, I judged, was about two hundred yards—not close, but plenty close enough if you had a rifle like Pappy's. I took a practice aim, judging the distance and the wind, and adjusted the leaf sight on the rifle.

I won't be easy, Tall, he'd said. Well, we'd see about that.

I waited until he reached the top of the grade before I brought him into the sights again. And then I had him, the center of his chest framed in the V of the rear sight, the knob of the front sight resting on the bottom of his left shirt pocket. It was a beautiful thing, this rifle of Pappy's. Once I had thought that a man would almost be glad to get killed by a gun like that, if he had any kind of love for firearms. I wondered how Ray Novak would feel about that.

I drew my breath in until my lungs had all they would take. Then I held it. The sights were still on the target. All I had to do was squeeze the trigger.

But I waited. A few seconds one way or the other wouldn't make any difference. I studied the man in my gunsights, the man who had all the things that could have been mine. Security, respect, and most important of all, Laurin. If it hadn't been for Ray Novak, all of them could have been mine. Now was the time to pull the trigger.

But I didn't. Sudden anger caused the rifle to waver, and I had to let my breath out and go through the whole thing all over again.

Laurin ... I could have had her, if it hadn't been for him. Maybe I could still have her, with Novak out of the way for good. But that thought went out of my mind before it had time to form. She had showed clearly enough what she felt for me—fear, and maybe a kind of pity. I didn't want that.

For a moment, while the sights were settling again, I wondered what Laurin would do, what she would say, when they brought Ray Novak's body in with a bullet through his heart. I wondered if being hated was worse than being feared.

I told myself to stop thinking. Squeeze the trigger, that was all I had to do. But my finger didn't move. I had never thought of it that way before. It was little enough, but at least she didn't hate me. Not yet.

And she wasn't alone. That was important now, because I was beginning to learn what it was to be alone. And I guess that was when I began to understand that I wouldn't pull the trigger to kill Ray Novak. Somehow, in killing him it would be like killing a part of Laurin....

I snapped the leaf sight down on the rifle. I'm sorry, Pappy. I guess my guts are gone.

And up on that hilltop with the moaning wind and rattling grass, I imagined that Pappy smiled that sad smile of his.

I watched Ray Novak until he was out of range, out of sight, and I wondered emptily if he would keep looking for me until he finally found me. As long as he was a United States marshal he would keep looking. I knew that. The hurt and the hate would burn themselves out in time, but not that sense of duty that the Novaks prided themselves on.

Then I had a sudden, strange feeling that, somewhere, Laurin wasn't fearing me any more. Nor hating me. It occurred to me that a man didn't have to stay a United States marshal—especially if his wife was against it.

But there was little comfort in the thought. If it wasn't Novak, there would always be others. The army, the sheriffs, the bounty hunters. Or punk kids wanting to make reputations for themselves.

I thought of Pappy then, not with sorrow, but with a feeling near to envy. I went over to that big black horse of his and stroked his neck for a moment before climbing on. I holstered the rifle, checked my pistols, and then we headed west.

THE END

A Noose for the Desperado

· · · · · · · · · ·

Clifton Adams

Chapter 1

I scouted the town for two full days before going into it. There hadn't been any sign of cavalry, and I figured the law wouldn't be much because nobody cared what happened to a few Mexicans. There it stood near the foothills of the Huachucas, a few shabby adobe huts and one or two frame buildings broiling in the Arizona sun. But to me it looked like Abilene, Dodge, and Ellsworth all rolled into one.

It had been a long trail from Texas, and my horse was sore-footed and needed rest and a bellyful of grain. I was beginning to grow a fuzzy beard around my chin and upper lip, and I had a second hide of trail dust that was beginning to crawl with the hundred different kinds of lice that you pick up in the desert. I was ready to take my chances on somebody recognizing me, just so I could get a bath and a shave and maybe a change of clothes.

So that was how I came to ride into this little place of Ocotillo, on that big black horse that used to belong to my pal Pappy Garret. I had Pappy's rifle in the saddle boot and Pappy's guns tied down on my thighs. But that was all right. Pappy didn't have any use for them. The last time I saw him had been on a lonely hilltop in Texas. He had died the way most men like that die sooner or later, I guess, with a lawman's bullet in his guts.

It was around sundown when we hit this place of Ocotillo, and it turned out that it was on the fiesta of San Juan's Day. I didn't know that at the time, but it was clear that they were having a celebration of some kind. The men were all in various stages of drunkenness, some of them singing and pounding on heavy guitars. Some of the young bucks were dancing with their girls in the dusty street or in the cantinas. A fat old priest was grinning at everybody, and the kids were crying and shouting and singing and rattling brightly painted gourds. It was fiesta, all right. It was like riding out of death into life.

I pulled my horse up at a watering trough and let him drink while the commotion went on all around us. Three girls in bright dresses danced around us, giggling. The big black lifted his nose out of the trough and spewed water all over them and they ran down the street screaming and laughing. Everybody seemed to be having a hell of a time.

Another girl came up and slapped the black's neck, looking at me.

"Hello, gringo!" she said.

"Hello, yourself."

"You come to fiesta, eh?" she said. Then she laughed and slapped the black again.

"Is that what it is, fiesta?"

"Sure, it's fiesta. San Juan's Day." She laughed again. "Where you come from, gringo? Long way, maybe. You plenty dirty."

"Maybe," I said. "Can I find anybody sober enough to give me a shave and fix a bath?"

"Sure, gringo," she grinned. "You come with me."

I had been looking around, not paying much attention to the girl. But now I looked at her. She was young, about eighteen or nineteen, but she wasn't any kid. Her dark eyes were full of hell, and when she flashed her white teeth in a grin you got the idea that she would like to sink them into your throat. She wore the usual loud skirt and fancy blouse with a lot of needlework on it that Mexicans like to deck themselves out in on their holidays.

"Look!" she yelled. Then she started jumping up and down and laughing like a kid.

Somebody had turned an old mossy-horn loose in the street and everybody was scattering and screaming as if a stampede was bearing down on them. The old range cow shook its head, bewildered; then some kids came up and began prodding it down the street. The yelling and screaming kept up until the cow disappeared down at the other end. That seemed to be a signal for everybody to have another drink, so all the menfolks started crowding into the cantinas.

"Does that end the fiesta?" I asked.

"Just beginning," she said. "At night they go to church and burn candles and pray to San Juan that their souls may be saved." She laughed again. "Then they drink some more. Tomorrow they go back to the fields and work until next San Juan's Day."

"How about that bath and shave?" I said.

"Sure, gringo. Come with me."

I left my horse at the hitching rack, but I took the rifle out of the saddle boot. The girl led me between two adobe huts, then through a gate in a high adobe wall. The wall completely surrounded a little plot at the back of the hut.

A dog slept and some chickens scratched under a blackjack tree. "This is a hell of a place for a barbershop," I said.

"No barber," the girl grinned. "I shave." She cut the air with her hand, as if slicing someone's throat with a razor.

"No, thanks," I said.

She laughed. "No worry, gringo. I fix."

She took my arm and led me into the house. The thick adobe walls made the room cool, and there was a pleasant smell of wine and garlic. It was like walking into another world. There was nothing there to remind me of the fiesta, or of the lonesome desert, or Pappy Garret. In this house I could even forget myself. I felt a little ridiculous wearing two pistols and carrying a rifle.

"Whose house is this?" I said.

She stabbed herself with a finger. "My house." Then she yelled, "*Papacito!*" When she got no answer, she shrugged. "Come with me."

The house had only two rooms. The first room had a fireplace and a charcoal brazier for cooking and a plank table and three leather-bottom chairs. In one corner there were some blankets rolled up, and I figured that was where Papacito slept when he was home. The other room had a mound of clay shaped up against one wall with some blankets on it, and that was the bed. A rough plank wardrobe and another leather-bottom chair completed the furniture.

"Wait here," the girl said.

She went out and I heard her shaking up the coals in the fireplace, and pretty soon she came back lugging a big wooden tub. "For bath," she said. On the next trip she brought a razor and a small piece of yellow lye soap. "For shave."

I grinned. "I can't complain about the service."

"You wait," she said.

I was too tired to try to understand why she was going to so much trouble. Maybe that's the way Mexicans were. Maybe they liked to wait on the gringos. I was beginning to feel easy and comfortable for the first time since I had left Texas. I pulled off my boots, sat in the chair, and put my feet on the clay bed. I was beginning to like Arizona just fine.

"Say," I called, "have you got anything to drink?"

She came in with a crock jug and handed it to me. "Wine," she said.

I swigged from the neck and the stuff was sweet and warm as it hit my stomach. "Thanks," I said. Then I had another go at the jug, and that was enough. I never took more than two drinks of anything.

That was partly Pappy Garret's teaching, but mostly it came from seeing foothills filled with gunmen who could shoot like forked lightning when they were sober, but when they forgot to set the bottle down they were just another notch in some ambitious punk's gun butt.

The girl came in with a crock bowl of hot water. I got up and she put the water on the chair and a broken mirror on the wardrobe.

"Bath before long," she said, and went back into the other room.

She had a way of knocking out all the words except the most essential ones, but she spoke pretty good English.

I went over to the wardrobe and inspected my face in the mirror. It gave me quite a shock at first, partly because I hadn't seen my face in quite a while, and partly because of the dirt and beard and the sunken places around the cheeks and eyes. It didn't look like my face at all.

It didn't look like the face of a kid who still wasn't quite twenty years old. The eyes had something to do with it, and the tightness around the mouth. I studied those eyes carefully because they reminded me of some other eyes I had seen, but I couldn't place them at first. They had a quick look about them, even when they weren't moving. They didn't seem to focus completely on anything.

Then I remembered one time when I was just a sprout in Texas. I had been hunting and the dogs had jumped a wolf near the arroyo on our place, and after a long chase they had cornered him in the bend of a dry wash. As I came up to where the dogs were barking I could see the wolf snarling and snapping at them, but all the time those eyes of his were casting around to find a way to get out of there.

And he did get out, finally. He was a big gray lobo, as vicious as they come. He ripped the throat of one of my dogs and blasted his way out and disappeared down the arroyo. But I heard later that another pack of dogs caught him and killed him.

"What's wrong?"

The girl came in with a kettle of hot water and poured it into the tub.

"Nothing," I said, and began lathering my face.

I started to leave my mustache on, thinking that it might keep people from recognizing me, but when I got the rest of my face shaved my upper lip looked like hell. It was just some scraggly pink fuzz and I couldn't fool anybody with that. The girl poured some cold water in the tub on top of the hot, and filled it about halfway to the top.

"Ready," she said. "Give me clothes."

"Nothing doing. I take a bath in private or I don't take one at all."

"To wash," she added.

These Mexicans must be crazy, I thought. Why anybody would want to take a saddle tramp in and take care of him I didn't know. But it was all right with me, if that was the way she wanted it.

"All right," I said. "You get in the other room and I'll throw them through the door."

She stood with her hands on her hips, grinning. "Gringos!" But she went in the other room and I began to strip off. When I threw the things in the other room she picked them up and went outside.

I must have soaked for an hour or more there in the tub, twisting and turning and scrubbing every inch of myself that I could reach. It was dark outside, and the only light in the house came from the fireplace in the other room.

"Say," I called, "are those clothes dry yet?"

"Pretty soon," she said. Her voice was so close it made me jump. Instinctively, I made a grab for my pistols, which I had put on the chair and pulled up beside the tub, but she laughed and I stopped the grab in mid-air.

"Get the hell out of here," I said.

She was leaning against the wardrobe laughing at me, and with the red light from the fireplace playing on her face. She must have found my tobacco and corn-shuck papers in my shirt, because there was a thin brown cigarette dangling from one corner of her mouth. That shook me, because I had never seen a woman smoke before, except for the fancy girls in Abilene or Dodge or one of the other trail towns.

I saw that she wasn't going to get out until she got good and ready. I couldn't figure her out. One minute she seemed to be a simple Mexican girl, almost a child, with a straightforward eagerness to help a stranger out; and the next minute she was voluptuous and cynical and as wise as Eve. I didn't know enough about women to know what to do with her. I had looked into big-eyed muzzles of .44's without feeling as helpless as I did when I looked at her.

"All right," I said, "you've looked. Now how about getting my clothes?"

She dragged deep on the cigarette and let it drop to the packed clay floor. "Sure, gringo."

She went into the other room and threw my pants through the doorway. They were still damp, but I didn't care. I put them on. She came in with my shirt, threw it at me, and leaned against the wardrobe again.

"You look better after shave."

"I feel better."

She must have brushed her hair or combed it while I was taking the bath. It shone as black as the devil's heart in the red light of the fire, and it was pulled back tight away from her face and rolled in a bun at the nape of her neck. Her mouth was ripe and red and those eyes of hers seemed to be laughing at something.

"What are you looking at?" I said.

"I thought you was man," she said. "With beard gone you're just boy."

I thought quickly that maybe I should have left the mustache on. Maybe I should have left the beard on too. "I'll grow up," I said. I fished in my pocket and found a silver dollar and flipped it at her. "That's for the bath and shave."

I had my shirt and boots on now, and was buckling on my guns. I didn't know where I was going exactly. I just wanted to go out and look at people and see if I couldn't get to feel like a human being again. I picked up my rifle and got as far as the door.

"*Adiós*," she said.

"*Adiós*."

"I hope you shoot good," she said. "It is bad to die young."

That stopped me. "What are you talking about?"

"The man in the street, by your horse," she said calmly. "I think maybe he shoot you. If you don't shoot first."

I felt my stomach flip over. Could it be possible that the federal marshals had trailed me all the way from Texas? I went out the back door, across the walled-in yard, and through the gate. There was a lot of singing somewhere, and some drunken yelling and laughing. Fiesta was still going on. The adobe huts seemed jammed closer together in the darkness, but the Mexicans had a bonfire going out in the street, so I could see enough to pick my way between them. A dog barked. Somewhere in the night a girl giggled and a man made soft crooning noises. After a while I could stand in the shadows and see my horse across the street.

Sure enough, a man was there.

He wasn't Mexican and he wasn't anybody I had ever seen before. He was a big man with flabby features and he didn't seem to be much interested in the fiesta or anything else, except that big black horse of mine. Then somebody came up behind me. It was the girl.

"Who is he?" I said. "I never saw him before."

She seemed surprised. She seemed suddenly to scrap all the opinions that she had formed about me and start making brand-new ones. "You sure?" she asked after a pause.

"I tell you I never laid eyes on him before. What is he, somebody's hired gunny?"

She did some quick thinking. "I think Marta make big mistake," she said.

"Are you Marta?"

"*Sí.* You come with me, gringo."

She stepped out into the street, in the dancing firelight, but I didn't move. She crossed the street, waving her arms and yelling something to the big guy. I saw the man nod. Then she motioned for me to come on.

The man didn't look very dangerous to me. He had the usual pistol on his hip, but I figured that he was too old and too fat to be very fast with it. Anyway, I was curious, so I walked across the street.

The man didn't miss a thing, not even a flick of an eyelash, as I came toward him. As I got closer I began to change my estimate of him—he could be dangerous, plenty dangerous. It showed in his flat eyes, the aggressive way he stood. It showed on the well-worn butt of his .44. He wore a battered, wide-brimmed Texas hat with a rawhide thong under his chin to keep it on. His shirt was buckskin and had been pretty fancy in its day, but now it was almost black and slick with dirt and wear. He kept his hand well away from his pistol to show that he wasn't asking for trouble. I did the same.

The girl was standing spraddle-legged, hands on hips, grinning at us, but under that grin I had a feeling that there was disappointment. The man jerked his head, dismissing her, as I stepped up to the dirt walk. She melted away in the darkness somewhere.

"This your horse?" the man said, nodding his head at the black.

"That's right."

"I was thinking maybe I'd seen him somewhere before. Texas, maybe."

"You've had time to make up your mind, the way you've been standing here gawking at him."

He blinked his eyes. He was used to getting more respect than that, especially from boys not out of their teens yet. "A tough punk," he said flatly. "If there's anything I can't stand it's a tough punk."

The way he said it went all over me. It was like cursing a man, knowing that he was listening and not having enough respect for him to lower your voice. Before he knew what hit him I had the barrel of my pistol rammed in his belly almost up to the cylinder. "Goddamn you," I said. "I don't know who you are, but if you use that word again I'll kill you. That's one thing in this world you can depend on."

I had knocked the wind out of him and he sagged against the hitching rack gasping. His flat eyes became startled eyes, then they became hate-filled eyes. I should have killed him right then and got it over with, because I knew that he would never quite get over it, being thrown down on by a kid, and someday he would try to even it up. Pappy Garret would have killed him without batting an eye, if he had been in my place. But like a damn fool, I didn't.

"Jesus Christ!" he gulped. "Get that pistol out of my stomach. I didn't mean anything."

"Not until I find out why you were sucking around my horse. You were waiting for me to come out, weren't you? All right, why?"

"Sure, sure, I was waitin' for you to come out," he said. "Word got around that a stranger was in town, and we don't go much for strangers here in Ocotillo. Basset sent me down to have a look. He figured maybe you was a government marshal, or maybe one of them cavalry intelligence men."

"What gave him a smart idea like that?"

"That girl you was with. She come around a while ago and told Basset she was holdin' you at her house. It was her idea that you was a government marshal."

That was fine. While I had been taking a bath and thinking that she was quite a girl, she had been working up a scheme to get me killed.

"Who is Basset?"

"You haven't been in Arizona long if you don't know who Basset is. He about runs things in this part of the territory."

"What does the cavalry do while Basset runs Arizona?"

"Hell, the cavalry's too busy with the Apaches to worry about us. Now will you take that pistol out of my stomach?"

I pulled the pistol out enough to let him breathe. I hadn't bargained for anything like this. What looked to be just another little Mexican town was turning out to be a hole-up for the territory's badmen.

"What do you think about me now?" I said, "Do you still think I'm a government man?"

"Hell, no. I spotted that horse of yours right off. The last time I saw that animal was in Texas, about two years ago, and Pappy Garret was ridin' him. We heard Pappy was killed not long ago, but the"—he almost said "punk"—"the kid that was ridin' with him got away."

"Did the kid have a name?" I said.

"Talbert Cameron, according to the 'Wanted' posters. Jesus, I never saw anybody pull a gun like that, unless maybe it was Pappy himself."

Well, that settled it. I couldn't outride my reputation, so I might as well try to live with it. At least until I thought of something better. I holstered my pistol because it looked like the fuss was over for the present. The big man pulled himself together and tried to pretend that every thing was just fine. But no matter what he did, he couldn't hide the smoky hate in the back of his eyes.

"Let's go," I said.

"Where?"

"I want to see the man that runs things around here, Basset."

He didn't put up any argument, as I expected. He merely shrugged. And I unhitched the black.

The fiesta had left the streets and had gone into the native saloons, or maybe the church, wherever it was. The bonfire was dying down and the night was getting darker. The street was almost deserted as we went up to the far end, and the ragged Huachucas looked down on the desert and on the town, and I had a feeling that those high, sad mountains were a little disgusted with what they saw.

After a minute I got to thinking about that girl, Marta. What was she up to, anyway? First she tells a gang of outlaws that I'm a government marshal, and then she tells me that there's somebody waiting to kill me.

I said, "What about that Mexican girl back there, the one called Marta? What was her cut for going to Basset and telling him I was a government man?"

The big man darted a glance at me and kept walking. "She's crazy," he said. "Let her alone. If you want to get along in Ocotillo, let that girl alone."

He said it as if he meant it.

At the end of the street there was a two-story frame building that was all out of place here in a village of squat adobe huts. From the sound of the place I could tell that it was a saloon of some kind—one with a pretty good business, if the noise was any indication. On the other side of the saloon there was a circle corral and another frame building that I took to be a livery barn.

"My horse needs grain and a rubdown," I said.

My partner shouldered through the doors of the saloon and picked out a Mexican with a jerk of his head. "Take care of the horse outside," he said. Then to me, "Wait here. I'll see if Basset wants to see you."

He marched down to the far end of the saloon, opened an unmarked door, and disappeared.

It was quite a place, this saloon. There were big mirrors and glass chandeliers that must have come all the way around the Horn and then been freighted across the desert from San Francisco. Part of the place was done in fancy oak paneling and the rest of it finished out in rough planking, as if the owner had got disgusted after the first burst of enthusiasm and decided that it was a waste of money in Ocotillo. What surprised me was that anybody could have been so ambitious in the first place.

About half the customers were Mexicans, which was about right, since the Mexican border wasn't more than a day's ride to the south. There were four or five saloon girls sitting at tables in the back of the place, near the roulette wheels, chuck-a-luck, and card tables. There was even a pool table back there, and I hadn't seen one of them since Abilene.

It was a crazy, gaudy kind of place to be stuck out here in the desert, off all beaten trails and a hundred miles away from anything like civilization. I went over to the bar and ordered beer. The Mexican bartender served it up in a big crock mug and I pushed my face into the foam.

From the minute I walked into the place I became the main attraction, but I figured that wasn't unusual, considering what Basset's hired man had said about strangers. The customers all made a big to-do about carrying on with their talking and drinking as usual, but from the corners of their eyes they were cutting me up and down. They studied my two guns. They noticed that I used my left hand to drink, leaving my right one free. They didn't like me much, what they could see of me. They were thinking that I was damn young to tote so much iron. They were thinking that somebody ought to get up and slap hell out of me just to teach me not to show off—but nobody got up.

I finished my beer and let the customers gawk until my friend with the dangerous eyes came back.

"Basset says come on in," he grunted, and he went on out the front door without waiting to see if I had anything to say about it.

Chapter 2

I don't know what kind of man I expected Basset to be, but I never would have figured him as the man he really was. Basset, it turned out, was a greasy-looking man not much over five feet tall and weighing not much under three hundred pounds. He was sprawled out in a tilt-back chair, in front of a roll-top desk, as I came in. He peered at me with dark little eyes that were almost squeezed out between enormous rolls of fat.

"Sit down, sit down," he said, panting as if he had just finished a long run.

He was alone in the room. He looked completely harmless, but I shied away from him like a horse shying away from a snake.

"My man Kreyler says you're the Cameron kid," he wheezed. "Says you used to ride with Pappy Garret. Hell with guns."

"That's what your man Kreyler says," I said.

"What do you say?"

I took a cane-bottom chair, the only other chair in the room. "Maybe."

Basset shifted abruptly and sprawled in the other direction. "What did you want to see me about?"

I wasn't sure why I had wanted to see him. So I said, "I'm not sure. Maybe I just wanted to see what the boss of Arizona looks like."

"Ha-ha," he said, panting. He just spoke the words, he wasn't laughing. "All right, out with it, do you want a job?"

"That depends on what I have to do."

"Have you got any money?"

"Twelve dollars," I said. That was left from a job of trail driving I had done almost six months ago. I hadn't had a chance to spend it.

"Ha-ha," Basset said again. "Let me tell you something, Cameron. I knew Pappy Garret. If you can handle guns the way he could, I'll make a rich man out of you. A rich man."

"I don't hire my guns," I said.

I'd had about enough of Basset. Watching his enormous, shaking belly made my skin crawl. I made a move to get up, but he waved me down.

"Just a minute," he wheezed. "Let me tell you about our charming little village here, Ocotillo." He settled back, smiling and breathing through his mouth. His lips were red and wet and raw-looking, like an incision in a piece of liver. "Ocotillo," he said again. "It was just a little village of Mexican farmers, a few sheepherders, until a few years ago, when some sourdough thought he had discovered a vein of silver up in the foothills. Overnight, you might say, civilization came to Ocotillo. You wouldn't believe it, but two years ago this whole area was covered with tents and shacks and wagons, and fortune hunters crawled over the hills as thick as sand lice."

He chuckled for a minute, remembering.

"Well, it turned out there wasn't any silver there after all, except some 'fool's silver,' traces of lead ore and zinc. Before you knew it Ocotillo was as empty as a frontier church. The fortune hunters all moved on, and for a while I'll admit I was worried. You saw the wood in my bar out there? Redwood from California. My wheels, pool table, gambling equipment, shipped clean from New York around the Horn and freighted across the desert. Cost thousands of dollars, this saloon, and for a while it looked like it wouldn't bring a penny."

I rolled a cigarette while he talked. As I held a match to the corn-shuck cylinder, Basset smiled and nodded.

"I remember Pappy used to smoke his cigarettes Mexican style like that. Anyway, here I was with this saloon and nobody for customers except a few poor Mexicans. Then one day I got another customer."

He slouched back in the chair, smiling, waiting for me to ask the question. "And this customer was ..." I said.

"Black Joseph," he said with satisfaction.

I wasn't particularly surprised. I hadn't heard of the famous Indian gunman for a year or more, so I knew that if he wasn't making buzzard food of himself he had to be in New Mexico or Arizona. I had never seen him, but I knew him by reputation. The artists' drawings on "Wanted" posters always showed him as a hungry-eyed, hawk-nosed, Osage, with a battered flat-crowned hat pushed down over his black, braided hair. He had been a scout for the Union Army during the war, but it seemed that even the bloody battles of Shiloh and Chickamauga hadn't blunted his craving to kill. He was supposed to be fast with a gun. According to some men who ought to know, he was the fastest. I didn't know about that, and I didn't care. Black Joseph didn't have anything against me, and I had nothing against him.

Basset seemed to think that the Indian's name should have done something to me. Maybe I should have started sweating, or loosened my guns, or something. When I didn't, the fat man seemed slightly annoyed.

"You've heard of Black Joseph, haven't you?" he panted.

"I've heard of him," I said.

That seemed to make him feel a little better. "Well," he said, "I began to get an idea the minute that Indian murderer rode into Ocotillo— not that I've got anything against him," he added quickly. "It's just that he doesn't bother to think before he shoots. Anyway, I figured maybe there were a lot of boys like him, things getting too hot for them back in Texas."

He smiled that damp smile, as if to say, "You ought to know, Cameron."

I said, "Has all this got anything to do with me?"

"That depends on you," Basset said carelessly. "Now, you look like a man on the run. Would you like to have a place to settle down for a while and give the United States marshals a chance to forget about you?

Would you like to be sure that you won't run into my cavalry men? Would you like to have some insurance like that?"

"You can't get insurance from a United States marshal," I said, "or the cavalry, either."

Basset lurched forward in his chair, got a cigar from a box on his desk, and rolled it between his wet lips. "You just don't know the right man, son," he said, breathing heavily. "The cavalry—no. But, then, the cavalry is busy up north with the Apache uprising. There's no call for them to come down here unless somebody like a federal marshal put them up to it."

"And what makes you think that some deputy marshal won't do just that?"

He went on smiling, holding a match to his cigar, puffing until it was burning to suit him. Then he threw the match on the floor and shouted, "Kreyler!"

The door opened and the big, slab-faced man came in. The last time I saw him he had been headed out of the saloon—but when Basset called, he was there.

"Yeah?"

"Show this boy who you are, Kreyler," Basset said.

Kreyler frowned. He didn't like me, and whatever it was that Basset had on his mind, he didn't like that either. But he didn't have the guts to look at the fat man and tell him so. Reluctantly he went into his pocket and came out with a badge—a deputy United States marshal's badge.

"That will be your insurance," Basset said, as Kreyler went out, "if you choose to stay with us here in Ocotillo."

The whole thing had kind of taken my breath away. I had only known one United States marshal before. He lived, breathed, and thought nothing but the law. I hadn't known that a man like Kreyler could worm his way into an office like that.

Suddenly I began to appreciate the kind of setup Basset had here. In Ocotillo a man could live in safety, protected from the law, his identity hidden from the outside world. I thought of the long days and nights of running, afraid to sleep, afraid to rest, forever looking over my shoulder and expecting to see the man who would finally kill me. Here in Ocotillo I could forget all that—if I wanted to pay the fat man's price.

Basset smiled, puffing lazily on his cigar.

I said finally, "Insurance like that must come pretty high."

"Not for the right men, like yourself." He bent forward, his jowls shaking. "Have you ever heard of the Mexican smuggling trains?"

I shook my head.

"There are dozens of them," he said. "They come across the international line, taking one of the remote canyons of the Huachucas. Thousands of dollars in gold or silver some of these trains carry. They trade in Tucson for merchandise that they smuggle back across the border, without paying the heavy duty, and sell at fat profits. In a way," Basset smiled, "you might say that Kreyler is upholding his oath to the United States, for he is a great help to us in stopping this unlawful smuggling of the Mexicans."

I was beginning to get it now, but I wasn't sure that I liked it.

"Take your time," the fat man said. "Make up your mind and let me know. Say tomorrow?"

"All right," I said. "Tomorrow."

I was glad to get out of the office. The bath that I'd had not long ago had been wasted. I felt dirtier than I had when I first rode into the place.

I stopped at the bar on my way out and had a shot of the white poison that the Mexicans were drinking. Business had picked up while I was in the office. Most of the fancy girls had found laps to sit on, and their brassy, high-pitched giggles punched holes in the general uproar like bullets going through a tub of lard. I studied the men in the place with a new interest, now that I knew who they were and what they were doing here. I didn't see anybody that I knew, yet I had a feeling that I knew all of them. Their eyes were all alike, restless, darting from one place to the other. They laughed hard with their mouths, but none of the laughter ever reached their eyes. I didn't see anybody drunk enough to be careless about the way his gun hand hung. And I knew I wouldn't. My friend Kreyler, the deputy United States marshal, wasn't around. Probably he was in some corner, waiting for Basset to yell for him.

I stood alone at the end of the bar, wondering where I was going to sleep that night and listening to three Mexicans sing a syrupy love song in Spanish, when she said:

"Hello, gringo!"

I don't know where she came from. But now she was standing next to me, grinning as if nothing had happened.

"Get away from me," I said. "When I get tired of living I can get myself killed. I don't need your help."

She didn't bat an eye. "I think you plenty fast with gun," she grinned. "You don't be killed."

"I'll be killed if you keep telling people I'm a government marshal. What the hell did you do that for, anyway? And after that, why did you bother to warn me that somebody was waiting for me? Do you just like to hear guns go off and see men get killed?"

She threw her head back and laughed, as if that was the best one she'd heard in a long time. "Maybe you buy Marta drink, eh?"

"Maybe I'll kick Marta's bottom if she doesn't leave me alone."

But I didn't mean it and she knew it. She laughed again and I poured her a drink of the white poison. She poured salt in the cup between her thumb and forefinger, licked it with her tongue and then downed her drink in one gulp. She looked more at home here in the saloon than some of the fancy girls. And she was a lot better looking than any of the doxies. But I noticed a funny thing. None of the men looked at her. They seemed to go to a great deal of trouble not to look at her.

"Another one, gringo?" she said, holding up her empty glass.

"Not for me." But I reached for the bottle and poured her another one. She downed it the same way she had the first one.

"Where you go, gringo?"

"To find a bed. There's a big desert out there and I've been a long time crossing it. I'm tired."

She took my arm and pulled me toward the door. "Come with me, I fix."

"Isn't there a hotel over the saloon here?"

"You no go there. You come with Marta."

God knows she made it clear enough, and she was the best-looking girl I had seen for longer than I liked to remember—but there was something about it that went against me. I felt a sickness that I hadn't felt in a long time, and memories popped up in my mind, sharp and clear like a magic-lantern show I had seen once. We were outside now, on the dirt walk in front of the saloon. At the end of the building there was an outside stairway that went up to the second floor, and on the corner of the building there was a sign: "Rooms." For no particular reason I began to get mad. I gave her a shove, harder than I'd intended, and she went reeling out into the dusty street.

I headed for the livery barn to get my saddlebags and she cursed me every step of the way in shrill, outraged Spanish. But I didn't hear. I was listening to other voices. And other times.

Other times and other places.... I went through the motions of looking after my horse and getting my saddlebags and going up the shaky stairs over the saloon to see if I could get a room, but they were like the motions that you go through in a dream. They didn't seem to mean anything. I remembered the big green country of the Texas Panhandle, where I was born. I remembered my pa's ranch and the little town near it, John's City. And Professor Bigloe's Academy, where I had gone to school before the war, and the frame shack at the crossroads between our place and John's City called Garner's Store, where I used to listen to the bitter old veterans of the war still cursing Sherman and Lincoln and Grant, and reliving over and over the glories of the lost Confederacy. And, finally, I remembered a girl.

But she was just a name now, and I had said good-by to her for the last time. Good-by, Laurin. I had hurt her for the last time, and lied to her for the last time, and I tried to be glad that she was married now and had put me out of her life. Maybe now she would know a kind of quiet peace and happiness that she had never had while I was around. I tried, but I couldn't feel glad, or sorry, or anything else. Except for an aching emptiness. I could feel that.

At the top of the stairs I pounded on a door and woke up a faded, frazzle-haired old doxie, who, for a dollar, let me have the key to a room at the end of the dusty hall. The room was just big enough to undress in without skinning your elbows on the walls. There was a sagging iron bed and a washstand with a crock pitcher, bowl, and coal-oil lamp on it. A corner of a broken mirror was tacked on the wall over the washstand. There was an eight-penny nail in the door, if you wanted to hang up your clothes.

It wasn't the finest room in the world, but it would do. I raised the window and had a look outside before I lighted the lamp. I was glad to see that there was no awning or porch roof under the window, and there was nobody out in the street that I could see. I lighted the lamp, took the straw mattress off the bed, and put it on the floor in front of the door. I was dead tired and I didn't want any visitors while I slept.

Automatically I went through a set routine of checking my guns, putting them beside me on the mattress, stretching out with my feet against the door. If that door moved I wanted to know about it in a hurry. Small things, maybe, but I had learned that it was small things that kept a man alive. Trimming a fraction of a second off your draw, filing a fraction of an inch off your gun's trigger action, keeping your ears and eyes and nerves keyed a fraction higher than the next man's. A heartbeat, a bullet. They were all small things.

For a long while, in the darkness, I rocked on the thin edge of sleep while almost forgotten faces darted in and out of my memory, flashing and disappearing like fox fire in a sluggish swamp. Laurin's face. And Pappy Garret. The fabulous Pappy Garret whose name was already beginning to appear in five-cent novels, and history books, and maybe even the Sunday newspaper supplements back East. My pal Pappy, who had taught me everything I knew about guns. I tried to imagine what Pappy would say if he could see how famous I had become. Would he smile that old sad smile of his if he could see the bright look of admiration in small boys' eyes as they read the "Wanted" poster?

At some unsure point half thoughts became dreams, and then the dreams vanished and there was nothing for a while.

I don't remember when I first felt the pressure of the door on my feet, but when I felt it. I was immediately awake, wide-eyed, staring into the darkness. There wasn't a sound. Not even from the saloon below. At first, as I lay rigid, I thought that I must have imagined it, but then the door moved inward again, slowly, carefully.

For just a moment I lay there wondering who in Ocotillo wanted to kill me. Kreyler? Maybe, but I didn't think he would try it while Basset was trying to get me on his payroll. Could I have overlooked somebody in the saloon that had something against me? A brother or cousin or friend of somebody I had killed? That was possible. I managed to roll off the mattress without making any noise. I wasn't scared, now that I knew what was going on. I was awake, but whoever it was at the door didn't know it. When he found out, he would be too close to death for it to make any difference.

I eased the mattress away as the crack in the door widened. A figure slipped into the room without a sound. I still couldn't tell who it was. White moonlight poured on the bed, but the rest of the room was in darkness, and for a moment that empty bed confused the killer.

I don't know why I waited. I could have squeezed the trigger and killed him before he knew what hit him. But for some reason I didn't.

I saw a knife glint dully as he began to move forward. Then I saw who it was.

I must have given a grunt of surprise, because the figure wheeled quickly in my direction. I didn't see a thing, but instinct told me to do something and do it in a hurry. I started to dive, and as I moved to one side the knife flashed and glittered, cutting the air down over my head. There was a sudden thud as it buried itself in the wall. I heard the quivering, disappointed whine of well-tempered steel. Then I slammed into a pair of legs and we crashed to the floor.

The would-be killer was Marta, the Mexican girl.

I heard clothing tear as we went down. I made a grab for her arms but she jerked away and gouged bloody holes in my face with her fingernails. I grabbed again and this time I got her down, my hands on her shoulders and my knee in her stomach. Her body was smooth and hot, and somehow hard and soft at the same time, like gun steel covered with velvet. Neither of us made a sound. We had landed near the window, and cold moonlight fell on her sweating face. Her blouse had come apart in the fight, and from her waist up she was mostly naked. She twisted her head to one side and sank those white, gleaming teeth in my wrist.

I heard myself howl as she broke loose and dived across the floor for one of my guns. But I grabbed her hair and jerked her back, scratching and clawing like some wild animal. I could feel warm blood running down my arm, and when she tried to bite me again I hit her. I hit her in the mouth as hard as I could. I felt her lips burst on my knuckles and blood spurted halfway across the room.

"Goddamn you!" I heard myself saying. She was limp on the floor, but I still had a hold of her hair, holding her head up. "Goddamn you!" I let go of her hair and her head hit the floor like a ripe melon. She was as limp as a rag, and I didn't give a damn if she never got up.

I fumbled around the dark room in my underwear until I finally found my shirt and got some matches. After a while I got the lamp burning and poured some water into the crock bowl and began washing the blood off my arm. But I couldn't stop the blood that kept gushing out of the deep double wound on my left wrist. The pain went all the way up to my shoulder and down to my guts. Anger swarmed all over me like a prairie fire.

"Get up, goddamn you!" I said. But she didn't move. I went over and gathered up my guns and her knife, trailing blood all over the place. Then I jerked off half her blouse and wrapped it tightly around my forearm. Pretty soon the bleeding stopped.

After a while she began to stir. She lifted herself slowly to her knees, shaking her head dumbly like a poleaxed calf.

"Get out of here," I said tightly. "And stay out. So help me, if you ever try a thing like that again I'll kill you."

She looked at me for a long time with those stupid eyes. She looked like hell. Her mouth was bloody and her lips were beginning to puff. She didn't look so damned wild and deadly now.

I went over to the door and flung it open. "Go on, get out of here."

She managed to get to her feet, swaying, almost falling on her face again. She put one foot out, as if it were the first step she had ever taken. Then she tried the other one. After a while she made it to the hallway. I slammed the door and locked it.

I don't know how long I sat there on the springless bed, nursing my arm and letting the anger burn itself out. But finally the red haze began to lift and I could think straight again.

She had tried to kill me! That was the thing that got me, when I began to think about it. But why? I didn't know enough about women to answer that. A lot of people had tried to kill me at one time or another, but, before tonight, never a woman. Maybe she was just plain crazy. I remembered that Kreyler had said that when I had asked him about her. Maybe Kreyler knew what he was talking about.

My wrist was still giving me trouble. The pain was no longer located in any one particular spot; the whole arm throbbed and ached all the way to the marrow of the bone. I got up and washed it again in water and tried to do a better job of bandaging it, but I couldn't tell any difference in the way it felt. That was when I heard somebody on the stairs. Footsteps in the hall.

I found my pistol and blew out the lamp. When the footsteps stopped in front of my door I was ready. I jerked the door open and stepped to one side, my pistol cocked. It was the girl again, Marta.

She had washed the blood off her face but she was still a long way from being a beauty. Her face was swollen, her lips were split and puffed all out of shape. But she had found a clean blouse from somewhere to replace the one I had torn off of her—and in her hands she had a bottle of whisky.

"Whisky good for arm," she said flatly. "I fix."

There was no fight left in her. Her eyes had the vacant, weary look that you see in the eyes of very old people, or perhaps the dying. I felt like a fool holding a gun on her, and in the back of my mind I suppose I felt sorry for what I had done to her, even if she had tried to kill me. What could I do with a girl like that? I couldn't hate her. I couldn't feel anything for her but a vague kind of pity.

And I was dead tired and maybe I did need the whisky.

"All right," I said. "Wait until I light the lamp again."

I lit the lamp and she came into the room, almost timidly. She took the bowl of bloody water, threw it out the window, and filled the bowl up again from the pitcher. "Come," she said.

She unwrapped my arm and washed the wound again. Then she

opened the bottle and poured the whisky over my wrist and I almost hit the ceiling.

"Bad now," she said, "but good tomorrow."

"If I live until tomorrow. At the rate things are going, there's a good chance that I won't."

She began bandaging the wrist again, without saying anything. I turned the bottle up and drank some of the clear, coal-oil-tasting fluid. It was the raw, sour-mash stuff that the Mexicans make for themselves, and when it hit my stomach it was almost as bad as pouring it in the wound.

"Where did you get this?"

"My house."

"It may be fine for wounds, but it's not worth a damn to drink."

"Papacito drink," she said.

"You like saloon whisky, don't you? Saloons and saloon whisky and gringos. Why don't you stay in your own part of town?"

For a moment she looked at me with hurt eyes, then went on with her bandaging. I didn't give a damn what she did. I was just talking while the whisky cooled in my stomach. It occurred to me that it was a crazy trick, letting her back into the room. Maybe she had another knife hidden on her somewhere.

"That good?" she said.

She finished with my arm, then poured some whisky on a rag and cleaned the blood off my face.

I had a look in the mirror. "That's fine. My face looks like something left on a butcher's block. I might as well throw away my off-side gun, for all the good it's going to do me. What the hell's wrong with you, anyway? Are you just plain crazy or did you have a reason for trying to get that knife into me?"

She looked down and said nothing.

"Out with it," I said. "I'm not mad now, I just want to know what you've got against me."

She still didn't say anything, so I grabbed her arm and jerked her around. Then I got a handful of her hair and snapped her head back.

"Tell me, goddamnit! Did somebody pay you to try a trick like that?"

We stood there breathing in each other's faces. Finally she said, "No."

"Then why?"

She shrugged. "I hate you for a little while. You shove Marta away.

I think maybe I kill you."

It took me a minute to get it, and after I finally did get it I didn't understand it. Just because I hadn't wanted to go to bed with her, she tried to kill me!

She was looking down again. Her eyes still had that dull, beaten look in them, and I had a queer feeling that she was crying and the tears were falling on the inside. I didn't know what to make of her. It made me uncomfortable just looking at her.

She said flatly, "I go now."

"That's fine." I went over and opened the door. She waited a long minute, watching me, as if she thought maybe I was going to change my mind and ask her to stay.

I didn't. All I wanted was to get her out of here and never see her again.

After she had gone I lay a long while trying to figure her out. But I couldn't do it, and along toward dawn I lost interest and tried to get some sleep. And at last I did sleep, and dreamed restless dreams, mostly of my home in Texas.

Fiesta was over when I woke up the next morning. Most of the Mexicans had gone back to their one-mule farms or their sheep herds, or wherever Mexicans go when fiesta is over. My room was a mess, with blood all over the floor, and the bed knocked around at a crazy angle, and everything I had scattered from one corner to the other. My wrist was swollen stiff and hurt like hell.

I picked up some of the things, shirts and pants and a change of underwear that had been kicked out of my saddlebags in the scuffle, and put them back where they belonged. I stood at the window for a while, looking down on the gray scattering of mud huts that was Ocotillo, and for a minute I almost made up my mind to get out of there. The place was crazy, and everybody in it was crazy. I didn't want any more to do with it.

But where would I go? Back to Texas and let some sheriff's posse decorate a cottonwood with me? To New Mexico or California, and take my chances with the cavalry or United States marshals?

I didn't think so.

It looked like Ocotillo was the end of the line, whether I liked it or not. And that proposition of Basset's—I'd have to listen to that, too, whether I liked it or not, because I didn't have any money and I didn't know of anybody that I could go to for help.

For a week, maybe, I thought. Or a month at the most. I could stand it that long. When I got some money together I could find a place to hole up until the law lost interest in me. Maybe I'd go across the line into Sonora, or Chihuahua, or some place like that. But it would take money.

There was one pretty thing about this business of Basset's. Robbing Mexican smuggling trains wasn't like robbing an express coach or a bank or anything else that the local law had an interest in. The law didn't give a damn if a smuggling train was robbed. They probably took it as a favor.

But it's funny the way a man's mind works on things like that. I had never had anything to do with robbing people. Killing—that was different. A man had to kill sometimes in this wild country. In the bitter, hate-sick Texas that had been my home, it had been the accepted way of settling arguments between men. Life was cheap. The lank, quiet boys of Texas had learned that when they rode off to fight for the Cause and the Confederacy, when most of them didn't even know what Confederacy meant, or care. Killing had become a part of living. But robbing people—that was something new that I had to get used to.

There were only the bartender and one other man in the saloon when I got down there. The bartender was kicking the wreckages to one side and making a few passes with a broom, the other man was eating eggs and side meat at the bar. The place was dark and sick with the stale, sour smell of whisky and smoke and unwashed bodies. The man looked at me quietly as I came in and stood at the end of the bar. The bartender glanced at me and said:

"Eggs?"

"Fried on both sides, and some of that side meat."

The man smiled wearily and pushed his own plate away half finished and stood up. "Eggs and side meat," he said. "Side meat and eggs. It wouldn't surprise me if I didn't start cacklin' like a chicken before long, or maybe gruntin' like a hog. Sometimes I think I'll get myself a Mexican woman, like some of the other boys, and let her cook for me. But I can't stand that greaser grub, either." He smiled a thin, pale smile. "Lordy, what I'd give for a mess of greens and a pan of honest-to-God corn bread!"

"Eggs sound good to me," I said, "after living out of my saddlebag, on jerky, for a spell."

He smiled again, that sad, faraway smile. "Wait till you've choked 'em down as long as I have."

The bartender went back to the rear somewhere and I began to smell grease burning. The man who didn't like side meat and eggs glanced lazily at my scratched face and bandaged wrist, but his pale eyes made no comment. He was about thirty, I guess, but no more than that. His voice was as thick and syrupy as molasses—a rich black drawl of the deep South. Everything he did, every move he made, was with great deliberation, without the waste of an ounce of energy. Lazily he shoved a filthy, battered Confederate cavalryman's hat back on his head and a lock of dry, sand-colored hair fell on his forehead.

He smiled slowly. "Welcome to Ocotillo," he said as if he were reading leisurely from a book, "the Garden Spot of Hell, the last refuge of the damned, the sanctuary of killers and thieves and real badmen and would-be badmen; the home of the money-starved, the cruel, the brute, the kill-crazy...." His voice trailed off. "Welcome to Ocotillo, Tall Cameron." He waved a languid hand toward a table. "Shall we sit down? I take it you're one of us now. Perhaps you'd like to hear about this charming little city of ours while you eat your side meat and eggs."

I shrugged. He was a queer galoot, there was no doubt about that, but there was something about him I liked. We sat down and the bartender brought me three eggs and three limp slabs of side meat and some cold Mexican tortillas. I dug in, and while I chewed I said, "How did you know my name?"

He looked quietly surprised. "Why, you're a famous man, didn't you know that? The protégé of Pappy Garret, the wizard of gunplay, our country's foremost exponent of the gentle art of bloodletting. May I speak for our quiet little community and say that we are greatly honored to have you among us?"

I looked quickly into those pale eyes to see if he were laughing at me. He wasn't laughing. The thoughts behind his eyes were sad and far away.

"Let me introduce myself," he drawled. "Miles Stanford Bonridge, one-time cotton grower, one-time captain of the Confederate Cavalry—Jeb Stuart's Cavalry, suh—one-time gentleman and son of a gentleman. I hail from the great state of Alabama, suh, where, at one time, the name of Miles Stanford Bonridge commanded more than small respect. The boys here in Ocotillo call me Bama."

I said, "Glad to make your acquaintance, Bama."

He nodded quietly and smiled. He made a vague motion with his hand and the bartender came over and put a bottle of the raw, white whisky on the table. "One thing about working for Basset," Miles Stanford Bonridge said, pouring some into a glass, "is that he pays his men enough to stay drunk from one job to the other. Not that he can't well afford it—he profits by thousands of dollars from our smuggler raids." He downed the whisky and shuddered. "Have you ever been on a smuggler raid, Tall Cameron?"

"I didn't know there was such a thing until Basset mentioned it."

He poured again, held the glass up, and studied the clear liquid. "You were too young, I suppose, to have fought in the war," he said finally. "And there is no parallel to these raids of ours, except possibly some of the bloodier battles of Lee's eastern campaign. For days after one of our raids the sky above the battleground is heavy with swarms of vultures; the air is sick with the sweet, rotting stink of death; the very ground festers and crawls with unseen things wallowing in the filth and blood.... Please stop me," he said pleasantly, "if I am ruining your appetite."

"You're not."

He nodded again, and smiled, and drank his whisky in a gulp.

I had already decided that he was crazy—probably from too much whisky, and a sick conscience, and maybe the war. What it was about him that I liked I couldn't be sure. His manner of speaking, his slow, inoffensive drawl, his faraway, bewildered eyes—or maybe it was because I just needed somebody to talk to.

"Would you mind," he asked abruptly, "if I inquired your age, Tall Cameron?"

If it had been anybody else I would have told him to go to hell. But after a moment I said, "Twenty. Almost."

He sat back in his chair and closed his eyes and seemed to think. "The day I became twenty years old," he said, "I was a second lieutenant in the Army of Tennessee, General Braxton Bragg commanding. Holloway's Company, Alabama Cavalry." He opened his eyes. "Maybe you remember September nineteenth, 1863. There we were on the banks of the Chickamauga, which was to become the bloodiest river in the South, and old Rosecrans' Army of the Cumberland was on the other side, so close that we could see the pickets throwing up their breastworks." He broke off suddenly. "No," he said, "you wouldn't remember that."

"I remember hearing about the battle of Chickamauga," I said, "but I don't remember who was there—or exactly where it was, as far as that goes."

Miles Stanford Bonridge shook his head. "It doesn't make any difference now."

I couldn't help wondering how a man like Bama could wind up in this God-forgotten country of southern Arizona. He wasn't a gunman—I knew that—no matter how many men he had killed during the war. His pistol was an old .36-caliber Leech and Rigdon that looked dusty from lack of handling, and he wore it high up under his right arm where he would have a hell of a time getting to it if he ever needed it in a hurry.

He smiled that quiet smile of his while I looked him over, and I had a queer feeling that he was reading my mind.

"All I know about guns," he said, "is what I learned in the cavalry. I'm not a bad shot with a carbine. Not worth a damn with a pistol, although I killed a man once with one. A damned Treasury agent, after the war was over. He was trying to cheat me out of twenty bales of cotton, so I shot him four times right in the gut. Have a drink?"

"No, thanks," I said.

He poured himself another one and downed it. "Then I had to kill a Yankee soldier, and there was hell to pay after that. For a while it seemed like the whole damned bluebelly army was after me, but I had some friends and they got me up to New Mexico, and finally I wound up here." He laughed softly, without humor. "I was lucky I guess."

I knew how he felt. With a little switching around his story could have been mine, except that I had taken up with a famous gunman and got the same kind of reputation for myself.

"I had the prettiest little gal you ever saw," Bama said sadly, "but I had to leave her. I wonder what she's doing now...."

I wished he hadn't said that, because it brought back too many almost forgotten days, almost forgotten faces. And a name that I couldn't forget—Laurin.

I pushed my plate away and Bama watched as I rolled a cigarette and put fire to it. At last he said, "Do you mind if I offer a little advice?"

"I'll listen, but I won't promise to take it."

"Leave the girl alone," he said quietly. "The Mexican girl named Marta. She's poison, and a little crazy, too. I've been here for quite a while now, and every man she has looked at always ended up the same way, dead in some gulch or some alley, with a bullet in his back."

His face was deadly serious.

There was nothing I wanted more than to keep that female wildcat out of my life. But what was all the fuss about? First Kreyler had warned me to stay away from her, and now Bama. Curiosity was beginning to get the best of me.

"Does that mean that somebody's got a claim staked out on her?" I said.

Bama nodded slowly and poured himself another drink. "Black Joseph," he said. "And he doesn't like you. He doesn't like you at all."

I was beginning to get impatient with all this hoodoo.

"How the hell does he know he doesn't like me? I've never even seen this famous Indian gun-slinger."

Bama gulped his drink. "Maybe you ought to meet him," he said. "He's standing right behind you."

Chapter 3

When I turned, the first thing I saw was a pair of the darkest, emptiest, most savage eyes I had ever seen. There was absolutely no expression in them. They were like twin bottomless wells filled to the brim with black nothingness. His face was dark, angular, beardless, also without expression. A wide-brimmed flat-crowned hat sat squarely on his head, and ropy braids of black hair hung down on his chest almost to his shirt pockets. He didn't say a word. I couldn't tell if he were looking at me or through me. After a moment he turned and went through the door to Basset's office.

"He doesn't like you," Bama said again.

"I think you're right. Maybe I'll have a drink of that stuff, after all."

"He makes your flesh crawl, doesn't he?" Bama said, pouring a drink in his glass and shoving it over to me.

I felt cold, as if Death itself had just walked by. How he had managed to walk into the saloon and get that close without me hearing him I didn't know. I downed the whisky quick and in a minute I felt better, except that I somehow felt unclean just having looked at him.

"God, how does she stand it?" I said.

"The girl?" Bama raised his eyes sleepily. "She doesn't have anything to say about it. Black Joseph took a fancy to her, and that's that. Have you met Kreyler?"

I nodded.

"He's crazy about that girl—really crazy. You can see insanity crawl up behind his eyes and stare out like a wild beast when the Indian touches her. Kreyler would have killed him long ago if it had been anybody but Black Joseph." He stood up, cradling the bottle in his arms. "I think I'll try to get some sleep," he said. "Joseph's been up in the mountains scouting the canyons for smuggler trains. Probably he's spotted one and we'll be starting on another raid before long."

He weaved across the floor and out the door, still holding tight to the bottle.

I sat there for a while waiting for the Indian to come out of Basset's office. Some of the fat man's hired men drifted into the saloon to drink their breakfast, and along about noon the fancy girls sneaked in and began putting on their paint for the afternoon trade. I didn't see Marta, and the Indian still hadn't come out of Basset's office. I got tired of waiting, so I went back and knocked on the door.

It turned out that Basset was alone, after all, and Black Joseph must have gone out the back way. The fat man looked up impatiently when I came in. He was poring over a list of names, checking one off every once in a while after giving it a lot of thought. "Sit down," he wheezed, "sit down."

I sat down and he checked off one or two more names, then turned and smiled that wet smile of his.

"Well?"

"I'm here to talk about that job."

"Ha-ha," he said dryly. "Your twelve dollars didn't last long, did it? Well, that's all right. You'll have plenty of money before long, plenty of money."

"How much is that?"

He blinked. His little buckshot eyes looked watery and weak behind the folds of fat. "That depends," he said. "Whatever the smuggler train is carrying, all the boys get a cut, fair and square. Share and share alike."

"Including yourself?"

He blinked again. "Now look here, I'm the man that organized everything here. I see that you boys don't get bothered by the federal marshals, and I keep the cavalry off our backs. Everything's free and easy here in Ocotillo, thanks to me. I take half of whatever you get from the Mexicans. The rest you split among yourselves, fair and square, like I say." He paused for a few minutes to catch his breath. "Now, do you want the job or don't you."

"I have to take it whether I want it or not. You knew that to start with."

"Ha-ha. Well, all right. That's more like it. There's something I'd better tell you, though. Joseph didn't want me to hire you, even when I told him who you were. I'll tell you the truth, I wouldn't hire you if I wasn't short on men. The last raid cut us down. I want to tell you here and now that it's no fancy tea party you're going on, robbing smuggler trains. What has Black Joseph got against you?"

"I don't know."

Basset clawed at his fat face, looking faintly worried. "The Indian's a good man," he said. "Fastest shot with a pistol I ever saw. Dead shot with a rifle, too. He'd as soon kill a man as look at him—maybe he'd rather. I think he actually enjoys killing."

He sounded like a man who had a tiger by the tail and didn't know how to let go. He was afraid of the Indian. It showed in his watery eyes, on his sweaty face. It showed in the way his hands shook when he reached for a cigar.

He was afraid of the Indian and he wanted me to get rid of him. He wanted *me* to get rid of him, but he didn't know how to go about it. Maybe he figured that by just throwing us together he could manage it somehow.

I remembered those deadly Indian eyes and the way they had looked at me. It occurred to me that maybe Basset had already started dropping hints that I was making a play for Joseph's girl. That would throw us together, all right, if the Indian ever got wind of it.

And then Basset saw what I was thinking, and he didn't like that much. He changed the subject.

"Our scouts have spotted a smuggler train coming up from Sonora," he said. "So you'll be able to earn your money quicker than you thought. Have you got a good horse?"

"His ribs stick out a little, but he's all right."

"Good. That's one thing you need, is a good horse. And a good rifle."

"I've got them."

"Good," he said again. He sat back and breathed through his mouth. "You can start for the hills as soon as you get your horse ready. The boys pull out of town one or two at a time and meet in the hills with Joseph and Kreyler. We have to keep it as quiet as we can. You can't tell about these damn Mexicans. One of them might try to get to the smugglers and warn them."

He sat back and panted after the speech. "You can ride out with Bama and he'll show you where the meeting place is. You met Bama, didn't you?"

"I met him."

"All right, I guess that's all, then. You'll get your cut when you get back."

Everything was very businesslike, like sending a bunch of coolies out to lay a few miles of railroad. It was hard to believe that Basset had just explained his plans for wholesale murder.

I went out of the office, collared the bartender, and found out where Bama, the gentleman of the old South, slept off his drunks. It turned out that he was a neighbor of mine. He bunked over the saloon in a cigar-box room just like mine, except that it was dirtier. He was asleep on the bed when I found him, one boot off and one on, the dead bottle still in his hands. I got the front of his shirt and shook him.

"Wake up, Bama!"

He grunted and tried to fight me off, being careful not to drop the empty bottle. The whisky smell in the room was thick enough to carry out in buckets.

"Wake up. Basset says we've got to earn our keep."

He came out of it slowly and stared vaguely around the room. Looking into his eyes was like looking into the windows of a deserted house. After a while he brought me into focus, reached out like a sleepwalker, and took my shoulders.

"Ah, the famous Tall Cameron!" He smiled crookedly. "Welcome to my humble ..."

"Snap out of it," I said. "We've got a little job of robbing to do."

"Robbing?" He thought about it for a while. "Oh, you mean another raid. God, I need a drink."

"Your bottle's empty. Get your stuff together and we'll get a drink downstairs."

That brought him out of it. He pulled himself up, then went unsteadily over to the washstand and poured a pitcher of water over his head.

"All the damn stuff's good for," he said thickly. "Where's my other boot?"

I found the boot for him and helped him put it on. His pistol was under the bed. I found it and buckled it on him.

"Are you ready?"

He licked his dry lips with a coated tongue. "God," he said, "I wish I had the guts, I'd blow my brains out. This rotten, maggoty mess of filth and corruption and death that I call brains, I'd splatter them all over these filthy walls!" He made a sweeping gesture with his arm and almost fell.

"Come on," I said. "You need that drink worse than I thought."

He was better after he'd had a couple of glasses of the stuff. His eyes cleared, his hands became steady.

"How do you feel?" I said.

He looked at me. "How do I feel? I can't tell you, Tall Cameron, but maybe by sundown you'll know." He took the bottle off the bar and walked out of the place swinging it in his hand. He was the goddamnedest guy I ever saw.

We went around to the livery barn where our horses were, and as the liveryman saddled up for us he slipped boxes of cartridges into our saddlebags.

"Compliments of Basset," Bama said dryly. He swigged from the neck of his bottle and then put it in his saddlebag with the ammunition. As we rode out of town he began to sing in that thick, black drawl of his:

> "Oh, Susanna, don't you cry for me,
> For I'm goin' to Alabama with a banjo on my knee."

"But her name wasn't Susanna," he said. "It was Myra. And I won't be going to Alabama, with anything."

It wasn't a long ride to the foothills of the Huachucas. Bama knew all the short cuts, and before long the town was far behind and there were just those naked, dark hills of rocks and boulders and cactus and greasewood. We climbed higher and higher until we got into the mountains themselves, and the going got slower.

"We won't be able to make it today," Bama said. "It'll be near sundown before we'll meet Joseph and Kreyler and the rest of Basset's army. The battle won't start before tomorrow, I guess."

I wondered if it was going to be as bad as Bama made it out to be. I doubted it. But something kept me from asking questions.

We rode for a long while without saying anything. Every half hour or so Bama would take a belt at the bottle.

"You know," he said finally, "this stuff doesn't really do any good unless you've got enough to make you sleep the deep and dreamless sleep of the dead." He shook the bottle thoughtfully. "There's not enough here for that."

"Then why do you drink it?"

He smiled sadly. "I'm afraid," he said mildly.

"You're also crazy."

He bobbed his head up and down, soberly, as if I had just said something very profound.

"It's surprising how much of the stuff you can drink when you're afraid," he went on. "For instance," he said abruptly, "I was awake last night when hell broke loose in that room of yours. I heard the girl in there and I thought to myself, Well, there's one more scalp the Indian can hang on his belt. Of course, I didn't know at the time that my neighbor was the famous Tall Cameron. He'll kill you, you know. The first chance he gets."

"He can go to hell," I said. "I don't want any part of his girl. She's crazy, like everybody else in this Godforsaken place. Last night she tried to kill me."

For a moment Bama looked at me. Then he threw his head back and howled with laughter. "Hell hath no fury like a woman scorned!" he said when he got his breath. "No, my friend, I'm afraid your days are numbered. If the Indian doesn't kill you, there's always Kreyler. To get that girl, Kreyler would kill you in a minute, if Black Joseph was out of the way."

"I tell you I don't want anything to do with her. Joseph or Kreyler can have her."

There was another long silence while Bama studied the contents of his bottle. He allowed himself a short drink, corked it good and tight, and put it away. "Why don't you tell me about her?" he said finally. "Maybe it will do you good to get it off your chest."

"Tell you about who?"

"The girl you left back, in Texas, or wherever you came from. The girl you grew up with and loved and planned to marry. The girl who loved you once but can't stand the sight of you now because you're a killer. The girl who will be the mother of another man's children because—"

He must have seen the anger and sadness in my eyes because he stopped abruptly and dropped his head.

"Goddamn you," I said, "if you ever mention her again I'll kill you. *So help me God, I'll kill you.*"

We rode the rest of the way in silence.

We finally reached a place where a great stone ledge reached out over a barren canyon, and that was the marshaling ground for Basset's army.

An army was just what it was. There must have been fifteen or twenty horses grazing down the canyon on the short, dry sprays of bunch grass. And under the ledge the men hunkered or sat or slouched, like so many soldiers awaiting their orders to march into battle. There were a few small fires, and with the smell of horses and sweat there was the heavier, richer smell of boiling coffee and frying bacon. Kreyler was standing at the entrance of the canyon, tally book and pencil in his hands, checking the riders off as they came in.

Bama was watching me, smiling that lazy, crooked smile of his. "What do you think of our little army?" he said.

I shook my head. I hadn't expected anything like this.

We unsaddled our horses and turned them loose with the others; then we sat down to wait. Riders came drifting in from different directions, a few of them Mexicans, but most of them were run-of-the-mine hardcases and hired gunmen. They kept coming until there must have been thirty of them. As the sun began to die in the west I helped Bama build a small fire and we cooked some bacon that he had thought to bring along. We washed it down with some greasy coffee that we boiled in a skillet. Bama's eyes were twin, silent screams for whisky, but he made no move to uncork the bottle again.

At last, when the sun disappeared, leaving a cold bloody streak along the horizon, Kreyler passed the word along to saddle up.

"I thought the Indian was supposed to be Basset's right-hand man," I said.

Bama shook his head. "The Indian's guns keep the men in line, but Basset and Kreyler are the ones who really run things. It's a nice arrangement for Kreyler; that deputy United States marshal's badge makes him practically bulletproof. A man would think a long time before he killed a United States marshal in this country."

I knew what he meant. There are some people that you just can't kill and get away with it, and a United States marshal is one of them. Even a crooked one like Kreyler.

Well, it didn't make any difference to me. I didn't intend to kill Kreyler, or anybody else, if he kept his nose out of my business. Anyway, after this job was over I meant to leave Kreyler and the whole business far behind.

That gave me something to think about as we started riding west again, farther up into the mountains. To get away—that was what I wanted. To go someplace where nobody knew who I was, and stay there until things in Texas cooled off. And then I'd go back.

I'd go home.

The very word was enough to turn me sick with longing. The big country of Texas, the people I knew, the kind of life I wanted to live. And Laurin....

But I knew all along that I'd never go back. Not even to die.

The night was coming down on us now and the horses stumbled along Indian file over dangerous, almost forgotten trails. The men were silent as they rode, and some of them, I guess, were thinking as I was, of home. And some of them would be counting in their minds the money that they would get from their cut of the loot. Some of them, like Bama, would be scared sick, dreading death and somehow welcoming it at the same time.

But it was Texas that I thought of. Smoky nights as still as the grave. The fierce winters of blinding snow. The blazing summers. And the little town of John's City, which was as old as the Santa Fe Trail, as old as the West. I thought of the days of the war, and the bitterness after the war—the carpetbaggers, the treasury agents, the scalawags and turncoats. The blue-suited army. The State Police.

They were all on their way out now, and before long Texas would again be the kind of place I wanted it to be—noisy with giant herds of cattle, dirty with trail drivers, rich and head-high. The strong, patient men would live to see Texas that way again. But not Tall Cameron. And not Miles Stanford Bonridge, once proud landowner in the proud state of Alabama. And not any of the other men who rode in the dark, wrapped in their own thoughts. The impatient, the money-hungry, the kill-crazy. Basset's army.

At last word passed back that the column was halting and the men were to take their positions up ahead. We dismounted and turned our animals over to men that Kreyler had appointed horse-holders; then we climbed single file up a rocky trail until we finally reached the tip of a shallow canyon.

Everything was done with army-like precision, and every man but me, it seemed, knew exactly what was expected of him.

Bama said, "You might as well follow me. It's going to be a long wait until morning."

We picked our way along the rim of the canyon, and now I could see the war party splitting in two parts, half the men slipping silently down the wall of the canyon and up the other side. The rest of us spread out on our side at four- or five-yard intervals and got behind rocks or bushes or whatever protection we could find. Bama found a rock, and I lay down behind a clump of needle-sharp cholla not far from him.

"Now what?" I said.

"We wait," Bama, said quietly. "We wait, and we wait, and we wait. And finally the Mexicans will come down this canyon, and then we kill."

"Just like that?"

"It's not as simple as it sounds. We've had scouting parties out for days, following the Mexicans up from Sonora. They never take the same route twice, but once they've picked themselves a trail to follow, they're stuck with it. But everything has been taken care of now. All we have to do is wait here and pretty soon they'll come along."

"I don't get it. They must know that we're waiting for them. At least, they must *guess* that we're here. Do they plan to just ride along and let us shoot the hell out of them?"

"They know," he said. "And they'll do something about it. We'll just have to wait and see."

So we waited, like Bama said. A pale moon came out and washed those raw mountains with a false cleanness, and a stiffening, bone-chilling cold settled down on us. I wanted a cigarette but I was afraid of striking a match. I wanted a drink, but Bama had left his bottle in his saddlebags.

"How much of this waiting have we got ahead of us?" I said.

"Only the scouts could guess at that. I'd say they'll be along in the morning sometime. Maybe tomorrow afternoon."

I didn't think I could stand it that long. My legs became cramped from staying in one position too long. My wrist began to throb and I thought of the girl and cursed her. I checked the loading of my rifle over and over and up and down the line I could hear other nervous men doing the same thing. If this was the way wars were fought I was glad that I never had to fight in one. It wasn't so bad when it happened quickly, when you were mad at somebody or they were mad at you and all you had to do was shoot. But this waiting—that was something else.

Bama must have gone to sleep. There wasn't a sound from behind the rock as the night crawled by. The cold got worse and ate right into my guts, and I had a feeling that all this was unreal and pretty soon I would wake up and discover that it had been a dream.

But it wasn't a dream. Every minute of that thousand-year night was real. But finally it ended. Morning came in the east, bloodshot and angry, and after a while a broiling sun shoved itself over the ridges and beat down on us. By noon we were baked dry and there was no water anywhere. And if there had been water we couldn't have moved as much as a foot to get it. At every move, at every sound a man made, word would be passed down the line:

"Kreyler says goddamnit, be quiet!"

As we lay there, I learned to hate the Marshal. I hated every line in his dry, sun-cracked face. By noon I could cheerfully have killed him.

"Take it easy, kid," Bama said softly.

"Where does he get off bossing us around like that? He's just one of Basset's hired help, isn't he? Like the rest of us."

"Think of something else," Bama said. "This sun bakes a man's brains. It gives him crazy ideas sometimes."

For a while we lay there. I could see the Indian and his half of the party on the other side of the canyon, and I began hating them too, every damned one of their sweaty, grim faces.

"Listen," Bama said,

And after a minute we all began to hear the faraway sound of bells—small bells, cool little silver sounds in the blazing afternoon. Along the rim of the canyon there were brisk metal sounds of cartridges being jacked into rifles. Bama's face was tight and gray as he lay on his belly, sighting along the short barrel of his carbine. He looked as if death had already touched him—as if the grave and he were old friends.

Then the mule train rounded into the canyon. One after the other they came, as if there was no end—gray, sure-footed little mules with bells around their necks and tall, awkward-looking aparejos strapped to their backs. Along the flanks came the outriders, brown-faced, hard-eyed men, heeled up with rifles and pistols and knives, looking as if they were begging for a fight. In front of the whole business rode a grinning old Mexican on a pale horse, dressed fit to kill in a tall spiked sombrero decorated with silver bangles, flashing light and spitting fire every time he moved his head. His big-bottomed pants were of cream-colored buckskin with more silver bangles and pearl buttons down the seams. A bawdy serape and high-heeled boots finished off his outfit, along with a fancy-handled six-shooter at his side and a long-barreled rifle resting across the pommel of his saddle. He looked like hell, all right. He could have been a gay old ranchero on his way to visit the most beautiful señorita in all of Sonora, from the way he was dressed. I wondered how that grin of his would stand up if he knew that thirty rifles were aimed at the back of his head.

Still the mule train kept coming, and the outriders kept watching the hills with restless eyes. I wondered how they could fail to see us. Did they have any outriders up in the hills looking down on us? If they did, it would be too bad, because they already had more men than we had. Thirty-five, maybe forty outriders were in view by the time the tail of the train had rounded into the canyon.

Word came down: "Hold your fire until Kreyler gives the word."

Bama was dead white. He didn't even seem to be breathing. I wanted to look behind me, but I didn't dare move. The palms of my hands were wet. It seemed almost impossible that in the next few seconds I would be killing men I had never seen before in my life, killing them without giving them a chance in the world. The thought lay heavy and unreal and dull on my mind—but it didn't have time to become an idea.

From somewhere—I didn't know where at first—came a wild, savage scream, and suddenly rifles were beating down on us from above. In the back of my mind I knew that what I had been afraid of had happened: Some of the outriders had got behind us and had discovered us before we could open fire. The next minute I heard one of our own men scream, and Kreyler was yelling, and gunfire seemed to explode from everywhere. I saw Mexicans go down in the first volley, and we fired again and more went down before they could bring their guns on us. But the rifles up above were raising hell.

"Make for the canyon!" I yelled at Bama.

He was pumping bullets into the Mexicans as fast as he could lever and pull the trigger. After a minute he lay down and began to reload. A bullet whined, kicking dirt up at his feet.

"In the canyon!" I yelled again.

"You're crazy!"

"It's better than getting shot in the back!"

Another bullet slammed into the rock beside his head. "Maybe you're right!"

The others were pouring down the canyon walls now, shooting as they slipped and skidded and fell to the bottom. The Mexicans were shooting their mules and using them for breastworks. It was all a crazy uproar of shooting and screaming and cursing, and there didn't seem to be any sense to anything. I felt the slight tug of a bullet going through the sleeve of my shirt and I snapped a shot into a brown, grinning face. The bullet hit in his mouth and exploded brains through the back of his head.

The violence and noise worked like a fever, and men who had been afraid now seemed crazy to kill. They rushed at each other like idiots, and now and then there was the keen flash of knives in the swirling smoke. I lost track of Bama. I seemed to lose track of everything except the brown faces that kept coming out of nowhere and falling back again into nowhere as my own pistols added to the noise.

The old leader of the smuggler train had been the first to die. He lay under his pale horse with his insides shot out by a dozen rifles, and two members of Basset's army were fighting over his fancy pistol.

I don't know how long it went on. I remember dropping behind a dead horse to reload, and when I stood up again there were no brown faces to shoot at. Whitish, gagging gun smoke swirled around the figures of the men still standing. Occasionally a moan would go up, or a curse, or maybe a prayer in Spanish. A pistol would explode to startle the sudden quiet, and the Mexican voice would be stilled.

"Jesus!" a voice said. "What did you have to shoot him in the gut for? That was a solid silver belt buckle, and look at it now!"

I went over to a rock and sat down. For a minute thought I was going to be sick.

Bama came up from somewhere and sat beside me. Pistols were still exploding every minute or so as wounded horses or Mexicans were discovered and killed.

"1 wonder," Bama said flatly, "what General Sherman would have to say about our little war here today."

I didn't say anything. The men were cutting the aparejos open, laughing and gibbering and shoving as clank-streams of adobe dollars poured into the dust. I didn't know how much money there was, but I had never seen so much silver before. Twenty thousand dollars, maybe. It looked like that much.

But I was sick, and the thought of money didn't help. The ground was littered with the dead. I had never seen so many dead men before. They lay sprawled in crazy ragdoll positions, smugglers and bandits alike, and the horses, and the gray little mules with the bells around their necks.

"I've seen what they call major battles," Bama said, "without that many men getting killed." He stared blankly at nothing. He rubbed his hands over his face, through his hair. At last he got up.

"Where are you going?"

"To find my horse."

Now I knew why Bama had saved that half bottle of whisky.

Chapter 4

In the hottest part of the afternoon we started back for Ocotillo, what was left of us. Kreyler and the Indian had gathered the silver together and loaded it on pack horses that we had brought along for that purpose. There were several riderless horses, but I didn't take the trouble to count and see how many men we had left back there in the canyon. I guess nobody did. I made the mistake once of looking back, and already the vultures that Bama had talked about were beginning to circle over the battleground. It took everything I had to keep my stomach out of my throat. I didn't look back again.

Bama had finished the rest of his whisky and was riding slouched, chin on chest, deep in some bleary, alcoholic dream. I tried to keep my mind away from the battle, but I kept seeing those brown, grinning faces as they fell away in front of my guns. I wanted to think of my cut of that silver. I tried to remember that killing was necessary sometimes to save yourself—and that silver would save me.

Somehow, we got back to Ocotillo. We split up again when we came to the meeting place, and Bama and I rode back into town the same way we had left it. It was a long ride. Bama still didn't say anything.

It was almost dark by the time I got my horse put away. I went up to my room and fell on the mattress in front of the door. I was dog tired. Every muscle in my body screamed for rest, and every nerve was ready to snap. Then I turned loose with everything I had. I vomited until my guts were sore and there wasn't anything left in me to come up, but still I kept gagging.

When it was over I was soaked in sweat and shaking like a whipped dog. It was all I could do to get off the floor and pour some water in the bowl and wash my face.

It was then that I felt the draft float over the back of my neck and I knew that the door was open and somebody was standing there. I think I knew who it was before I looked up. Sure enough, it was Marta.

"What do you want?"

"I think you need Marta."

"I don't need anybody. Get out of here and stay out."

She looked at me for a moment, then turned and went down the hall. In a minute she was back with a pan and some water, and began cleaning the floor.

"I don't know why they bother to put locks on these doors," I said. "How did you get in here?"

She grinned faintly, took a knife from the bodice of her dress, and showed it to me.

"Is easy."

"It must be."

I didn't feel like talking or fighting or anything else. If she wanted to clean up after me, all right. All I wanted to do was rest and try to forget that I had taken part in anything that had happened today.

She worked quietly, not looking at me. After she had finished I could feel her standing beside me.

"You need eat," she said.

"I need nothing."

She went out of the room, taking the dirty water with her. I didn't bother to close the door.

Maybe five minutes went by, and then she came back with two hard-boiled eggs and a pitcher of cool beer. "Here."

"You're crazy as hell," I said.

She cracked one of the eggs and peeled it. I took it and bit into it. It tasted good. I washed it down with some of the beer, then reached for the other egg.

"Good?" she said.

I nodded and had some more beer.

"You sick. Why?"

How could I tell her why I was sick? Maybe I wasn't even sure myself. But somehow I felt that the last decent thing in me had been fouled in that massacre. A myth had been shattered. I could no longer tell myself that my killing had been done in self-defense. I was sick with myself, but how could I tell anybody that?

"It wasn't anything," I said.

"You better now?"

"Sure. Have some beer."

She grinned uncertainly, then swigged from the mouth of the pitcher. I was beginning to be glad that she had shown up. I needed something or somebody to take my mind off of things. It was just the shock of seeing so much cold-blooded killing, I tried to tell myself. Pretty soon I would get over it, but now it was just as well that I had somebody to help me get my mind on something else.

"Don't you ever take no for an answer?" I said. "Do you always hang on until you get what you want?"

She shrugged as if she didn't understand me.

"What do you want me for, anyway? I'm not such a prize—not even in this God-forgotten place where almost anybody would be a prize."

She shrugged again and grinned. Sitting cross-legged on the floor, she took my wrist and began inspecting the bandage on my left wrist.

"I am sorry," she said.

"It's all right now."

But it still hurt, and it gave me a vicious, animal-like satisfaction to see that her mouth was still swollen and bruised where I had hit her.

It was dark now. Night had come suddenly down on Ocotillo, and we could hear the noises in the saloon below, and in the dusty street there was the rattle of high-wheeled cars as the Mexican farmers came in from the fields, and the lonesome, forlorn chanting of the native herdsmen. I rolled a cigarette and gave it to the girl, then I rolled one for myself and fired them with a sulphur match.

"Where you learn smoke like this?" she said suddenly.

"A friend of mine. He used to roll them this way, in cornshucks. He's dead now," I added, for some reason.

"You love this friend very much," she said.

"What makes you say that?"

"You are sad when you say he is dead." Then, "He was good man?"

I listened to the night and remembered Pappy Garret. "He was good at one thing," I said. "He could draw faster and shoot straighter than any man who ever lived. He picked me up when I was just a kid running from the State Police and taught me what he knew. I used to wonder why he bothered with me—but I know now that he was a lonely man."

I knew that she wasn't really interested in hearing about it, but she kept quiet and I went on. "He wasn't really a bad man," I said, "but once you start a thing like that, there's no end to it. A gunman kills a friend of yours, then you kill the gunman. Then the gunman has a friend and you have to kill him, or be killed, and it goes on and on that way until you think there isn't a man in the world that doesn't have a reason to shoot you."

Marta stroked my bandaged arm with her cool fingers. "You no bad," she said.

"I'm rotten to the bone, or I would never have done what I did today, no matter how much money there was in it."

She looked up, but I couldn't see what she was thinking. "I think you be rich man pretty soon."

"I'm as rich as I'm going to be, as soon as I get my cut of the silver. I'm through with Basset. I'm going to throw my guns in the deepest river I can find."

It was dark and I couldn't tell much about her face, but I knew that she was smiling. I started hating her all over again. She didn't believe that I would ever throw my guns away, that I would ever quit Basset. What she believed was what I had said before—that I was rotten to the bone—and it didn't matter a damn to her one way or the other. I was going to be a rich man. I felt her arms crawling around my neck like soft warm snakes and she dug her fingers into my hair and pulled my face down to hers.

I brought my arms up and broke her hold and she hit the floor with her rump. I stood up and for a long moment and neither of us said anything. Then I tightened my pistol belt and started for the door.

"Where you go?"

"I don't know."

I went down the stairs and heard the noise and laughing in the saloon. The girl was beside me as I pushed through the batwings and went to the bar, and I didn't try to get rid of her or hold her. I didn't care what she did.

The bartender came up and I said, "Tequila. You might as well bring the bottle."

He brought the bottle and two glasses and I took them over to a table where Bama was sitting by himself. The girl was still with me.

Bama blinked his bleary eyes as we sat down. "I knew you were crazy," he drawled, "but I never figured you'd be this crazy. Don't you know that Black Joseph will shoot you on sight if he catches you with his girl?"

"To hell with Black Joseph."

He blinked again. Then he shrugged, smiling that lopsided smile of his. "To hell with him," he said. "Well, I guess another killing, more or less, won't make much difference on this day of days." He chuckled dryly. "The funny thing about this place is that everybody thinks that everybody else is crazy—and probably they're right. But there's one good thing about these raids of Basset's. A man can afford tequila for a while instead of that poisonous slop the greasers drink. Here's to bigger foothills!"

He filled his glass and drained it, using the bottle I had brought because he had already emptied his. "May the best man win, señorita," he said, nodding in mock politeness. "And may it be entertaining and bloody. Most of all, let it be bloody."

Marta sat stone-faced while I poured a round. "Don't you ever sober up?" I said.

"Not if I can help it. Tequila is good for the soul. It reverts man back to the jungle from whence he came, as they say, back to the vicious, lewd, wild beast that he was before somebody told him that he had a soul. Remember the old camp-meeting hymn that backwoods preachers used to bellow at the top of their lungs? 'I'm Washed in the Blood of the Lamb.' Blood with a mile-high capital B. Did it ever occur to you that the Bible is one of the bloodiest manuscripts ever written? Most of its heroes either are killers or died violent deaths themselves. Blood, I've seen enough of it. I'll wash my soul in the clean, destroying liquid of tequila."

"You're crazy," I said.

He chuckled. "See what I mean?"

Marta was watching him strangely, almost fearfully. Bama slouched back in his chair and smiled at her, his eyes flat and empty. I drank my tequila down, poured another glass, and downed that. My insides began to settle down and I began to feel better. I could feel Bama watching me. Without interest, without feeling.

Pretty soon I began to notice things that I hadn't noticed before. Basset's customers had given us a whole corner of the saloon to ourselves. The area around our table was quiet, as if some kind of invisible wall had been put up around us.

"You can't blame them for moving out of the line of fire," Bama drawled. "As long as you're with that girl we're poison. Have another drink?"

Until now I hadn't really believed that men would kill over a girl like Marta—over money, or pride, or almost anything else, but not over a girl like that. But I saw that I was wrong. Everybody in the place accepted it as a fact that before long either the Indian or I would be dead. The talking and laughing and drinking and gambling went on as usual, but there was a nervous sound to it, a tight feel in the air.

I already had my limit of two drinks, but I took the third one that Bama poured and downed it. I tried to reason with myself. What was the good in taking a chance on getting killed over a Mexican hellcat that was no better than a common doxie? All I had to do was tell her to get away from me, and tomorrow after I got my cut of the silver I'd get out of Ocotillo for good.

But I couldn't do it. I'd never backed down from an Indian or anybody else in my life. In this business you took one step back and you were done for, the whole howling hungry pack would be on you.

So I sat there while Bama smiled that crooked smile of his. But he seemed more interested in the girl than in me. He watched her steadily, and all the time a change was taking place in Marta's eyes. First fear, then uncertainty gave way to a brighter fire of self-satisfaction and conquest. It struck me then that she was actually enjoying this! She wanted to be fought over. She wanted blood at her feet. At every sound her head would turn, her eyes would dart this way and that in excitement. I began to understand why most men wanted no part of her.

Bama took another drink and lifted himself unsteadily to his feet. "Like the darky says," he said, "I'm tired of livin' but 'fraid of dyin'. You don't mind if I just step over to the bar until this is all over, do you?"

I didn't say anything. Bama drunkenly doffed his Confederate hat in Marta's direction, turned, and weaved across the floor.

She was actually smiling now. She reached across the table to take my hand and I pulled away as if she had been a coiled rattler.

"Just let me alone," I said tightly. "There's no way of stopping this thing now, but there's one thing you'd better understand. I'm not getting into any trouble on account of you. And when it's over, I'm telling you for the last time, let me alone."

I don't think she even heard me. Her eyes were darting from one side to the other, and her mind was so hopped up with excitement that she couldn't sit still.

I could feel the change in the place the minute he walked in. It was nothing you could put your finger on at first—there was no change in the way people acted, or in the noise, but I had the feeling that somewhere a grave had been opened and Death itself had walked into the saloon.

In a minute the others felt it, and their heads turned toward the door as if they had been jerked on a string. Saloon sounds—the rattle of a roulette wheel, the chanting of the blackjack dealer, the muffled slap of cards on felt, the clank of glasses behind the bar—all went on for a few seconds and then suddenly played out. I shoved my chair back and there he was standing in front of the batwings. He was looking at me. For him there was no one in the saloon but me.

I didn't know whether to get up or stay where I was. If I had been smart I would have had my right-hand gun pulled around in my lap for a saddle draw—but I hadn't been smart, and it was too late to worry about it now. He started forward, and I could feel the customers pushing back out of the line of fire. This is a hell of a thing, I thought. Here's a man I never saw but once in my life, a man I've never as much as said "Go to hell!" to, and now he's after my hide!

He came forward slowly, in that curious toe-heel gait that Indians have, as if he had a long way to go and was in no particular hurry to get there. Just so he got there. Well, anyway, I was glad the waiting was over. Now that I could look at him, he didn't look so damned tough. He looked like any other Indian, except maybe a little dirtier and a little uglier, with eyes a little more deadly. He had just two hands, like anybody else, and he had blood in his veins that would run out when a bullet went in. That first feeling of doom passed away and I was ready for him.

The smart guys along the bar and against the wall were grinning as if they expected me to fall on my knees and start begging him not to shoot me. They would have loved that. There's nothing that would make them happier than to see me spill my guts. There wasn't a man in the place, with the possible exception of Bama, who wouldn't have taken a shot at me if that had happened.

That's a pleasure they'll be a long time seeing, I thought grimly.

I stood up carefully as he stopped at the table, beside Marta.

"There's something you want?" I said.

For a minute he just looked at me. Or through me. There was no way of telling about those eyes of his. Not a muscle twitched in that stone face, but I noticed that his right hand was edging in toward the butt of his pistol—not much, but enough to carry on through when the time came. He didn't even look at Marta. He just reached with a big hand, grabbed her by the hair of the head, and jerked her half out of the chair.

The smart guys sucked in their guts, laughing to themselves. They already had me dead and buried. They didn't like the Indian much, but they hated punk kids like me even more. They figured I had got my reputation the easy way, and they figured I knew it. I guess I jarred them when I said:

"Take your goddamned hands off of her if you want to go on living."

Even the Indian showed surprise. His eyelids raised about a millionth of an inch. The next thing I knew his gun was coming out of the holster.

I made my grab and didn't bother to aim. There wasn't time to aim, and when you're standing belly to belly, the way we were, there's no sense in it anyway. I just got the muzzle of my pistol over the top of my holster and fired. I didn't hit him. I didn't even come close. The bullet slammed into the floor somewhere, but I wasn't worrying about that.

The muzzle blast from a .44 is a powerful thing. At that range it can deafen a man, paralyze him, burn him, shock him, throw him off balance. That was what I was counting on. I didn't need that first bullet, just the muzzle blast. And the Indian knew it. His mouth flew open as he slammed back under the impact, and before he could get his balance, before he could swing that pistol on me again, he was as good as dead.

I had all the time in the world after that first shot. I shot him twice through his left shirt pocket and he jerked like a monkey on the end of a string. He hit the floor, flopping around like a fish with a broken back. I don't know what kept him alive, but he wouldn't die until he managed to lift his pistol again and try to fix it on me.

Sweat poured off his face as he lifted the pistol, slowly, an inch at a time. For him, it must have been like lifting the south end of Texas, but somehow he did it. There was no fear of dying in those eyes of his. They were completely savage, kill-crazy. Then I stepped in and kicked the pistol out of his hand. I slammed the toe of my boot in his ribs.

"You sonofabitch! You filthy sonofabitch!" And I kept kicking him until somebody came up and pushed me back. It was Bama.

"That's enough!" he said. "Jesus Christ, you can't kill a man but once!"

All the anger and hate seemed to rush out in me all at once. I swung on Bama and knocked him sprawling with the barrel of my pistol. "Goddamn you," I said, "don't tell me what I can't do!"

He was on all fours, shaking his head like a poled steer. Blood was welling up at the corner of his mouth and I could hear every drop hit the floor and splatter. The saloon had been shocked and jarred and stunned to a deathly quiet. The smart guys weren't so smart now. They stood with their mouths hanging open, staring stupidly.

As suddenly as it had hit me, my anger was gone. I put an arm around Bama's shoulder and helped him up.

"How do you feel?"

"I'm—all right."

But he was looking at me strangely. First at me, then at the dead Indian, then at me again. He said, "I think I need a drink."

"Sure." I poured him a drink with my left hand, keeping my gun hand ready in case the Indian had some friends that wanted to take up the argument.

Bama downed the drink and wiped his mouth with a shaky hand. "Put your pistol away," he said hoarsely. "Nobody wants to fight you. Not now, anyway." He took a step forward, and a step backward, then he began to fall.

I caught him before he hit the floor and wrestled his dead weight up to something like a standing position. "Give me a hand," I said to the girl.

She had a stupid, idiot's smile on her lips. She was half crazy with excitement and power and lust and God knows what else. She couldn't take her eyes off the dead Indian. Some insane, morbid love of blood and violence held her entranced, hypnotized her, charmed her.

"Goddamnit!" I said. "Help me get him out of here!"

Her head jerked up. The idiot's stare went out of her eyes and she got her shoulder under one of Bama's arms and we began to drag him out of the place. We dragged him right over the corpse, the rowels of Bama's spurs raking across the Indian's bloody chest and then clanging to the floor. Nobody made a move. I don't think anybody breathed. From the corner of my eye I glimpsed Basset standing in the doorway of his office, his fat face bloated and pale-looking in the orange light of the coal-oil lamps. I think he was smiling, but I wasn't sure, and I didn't care. There was somebody standing behind him looking out with wild, pale eyes. I think it was Kreyler.

Somehow we got Bama out of the place and up the stairs and into my room. I got the mattress off the floor and put it on the bed, then we stretched Bama out and began to work on him.

He was just drunk, mostly, but there was an ugly lump over his ear and a fine red thread of blood was taking quick long stitches across his face and down his neck, ending in a spreading red blotch on his collar.

"Get me some water," I said.

The pitcher was empty, so she had to go around to the back of the saloon, where the pump was. In a minute she was back, and I dipped a rag into the water and washed the blood off Bama's face. He still didn't move.

"Is there a doctor in this place?" I said.

She shook her head. She came over to the bed and put a hand on his chest, on his throat, on his forehead. "No need doctor. Too much tequila."

Maybe she was right, but it made me uneasy seeing him stretched out there, not making a move, hardly breathing. I hadn't meant to hit him. But, goddamn him, why couldn't he have kept out of my way? Why did people always have to make my business their business? If they got hurt they had nobody but themselves to blame.

"Well, I guess there's nothing else we can do. Maybe he'll sleep it off."

I sat on the bed, staring at nothing, thinking of nothing. Downstairs, they were probably dragging the Indian out and maybe getting ready to bury him, but it didn't mean a thing to me one way or another. The Indian could never have been born, as far as I was concerned. I had no feeling for him at all; no hate, no anger. And in the back of my mind I knew that somebody—Basset, Kreyler, one of the Indian's friends—was probably planning a way to kill me. That didn't seem important either.

I was getting out of Ocotillo. I was getting out tomorrow.

The girl was standing there beside me, looking at me and not saying anything. She was still smiling, but it was a different, sweet, almost holy smile. It reminded me of old women on their knees in front of altars saying their prayers. It made me uncomfortable having her look at me that way.

I got up and went out of the room and went into Bama's room and lay across the bed in the darkness. I knew that she would be there in a few minutes. And she was.

She didn't say a word. She just lay down beside me and pressed that hot animal self of hers against me and waited. We both waited, and nothing happened. She came closer and those soft arms crawled over me, and then she was breathing her hot breath in my face and mashing her bruised mouth against mine. Still nothing happened. I could have been kissing a stone statue and it would have been about the same. For a while we just lay there. Maybe she thought that it was the excitement of the fight that made me the way I was, but it was more than that. She just wasn't what I wanted. After a while she went away.

Chapter 5

The next morning I awoke to the sound of sloshing water behind the thin partition that separated Bama's room from mine. I got up and sloshed water on my own face, drying it on the tail of one of Bama's shirts. Then I went into the hall and knocked.

"Bama, are you up?"

He opened the door, bleary-eyed, licking his cracked lips. "Well," he said. "I was wondering what happened to you."

"I spent the night in your room. It seemed easier than trying to move you. How do you feel?"

"Fine," he said thickly. "Like I always feel on mornings like this." He touched the knot behind his ear and winced.

"That's where I hit you."

"I know," he said. "You didn't bring a bottle along, did you?"

"Don't you think it's about time to lay off the stuff for a while?"

He looked at me hazily. He sat on the bed, holding his head as if he thought maybe it would roll off his shoulders if he didn't. "God," he said flatly, "what a rotten, lousy life. You killed the Indian, didn't you?"

"The sonofabitch asked for it."

Then he thought of something. "The girl—Marta—where is she?"

"How should I know? I guess she went home, down in the Mexican section. I don't care where she went."

"She—she wasn't with you last night?"

"Not after we got you up here."

He thought for a while, then he said a funny thing. "Maybe there's some hope for you, Tall Cameron. As unlikely as it seems, maybe there's some hope for you, after all."

"What the hell is that supposed to mean?"

But he seemed to have forgotten what he was talking about. "Sometimes I think that memories are the only things that are real. I wish they were. Are you sure you haven't got a bottle?"

Then I remembered that bottle of greaser poison that Marta had used on my wrist. I dug it out from under some dirty clothes and poured him a small one. "I'm sorry about that lick I gave you," I said. "But you butted into something that was none of your business."

"Yes," he said, "I suppose I did." And then he polished off the drink and shuddered. "But that temper of yours," he said when he got his breath, "you ought to learn to control it. It'll turn on you like a bad woman, and that will be the end of Tall Cameron."

"Let me worry about my temper," I said. Suddenly I began to get an idea—or rather, an old idea that had been floating around in the cellar of my mind suddenly came to the top. I said, "Bama, if you hate this place so much, why don't you get out of it?"

He just looked at me.

"What's holding you here?" I asked. "Take your cut of the silver that we got off the smugglers and go down to Mexico somewhere like I'm going to do."

I was telling Bama something that I hadn't even admitted to myself. I was telling him that I was tired of being alone, that I was even afraid of being alone. I was asking him to ride with me. God knows why a man like me would want Bama with him. He would be no earthly good, and his drinking would probably cause trouble wherever we went.

Then it hit me that maybe I could feel the day coming when I would look around me and discover how far down I had gone. When that day did come I would want somebody around that I could still look down on. And that somebody was Bama.

I think he could see the way my mind was working, but there was no anger in his eyes, except possibly an old anger at himself. He started to say something, but he changed his mind at the last moment and had another drink.

"Think it over," I said. "Maybe I could use some company if you want to ride along."

Looking at the bottle, he said, "Do you really think you'll get out of Ocotillo?"

"Why shouldn't I? I've got enough money coming to keep me below the border for a while. After that, something will show up." Then I said, "Speaking of money, I think I'll go down and pick up my cut from Basset. Do you want to come along?"

He reached for the bottle again. "I think I'll just sit here for a while, if you don't mind. Anyway, I got my cut last night."

So I left him sitting there, getting an early start on the road to nowhere.

The bartender was leaning on a broom, contemplating a dark brown splotch on the saloon floor, when I came in. I said, "I want to see Basset," and his head snapped up as if he had never seen me before.

"Sure. Sure," he said. "Wait a minute, I'll see if Basset's up yet."

He went back to the rear of the saloon, where I guessed Basset had a sleeping room next to his office—he struck me as being the kind of man that wouldn't like to get too far away from his business. After a minute the bartender came back.

"It's all right. He's in the office."

He was still sitting, fat and sweaty, behind his desk when I went in, looking exactly the same as the last time I had seen him. "Well," he wheezed, "I guess you came by your reputation honest. You can handle guns, I'll say that for you. You've got a bad temper, though. You'll have to learn to hold onto that if you're going to work for me."

"I'm not going to work for you," I said.

He sat back, blinking folds of fat over those buckshot eyes. "Now, look here," he panted. "What's the matter?"

"I don't like wholesale murder and I don't like robbing people," I said. "I just want to get out, like I told you. Now if you'll just figure out my cut of the silver ..."

He lurched his hulk over in the chair and sat there blinking those eyes at me, breathing through his mouth. "Well," he said. "If that's the way you feel about it. Sure, you can have your cut. No hard feelings."

He pulled out the big bottom drawer of his desk and opened a strongbox with a key. He took out a heavy-looking, clanking canvas bag and shoved it across the desk toward me.

"Here it is," he said. "You sure you don't want to change your mind?"

"I'm sure," I said. I didn't bother to count the silver. I just picked it up and walked out, hoping that I had seen the fat man for the last time.

I went back up to my room and Bama was still there, drunk, as I had expected. I heard him talking to somebody as I came up the hall, and when I got to the door I saw that it was Marta.

"What's she doing here?"

Bama shrugged, "Maybe she's in love with you," he said, waving his arms. "Maybe she can't bear to have you out of her sight."

"She'd better start getting used to it, because I'm going to put Ocotillo behind me."

I threw the sack of silver on the bed and she stood there looking at me. She seemed to come and go like night shadows, and every time I saw her she seemed to be a different person. I tried to remember how she had looked the first time I had seen her, there in the dusty street with fiesta going on all around us. I couldn't remember.

"I think the girl's got the wrong idea about you," Bama said. "She thinks you killed the Indian because of her. It wasn't that at all, was it, Tall Cameron?"

"No," I said, "it wasn't."

"See?" Bama said, waving his arms again, as if he had just proved something.

The girl didn't say anything. She just stood there looking at me, and I had a feeling that overnight she had grown from a wild animal into a woman. And not a bad-looking woman, at that.

But I still wasn't interested. "You really ought to do something about her," Bama said. "Tell her to go home. It's not decent the way she walks in and out of this place any time she gets the notion." Bama lay back on the bed, holding the empty whisky bottle before him, staring into it as if it were a crystal ball and he were about ready to give us the beginning and end to everything. But, instead, he dropped the bottle and dozed off.

I began digging in my saddlebags, getting my stuff together. "Why don't you do like he says?" I said. "Go home or somewhere. Why don't you stay down in the Mexican part of town with your own people?"

"You need Marta," she said.

"I don't need anybody." But she didn't believe me.

And I didn't believe myself, for that matter. An old, half-forgotten memory began to shape in my mind, and I remembered what Bama had said the day before. "Why don't you tell me about the girl you left in

Texas? The girl you grew up with and loved and planned to marry."

For a moment bright anger washed over me, a hurting, twisting anger that made me want to kill Bama as he lay there in his drunken stupor. But then I remembered Bama's own lost love and the anger vanished. We weren't so different, at that, Bama and me. We both lived in the past, because men like us have no future.

The mood hung on and I couldn't shake it off, and I felt completely lost. A bundle of loose ends dangled in a black nothingness. There was no turning back, and I wondered if maybe Bama had found the answer in whisky.

It even occurred to me that maybe Marta was the answer for me, that maybe she was right and I needed her. But that wouldn't work either, and I knew it. The best thing to do was to get out of Ocotillo.

I threw some more stuff into the saddlebag, then I went over to the bed and rolled Bama over to give me room to count the silver. I hadn't bothered to guess how much my cut would be, but I had seen the pile of money we had got off the smugglers and I knew that a fair cut would be enough to take care of me for quite a while.

Bama grunted and lurched up in bed as I untied the sack and dumped the contents on the blanket.

For a minute I just looked at it. There were some adobe dollars there, all right, but there was a lot of other things too. I scattered the stuff around and picked up a handful of round brass disks with holes in the middle. On one side they had the name E. E. Basset stamped on them, and on the other side there were the words "Good for One Dollar in Trade."

For a minute I thought there had been a mistake and Basset had given me the wrong sack. But then, from the look on Bama's face, I knew that it was no mistake. This was the way the fat man paid off: He collected the silver and gave his men a pile of worthless brass buttons. Quickly I scattered the stuff some more and sorted it out, and when I had finished I had thirty-five adobe dollars and sixty-five pieces of brass.

Finally I straightened up, and what was going on inside of me must have been written on my face.

Bama seemed suddenly sober. "Take it easy, kid."

"Is this the way Basset pays all his men?"

"I thought you knew," Bama said.

"Look at that!" I kicked the bed and brass and silver went flying all over the room. "Is that what he calls a fair cut? I saw the money they sacked up on that raid—fifteen thousand dollars, at least. Maybe twenty thousand. And he hands me thirty-five dollars and sixty-five pieces of brass. Even if it was all silver. It would still be a long way from a fair cut."

By the time the money hit the floor, Marta was on her knees gathering it up in her skirt. Bama sighed deeply.

"That's the way it is when you work for men like Basset. That's why I was wondering how you meant to get out of Ocotillo. Anyway, that brass is as good as the silver, if you spend it in the saloon."

"I don't intend to spend it in the saloon," I said. Then I wheeled and headed for the door. Marta was standing there, the silver and brass in her skirt, holding it out.

I said, "Keep it. Spend it on saloon whisky, or take it home, or throw it to the chickens. I won't need it."

Her eyes lit up and she smiled a smile like a kid who had just found a wagonful of candy.

Bama lurched across the room and grabbed my sleeve as I was about to walk out. "Don't go down there half-cocked," he said. "Don't you think Basset has had this kind of trouble before? He knows what he's doing and he knows how to take care of himself."

"I don't want any trouble," I said, "but I'm going to get what's coming to me if I have to choke the stuff out of him."

I shook Bama off and went down the stairs three at a time and burst into the saloon. The bartender was still leaning on his broom. He didn't seem exactly surprised to see me and he didn't try to stop me when I marched straight on back to Basset's office. I kicked the door open and said, "Goddamn you, Basset, I want what's coming to me ..."

But I left the words hanging. Basset had been receiving company while I'd been upstairs jawing with Bama. Kreyler, the fat man's right-hand gun, was leaning against the wall near the door. I guessed that Bama knew what he was talking about; Basset had experience in handling situations like this.

Kreyler didn't have his guns out, but he had his thumbs hooked in his gun belt, and all he had to do was cup his hand around the pistol butt if there was some shooting to be done. Basset was still sitting where I had left him, smiling that wet smile of his. He sat back, wheezing and coughing.

"Why, son, what seems to be the matter? Ha-ha. You look all worked up about something. Doesn't he, Kreyler?"

Kreyler didn't say anything; he just looked at me with those flat, hate-filled eyes.

I said, "I came after my cut of that silver that we took in the smuggler raid. And don't try to talk me out of it, because I'm going to get it one way or another."

I told Kreyler with a look that he could go to hell. If he wanted to make his draw, it was all right with me. But nothing happened for a minute. The fat man and the Marshal looked at each other and I began to get the idea that they were cooking something between them, but I didn't know what. Basset wasn't armed, as far as I could see, and even if he did have a gun on him, I figured it would take him a week to find it among all the folds of fat. If it was just Kreyler's shooting ability that I had to worry about, I was all right.

"Well, now," Basset said, "this is very irregular. Very irregular indeed, isn't it, Kreyler? I was under the impression that you had picked up your cut this morning, Cameron." He didn't seem worried, and that in itself was something for me to worry about. "However," he went on, "we always try to keep the men happy here in Ocotillo. Even the ungrateful ones. Of course, it will mean going into my own pocket, but just so there won't be any hard feelings, I'm willing to add a little to your cut. Say another thirty-five dollars. In silver."

I said, "I was thinking that five hundred dollars would be about right."

He didn't like that. Those little eyes began to narrow and I got the feeling that this was the time to be careful.

"Well, now," he said, "that's a lot of money. But, like I say, we try to keep the men happy."

Grunting, he reached across his desk and pulled the cigar box over. "I think maybe it can be done," he said vaguely. "Five hundred. Yes, I think it can be done, don't you, Kreyler?"

And while he was talking he was opening the cigar box and fumbling around in it. I had seen him do it before, just the way he was doing it now, and it hadn't meant a thing. But this time it did. Something prodded me in the back of my mind and I knew that it wasn't a cigar that he was fumbling for.

It was a little double-barreled derringer, probably, but he didn't get to use it. I guess he intended to let me have both barrels right through the lid of the box, and it wasn't such a bad idea, at that, because one of those little belly guns can do damage out of all proportion to its size. It was a nice setup, all right. In another second he would have shot my belt buckle right through my backbone. If he had lived that long.

At times like that you appreciate your training, and when it came to guns I had one of the best educations in the world. My right hand took over where my brain left off, and what came next was as natural as reciting the multiplication tables. More natural for me.

So I shot him. It was as simple as that, and I didn't wait to see where the bullet hit, because I already knew. When Pappy Garret trained a man, he didn't leave any margin for doubt about things like that. After I had pulled the trigger I moved one foot just enough to pull my body around and lay the pistol on Kreyler.

As a gunman, maybe the Marshal was all right as long as he stayed in his own class, but he hadn't had the advantage of studying with an expert, the way I had. As it was, I had all the time in the world. I could have shot him twice before the front sight of his pistol cleared his holster, and Kreyler knew it. I guess there was an instant there when he was already seeing himself frying in hell, because his eyes got that sick look and he lost heart and didn't even try to get his pistol out.

There's one thing about gun fighting, when you start shooting it's hard to stop. The first thing a gunman learns is to start shooting the minute his hand hits the gun butt—that is, he starts cocking his pistol the instant he starts his draw. If he's good enough he's got his pistol cocked and is squeezing the trigger by the time he clears leather, and from then on it's almost automatic. You cock again as the gun goes down from recoil, shoot again, cock again, until you're out of ammunition.

That's the way it usually goes. That's the way Kreyler expected it to go this time, and from the way he looked, he was already feeling the shovels hit him in the face as they covered him up in some boothill grave. But about that time something stopped me. I broke off right in the middle of the cock-trigger action and just stood there looking at him.

For a while he didn't believe it. And neither did I. I couldn't think of any good reason why I shouldn't shoot him. He had been drawing on me. He and the fat man had set a nice little trap for me. On top of that, I should have shot him just because of the principle of the thing, if for no other reason, because in the school I had attended they taught never to pull a gun on a man unless you meant to kill him.

This was the second time I had pulled on Kreyler. And he wasn't dead yet.

But finally I began to understand what had happened. In the heat of the fight I had forgotten that Kreyler was a U.S. marshal, and I guess it was instinct alone that held my trigger finger just in time.

After a minute Kreyler began to realize why I hadn't killed him, and

I think it crossed his mind that maybe he could make his draw and shoot me while I was worrying about it. But it was just a fleeting thought. I didn't want to kill him, but I would if he forced it. And he knew it.

No more than two or three seconds had passed since I had put a bullet into Basset, but at that moment it seemed like years ago. I realized that I had been holding my breath, so now I let it go.

I said, "Just move easy, unbuckle your belt, and kick your pistol over here."

He hesitated a moment, then his pistol hit the floor and he kicked it over. I heard somebody running in the saloon, so I stepped over to the door and saw the bartender diving under the bar. After a shotgun, I figured. But he got peaceful when he saw me standing there, and all he came up with was a rag.

"Go over to one of those tables," I said, "and sit there until I think of something for you to do."

His Adam's apple went up and down a few times, as if he were trying to swallow his stomach, then he went over to a table and sat down, still holding onto the rag. Then there was a commotion outside the saloon and in a minute Bama and Marta came bursting through the batwings. They hurried on back and stopped at the doorway of Basset's office, looking in.

"My God," Bama said weakly. He wiped his hand across his mouth, looking as if he needed a drink. Marta didn't do anything except stare at me.

I said, "Keep an eye on the bartender, Bama. How much racket did I make?"

"Plenty," he gulped. "My God, did you have to kill him?"

"Of course I had to kill him. He was getting ready to shoot me with that derringer in his cigar box."

I turned then and glanced at Basset for the first time. He was sprawled out in his chair, as formless as three hundred pounds of lard in a hot room, and getting more formless all the time. There was a black little hole about nine inches below his left shoulder, but there wasn't any blood to speak of.

I said, "You've been around here a while, Bama. How much excitement is this going to cause?"

"Plenty when Basset's men find out. That will take a little time, though. We heard the shooting upstairs, but I doubt if anybody else did."

"Anyway, that gives us some time to figure out something. First there's the silver. I'm going to get my cut of that before I do anything else."

Bama had opened Basset's cigar box. Something happened to his face as he stared into it. I don't know just what it was, but suddenly he looked very tired and very old. I pulled the box over and had a look at it. Then I heard myself saying, "Well, I'll be damned."

There hadn't been any derringer in it, after all.

It was a shock at first. Then occurred to me that it had been a lot bigger shock to Basset. There was something in it that seemed funny to me at just that moment, and I laughed a little and said again, "Well, I'll be damned. There wasn't any gun in there at all, he was just reaching for a cigar."

Bama looked at me with those old eyes. "You can kill a man like that, and then laugh at it?"

I was keyed up, I guess, or I wouldn't have paid any attention to him. But as it was, it went all over me.

I said, "What are you crying about? You shoot Mexicans in the back, don't you, for a few lousy pieces of silver? What makes you think that you've got a right to read a sermon to me?"

It hit him like a kick in the gut, and I was sorry after I had said it. I would have taken it back if I could, but I couldn't, so I tried to pass it off the best way I could.

"Why don't you go on out and take a look at the bartender?" I said. "If anybody comes into the saloon, let me know."

That left me with Kreyler, and the problem of what to do with him. But first there was the silver, so I said, "All right, where does Basset keep his money?"

Kreyler gave me a flat look. "He doesn't keep any money, not here. After a raid he has it expressed to a bank in Tucson, under another name."

"But he must have some money here," I said. "Enough to pay me what he owes me." I dumped Basset out of his chair and he hit the floor like a wagonload of mud. Then I began going through the drawers of his desk until I found what I was looking for.

It was in the strongbox that I had seen earlier in the morning, and I had to go through the dead man's pockets to get the key. After I got the box open, there it was, about five hundred adobe dollars.

"That will just about do it," I said, and I sat down in Basset's chair and raked the silver coins into a canvas sack.

Kreyler was watching me, and he didn't look exactly brokenhearted because the fat man was dead. But I could understand that. With Basset dead, and the Indian dead, I had opened the road for the Marshal to sit down at the boss's desk and take over the business for himself.

"You really owe me a great deal," I said. "I've done you two big favors since I've been in Ocotillo, getting rid of Basset and the Indian. To say nothing of not shooting you when I should have."

"You haven't got the guts to shoot a United States marshal," he said flatly.

Every man makes a mistake once in a while, and Kreyler made one right then. I had my money gathered up and was ready to leave everything just the way the Marshal wanted it—but when he opened his mouth he ruined it.

The idea must have been in the back of my mind all the time. Maybe it was even there when I shot Basset. I don't know for sure, but the idea jumped up too fast and too full-blown to have come from nowhere, and I guess I was just waiting for a chance to do something about it.

"Bama!" I yelled. "Come here!"

I was sitting at the fat man's desk, feeling pretty pleased with myself, as Bama came up and stopped in the doorway.

"Bama, how do I look?"

His eyes were puzzled. "You look all right, I guess. Why?"

"I mean how do I look sitting here at Basset's desk?"

"I guess I don't know what you're talking about."

But Kreyler did. I grinned at him and he started swelling up like a toad and you could fairly see the angry fires behind those eyes of his.

"Bama," I said, "I want you to go out and pass the word around that Basset is dead. Find all his men you can. Tell them I killed Basset and from now on I'm the boss of these smuggling raids. If they don't like it, just remind them what happened to the Indian. Oh, yes, and tell them that from now on they get the fair cut that Basset promised them but didn't 'give them, and that it will all be in silver or gold, whatever the smugglers have on them. But the thing I want you to impress them with is that I'm the boss. And I'll be the boss until a faster gunman comes along to change my mind."

Chapter 6

It was kind of funny the way it all happened. One minute I was just another wanted gunman on the run, and the next minute I was all set up in business as the boss of a band of cutthroats. It happened so fast and so natural that I didn't have time to give it much thought. I just saw the opening and took it. That, I realized later, was the way bosses were made.

There was one thing, though, that complicated things, and that was figuring out what to do with Kreyler. The Marshal was the key to the whole thing here in Ocotillo. He gave the business the protection and the freedom to operate that it had to have, and without him the whole thing would fall down around my shoulders. However, that worked itself out along with everything else.

I started with the bartender, by putting him back to work as if nothing had happened. Then I marched the Marshal back into the office, and there we waited for things to begin to happen.

"You'll never get away with it, Cameron," he kept saying.

But I would, and he knew I would. Then I began going through Basset's things again and finally I found the thing that would nail Kreyler down just the way I wanted him. It was a big ledger book that the fat man had used to make his bookkeeping entries in, and every penny of smuggled silver was accounted for right there, along with the money he had paid out to Kreyler and the Indian and all the rest. I looked at it and sat back and grinned, and the Marshal knew it was all over.

"Now," I said, "I think we can do business together, Marshal. We'll keep things just like they were when Basset was running things. You furnish the protection and I'll see that you get a good share of the profits. What do you think about that?"

"I think you're crazy. You're wanted in every state west of St. Louis. It would be suicide for a United States marshal to try to do business with you."

"Maybe," I said, "but it would be slow and you'd have a chance to build up a stake." I tapped the ledger. "Here's something for you to think about. Say I turned this ledger over to somebody in Tucson—say a lawyer that I could depend on, or maybe even a sheriff—with instructions that the book was to be turned over to the United States marshal's office if they didn't get the word from me once a month to hold onto it. Of course, I wouldn't ride into Tucson myself, but I could get somebody else to do it."

He could cheerfully have cut me into pieces and thrown me to the dogs. But I had him where the hair was short. And he knew it. For a long while he just sat there, angry thunderheads boiling behind his eyes.

At last he said, "I'll have to think it over."

"Think it over, but the answer better be yes. And in the meantime don't try to beat this ledger to Tucson and put the law on my tail."

He didn't say anything, so I sat there and let him hate me until Bama got back.

"I don't know," Bama said wearily. "Some of the men don't like it. They didn't care much for Basset, but they just don't like the idea of somebody coming in and shooting his way to the top."

"Did you tell them about getting a full cut in silver?"

"I think maybe that will do it," he said. "They're talking it over now among themselves, and we'll know within an hour or so if they're going to work for you." He looked at Kreyler and then at me. "No matter what they decide," he went on, "you'll never get away with it."

"Kreyler's been telling me the same thing," I said, "but look at this." And I showed him the ledger and after a minute he caught on what I was going to do with it.

"I think I'd better have a drink."

"I'll have one with you. We've got something to celebrate here. Kreyler?"

"If it's all right with you," the Marshal said flatly, "you can celebrate by yourself."

"Sure, if that's the way you feel about it." Then I picked up his gun and threw it at him. "You can have this, only don't get any funny notions. That Marshal's badge won't stop a bullet."

Kreyler buckled his belt on and walked out of the place, and Bama and I went out to the bar and had the bartender bring us a bottle. Bama downed three fast ones, then leaned on the bar and held his head in his hands.

"What's the matter with you?"

"I guess I'm just a little sick."

"You'll get over it. In a few weeks we'll have all the money we need and we'll leave this town behind."

"Are you sure?" he said, looking at me. "What happened to you, anyway? Yesterday you were as sick of this mess as I was and all you wanted was to get out."

"I still want to get out," I said. "It's just that I've found a better way to do it. What's the sense in going off half-cocked? This business of Basset's fell right in my lap. Why shouldn't I take it long enough to get a little money?"

"No reason, I guess," he said. "I was just hoping that it wouldn't work out this way. But then, nothing ever seems to work out, does it?"

I couldn't figure the guy out, and I never did figure him out completely. I didn't say so in as many words, but here I was offering a partnership in a well-paying business and he seemed to be sorry about the whole thing. It wasn't the prettiest business in the world—I could see that— but what the hell, he had been in it longer than I had.

After a while we heard boot heels hit the dirt walk outside the saloon and we had company. Four men pushed through the batwings and stood looking at us.

"Basset's scouts," Bama said. "They're probably acting as spokesmen for the other men."

One man stepped out in front of the others, then walked around the tables till he could see Basset where he was still sprawled out. For a long minute he just looked at the dead fat man, and then he said, "By God, he's dead, all right."

Then he walked over to Bama and me and poured himself a drink from our bottle.

"I hear you're the one that did it," he said to me.

I didn't say anything. He was a lean, leathery man with about fifteen cents' worth of tobacco working in one cheek, causing a brown dribble at the corner of his mouth, which disappeared into a bushy, dirty beard. He looked about as excited as a dead armadillo. He sure didn't look like a man stricken with grief.

"Well, maybe you done us a favor, but that's to be found out later, I guess. I hear you're settin' yourself up in Basset's place."

"That's right."

"What makes you think you're big enough to hold a job like that?"

"Any man that feels bigger can take it from me the way I took it from Basset."

He considered that carefully, over another drink. He studied my guns. He studied the dead man. "Look," I said. "I'm offering you men a better deal than you ever got out of Basset. You'll get a fair cut from every raid. The men can watch the money while it's being counted and split up. And, starting now, those brass buttons of Basset's are no good. I'll buy them up with real silver."

He sipped his drink thoughtfully. "How about Kreyler? We can't do anything without him!"

"Kreyler's staying with us. Never mind why, but he'll be with us to the end."

Another long minute went by while the scout weighed things in his mind. He had the power to make or break me, and we both knew it. I hadn't made up my mind what I was going to do if he said no.

Luckily, I didn't have to worry about it. The scout shifted his cud and said, "Well, I never liked the sonofabitch much, anyway." And he motioned to the men standing in the doorway. "You might as well come on in, boys, and have a drink with the new boss."

There wasn't anything to it after that. We buried Basset in a gully near the Huachuca foothills, and by night the saloon was doing business as usual. I threw Basset's things out of the back end of the place and moved my things in, what there were of them, and called Kreyler and Bama and the scouts together for a pow-wow.

"I haven't been here long enough to know just how Basset ran things here," I said, "but what I saw of it I didn't like. First, there's that business of letting the smuggler outriders get behind us while we were sitting in ambush. I want a map drawn of those mountains and foothills, and I want every cut and gully and rock and sage brush on it. Like the maps they use in the Army when they're getting ready to plan a battle. Bama, you used to be a soldier. Can you draw a map like that?"

Bama shrugged. "I guess I can try."

We were sitting in the office, the four scouts, me, Bama, and Kreyler. The door was closed but we could still hear the saloon noise on the other side. The scouts looked sleepy. Bama looked thirsty. Kreyler didn't look any way in particular, but I had an idea of what was going on inside him.

I said, "Bama, it will be your job to do the map. In the morning you can take two scouts into the hills and go to work on it. I don't care how long it takes, just so you get everything on it. The other two scouts can ride off toward Mexico and see what you can find in the way of smuggler trains."

Kreyler looked up at that.

"You can't push too hard on a thing like this," he said. "We can't attack every smuggler train trying to make its way to Tucson. They expect a few attacks, but if it happens too often they'll change their route and that will be the end of a good thing."

I could see the scouts agreeing with him, and Bama too. "We're not going to try to get them all," I said, "but the ones we do go after, we're going to do it right. That's the reason I want the map. If we pick our spot right, there's no reason why we should get shot up. And besides, we won't need so many men if everything is done right, and that means a bigger cut for everybody."

They liked that, especially the scouts, and after a while we got down to details.

"How long have you been thinking about this?" Bama asked after the others had gone.

"Just since this morning. How long do you think I've been thinking about it?"

But he only shrugged and let it go.

"The next thing we've got to do is take care of this ledger," I said. "We can't follow Kreyler around with a gun all the time, and anyway, this thing is better than a gun. It keeps the Marshal tied to us and keeps him from putting a bullet in my back at the same time."

"You're really going into this, aren't you?" Bama said, and I tried to read some meaning into it, but there wasn't anything there but a thick, heavy drawl.

He sat there looking at me with no expression at all. At that moment he looked as if he had lived a hundred years and every year had been a hard one. "If I had the guts," he said, "I'd tell you to go to hell. But I haven't got the guts. So if you'll get me a bottle of whisky I'll tell you what you'll have to do about Kreyler."

I think at that moment he really hated me. But, like he said, he didn't have the guts to do anything about it. Anyway, I was getting used to his moods and the way he talked, so I slapped him on the shoulder and said, "It's not going to be as bad as all that."

I opened the door and yelled to the bartender, and in a minute we had a bottle and a couple of tumblers on the desk.

Bama said, "I know a lawyer in Tucson who would handle the ledger for you, but I couldn't risk showing myself in a place like that. And neither could you. What you've got to have is a man who isn't wanted by the law here in Arizona. It would be better if he wasn't wanted at all, but it's not likely we'll find a man like that. I think I've got the man you want."

I waited until Bama finished his drink, then he went on. "He's just a kid—much more of a kid than you are. He came riding into town today sometime after the shooting. From Texas, by the look of his rig. He's out in the saloon and you can talk to him if you want to."

"If you think he's the one we need."

So Bama got up and went into the saloon, and after a minute he came back with a hay-haired kid who looked to be about seventeen years old. He wore blue overalls that had been patched several times around the rump and knees, and heavy brogans, and a dirty felt hat that had part of the brim torn off. He sure didn't look like much, but there was something about him that gave me kind of a shock.

It was almost like looking into a mirror and seeing myself as I had been at that age—except that I had never worn those nester's overalls and brogans. But it was his face, I guess, that got me, and his eyes. His eyes were pale blue and they were kind of bewildered and they didn't know much of anything. And maybe there was a little fear in them, and uncertainty.

"Well, son," Bama said, reaching for a drink, "how does it feel to be in the presence of the mighty? Of course, you've heard of Talbert Cameron, desperado, killer, as they say on the 'Wanted' posters. The fastest gunman ever to come out of Texas, the scourge of lawmen, soldiers, and just plain downright honest citizens."

I wished to hell that Bama would shut up, but he kept running on and the kid's eyes got bigger and bigger. And I couldn't get away from that feeling that the kid was myself standing there, getting my first look at a real gunman and being a little stunned and awed by it.

I said, "For Christ's sake, Bama, shut up."

Bama grinned a little, sadly, and shrugged. "Go ahead and sit down, son. I don't reckon he'll bite you." The kid sat down on the edge of a chair and stared at me. He swallowed a couple of times and his Adam's apple flopped around while he tried to think of something to say.

I said, "Bama tells me you're from Texas. What part?"

He gulped. "South," he said faintly. "Along the Nueces River."

I'd never been in the brush country, but by looking at the kid I got a pretty good idea of what it was like. It would be blazing sun and blistering wind and men grubbing for a living on land that was never meant to be worth a damn for anything. But those men would love the land, and they would live on it, and fight on it, and die on it. I wondered what had made the kid leave it.

"Have you got a name?" I said.

"Yes, sir." He was beginning to find his voice now. "Rayburn. John Rayburn."

Bama was sitting on the desk, soberly studying the kid, and I guessed that Bama was also seeing something of himself in this lost, bewildered-looking kid who called himself John Rayburn. After a minute he spoke quietly, with a gentleness in his voice that I had never heard before.

"Do you want to tell us about it, Johnny? We're all pretty much in the same fix here, as far as the law goes. And you are running from the law."

"I've been doin' that, all right," the kid said, and he looked at me and Bama, "but I sure never figured to wind up in any place like this." His gaze settled on me. "Are you really the Tall Cameron that they talked so much about in Texas?"

I started to ask him what they were saying about me, but I changed my mind and said, "That's right. Now, who are you, besides just somebody by the name of John Rayburn?"

"Well, gosh," he said, "I'm not anybody much. My pa owns a little brush-poppin' outfit down on the Nueces, like I said, and I was born there and lived there all my life—until the last month or so." He hesitated until he became convinced that it was all right to talk. "Well, hell," he said, "I guess I got into some trouble. There was a dance in Lost Creek—that's a town by our place—and I guess some of the boys kind of got liquored up and there was a fight. The first thing you know there's a deputy sheriff dead on the floor, and then the first thing I know they're claimin' I was one of the boys that done it."

He looked at us to see what we thought about it. "I didn't have anything to do with it," he said, "but they locked me up anyway, along with the others. And when they have the trial the jury says manslaughter and sentences all of us to three years on the work gang." He grinned uncertainly. "But the jail they was holdin' us in wasn't much, so I lit out of there as fast as I could. God knows how I wound up in Arizona."

For a minute there was silence and I sat there thinking about myself, a kid who had started running just about the same way, and was still running. Then, for no reason I could think of, I began to get mad, and I wanted to get up and shake that kid until his teeth rattled and knock some sense into his head. I wanted to tell him that there were worse things than the work gang. I wanted to tell him how it was when you ran and ran until you couldn't run any more, but you knew that if you stopped it would be all over. There were a lot of things I could tell him— things I wished somebody had told me.

I think Bama's mind was working about the same way mine was, but he just sat there waiting for me to do something. But all I did was to sit back in the chair and say, "Do you want a job?"

"With you, Mr. Cameron? Gosh, yes!"

I looked at him and then looked away. He was building me up in his mind as a big hero, but I didn't feel like a hero right then.

I said, "Bama, give him the ledger and tell him what to do," and I threw out the sack of Basset's with the five hundred adobe dollars in it. "This ought to be enough to take care of the lawyer."

Bama took the money and waited a minute for me to look at him. But I didn't look at him.

That night after the saloon had emptied and things had quieted down, I went back to my new quarters behind the office and tried to get things straightened out. The room was a plain affair with the usual bed and chair and washstand. On one wall there was a big framed picture that showed a bunch of battered, dejected, half-frozen soldiers marching through the snow. They had rags tied around their heads and rags on their feet, and they looked as if they had about a bellyful of war. But off to one side there was a cocky little man sitting on a big white horse, and just by looking at him you knew that he was the boss and the war wasn't going to be over until he said so. Down at the bottom of the picture there was some small print that said, "Napoleon in Russia."

There was a bookshelf beside the bed, and a coal-oil lamp. I picked up one of the books, and it was *The Complete Works of William Shakespeare*. There was also a limp-backed Bible there, and I tried to imagine Basset reading a few chapters of Luke or John before going to bed every night, but the picture wouldn't work out. There were also two big volumes of Dante's *Divine Comedy* and pictures of devils and angels and a lot of people suffering in one kind of hell or another. Well, I thought, Basset ought to be right there among them about now.

There were a lot of other books there, but I didn't look at them. I began to count the money that the saloon had taken in for the night, and it was a little over two hundred dollars. I was just beginning to appreciate what a good thing I'd come into. I made a mental note to ask somebody where Basset had got his whisky supply for the saloon, but I figured it would probably be Mexico. Then I started figuring how money would be coming in every month from the saloon and the smuggler trains, and the amount it came to was staggering.

I paced up and down the room with figures running through my mind, and every once in a while I would stop and look at that picture of Napoleon and I knew just how he felt. There was only one way to look—straight ahead.

That was before I found out what happened to Napoleon in Russia.

But I was feeling pretty good about it then, and the feeling hung on as long as I kept thinking of money and had that picture to look at. It was only after I had undressed and blown out the lamp that something different began to happen.

There in the darkness things began to look different. I began to think about the day and the things that had happened and I couldn't believe it. Here I was in Basset's room, in Basset's bed, and the fat man was dead and buried—but none of it seemed real.

Maybe, I began to think, it was because I didn't want it to be real. I lay there for a long time and I could hear Bama saying, "What has happened to you?" And that was what bothered me. I didn't know. Things had happened too fast to know much of anything. It was like having a comet by the tail and not being able to let go.

Abruptly, I got out of bed, fumbled for matches, and lit the lamp. I looked at the picture again, but that didn't help. The cocky little man on the white horse didn't seem so cocky now, and I doubted that he was as sure of himself as he tried to make people believe.

I went into the office and fumbled around in the dark until I found the whisky that Bama had left. I poured and downed it. I poured again and downed that. I began to feel better.

I took the bottle and glass back into the room and sat on the bed and had another one. I was beginning to feel fine. Another drink or two and I would be ready to kick Napoleon off that white horse and climb on myself.

I don't know how long I sat there, with my mind going up in dizzy spirals, skipping from one place to another like a desert whirlwind. But after a while it hit me and I realized what I was doing. Nothing ever hit me any harder.

Suddenly I could understand Bama, because I was on the road to becoming just like him. Miles Stanford Bonridge, gentleman and son of a gentleman. Now I understood how a man could be so sick of himself that the most important thing in the world could be just forgetting.

But not for me. I hammered the cork into the bottle and took it back into the office and there it would stay. Not for me. But the effort left me weak as I went back and sat on the bed and tried to piece together a lot of loose ends that didn't seem to fit anywhere.

But they did fit when you worked at it long enough. And the first loose end was that smuggler raid. Killing was one thing, but killing like that was something else and would never really be a part of me. I should have known that when I went back to my room and messed up the floor, and maybe I had known, in the back of my mind.

I sat there for a long time, getting a good look at myself, and it wasn't very pretty. It was like that first day that I rode into Ocotillo and Marta had taken me to her house and fixed me up with the stuff to shave and take a bath with. I remembered the shock I'd got when I looked into that mirror. The face I'd seen was a stranger's face, and I guess I was experiencing the same thing all over again.

Except that I was looking deeper. Maybe I had a hold of that dark, illusive thing that they call a soul. But I turned loose of it in a hurry, just as I had looked away from the mirror,

Chapter 7

It's funny how everything seems different in the light of day. Most of your doubts and fears go with the darkness, and after a while you forget about them completely.

The kid, Johnny Rayburn, got back to Ocotillo late the next day. I came out of the office and there he was standing at the bar, gagging on a shot of tequila.

I said, "You made a quick ride. Did things work out all right in Tucson?"

"Sure, Mr. Cameron."

Then Kreyler came into the saloon and I said, "Wait a minute. All this is for the Marshal's benefit, so he might as well hear about it."

The three of us went back to the office, and I could feel Kreyler's eyes on my back, looking for a soft spot to sink a knife in. But he didn't bother me now. I had him where I wanted him and he knew it. Or he would know it pretty soon.

I said, "All right, kid, let's have it. Tell Mr. Kreyler just exactly what you've been doing for the past day and night."

The Marshal gave the kid a quick look. Then he sat in a chair and waited, and he might as well have been wearing a mask, for all the expression you could read on his face.

"Well," the kid said, "I rode into Tucson, like you said, and I gave the ledger to—to the man Bama told me about. I gave him five hundred dollars and asked him if he would hold onto the book as long as I kept coming back every month to give him another hundred, and he said sure, he'd be glad to. Then I came back to Ocotillo."

I said, "Tell us what's going to happen if we miss giving him the hundred dollars every month."

"He'll turn the book over to the U.S. marshal's office," the kid said.

I expected Kreyler to do something then, but he didn't. He just sat there with that slab face not telling me a thing.

"Well," I said, "it looks like you're working for me, Kreyler, whether you like it or not."

"It would seem that way," he said flatly.

"It doesn't seem any way. You're working for me and you'll keep on working for me until I get tired of having you around."

"All right, I'm working for you."

I didn't like the way things were going. I had expected a hell of a racket about that ledger, but there he was sitting there as if he didn't care about it one way or the other. There was something going on behind those eyes of his, and I thought I knew what it was.

He kept looking at the kid, and then I realized that just three of us knew where that ledger was, me, Bama, and Johnny Rayburn, and if Kreyler wanted to find out where it was he would have to get it out of one of us. I didn't have to do much figuring to guess which one he would work on.

I jerked my head at the kid and said, "Go somewhere and get some sleep." Then it hit me that just "somewhere" wouldn't be good enough. He had to be someplace where Kreyler wouldn't have a chance to work on him. So I said, "Get your stuff and bring it down here. We'll put up a cot or something and you can bunk with me until we figure out something better."

"Well, gosh," the kid said. "Sure, if you want me to, Mr. Cameron." As he went out of the place he seemed to be walking about a foot off the floor, and he had suddenly developed a curious kind of toe-heel way of walking that reminded me of a cat with sore feet. It wasn't until later that I realized that I walked the same way, because I had learned that it was the quietest way to walk. And with a gunman, the quietest way of doing a thing is the safest way.

It began to dawn on me that Johnny Rayburn was imitating me. A thing like that had never happened before. I had never thought of myself as much of a hero, and it had never occurred to me that anybody would want to pattern his life after mine. But there it was, and there was something about it that pleased me—the same way, I guess, that a man is pleased to have some bawling, yelling brat named after him.

It was something like being assured that a part of me would go on living, no matter what happened to Talbert Cameron.

I thought about that, and then I became aware of Kreyler sitting across the desk from me, watching me, reading the thoughts going around in my mind.

"There's something we'd better get straight right now," I said. "If anything happens to that kid, I'll kill you. All the cavalry and United States marshals in Arizona won't be able to save you."

He sat there for a while, half smiling. Then he got up and walked out.

It took Bama and the two scouts eight days to make the kind of map I wanted, but when they finally got back and put the finished product on my desk I saw that they had done a good job. The chart was drawn in six different sections, but Bama had the pieces lettered and numbered and the whole thing made sense when he put it together. There were almost a dozen natural traps that Bama had already marked, and there wasn't much for me to do except to post scouts along the various canyons and wait until a smuggler train was spotted.

"And what do we do," Bama asked, "if the Mexicans decide not to use one of these particular canyons?"

"We'll wait. They'll take one of them sooner or later, and when they do, they won't have a chance."

"No," he said wearily, "I guess not. Do you want a drink?"

"No."

"Well, I do." And he went to the bar and came back with a bottle and glass. "Did the kid take care of the ledger all right?"

"Sure, he did fine."

Very deliberately, Bama poured the tumbler brimful and then sat there looking at it. "I saw him out in the saloon," he said, "when I came in. I thought he was you at first. He walks like you, talks like you, even dresses like you."

I knew that it didn't mean a thing, but still I couldn't help being pleased that somebody else had noticed. "He picked the new rig out in Tucson," I said, "with his own money. It's funny that he'd get just the kind of things I wear."

"Funny?" Then Bama picked up the glass and drained it without taking a breath. He was tired and dirty and his eyes were red-rimmed from long hours of riding in the sun. He said, "I guess I don't see anything very funny about it."

"What the hell's wrong with you, anyway? You know what I mean."

"I don't know anything," he said, "except that I just saw a kid out there blown up with his own conceit and making a goddamned pest of himself. Eight days ago he was just another punk kid who had got off the right track but not so far off that he couldn't have been put back on again. Now he's swaggering like a fighting rooster that hasn't got sense enough to know that he hasn't been equipped with gaffs. But I suppose you're doing something about that. What are you doing to him, anyway—giving him lessons in gun slinging?"

"I'm not doing a damn thing to him," I said, and in spite of all I could do I was letting him get under my skin again. I stood up and grabbed the front of his shirt and twisted it. "Look," I said tightly, "there's something we'd better have an understanding about. You're just working for me, like Kreyler and all the others. When I want you to say something or do something, I'll let you know. Until that time, you'll keep your goddamned mouth shut."

As usual, I was sorry after I had said it. He just stood there looking at me with those sad old eyes and I knew that I would never be able to hate him.

"I'm sorry, Bama," I said. "I didn't mean what I said, but why do you have to keep prodding me until I fly off the handle that way?"

He kept looking at me and I had the uncomfortable feeling that he was pitying me, and if there was anybody in the world that I didn't want pity from, it was Bama. I sat down and said, "Go on, have another drink and forget it."

I poured one for him and shoved it across the desk, but he shook his head and said, "I can forget about us because I guess we're not very important to anybody now. But that kid is different."

I was getting impatient again, but I forced myself to sit tight until he got it off his chest.

Bama said, "Why don't you send him back to wherever he came from? He'd listen to you. Just tell him to go back and put in his time on the work gang and give himself a chance to live like a human being."

I said, "I'm not holding him here. He can do anything he wants to do." But that wasn't answering Bama's question and we both knew it. "Anyway, he's the one who has to take care of that ledger."

Bama sat back and closed his eyes. "Of course, what I think doesn't amount to much, but I was wondering if it wouldn't be better for all of us if we let the kid go—and the ledger, and the smuggler trains, and all the rest of it."

"Now, that's a hell of an idea. Look, one raid is all we need to make. That will give us enough money to keep a hideout until the law forgets that we were ever alive. But that money, we've got to have that."

"But is money the most important thing?"

I got up, tired of the senseless bickering that was getting us nowhere. "By God, you're crazy," I said. "That's the only way to explain the way your brain works."

And Bama smiled that faraway smile and I knew that he wasn't mad at me, and never would be, really. "Sooner or later it always gets around to that, doesn't it? Everybody's crazy." He finished off the drink I had poured for him. "Well, maybe that's the right answer. I don't know any more."

I got to thinking about it later and decided that maybe Bama had been right on a few points. For one thing, the kid was carrying this imitating business too far. God knows where he found them, but somewhere he had picked up a couple of old Prescott revolvers. Navy revolvers, they were called, but the Navy had never bought any of them, and neither had anybody else who had any idea what a good pistol was supposed to be. But the kid had them buckled on with a couple of cartridge belts that I figured he had made himself, and he had his holsters cut away like a real badman and tied down at his thighs.

He was in the saloon talking to Marta when I first saw him in that getup, and I figured it was about time we had a talk.

Marta was laughing at something when I came up, and I said, "I'm glad to see that everybody's in a good humor for a change."

She laughed again and pointed at Johnny. "Juanito say he be big man like you someday." The kid's face turned red and he fiddled with a whisky glass that was about a quarter full of clear tequila. "Maybe bigger, he say," and Marta's eyes had the devil in them again, that look she got whenever she got two men together. It was the kind of look that you see in Mexicans' eyes when they take their roosters to the fighting pit and start roughing them up before the battle.

But I knocked a hole in some of her fun when I said, "Yes, he'll be a bigger man than me." Which, after all, wasn't saying so much. "But not the way he means," I went on. "Not with guns."

The kid's face had started to brighten, but it fell quickly. Then it took on a half-angry, defiant look. "I never said anything about it," he said, "but I was considered a pretty good shot down in the Nueces River country. I guess I know as much about guns as most people."

"You don't know a hell of a lot," I said, "or you wouldn't be making a fool of yourself with those old Prescotts."

Blood rushed to his face as if I had just slapped him. "Look," I said, and my voice was as deadly serious as I could make it. "I hired you on as a messenger boy, not a gunman. When you're heeled you're just advertising for trouble. On the other hand, there aren't many men—not even in Ocotillo who would take a shot at a man who didn't have a chance to shoot back."

The kid stiffened. "Mr. Cameron," he said, "I guess you don't know much about Ocotillo, even if you do run it."

"What is that supposed to mean?"

Then he took off his hat and I saw the bump over his left ear, and an open cut about an inch long that was just beginning to scab over.

I must have sat there for a minute or more before I could think of anything to say. The thing jarred me because I thought I had everything under control—I had Kreyler nailed down, most of the men were satisfied, and I had two men, the kid and Bama, that I could trust. And still somebody was working against me.

At last I jerked my head at Marta and said, "Go home or somewhere. I want to talk to Johnny alone."

She didn't like that much, being brushed away like a bothersome fly. But then she saw that I meant business and she got up from the table and sort of melted away.

"All right," I said. "Tell me about it and don't leave out anything."

He shrugged. "Well, it was last night. I was in the saloon for a while, and—well, I guess I kind of made friends with that girl, Marta. After a while she said why didn't I walk to her house with her, down in the Mexican part of town, and I said sure, I'd like to. That was the way it started. I got to her house, all right, but her pa raised such a hell of a racket that I didn't stay." He grinned a little. "I don't understand much of that greaser talk, but I understood enough to know that her old man doesn't like gringos. Well, after that I started back for the saloon, and the streets down there are as dark as hell. That's where they jumped me."

"Who jumped you? Mexicans?"

"If they were Mexicans, they knew a lot of English cuss words. There were three of them, I think, and I still don't know what the hell they wanted. I didn't have any money. And if it was somebody with a grudge against me, why didn't they shoot me instead of hitting me over the head?"

"How did you get away from them?"

"I guess they weren't expecting much of a fight. Anyway, we stirred up the Mexicans. The next thing I knew I was in one of those adobe houses and Marta was taking care of this cut on my head."

Slowly I began adding things together. Kreyler and that Mexican girl—they might have something to do with it. Maybe the Marshal was just crazy enough to fight for that girl when he didn't have guts enough to fight for himself. I was beginning to understand that women could make men do crazy things. Anyway, I put Johnny Rayburn and Marta together in my mind and I didn't like it at all. Even if it had nothing to do with that ambush.

"It's about time we had an understanding," I said. "That girl, Marta, is not for you. The sooner you get that through your head, the better off you'll be."

I had expected an argument, but instead of arguing he just sat there looking puzzled. "Why, gosh, Mr. Cameron," he said, "I never even thought about her. Not the way you mean." And he began to look uncomfortable. "Well," he said, "to tell the truth, I've got a girl down in Texas waiting for me, and I guess she's the only girl in the world as far as I'm concerned. Do you know what I mean?"

He hit me with it and I hadn't been expecting it. It knocked me right out of Ocotillo and into the big, wild Panhandle country, which had been my country once—but that was long ago. There had been a girl there too, and she had waited as long as any girl could be expected to wait, I guess. But I hadn't got around to going back until it was too late.

My first impulse was to strip those guns off him and make him go back to Texas and give himself up. But then I remembered the ledger, and the kid was the only one who could take care of that for me. And that had to be taken care of. I had to keep my hands around Kreyler's throat.

Until after one more raid. My visions of riches were gone. Kreyler had found my soft spot—the kid—and he was already beginning to shove the knife in.

"Is anything wrong, Mr. Cameron?"

"Wrong?" For a moment I forgot what we were talking about. "No, nothing's wrong. Just see if you can find Bama, will you, and tell him to see me in the office."

Bama took his time about coming, but finally he did come, and the world felt like a saner, safer place with Bama around. He helped himself to one of Basset's cigars on the desk, then he pulled up a leather-bottomed chair and sat down.

"You look worried," he said. "That's not much like you, Tall Cameron."

Why the hell he couldn't just call me Tall I don't know. But he always used my full name, and for some reason it always reminded me of the first time I ever saw my name on a "Wanted" poster.

But that was just a passing thought, as he sat there looking at me, and I was surprised to see that he was almost sober—or as sober as I had ever seen him, anyway.

I said, "I think Kreyler has already gone to work on the kid. It was a mistake letting Kreyler know who was going to take care of the ledger for us, but I guess it's too late to worry about that."

And I told him what the kid had told me, about the bushwhacking and the way they had tried to brain him, and Bama sat there rolling the cigar from one side of his mouth to the other and not saying anything.

"If they get their hands on him again," I said, "they'll beat the information out of him and then put a bullet in his skull." Bama still didn't do anything, so I said, "Why don't you say something?"

"What good would it do? It's your show now. You've got everything just the way you want it. Of course, you could send the kid back to Texas if you wanted to."

"You know we can't do that. Everything here depends on Kreyler, and Kreyler depends on the kid."

Bama sighed. That was all.

"How many men on my payroll would fall in with Kreyler?"

"Five, maybe six. You find malcontents wherever you go, but I couldn't point them out for you."

Then I went to the map that I had tacked on the wall of the office and said what I had meant to say in the first place.

"We've got a scout report that a smuggler train has entered here, at a place called Big Mouth Canyon, about twenty-four hours ago. Heavily loaded, according to the scout, with maybe a record load of silver or gold. How soon can you get the men together?"

Bama stared at me. "You can't attack in a place like that. They'll be traveling over open country. Their outriders will be fanned out and they'll shoot us to pieces."

"We can't string it out any longer," I said. "This is the raid we have to make. And it will be the last one."

Bama looked at me, and then at the map, and then he sighed again and got up from his chair. "Well, I'll round up as many as I can find," he said, "and tell them we'll meet at the same place tonight."

That was one thing about Bama, you didn't have to talk all day to get an idea across. One raid, that was all I wanted, and then we'd find a place to start all over again—not, as Bama had said, that it made much difference about us. But the kid still had that girl waiting for him, and Bama knew how I felt about that.

It all began much the same as the last raid, except that I was the boss now and not just another rider. But I didn't have the knack for organizing the way Basset had had. I didn't have the patience to sit down with paper and pencil and check off all the names of men I could depend on. I left that job to Bama while I took Johnny Rayburn around to the livery barn to get our rigs in shape.

I didn't like the idea of bringing the kid along on the raid, but I couldn't very well leave him back in Ocotillo making bullet bait of himself. The stableman brought my black in, and a bay for Johnny Rayburn, and then we heard a commotion outside and Bama came in.

His face was worried and he was wiping nervous sweat off the back of his neck with a dirty handkerchief. I waved the stableman out of the place and said, "What's going on out there?"

"You've got to send somebody out," he said, "and call your men in, because the raid is off."

"Like hell," I said.

He wiped his neck some more and then brought the handkerchief across his mouth. "Maybe you'd better come out and see for yourself."

I went out, with the kid on my heels, and saw maybe a dozen men ganged around in front of the saloon. In the middle there were two horses, and it didn't take me long to see what the excitement was about. As I began to shove men aside I heard Kreyler saying. "Morry, get yourself a partner and ride out to the meeting place and tell the men to come back in."

By that time I was in the middle of things. I said, "Just stay where you are, all of you." One of the horses was nervous, snorting and pawing the ground, the way animals will do at the smell of blood. He started to rear up but I grabbed the reins and jerked him down good and hard, and then I stroked his neck for a minute until he quieted down. After all that I finally got around to inspecting the thing in the saddle.

It had been a man once, but now it wasn't much of anything. He lay belly down across the saddle, his feet and hands tied with a strip of rawhide under the horse's belly to hold him in place.

"Somebody give me a knife."

A knife appeared from somewhere and I cut the rawhide thongs. The body slid out of the saddle and sprawled out in the dust at my feet. He was one of my scouts, a little man with a mangy beard and a pair of wide-open eyes that seemed to be staring about a thousand miles into space. He had been shot all to pieces and there was no use feeling of his pulse to see if he was dead.

I went around to the other horse where the second body was, and I cut him down. This one had been my chief scout, the lanky, tobacco-chewing man who had thrown his weight on my side the day I shot Basset. He was bleeding from almost a dozen wounds, wounds that at first looked as if he had been caught in the haphazard blast of a scatter gun. But then I saw that there was nothing haphazard about it. He had been shot to death scientifically, by an expert rifleman, with the bullets just missing the really vital parts of his anatomy. It was the hard way to die, the way he had died. It was the long way.

I don't know how long I stood there looking at him before I began working up some kind of feeling about it. I had never known him very well. He was just a man on the run, like the rest of us, and his name was Malloy, and he was a pretty good scout who did his job without asking too many questions. That was about as much as I knew about him. But, seeing him sprawled out in the dust, I seemed to know him better that I had ever known him before. And for a moment something like fear struck in my guts, and I had the crazy idea that it was myself that I was looking at. I could almost feel the pain that was still a silent scream in the scout's eyes, I could almost feel the darkness closing in....

Then Bama said hoarsely, "My God, he's still alive!"

I snapped out of it, and I looked into the scout's eyes, and I saw that Bama was right.

"Get hold of him and take him into the saloon," I said. "Take him back to the office and put him on my bed. Bama, see if you can find Marta. She's pretty good at this kind of thing."

But I knew that neither Marta nor anybody else could help him now.

Four men picked him up as easily as they could and took him into my room and put him on my bed. Somebody brought some water and rags.

"Whisky."

Somebody brought the bottle, but I knew that the scout would never be able to drink it. I soaked a rag and washed his face and that was about all I could do for him. It occurred to me then that it had been meant all along for him to live until he got back to Ocotillo. Such carcful shooting wouldn't have been necessary if they had meant only to kill him.

"How do you feel, Malloy? Can you swallow some whisky?" They were both stupid questions, but I couldn't think of anything else to say. For a moment his eyes lost their glassiness, and he looked at me and at the men crowding into the room.

"Who did it, Malloy, can you tell us that?"

It took a long time to get his mouth working, and when he finally did get it working, no sound would come out. I put the wet cloth to his face again and squeezed a little of the water between his lips. He tried again, and this time I could make out the words "Smugglers ... Indians ..." His mouth kept working, but those were the last words he ever said.

I turned around and said, "Get out of here, all of you." Then I saw that Bama had come back with Marta and I motioned for Bama to come in.

The girl came in with him and I said, "Not you. He's already dead."

She looked at me in that flat way of hers, and then she crossed herself. "I say prayer."

It looked like it was a little late to pray for Malloy, but what difference did it make?

She knelt down by the bed where the dead man was and I turned to Bama. "Smugglers. Indians. What the hell did he mean by that? Apaches don't run in this part of the country."

"Mexican Indians," Bama said. "They're even more expert at torture than Apaches."

"Do these Indians run smuggler trains of their own?"

Bama shook his head. "The Mexicans hire them sometime, when they have to, as guards, and that's what we've run into this time. The Mexicans don't like them, but your men like them even less. They won't go up against a smuggler train with an Indian guard, if they know about it."

I thought a minute. "They will this time, because we can't wait for another one."

Bama didn't believe me. He thought that I had run up against something that I couldn't knock over.

I said, "You'd better be getting your horse ready."

He just stood there. "They won't follow you. They won't go up against those Indians. They're scared to death of them."

"They'll be scared of something else if they don't."

I walked into the saloon and Bama came after me, more out of curiosity than anything else. The men were ganged up at the bar pouring whisky down their gullets to settle their guts. I saw Johnny Rayburn and motioned him out of the way, and then I heard Kreyler saying:

"Mexicans are one thing but Indians are something else. If you men want to follow Cameron and wind up like those two scouts, that's fine, but not me."

I was behind him before he knew it. Instinct told me that arguing with him would only be a waste of time, so I stepped in and hit him as hard as I could behind the ear.

It stunned him. It stunned all of them. From the corner of my eye I saw that Bama and Johnny had their hands on their guns, in case it came to that.

But it didn't. I jerked Kreyler around before his head cleared and hit him in the face. I slammed the heel of my hand on his chin and snapped his head back, then I hit the corner of his square jaw. It was a fool thing to do, maybe, using my hands when I had guns, but I was still remembering that he was a United States marshal. And I didn't want to kill a United States marshal, no matter who he was.

The way it turned out, I didn't need the guns. It hurts to get hit like that, behind the jaw when you're not expecting it. It hurt Kreyler. I could see pain flare up in those dull eyes as his head snapped back. He began to go down, gasping for breath and grabbing for something to hold to. But there wasn't anything there, and he fell to his knees, and then he went over on his side.

I stood back for a minute, panting, and looking at the men.

"Has anybody else got any ideas about not going on this raid?"

Nobody said anything for a minute. Then Bama yelled: "Look out!"

But I had already seen Kreyler making a grab for his gun. I could have shot him, or I could have kicked the gun out of his hand, but I didn't do either one of those things. I stepped in and slammed the toe of my boot in his gut.

His mouth flew open and his face went from a dead white to an ashy gray. He folded up like a jackknife and began to gag. The Marshal would never be any sicker than he was at that minute, not if he lived to be a hundred. All the fight had gone out of him. The fight seemed to have gone out of everybody.

I said, "Bama, have you got a list of the men who are to make this raid?"

"I've got it," he said.

Then I looked at the men, still standing at the bar with their mouths hanging open stupidly. "We'll check the list at the meeting place," I said. "Any man who's not there by sundown, I'll find him. I'll find him if it's the last thing I do."

They began to get the idea that this raid was coming off, no matter what Kreyler or anybody else thought about it. They stood there for a minute, shuffling uneasily. Then one of them hitched his belt and started for the door, and the rest of them followed, one and two at a time.

"Well," Bama said, "I guess that takes care of that. You always get what you want, don't you?"

"If I want it bad enough."

Kreyler was still doubled up on the floor, too hurt and sick to move. I said, "What I told the other goes for you too. You'll meet with the rest of us, before sundown." Then the three of us, me and Bama and Johnny Rayburn, walked out of the place. Bama stopped at the bar just long enough to take a bottle out of the bartender's numb hands.

Chapter 8

We didn't say much as we rode out of Ocotillo and into those barren, angry-looking foothills of the Huachucas. Bama was nursing the bottle again, and the kid wasn't doing much of anything, except that once in a while he would look wide-eyed all around him as though he couldn't understand how he had ever got here. I tried to do some thinking and planning, but my mind kept shooting off on sharp tangents and winding up in strange, long-forgotten places.

I guess we were all thinking pretty much the same thing—the wild Nueces River brush country, the wide green lands of the Texas Panhandle, and Miles Stanford Bonridge's state of Alabama. Home, for all of us, was a long way off. Farther than the poles, farther than those foreign lands on the other side of the ocean, because the distance that separated us from home was more than miles. It couldn't be measured and it couldn't be crossed.

The sun was about two hours high when we finally reached the big rock ledge, and there were six or eight horses already grazing down the canyon while the riders hunkered together under the shelf, waiting. We unsaddled and unbitted and put our horses out to graze, and then Bama went up to the head of the canyon to check off the names as the men rode in.

Johnny Rayburn said, "Is there anything I ought to do, Mr. Cameron?"

He still had that lost look and I began to wish that I had left him back somewhere.

I said, "There's nothing to do now but wait."

I went up for a while to see how Bama was doing. The men were coming in slowly, grim-faced, reluctant.

Bama checked off a name and said, "Twelve. They're coming, but they don't like it worth a damn."

I said, "They're getting paid for it. They don't have to like it."

"Just the same, I've got a feeling that all our trouble won't come from the smugglers. This isn't exactly the smartest play in the world, and the men know it. They're beginning to say that they should have put Kreyler in as boss."

"The more they talk, the less they'll do."

But I wasn't so sure.

"It's the Indians they don't like," Bama was saying. "It would be better if you called this raid off and waited for another train to come up."

"And give Kreyler a chance to work on the kid in the meantime?"

Talking about the kid reminded me that Kreyler's men could be working on him right now, for all I knew. I turned and half ran down the canyon. But nothing had happened. He was squatting with his back against the rocky wall. There was a ragged tally book on his knee, and he was writing painfully in it with the nub end of a pencil. He didn't see me until I was right in front of him, and when he looked up his face got red, as if he had just been caught stealing pennies from a poor box.

"I—well, I guess I was kind of writing my girl a letter," he said. "I know there's no place to mail a letter around here, but when I get back to Tucson I can do it."

I don't know why he thought it was necessary to tell me about it, but he kept stumbling on, telling me about his girl. I guess he didn't notice the look on my face—or maybe I had learned to hide the things I felt.

"You think a lot of this girl, don't you?" I put in.

"Why, sure. Well, we've even got it planned to get married—sometime."

Sometime....

I should have done something right then. I should have put him on a horse and sent him back to Texas. And I caught myself thinking, That's exactly what I'll do—sometime.

It wasn't Johnny Rayburn that I was interested in, it wasn't even the money—because if this was to be the last raid it didn't make any difference what happened to the ledger. I was afraid—I admitted that. But the queer thing about it was that it wasn't the prospect of getting killed that scared me, it was the business of living and being alone.

It was crazy, and I guess there's no good way to explain it, but I didn't have the feeling when the kid was around. I guess he was what they call a symbol. A symbol of other times. Better times.

The kid was still talking, rambling on. Now that he had got started, he didn't seem to know how to stop.

"I wouldn't expect anybody else to know how I feel about that girl of mine," he said. "Maybe you wouldn't think she was so much to look at, but she's prettier than a new colt to me. Yes, sir, I'm going to go back there someday. We're going to stake out a little place down on the Rio Grande that I know about and raise some beef cattle and some grain." He laughed. "And some kids too, I guess."

"What you do is your own goddamned business," I said, "except just keep it to yourself. I don't want to hear about it."

The bitterness in my voice surprised me almost as much as it did the kid. I didn't know why I had said it and I didn't know how to explain it. I just knew that I didn't want to hear about his girl, or his plans, or anything else.

I left him sitting there with a startled, bewildered look in his eyes. As I turned I almost ran into Bama, who was standing behind me.

"Well, what do you want?"

Bama ran a hand over that bearded, weak-looking chin of his. "It looks like the last of your men are in," he said. "Kreyler came in just a while ago. The scouts just got in, too." He rummaged in his shirt pocket and took out a section of the map that he had drawn. He put his pencil on the throat of a funnel-shaped canyon. "Here is where the train ought to be around noon tomorrow, according to the scouts. It'll be an all-night ride, and then some, if we get there in time."

"We'll get there."

"Look at this," he said, holding his tally book in front of me. "Twenty men is all we've got, and they're already beginning to lose their guts for this thing. According to the scouts, the smugglers have around thirty outriders, most of them Indians."

I looked up and the sun was almost gone, and, long, cool shadows were reaching into the canyon, and pretty soon it would be dark. I said, "Out of these twenty men of mine, is there anybody we can trust if the going gets tough?"

Bama thought about it. "There's maybe four or five that ought to string along."

"All right, this is what we'll do. When we ride out of here you'll stay with Kreyler in the van of things, and you'd better keep a couple of those men with you. Have the others somewhere in the middle of the column when we hit the mountain trails, and tell them to report to me it anybody starts acting up. I'll be back in the drag with the kid."

We didn't move out until Bama went through the motions of contacting the boys he thought would stick; then finally he gave me the sign and we began to round up our horses.

It was dark by the time we rode out of the canyon, traveling in a column of twos and looking like the ragged, whipped-out remnants of some defeated army. After a while a pale moon came out, looking aloof and cold as only a mountain moon can look, and I began to feel the uneasiness of the men.

Maybe an hour went by, and then we reached a wide place in the trail where one of the men had dropped out to tighten his girth.

"Cameron."

I got a look at his face in the moonlight and recognized him as one of the men that Bama had singled out to be trusted. I motioned to the kid to pull up beside me and I said, "Yes?"

He looked all around as the column wound on down a rocky grade, and he lowered his voice.

"In about an hour," he said, "we're goin' to hit a flat stretch of country at the bottom of this grade. There's talk up ahead, among the men."

"What kind of talk?"

"They're goin' to make a break for it. They haven't got the guts for a raid like this, I guess. They plan to leave you sittin' high and dry."

For a minute I just sat there. "Who's behind this talk? Kreyler?"

"Kreyler's in no condition to do anything. It's all he can do to stay on his horse." He pondered for a minute. "Maybe he's behind it, at that. I guess he is. But it's Bucky Fay that's doin' the talkin', gettin' the men stirred up."

I guessed that Bucky Fay was one of the men I had inherited from Basset, but I didn't know him. Not by name, anyway. I figured it was about time we got acquainted.

I said, "I don't think they've got the guts to make a break for it, but I'll ride up just to make sure. I'll see that you get taken care of when we make the cut on the silver."

He grinned. That's what he had been waiting for. He was about as dependable as a cardboard dam in a flash flood. But maybe the silver would hold him as long as I needed him.

I brushed my black horse with the rowels of my spurs and we spurted toward the head of the column. We threaded in and out between riders along the narrow trail, and it didn't take long to see that something was going on. I rode up behind one man and heard him saying:

"By God, it's suicide. Nobody but a damn fool would try to attack smugglers in Funnel Canyon. Personally, I never took myself to be that kind of fool. How about the rest of you boys?"

By that time I was riding alongside him, and I said "Are you Bucky Fay?"

His voice shut off suddenly, like the squawk of a chicken on a chopping block. I had seen him in the saloon and his face was familiar, even if his name wasn't. He was one of Kreyler's buddies, all right, just like I figured—one of those tight, nervous, flint-faced little bastards that I never liked anyway, and that was going to make my job that much easier.

We were on the moon side of the mountain and everything was light enough to see what was going on. The column limped along like a dollar watch with a busted spring, then suddenly it stopped. Everybody was looking, and that was the way I wanted it.

"Bucky Fay?" I said again, and I found that it was getting harder to keep my anger shoved down where it ought to be.

He got over his first shock of seeing me there beside him. He started to sneer—it was just the beginning of a downward twitch around his puckered little mouth, and I guess he thought he had me just where he wanted me. His eyes shifted from one side to the other and he saw that most of the men were on his side and that gave him the confidence he needed.

He started to say something—maybe it was to answer my question, or maybe it was just to hold my attention while somebody else tried to put a bullet in me. It doesn't make any difference now, because he never got it said.

There's only one way to handle things like that. I would have shot him, maybe, if it had been another time, another place, but now I didn't want to rouse half of Arizona by burning a cartridge uselessly. I had him on my near side and my pistol was in my lap for a saddle draw. I leaned over slightly, my pistol jumped in my hand, and I slammed the heavy barrel across his head.

It made a sound like dropping an overripe pumpkin on a flat rock, and his eyes popped out as if they had been punched from behind with a pool cue. I didn't know if I had killed him and I didn't particularly care. I just knew that when he fell out of the saddle he was going to lie there for a long time and he wasn't going to bother me or anybody else.

It all happened pretty fast, without the bickering back and forth that usually goes before a fight. I raised up in the saddle so that I could see every startled, gutless face in the column, and I knew the less said about it, the better. Let them think about it. By the time they got through thinking about it the raid would be over.

I noticed Kreyler up near the front and he looked pretty sick about the whole thing. I couldn't tell what hurt him the most, his sore groin or seeing his plans blow up in his face. I motioned down the line for Bama to get things started again.

"Forward ho-o-o!" Bama called, as if he were still Lieutenant Miles Stanford Bonridge of the Army of Tennessee.

There wasn't any trouble when we hit the flats at the bottom of the grade. We crawled on up into the mountains and around daybreak the column halted again and Bama lifted his arm.

"All right, kid," I said, "let's have a look."

"This is it," Bama said when we reached the point, and he made a vague gesture toward the rocky lowlands below us. At first I didn't believe him, because there was no canyon there at all; it was just a rocky tableland between two small mountain ranges a mile or so apart. Bama must have seen the dismay on my face, and he didn't look very happy about it himself.

I said, "By God, this is a hell of a place to try to ambush somebody."

He grinned, but it looked a little sickly to me. "That's what the men have been thinking all along. Do you want to go through with it?"

"We've got to go through with it."

But I didn't like it. We'd have to go right down and meet the smugglers on their own battleground, and I didn't like to think what the odds would be on getting out alive.

"Isn't there a better place than this?" I asked. "That map of yours showed a neck on this canyon."

Bama wiped his face. "What looks to be a neck on paper can cover a lot of land on actual ground." He was on the verge of telling me, "I told you so," but he didn't. He just sat there and let me sweat.

"Well, we can't sit here and let the men lose what few guts they've got left." I motioned for the column to start moving and we began slipping and sliding down the side of the mountain.

When we hit bottom it didn't look much better, but at least there were a few rocks and bushes that the men could hide behind.

"Maybe you ought to wait and hit them tonight," Johnny Rayburn said, and it seemed to me that it was the first time he had opened his mouth in an hour or more.

"By night they'll be out of the mountains and into the desert," Bama said. "We couldn't get within a mile of them."

I rode out a hundred yards or so to get the lay of the land, and after I had done that I decided that the situation wasn't hopeless. I motioned for the men to come after me and we rode right out to the middle of the rugged mountain valley.

"It stands to reason," I said as Bama pulled up alongside. "That they'll come right down the middle of this draw, fanning their outriders a hundred yards or so on both sides. Anyway, we've got to count on that and make our lines." I motioned for Kreyler to come up, and his face was gray with sickness and hate, and maybe fear.

"Here's where we make our stand," I said. "When the smugglers come down the middle we'll hit them from both sides from behind rocks and bushes or whatever you can find to get behind. We'll have to depend on surprise. Come to think of it, maybe this isn't as bad as it looks, because they're not going to be expecting an attack in a place like this. Anyway, Kreyler, you take half the men and I'll take the others, and we'll leave about four hundred yards of open space between our lines. When you begin to lose your guts, just think of that silver."

He didn't say a word, but he cut me wide open with a look that was barbed with hate.

"All right," I said, "get your men and move out."

There was one thing I almost forgot—the horses. I called to Johnny Rayburn and my dependable man, whose name was Lawson, and got them to round up the horses and take them up to the high ground until the fracas was over. Anyway, that would keep the kid out of the line of fire and away from Kreyler.

It took about a half hour to get everything set, scattering the men out in a wavery line and piling brush in front of them and on top of them to make them as inconspicuous as possible. On the other side of the flat I saw that Kreyler was doing the same thing, and finally everything was set. All we needed now was the smugglers.

By the time the sun was well on its way to looking like a blast furnace, and Bama was lying belly down behind a rock, mopping his face nervously with his neckerchief.

"Pull your guts together," I said, and dropped down beside him. "Hell, we should have picked places like this all along. These narrow canyons practically advertise an ambush, but they sure won't expect anything in a place like this."

But Bama wasn't happy. His lips were dry and cracked and his eyes had a desperate look to them. "I wish you'd told me you were going to drive the horses off," he said.

"If it's the bottle you're worried about, you can get it when this business is over."

He licked his lips. "I'm not sure that it will do me any good then."

Up until now I had been too busy keeping the men under control to find time to be scared. But now there wasn't anything to do but wait and think about it, and I began to get some of that uneasiness that I had felt on all sides of me.

"Was that smart," Bama said, "giving Kreyler half the men? Do you think they'll fight?"

"They'll fight," I said. "They'd better."

Bama sighed and I knew he was still wishing for his bottle. I jacked a cartridge into the chamber of my rifle and said, "I don't like this any more than you do, but we've got to have that silver."

"Sure," Bama said.

"What's the matter with you? Don't you want to get away from this? Don't you want the safety and security that silver can buy?"

"The things I want can't be bought," he said.

I lay there for a long while looking over my rifle, across the field of fire. He was right, of course. Bama was almost always right, and that's what made me so mad at times.

Bama looked up at the sun and said, "It won't be long now."

As if that had been a signal, we began to hear the metallic sounds of cartridges being jacked into rifles. They would fight, I thought grimly. Maybe they wouldn't like it, and maybe their guts were crawling like a bagful of snakes, but goddamn them, they would fight because they were more afraid of me than they were of the smugglers.

I looked up and Bama was staring at me in that disconcerting way of his, as if he had been reading my thoughts. But he didn't say anything. He lay down again, motionless, looking over his rifle, and after a moment he began singing softly:

"The years creep slowly by, Lorena,
The snow is on the grass again ..."

It was an old war song, sugary and sentimental as most of those songs
were. I had heard the long, awkward boys of Texas singing it as they
marched the dusty roads with Hood to fight in strange and foreign
lands for the Confederacy. I had heard it again as they came straggling
back after Appomattox, what was left of them.

"We loved each other then, Lorena,
More than we ever dared to tell;
And what we might have been, Lorena,
Had but our lovings prospered well...."

I don't know, maybe it was the song that started me thinking about
Texas again. "And what we might have been, Lorena." It was so goddamned cloying and sickeningly sentimental that it was almost enough
to make a man throw up—and still, that just about summed it up...

Sometimes, after I had finished with my ranchwork, I used to ride over
to Laurin's place, which was only about two miles from our own Panhandle ranch house.

And more than likely I would use the excuse of looking for strays, because her brother thought I was wild, as he called it, and never liked
for me to be hanging around. But he couldn't keep me from seeing her.
We were both pretty young then and we didn't do much except talk a
little, but we understood from the first the way it was. I remember on
my seventeenth birthday Pa had given me four head of beef cattle and
I couldn't wait to tell her about it. "This is just the start," I said. "Those
four cows will grow into one of the biggest ranches in Texas. It'll be
our ranch."

I guess we were pretty happy then.

It wasn't my fault that there was a war. It wasn't my fault that the carpetbaggers and bluebellies moved into Texas looking for trouble. I had-
n't been the only hothead who decided that it was better to live a life
of my own outside the law than to live within the law and have a blue-
coat's boot heel on my neck.

But I hadn't known that it was going to work out like this. In the back
of my mind I had always planned on going back and having that ranch
and family just the way we had planned. But I never would. It was too
late.

"It matters little now, Lorena,
The past is in the eternal past...."

"Will you stop that goddamn noise!" I said, and my voice was shriller, louder than I had intended.

Then we all began to hear the bright, faraway little sounds of bells, and I heard somebody say, "Get ready, here they come," and the word was passed all along the line. I looked around and everything seemed to be all right. All the men were down, covered up with brush. Nothing looked out of place.

The bell sounds became mingled with the clatter of hoofs on the rocky ground, and then I could see them coming.

"By God, it's just like I figured. Right down the middle."

Bama didn't say anything. He looked frozen, and he was gripping his rifle hard enough to put dents in it. The smugglers' advance guard was getting close now, three Mexicans riding in line with about twenty yards between them. Behind them came a fat old geezer on a dappled horse, all decked out in a white sombrero and a scarlet sash and silver bangles. He was almost as fat as Basset, but he was mean and tough and he carried two six-guns and a knife and he had a scar from the top of his left ear to the point of his chin to prove it. Flanking him there were a couple of saddleless riders with dirty rags around their heads, and I guessed they were the Indians who were scaring everybody to death.

They didn't look so tough to me. They rode heavily, slouched on their ponies, in the way of all Indians. Most of them wore dirty hickory shirts that they had picked up somewhere, and a great variety of pants, most of which were torn off or cut off just below the knee. There were a great many knives and hatchets and a few old cap-and-ball pistols that must have been relics of the Mexican War.

After the advance guard, and the head smuggler and his personal bodyguard, there came the train of little gray mules and the outriders. It was pretty much my first raid all over again, except for the Indians. There was nothing much we could do now except lie there and hope that they didn't see us until we had the whole train in our field of fire.

After they all came into line I saw that the picture wasn't as bad as the scouts had painted it. After some fast counting I saw that there were only twenty Indians and four Mexicans, including the head man, so they only had us outnumbered twenty-four to twenty. Which wasn't bad, considering that we had our twenty in ambush.

I could feel Bama tighten up as the outriders began to come by. They were damn near close enough to shake hands with.

I let about half the train go by and said, "Suck your guts in and pick out a target." Then I got an Indian's head in the V of my rear sight. I waited an instant while the knob of my front sight settled on his ear. I should have squeezed the trigger. Bama was waiting for it, white-faced, but I couldn't seem to make my finger move.

This was a hell of a time to think about ethics, but I simply couldn't kill a man like that, without giving him a chance in the world to fight back. I lowered my rifle. Before I realized what I was doing I was standing up and yelling—and that, I guess was when hell moved to Arizona.

Chapter 9

It didn't take long to see why the men held such a deadly respect for the Indians' fighting ability. There was no period of surprise when I stood up and yelled, there was no time wasted in shock, and they didn't wonder what to do. They just did it. One instant they were riding in deep lethargy under the broiling sun, and the next instant they were screaming insanely and firing point-blank down our throats.

I had never seen anything like it. I fell back and lost sight of my target completely, and the next thing I knew, an Indian was trying to split my skull with a hand ax. I must have shot him, but I can't be sure about anything that happened then. I had dropped my rifle somewhere and was clawing for my pistols, and across the flats I could hear the sharp volley of fire as Kreyler's men let go with their first rounds.

Vaguely, I saw the fat old smuggler slide from his horse and come charging at us with both pistols blazing. He went down holding his gut. The Mexicans milled senselessly, wondering what had hit them, but the Indians were chopping us to pieces. And the crazy thing about it was that you could shoot them but they would keep coming and slash your throat and laugh at you before they died. It was a nightmare of screams and smoke, and men wandering aimlessly with bullet holes in them like lost souls in limbo.

It couldn't have lasted long, but time like that isn't measured by the ticks of a clock. A lifetime can be lived by the time a bullet travels twenty paces. In the instant it takes a hammer to fall and a cartridge to explode you can grow to be an old man. I felt like an old man right then. My hands shook. I wasn't certain of anything. I kept falling back and more Indians went down in front of my guns. Then my pistols were empty and I scooped one out of a dead man's hand and kept on firing. Then I heard Bama yelling, and I looked around and saw him kneeling behind one of those little gray mules, his rifle to his shoulder.

Somehow I got over to him and he gave me covering fire while I punched out my empties and reloaded. We seemed to be the center of attention now as four or five Indians spotted us and rushed us. We beat them off that time. I dropped one and Bama got one with his rifle, and they turned and got behind rocks to think up something better. That was when I began to notice that we were all alone out there.

I didn't see any of the men anywhere. It was just me and Bama and maybe a half-dozen Indians. And I had a feeling that pretty soon it would be just the Indians.

"My God," I said, "are all the others dead?"

Bama laughed. It wasn't a pretty sound. He pointed behind us, and the men were running—what was left of them. They were running for the high ground and the Indians had decided to let them go and concentrate on us.

For a long moment I cursed. I used all the vilest words I'd ever heard, and they weren't half enough to say what I wanted to say. And then our friends the Indians were coming again. This time they had spread out and were coming at us from three sides, and they must have picked up some of our rifles because their shooting was getting better all the time.

They had changed their tactics too. They had learned that charging us wasn't the answer, so they were creeping up on us from behind rocks and bushes, and even dead animals and men. They seemed to flit across the ground like cloud shadows in front of a racing wind, and they were gone before you realized they were there.

I took some shots just to keep my nerve up, to feel the pistols in my hands, but I wasn't doing any good. I looked back at the high ground just in time to see Kreyler and his men clawing their way up the steep embankment.

"The bastards! The goddamn no-good bastards!" Bama laughed that wild laugh again.

"Shut up, goddamn you! Shut up and let me think!"

The wildness went out of Bama's face and he just looked tired. Very sober and very tired, and he looked as if he didn't give a damn what happened.

"I'll get them," I said tightly. "If it's the last thing I do, I'll kill every last one of them."

And Bama said flatly, "Yes, I guess you would, Tall Cameron."

"I *will!*"

Somehow I would get out of this mess. I didn't know how yet, but I would, and when I did ...

"Watch it!" Bama said.

I caught just a glimpse of an Indian as he shuttled from one rock to another. I burned a cartridge just because I wanted to shoot at something, not because I thought I would hit anything. I started reloading again, filling the cylinders all the way around, six cartridges to a pistol. I finished one gun and got three in the other one and that finished my belt.

That was when the sun stopped giving off heat. That was when cold sweat started popping out on my neck and my insides felt as if it had been washed with ice water. Bama's .36-caliber ammunition wouldn't fit my pistols, and anyway, he was out too.

"How many rounds have you got for that rifle?" He checked the magazine and there were two.

"Well, that gives us eleven shots between us. Have you got any ideas?"

"I guess you could pray, if you go in for that sort of thing."

That seemed to end the conversation. Things didn't look too bright, but they could be a lot worse. For one thing, Bama was getting his guts back—I could tell by the way he talked—and guts was just the thing that might save us. My brain still burned when I thought of Kreyler and his boys running out on us, but I'd have to wait a while to take care of that. The Indians moved in a little more.

"How many do you make out there?" I said.

"Six, seven, eight, maybe more."

He was a big help. But he still had his guts, and a rifle and two cartridges, and that was something. "When they get close enough, they'll have to rush us," I said, "I guess that will tell the story."

"I guess so," Bama said. He didn't even sound interested. He scrunched down behind the little mule and began fumbling at his pockets. After a while I got my own makings out and gave them to him. It seemed that the whole world held its breath while he built a cigarette and held a match to it, and I caught myself jumping every time the wind rattled a piece of dry grass. Take it easy, I told myself. Just take it easy and let them come. There won't be anything to it then; all you have to do is shoot.

I took my guns out and laid them on the mule where they would be handy and then I took the tobacco and corn-shuck papers and built a cigarette for myself. It was so quiet that I began to wonder if the Indians were really out there. I looked out at the battlefield and for the first time I saw it as it actually was. The most pitiful things there were the little mules with the bells around their necks. The men didn't seem to mean much, dead or alive—but those mules, they hadn't asked for any of this.

As far as I could see, they were all dead. The ones that hadn't been shot for breastworks had run into stray bullets. When I thought back on it, it seemed a wonder that anything was still alive. The battle seemed long ago. I had to keep reminding myself that it wasn't over yet.

"Watch it!" Bama hissed.

And about that time four Indians jumped up and started at us in a crazy-legged gait, as silent as ghosts. It didn't seem right that they didn't make any noise. They ought to yell, I kept thinking, but they didn't. One of them had a rifle and he fired once, and that snapped me out of it. The other three could have had guns if they had wanted them— there were plenty of them scattered around but they seemed to favor knives and hatchets. They were almost on top of us before I got my guns to working. I heard my pistols roaring, and after a moment I heard the empty click of my off-side gun, so I dropped that one.

I stopped the one with the rifle and two of the others. I thought Bama had the last one, but the bullet went in and out without even slowing him down. He came charging over the mule, a bloody mess and a scream. Then Bama swung his rifle and the stock made a sickening, mushy sound as it smashed into the Indian's skull.

I thought we would be swarmed then, but the others decided to sit this hand out. When I turned around Bama was wiping the blood off his rifle and making a higher breastwork by putting the Indian on top of the mule.

I had three rounds left for my right-hand pistol, and Bama had one for his rifle. I wondered how many Indians were still out there. There was no way of telling. They seemed to come out of the ground like weeds.

Bama was puffing and blowing after his skirmish. He hunched down in an awkward, one-sided position, his face as white as a frog's belly, and that was when I noticed that he had been hit.

It was his leg, about halfway between the knee and the hipbone. The Indian rifleman, I guessed, must have done it with that single shot that he let go with.

"Well," Bama said between puffs, "I guess this about frays it out, Tall Cameron. You'd better make a run for it. There can't be many more of them left. I've still got a bullet. I can stop one of them."

"Shut up and give me a knife."

He didn't have a knife, but the Indian on top of the mule had one, and I used it to slit Bama's trousers up to the hip. There was a lot of blood and it was coming out in spasmodic little spurts, and I figured that an artery or something had been hit. But still it wasn't too bad, everything considered. There was a clean hole where the bullet had gone in and come out. There didn't seem to be any bones broken.

I said, "Just keep your eyes open and watch our friends out there." Then I hacked off the leg of his trousers, wound it up, and tied it loosely above the bullet hole. I got my empty pistol between the leg and the bandage for some leverage, and began to twist. After a minute the spurting stopped.

I took his rifle and put it on top of the mule where I could get to it. "Just take it easy for a few minutes and we'll be out of here."

But Bama didn't believe it, and I guess I didn't either. As Bama had said, it began to look as if our string had about frayed out. I could see them moving around out there again—or rather, I could feel them. They were getting closer all the time, but they never showed enough of themselves to shoot at. It was very quiet.

And then it wasn't quiet any longer because they were coming after us.

Bama just sat there looking at them. They split the afternoon wide open with their yelling and shooting—six of them, and I remember thinking that it might as well be six hundred.

They came at us from three sides and it seemed to take them a year to reach us. I had the impulse to shoot as fast as I could at anything that moved, but I choked it down and took my time. I made the one cartridge in Bama's rifle good, but it didn't even slow them down. Bama seemed to have completely disconnected himself from the whole business. He sat there smiling that half-smile of his, as if a hole had suddenly opened up for him and he could look right through that impenetrable barrier that separates the living from the dead. I don't know what he saw there on the other side, but whatever it was, he had reconciled himself to it, and he was waiting for it with no bitterness and no regret.

But not me. I hadn't gone to all this trouble only to be cut down by a few savages. All I had to do was hold onto my guts. I raised my pistol and waited until it seemed that I had the muzzle in an Indian's mouth. Then I pulled the trigger. He was the fast one of the bunch. He was the eager one with a whetted taste for blood, and I could almost smell his rancid breath in my face as the pistol jerked in my hand.

I could count him out. He was traveling the road to hell on a fast horse, and now I could turn my attention on the others and try to figure out a way to make two bullets do the job of one. That was what I was thinking, and the next thing I knew he was hacking at my skull with a hand ax.

I don't know how he did it. I'd never seen a man take a .44 bullet in the face before, and keep coming after you, still determined to kill you. We went down in a bloody tangle of arms and legs and my pistol went flying out of my hand. Something hit the side of my head then. It felt like a mountain falling on me, but I guess it was just a glancing blow from the Indian's hatchet. A smothering black fog rolled in. It was a cool, comfortable fog where there was no noise and no pain, and the most pleasant thing in the world would be just to lie down and let it wash over me.

But I kept fighting. Reflex, I guess, took over where the brain left off, and I grabbed hold of an arm and held on until the fog drifted off somewhere. We seemed to wrestle for a week, kicking, biting, scratching there on the rocky ground. He was gouging at my eyes and giving me the knee every chance he got, but I still held onto that arm. I seemed to be covered with blood and I couldn't tell if it was coming from me or him, or maybe both of us. I held onto that arm.

When it was over it was over all of a sudden. He went limp and the hatchet dropped out of his hand and that's all there was to it. I shoved him away. I knelt on my hands and knees and tried to gulp all the air in Arizona into my lungs. "Well," I heard somebody say, "the sonofabitch finally decided to die." It didn't sound like my voice, but it was, I guess. And then—finally—I remembered the other Indians.

I couldn't move. I squatted there like a poled steer and wondered why I wasn't dead. What had happened to the other Indians that had been in on the charge? It worried me, but I didn't have the strength to do anything about it.

I gulped some more air into my lungs. My stomach was sick and fluttery and the muscles in my legs were as weak as buttermilk. Maybe a minute went by while I got a hold on myself. I was pretty sure that those Indians hadn't decided to knock off work and go home just when they had us where they wanted us. Maybe it was one of those miracles that you hear about but almost never see. Like Daniel and the lions. But I didn't put much stock in it. I hadn't led the right kind of life for that sort of thing.

I had a few more theories, but I discarded them. It was time to take a look.

The first thing I saw was Bama. He was still sitting there behind the mule, holding onto the bandage around his leg. He looked as if he knew the answer, but he wasn't saying anything unless I asked him, and I was still too addled to think up words to put into questions. I stood up, finally, and saw that the Indians had been taken care of. They were scattered around carelessly like dirty laundry in a bunkhouse, and just as lifeless. One of them had reached our mule fortress and had died with a knife in his hand just as he was about to go over the top. His trouble had been two rifle bullets in the chest, spaced almost a foot apart. Not very good shooting. But good enough.

By that time I had the answer. Johnny Rayburn was walking across the flat with a rifle cradled in the crook of his arm.

I don't know how he did it, but he must have slipped down from the high ground some way and then crawled for about a quarter of a mile on his belly across the flats. The important thing was that he had done it. While all the others had been running, he had been figuring out a way to save my hide.

I guess I hadn't realized before just how close I had been to dying. The thought of it put a watery feeling in my guts.

"He's going to be a big help to you, isn't he, Tall Cameron?" Bama said dryly.

The words jarred me, because that was exactly what I was thinking as the kid came toward us. With some training, with some of the greenness rubbed off and some experience rubbed in, he would be a big help. He would be somebody I could trust; that was the important thing.

That was when I started changing my plans, putting the kid into them, taking Bama out of them. Bama couldn't help me. Not with that leg. But the kid ... That was something else again.

Johnny Rayburn grinned nervously as he came up to where we were. He looked awed by the thing he had just done.

"I thought I told you to stay with the horses," I said.

"Well," he said, "I figured the horses could take care of themselves. Anyway, I wasn't crazy about staying up there on the bluff with Kreyler's men." He shifted hands with his rifle. "I didn't do wrong, did I?"

I laughed, not because anything funny had happened, but just because it felt good to have a kid like that on my side. I said, "No, you didn't do anything wrong."

"I told you once I was a pretty good shot."

"Not too damn good," and I nodded at the dead Indian, "when you space them a foot apart." I knew that Bama was listening. And I didn't give a damn. I said, "But there's nothing wrong with your shooting that can't be fixed. And I'll fix it."

He couldn't have been more pleased if I had just handed him Texas with a fence around it.

From that moment, I guess, it was just me and Johnny Rayburn against the world. Or rather me and Johnny Rayburn, and a fortune in silver. That reminded me—we had to do something about the silver.

We didn't have any horses, and we sure couldn't carry the stuff on our backs. I looked up at the high ground and saw that Kreyler and some of his boys were still up there. I guess they had time to get their guts in shape, and probably they had just been waiting for me and the Indians to finish each other off so they could come back down and take the silver for themselves. But I had something else planned for them.

I stepped out in the open and cupped my hands around my mouth and yelled for them to come on down. I hadn't forgotten the way they had run out on us, but I could take care of that when the time came. This wasn't the time.

They must have been pretty disappointed to see me come out of it alive, and they must have had a pretty good idea that it wasn't purely an act of brotherly love that prompted me to call them back into the fold. I could see them talking it over. There was some arguing, I guess, but in the end they came down, as I knew they would. The silver was still down there and they couldn't resist the temptation of that easy money.

As they started down the slope, I went over our battlefield and found my rifle and salvaged some .44 cartridges for my pistols. I was ready for them by the time they rode up, and there wasn't much doubt as to who was still boss.

Kreyler looked like a man who had been outvoted. Silver wasn't as important to him as it was to some of the others, but he couldn't very well tell them to go to hell, because he still had ideas of running the business himself someday.

I said, "Well, men, we did it. All we've got to do now is get this silver back to Ocotillo and split it up. Let's get at it."

That jarred them a little. They had expected a good cussing at the very least, and here I was practically patting them on their backs. But they got over their shock. A yell went up and they went scurrying over the battlefield, cutting open the silver-filled aparejos and stuffing the adobe dollars into saddle pouches and war bags. But Kreyler wasn't fooled. He knew that I had to have them, if I wanted to get that money back to Ocotillo.

But there was nothing much he could do about it. Anyway, all that silver was putting a hungry look in his eyes, and the first thing I knew, he was as busy as any of us. Bama sat quietly through all of it, his face getting whiter and whiter. After a while I had the kid bring the horses down, and I found Bama's bottle and gave it to him.

"Here," I said, "you'd better have a drink of this."

He took the bottle and looked at it blankly. He turned it up and drank as if it were the last whisky he would ever see. Then he sloshed a little of it on his wound. But not much.

He sat back and closed his eyes for a minute until the pain let up. "You're not fooling Kreyler," he said.

"I'm not fooling anybody."

"You're not going to split that silver, are you, when you get back to Ocotillo?"

I just grinned.

"That's what I thought. I guess there's no use telling you that the men won't stand for it. But they won't. You've pushed them around about as long as they'll take it."

"Why don't you let me worry about that?"

He hit the bottle again. Loss of blood and shock and whisky were beginning to hit him. His eyes were bleary. His mouth didn't seem big enough to hold his tongue. He took another long drink and let the empty bottle slip out of his hand. "You and the kid," he said thickly, "ought to make quite a team."

"We might, at that."

He looked at me for a while. Then he slid over on his elbow. He must have passed out then, because his arm gave way and he fell on his face.

The tourniquet on his leg came loose and blood began spurting again. I grabbed it and tightened it, and stretched him out as well as I could. I looked up and the kid was standing there beside me.

"Get the horses," I said, "and bring them over here. Then find one of those Indian hatchets and cut a pair of blackjack poles long enough to make a travois."

He didn't ask a lot of fool questions. In a few minutes he was back with the horses and poles. The poles weren't nearly long enough, but it was the best he could do in this kind of country. We lashed them to Bama's saddle and laced them with a reata that one of the men had. Then we tied Bama on it.

By the time all that was done, the men were ready to go. The silver had all been gathered up and they were anxious to get home and make the split.

So we rode out of the valley and into the high Huachucas, the thud of hoofs mingled with the heavy jouncing of silver. I didn't look back this time. The death and stink of battle seemed a long way off, and I wanted to keep it that way if I could. The kid rode beside me, his eyes thoughtful, and I could see the question coming long before he got up nerve enough to ask it.

"I was just wondering about something," he said finally. "Did you really mean it, what you said back there? When you said you'd fix up my shooting?"

We rode on for quite a while before I answered. And in my mind there was the memory of empty days and long nights. Tight-wound days and tighter nerves, when the sound of a snapping twig or the rustle of brush was always a cavalryman, or a marshal, or maybe just a reputation-hunting punk anxious to get a notch in his gun butt. Sounds were always sharper when you were on the run, and alone.

But who could you trust when you had a price on your head?

Well, I guessed I had found somebody at last. So I said, "Don't worry about it, kid. I meant it, all right."

Chapter 10

It was dark again when we got to Ocotillo, and the town seemed nice and peaceful and sleepy-looking there at the bottom of the foothills. It seemed a shame to ride in there and get everything all stirred up again. But it had to be done. A few Mexicans came out and watched as we rode into town, and I imagined that their faces had a dull, angry look.

It was a funny thing, but I had never thought of the Mexicans resenting us and hating us. Well, I thought, they wouldn't be bothered long with me and the kid, and if they got tired of Kreyler and his bunch they could rise up and knock them down. I wondered why they hadn't done it before now.

As we pulled up in front of the livery barn, beside the saloon, the Mexicans sort of melted away in the darkness and I forgot about them. I watched the men while they unsaddled and lugged their saddlebags and war bags back to the rear of the saloon and into the office. After they were all finished we had silver scattered all over the middle of the room and it looked like a hell of a lot of money stacked up there in one big pile. The men were all ganging up in the room to watch the split. Something had to be done about that.

So I said, "It looks like a pretty good haul, doesn't it?" And everybody agreed. I laughed and kicked the saloon door open and yelled for the bartender to set them up.

That broke it up. They all flocked out and ganged up around the bar—all but Kreyler, that is. He stayed in the office with me and the kid, and I had an uneasy feeling that he had picked my brain and knew as much about my plans as I did.

I said, "You might as well get your share of the free drinks."

But he shook his head. He leaned against the doorjamb, looking careful and crafty, but not very healthy.

"Well, I am," I said. I looked at the kid and we went into the saloon and left Kreyler in the office. He couldn't carry off much of that silver by himself, if that was what he had in mind.

Everybody had had a round or two by the time we got to the bar, and it looked like a real celebration was on the way. I motioned to the bartender and he slid a bottle down, and I guess it was the bottle that reminded me.

"By God, we forgot Bama!"

I went out the door and the first thing I knew a couple of arms came out of the darkness and grabbed me. Probably I would have killed her and learned who it was later, if she hadn't laughed. But she did laugh and I knew it was Marta.

"Goddamnit, don't you know better than to jump on a man like that?" She was pawing me and kissing me and she seemed as happy as a pup with a bone.

"You glad to see Marta?"

"Sure," I said, "I guess I'm glad."

But just the same I shook her off and got my back against the wall and got my gun hand ready. In the back of my mind I was reasoning that somebody out there in the darkness could have put a bullet in me while a fool girl was hanging around my neck. It was just a passing thought, but I didn't like it.

Marta's laughter lost its bright edge. "What's the matter?"

"Nothing's the matter. I just like to be careful."

"You no trust Marta."

"I no trust anybody. That's how I got to be as old as I am."

"You no like Marta."

I was beginning to get tired of this. "Sure I like you," I said. "I'm crazy about you. Now, just come along with me. I've got a job for you."

"What job?"

"Never mind, just come along."

I took her arm and led her around toward the livery barn, the kid right behind us like a shadow. We found the horse, and Bama was still lashed to the stubby travois poles. He was pretty shaken up but his tourniquet was still in place and the bleeding had stopped. We left him on the travois but untied the poles and lowered him to the ground. The kid felt of his face and forehead while I loosened the tourniquet.

"He's got a fever."

"Then he's all right. What we've got to do is get him somewhere and keep him warm before the chills begin." I thought for a minute and began to get an idea. "Kid, do you think you and Marta can get Bama down to her house without advertising it?"

He rubbed his chin. "Well, sure, I guess so. She can take the feet and I can—"

"That's all I want to know. Marta, have you got some friends—friends with strong backs and not too many brains?"

She nodded, frowning.

"Round them up," I said. "Have them come around to the back of the saloon where the office is. I've got some things I want them to carry down to your place, and I want them to be quiet about it. Tell them it's worth five dollars in silver after the job's over."

She began to get it then, and so did the kid. Marta's face broke up in a grin. "Marta think you plenty rich!"

"Marta thinks too damn much."

"You leave Ocotillo, maybe?"

"My plans are my own. Now, pick up that travois before we have a dead man on our hands."

"You take Marta with you?"

"Good God, yes, I'll take you with me. Anything, just get going."

The last thing in the world I wanted was to be tied down to a girl like that, but I had to tell her something. And it seemed to satisfy her.

Johnny Rayburn hadn't decided if he was satisfied or not. He was thinking about Bama, I guess, and wondering how we were going to get out of Ocotillo with a wounded man and several hundred pounds of silver. He didn't know it yet, but Bama wasn't going with us. I hadn't figured out a way yet to take care of the silver. But I would.

Using the travois like a stretcher, they picked it up and marched off into the darkness. I waited a few minutes until I was pretty sure that they were going to make it, and then I went back to the saloon.

Kreyler was standing in the doorway. I was going to walk right past him, but he turned and followed me to the bar. His face was grim as he said: "Wasn't Marta with you out there?"

I had almost forgotten that the Marshal was still crazy about the girl. Well, he could have her as soon as I got out of Ocotillo.

I said, "There wasn't anybody out there. I was just looking after Bama."

"Didn't the kid go out with you?"

"What the hell is this? If you've got something in your craw, spit it out."

Suddenly he smiled, and I didn't like that at all. What if he had his boys out there laying for the kid? It was something to worry about, but there wasn't much I could do. Of course, I could have gone running after them, but that would have given the whole thing away. There was still the silver to be taken care of. Not even Johnny Rayburn came ahead of that.

I went back to the office and locked the door and put a chair against it. Then I walked the floor, waiting for something to happen. From the sound of things, the men were getting pretty drunk in the saloon. But there was still Kreyler, goddamn him.

Well, I could still take care of him. When he ran out on me I swore I would kill him. And I might do it yet.

Somewhere in that confusion of thoughts there was a knock at the back door. I opened up and there stood four grinning Mexicans, all teeth and eyes in the darkness. They all started jabbering that spick lingo at me, and I told them to shut up and start moving those bags.

They grunted, surprised at the weight of the stuff. But I finally got them loaded up and they went staggering off into the darkness. They only got about half of it the first time around, and I waited for what seemed a week for them to come back. What if they got curious as to what was in those bags? You can't trust Mexicans. You can't trust anybody with that much money.

But I guess they weren't the curious kind. They came back finally, puffing and grinning, and I loaded them up again. I went around to the livery barn and got that black horse of mine and a sturdy little bay for the kid, and I headed down the alley toward the Mexican part of town.

I knew that part of town pretty well by now, so I went around the back way and came in between the high adobe walls to the back door of Marta's place. Through the open door I could see the Mexicans puffing and wiping their faces as they stared blankly at the pile of silver on the kitchen floor.

"Mr. Cameron?"

"Are you all right, kid?"

"Sure," he said, and came out into the little walled-in yard where I was.

"How's Bama?"

"He looks pretty good," he said. "That girl washed the wound and bandaged it up and gave him some broth. He looks better than he did on that travois."

"Let's go in and look at him," I said. "We haven't got much time, though."

The kid held back as if he weren't any too anxious to go back inside.

"What's the matter?"

"It's the old man," he said. "Marta's pa. He doesn't like gringos to start with, and he especially doesn't like them coming in and taking his house over."

We could fix that, I thought. I'd give him a handful of silver and that would shut him up. Anyway, we went in and there was Bama stretched out on the earth bed with a cigarette between his lips. His face had been washed and his leg had a clean bandage. He looked like a new man.

But he hadn't really changed. He spat the cigarette out and drawled, "Welcome to our little sanctuary, Tall Cameron," and I remembered that long spiel he had made the first time I saw him. "Welcome to Ocotillo, the last refuge of the damned, the sanctuary of killers and thieves and real badmen and would-be badmen; the home of the money-starved, the cruel, the brute, the kill-crazy...." At the time I thought he had been joking. But it was no joke. I had seen them and lived with them. I was one of them.

"How's the leg?" I cut in on him.

He closed his eyes. "The leg's all right. It's a hell of a thing, isn't it, to have a body that's seemingly indestructible, when you're dead inside?"

"I guess you're all right. You still talk crazy, which is normal for you,

I guess."

Bama laughed. "How about Kreyler and the boys? Are they going to let you just walk out with their silver?"

"They don't know yet that I've walked out with it. By the time they find out, I mean to be on my way to Mexico."

Bama had no comment to make on that. He just lay there with his eyes closed. All the time we had been talking there had been a lot of jabbering going on in the other room. I went to the door and saw that it was Marta paying off my baggage boys. They backed out of the house, grinning and bowing, clutching the silver in their hands.

"Where are they going?" I asked.

Marta laughed. "They go cantina."

That was fine. Tomorrow morning they would wake up with a headache and a bad memory.

I wondered how long it would take Kreyler to discover that I had pulled out with the silver. Not long, probably, but after he did find out he would have to find us to do anything about it. We had an hour, I figured, to take care of the silver and get out of Ocotillo.

They say that money can be a burden, and for a minute it looked as if that was what that silver was going to be to me. We couldn't load our horses down with it. And we couldn't put it on a pack horse and take it with us, because that would slow us down, too. The only thing to do was to go somewhere and have the silver shipped to us.

But how? No freighting company would touch it, even if there had been a freighting company in Ocotillo. We could bury it, maybe, and come back after it later. But we needed the money now. Anyway, I'd had enough of Ocotillo to last a lifetime.

Then the whole thing exploded pretty and clean in my mind and I knew how we were going to take care of that silver.

I yelled, "Marta!" and she was standing right at my elbow. "Look," I said, "do you still want to go with me?"

Her head bobbed. There was nothing she would like better—especially since I had come into a fortune of silver. Marta's old man had been quiet through the whole thing until now. He had been sitting at a rough plank table holding his head in his hands. Every once in a while he would fumble at some wooden beads around his neck and mumble a prayer, and from the look of hate in his eyes I figured he was praying for lightning to strike us all. Now his head jerked up and he glared at me. He didn't understand a word of what I had said, but somehow he knew.

"This is what we're going to do," I said. And I was talking to the old man as much as to Marta. "We've got to get out of Ocotillo and we've got to leave the silver here. The old man's got some burros, hasn't he?"

She nodded, puzzled.

"All right, we'll go somewhere—" And then I remembered a place on that map that Bama had drawn for me. "We'll go to Three Mile Cave down near the border. Do you know where that is?" She knew. "We'll go there and wait two days, and in the meantime Papacito can load the silver and bring it to us. He can cover it with wood or something to fool anybody who may get curious. I don't care how he does it, just so he does it."

She was beginning to get it now. Her eyes lit up, and I guess she was seeing herself as the belle of Sonora, dressed in silks and satins and cutting quite a figure. The real reason I wanted her along never occurred to her.

But it did to the old man. He jumped up from the table and began to jabber in that spick language, and I could see that he was telling Marta that he wasn't going to do it. But Marta was still seeing herself with all the things that silver could buy. That was one picture that she liked, and she wasn't going to have it ruined, Papacito or no Papacito. Before I knew it, the whole thing got out of control. Marta's eyes spat fire and they stood there in the middle of the room yelling at each other.

I had to break it up myself. I stepped in and shoved Marta against the wall. The old man yelled louder than ever, so I shoved him down in his chair and whipped my hand back and forth across his mouth, crack, crack, like a mule skinner two days behind schedule and laying on the leather.

That quieted things down for a minute. Marta stood against the wall, her eyes still flashing. She hadn't liked the way I shoved the old man around, and I hadn't enjoyed it much myself. But sooner or later somebody was going to have to step in and declare himself boss. So that was what I did.

I got hold of Marta's arm and quieted her down. "I'm sorry," I said. "But we can't stand here yelling at each other. We haven't got time for it. For all I know, Kreyler and his boys may be right outside the door getting ready to shoot hell out of everything."

I said, "Has the old man got it straight what he's to do with the silver? We pull out of here tonight and head for Three Mile Cave. Tomorrow he loads the silver on his burros and meets us at the cave the next day. Tell him again."

She shrugged and told him again, and the old man didn't like it any better this time than he had the first.

"We'd better do something to impress it on his mind," I said. "Tell him we're taking you as hostage. If he doesn't show up with the silver he'll never see you again."

She wasn't so sure that she liked that, but she understood that it was the only way of being sure of that silver. So she told him.

The old man stared at me for a long while with those hate-filled eyes, and then he started breaking up in little pieces. He dropped his head on the table and his shoulders began shaking. The silver would arrive on time.

But in the meantime we couldn't just leave it piled up in the middle of the room. I walked around the house, but there wasn't any place there to hide it. I went out in the yard and kicked around for a few minutes, waking up a hound dog and a few chickens. The chickens gave me an idea.

"Bring the stuff out here," I called. "Johnny, give Marta a hand."

I had the chickens scattered and squawking all over the place by the time they came out with the first load, but I also had a couple of empty chicken coops, which were just what we needed. We piled the silver in the back of the coops and shooed the chickens back in.

That about nailed things down. All we had to do now was to get out of Ocotillo, and we couldn't do it too fast to suit me. We went back in the house and I said, "Well, Bama, I guess this is good-by."

He opened his eyes and looked at me. "Good-by to Ocotillo," he said lazily. "I've been saying that ever since I got here, but I never left the place. Maybe I never will now."

"Sure you will," I said. "I'll have the old man give you some silver. All you can carry. When your leg gets better you can pull out of here. Maybe we'll meet up in Mexico sometime. You can't tell who you'll run into down there, they tell me."

The kid came into the room just as I was finishing my speech. I turned and said. "We've got to get a horse for Marta. I'll have to see if I can get back to the livery barn—if Kreyler's men haven't already missed us and started tearing things, up."

"You mean two horses, don't you, Mr. Cameron?" the kid said. "Bama hasn't got a way to travel."

"Bama's not going," I said.

I don't think he even heard me, or if he did, he didn't believe me. "He sure can't stay here," he went on. "He would be the only one left who knew about the ledger, and you know what Kreyler would do to him about that."

"Kreyler can have the ledger," I said. "It doesn't make any difference now."

But he still couldn't believe that I was going to leave Bama behind. Bama was my friend. Bama was a man you could put your trust in. You didn't go off and leave friends to wait for what was almost certain death.

"Look," I said. "We've got a long ride ahead of us and it's no kind of trip for a man with a hole in his leg." I could have gone on arguing, trying to justify it, but what good would it do? It was a hard world, and sooner or later the kid had to learn that.

He began to get a stubborn look. He wanted to argue. Bama was watching us in a disinterested sort of way, as though he thought it might be kind of interesting to see how it came out. But not too interesting.

Nothing at all happened, the way things worked out. Outside, I heard one of the horses stamp nervously. It wasn't anything out of the ordinary. But just the same, it gave me a funny feeling. Uneasiness started walking up my back with cold feet, so I went to the door and looked out.

Things were pitch-dark out there and I couldn't see a thing. But that feeling was still with me. I stepped outside, brushing my palms against the butts of my pistols, just to make sure that I had them.

That wasn't enough. I should have pulled them and started shooting.

Chapter 11

You never know, I guess, just what's the right thing to do. You either do it or you don't. And that time I didn't do it.

I stepped outside and something hard and solid connected with the back of my head and bright showers of pain flew out in all directions. I took another step—or thought I did—and I walked right into that black pit that has no sides and no bottom and I started falling.

It was a long trip. My head hit something two or three times on the way down. Then something slammed in my middle and my stomach jumped up and tried to shove my Adam's apple out of the way and get in my mouth. I fought it, but after a while it didn't seem to be worth the trouble. I let the darkness have its way.

We got to be old friends, me and the darkness. I got to like it down there. It was cool and comfortable and the smothering black fog closed over me and around me and all I had to do was sleep. The trials and tribulations of the world were away and gone and I didn't have to worry about scrabbling around in the dirt for money or life, because money and life didn't mean anything down there. I should have stayed there. And maybe I would have if I had known what it was going to be like when I got back. But I didn't know it then. I didn't know anything.

I started fumbling in the blackness, and after a while I found a little slit of light about an inch long and about as wide as a thread of silk split four ways—and that was my consciousness, I suppose. Anyway, I clawed and scratched until I got a hold in the slit, and then, with an effort that left me sweating, I ripped the darkness wide open.

I was sprawled out in Marta's kitchen, and a lamp was being held over me. The sudden light hit my eyeballs like hammers and I rolled over and tried to curse, but all that came out was a groan. I heard somebody saying, "By God, he's got a hard head, all right. That's one thing you can say for him." Somebody else said, "Just watch him, and if he tries to get up let him have it again."

I didn't recognize the first voice, but the second one belonged to Kreyler. I lay there for what seemed a long while, trying to get the mud out of my brain. Kreyler ... It looked like I had fooled away too much time in Ocotillo when I should have been on the road. The Marshal was either smarter than I thought he was, or I was dumber than I thought I was. It didn't make much difference now. He had found out about the silver, and he had caught up with me, and somebody had damn near beat my brains out with a pistol barrel—if I'd had any brains to begin with.

I tried to move again, and that was a big mistake. The stupor that had me sealed up in a little world all my own, like sod on a grave, suddenly disappeared and I broke into the world of reality, full of aches and pains. My head was the big trouble. It felt like an October gourd that had been stepped on—smashed and empty.

The room began to swim, and my stomach started crowding into my throat again. I raised my head as high as I could, but all I could see was boots and spurs and the packed clay floor. I was ready to give up. I was sick, and tired to death, and blood was getting in my eye, and I couldn't figure out a way to stop it. Kreyler could have the silver. He could have the girl. All I wanted was to be left alone.

But it wasn't as simple as that. Through the sickness I heard the sodden sound of bone and flesh hitting more bone and flesh. Somebody laughed—the man who was supposed to give me another pistol whipping if I tried to get up, I guess. I heard Marta make a tight little sound, and then something hit the floor, solidly, like a sack of oats being dumped off a wagon.

I had a pretty good idea what was happening, but I was in no position to do anything about it. I lifted my head again and the room tilted up on one corner and spun around a few times. Finally it settled down. Things came into focus.

It was about the way I had figured it. Johnny Rayburn was sitting on his rump, with a bloody mouth and a dazed look in his eyes, and Kreyler was standing over him, grinning, rubbing his right fist in the palm of his left hand. "I can keep this up all night, kid," the Marshal said. "Do you want to tell me who has that ledger, or do you want to go through this all over again?"

The kid just sat there looking stupid. Kreyler jerked him up by the front of his shirt and hit him again. Away down in the cellar of my mind a spark set off an explosion of anger. I rolled over on my face. I got my hands under me and began to push. My stomach turned over and tied itself into a knot. I pushed some more and sweat popped out all over me. Somebody had gone to Austin and brought the capitol building to Arizona and tied it on my back. But I was going to get up anyway. And when I did, I was going to see if Kreyler could take it as well as he handed it out. I wanted to see how he would stand up under a pistol whipping. I was going to find out—as soon as I managed to get off the floor.

My intentions were all right, but something went wrong with my arms. They gave away and I fell on my face again. For a moment I just lay there with my head ringing, blowing as if I had run all the way from El Paso. I must have put on quite a show. Anyway, it seemed to amuse Kreyler and his pal. They had a good laugh about it. Then Kreyler came over and turned me on my back with the toe of his boot. "Well," he said, "the great Tall Cameron doesn't look so tough now." And everybody had another round of laughs.

Anyway, I had pulled Kreyler's attention off the kid for a few minutes. And I finally got a look at the Marshal's pal.

He was a frail little man not much over five feet tall, with pale watery eyes and a thin little mouth that was always just about to break into a smile, but never quite made it. When he laughed it was just a sound that he made with his mouth, ha-ha, something like the kind of sound that Basset used to make. He was standing over me with the muzzle of a .44 shoved in my face, looking as big as a rain pipe. I think he would have pulled the trigger just to feel the gun buck, if Kreyler hadn't stopped him. Well, I wasn't the only one in the company with a hard head. Kryler's gunny was Bucky Fay, the man I had knocked out with my pistol barrel and who was supposed to have been stretched out in the mountains somewhere with his skull split open.

"Not yet, Bucky," the Marshal said soothingly, as though he were talking to a backward child, "I'll tell you when, Bucky, but first we've got some things to do. Remember?"

Bucky thought about that for a while, and finally he did remember. He stepped back one pace, almost smiling, and held his pistol just about on a line with my heart.

"Now, let's see," Kreyler said looking at me. "Would it be better to work on you or the kid?" He wasn't in any hurry. He seemed to have all the time in the world, and this was a delicate problem and he was going to figure it out if it took him all night.

"I think the kid," he said finally. "You're right fond of him, aren't you, Cameron? You wouldn't like to see him with his face all messed up and maybe an eye knocked out, now, would you, Cameron? Well, I'll tell you what I'll do. You just tell me where that ledger is and I won't even lay a hand on him. I give you my word."

Kreyler's word would be about as good as a counterfeit dime. But I couldn't tell him that now. He had guessed right about the kid. I wasn't going to let anything happen to him, if I could help it.

"Can I sit up?" I said.

Kreyler shrugged. "Sure. Let him sit up, Bucky."

Bucky took another step back and lined his pistol up again, this time at some invisible spot between my eyes. My co-ordination must have been getting better, because I made it all the way to a sitting position the first try. But it wasn't without effort. I sat there gulping in air and wiping blood off the side of my face. I felt of my head, and there were two good-sized bumps and a nasty cut, but I figured I would live. For a little while, anyway.

Marta was over by the cook table trying to comfort her old man. Papacito seemed to be taking it harder than anybody in the room. Tears were rolling down his face and getting into his dirty mustache, and he kept fumbling at those wooden beads around his neck and jabbering some kind of prayer over and over, and for some reason that made me madder than anything else. What the hell did he have to cry about?

"For God's sake, shut him up," I said to Kreyler. "How can I think with that racket going on?"

It must have been getting on Kreyler's nerves too, although he hadn't shown it. He said, "Watch things, Bucky." Then he stepped over and knocked the old man clear off his stool and sent him rolling against the wall. Marta was on him like a panther, clawing and scratching and spitting out curses in that language of hers. But this was the Marshal's night to do all the things that he had been wanting to do for a long time. Me, the kid, the old man and now Marta. He was taking care of all of us and loving it. Every dog has his day, they say. This one belonged to Kreyler.

He made short work of Marta. He backhanded her hard enough to cross her eyes and then he grabbed her shoulder and shook her until her teeth rattled. "Goddamn you!" he said hoarsely, and I didn't realize until then how mad he really was. Maybe he would have killed her if she had kept fighting. But I guess she had all the fight knocked out of her. He let her go and she dropped down at the table and started crying.

That surprised me. I wouldn't have thought that there were any tears in a girl like that.

Anyway, Kreyler had quieted things down. Now he came back to me.

"What's it going to be, Cameron? Are you going to tell me about the ledger or do I work on the kid some more?"

By now I had discovered that my guns were gone, which was no surprise. What was I going to tell him? I couldn't take much more. And neither could the kid. Of course, there was Bama in the next room, and they could work on him if they killed both of us.

I said, "What good is it going to do me if I tell you where the ledger is?"

Kreyler smiled. "You can go, after that. The ledger's all I want."

"And the silver?"

"You can have that, too, if you can figure a way to get it out of Ocotillo."

He was lying and we both knew it. Once he knew where the ledger was, he would kill all of us—except Marta, maybe—and take the silver for himself, the way I had been going to do. It would be easy. He could tell the men that I had double-crossed them, and not even Bucky would be alive to tell them any different.

I said, "Would you mind telling me why the men aren't yelling their heads off about their cut? They must have found out by now that the silver's gone."

"The trouble with you, Cameron," he said, "is that you don't know how to handle men. I knew what happened to the silver as soon as I found out it was missing. But I didn't tell the men about it. I told them to go on drinking and we'd make the cut in the morning."

It was all very pretty. I would be missing, and so would the silver, and two and two is always four—anyway, most people think so.

Bucky was still standing there with his .44 pointed at a place between my eyes, and he was probably thinking what a lucky guy he was, because Kreyler was going to split that pile of adobe dollars with him.

Like hell Kreyler was going to split with him. Bucky would wind up with the rest of us, in some shallow grave where we would stay until the coyotes dug us up a year or two from now.

For a minute I thought maybe Marta could help us. I could get a signal to her and she could rush Bucky. Then the kid could keep Kreyler busy for a minute while I got Bucky's gun and finished the job. That was the way things were beginning to shape up in my mind. Johnny Rayburn seemed to be reading my thoughts, because he nodded his head when I looked for just the right spot to make the tackle. But when I looked at Marta I tore the plans up and threw them away.

Marta was a smart girl. I had forgotten how smart.

Marta was through with me. She was through with me, and Bama, and Johnny Rayburn. The money was blowing in a new direction, and Marta was drifting with the wind. The Marshal was her man now.

She had stopped her bawling and thought things over, and she had come to the conclusion that Tall Cameron's future wasn't exactly the bright and shining star to hitch her ambitions to that she had once thought. But Kreyler—that was something else again. From here on out, Kreyler would be boss. Besides that, he would have that pile of silver and could buy her all the pretties her black heart desired.

She thought about that. She liked it. She looked at me and sneered, and she looked at Kreyler and smiled.

But Kreyler wasn't dumb. It was a fact I had overlooked at first, but I was making no mistake about it now. He could look into those eyes of hers and read the lies as plain as anybody and for a minute I thought maybe he was going to tell her to go to hell.

But he didn't. He had wanted her too long, I guess, and she was in his blood. Well, I thought, they would make a nice couple. It would be interesting to stick around and see who would be the first to stick a knife in the other's back.

That was as far as my thoughts got. About that time Kreyler's patience played out, and he stepped over to the kid and jerked him off the floor and hit him across the mouth.

"The ledger," he said coldly.

The kid said nothing, and that got him another slap across the face. Anger almost made me do something foolish, like getting off the floor and trying to punch a fist through Kreyler's thick middle. The thought was there, but it never got to be more than a thought. My glance ran head-on into that half-smile of Bucky's, and that was a great settling influence.

It was getting bad now. That ham-sized fist of Kreyler's would spat sickeningly in the kid's face.

"The ledger!"

The kid would say nothing.

Then the spat again.

But the kid didn't break. I was the one that broke. I stood it as long as I could and then I yelled, "Goddamnit, let him alone! I'll tell you about the ledger."

Kreyler paused for a moment. His fist was bloody, and he was grinning, enjoying himself. There are men like that.

He grinned at Bucky. "Mr. Cameron wants to tell us all about it. He doesn't like to see his little pal knocked around. What do you think about that, Bucky?"

Bucky laughed, but there was no comment behind his laugh, and no humor.

"I don't much like to stop in the middle of a job of work like this," Kreyler said pleasantly. "I figure the kid will tell me what I want to know, Cameron. It may take a little time. But I'm in no hurry." He grinned again and jerked the kid's limp body up with a big left hand, and I guess that was when I threw caution away.

I started gathering myself. I was going to jump and Bucky knew it and was waiting for it. He opened his thin lips and breathed through his mouth. He was going to shoot me right between the eyes because that was the spot he had been concentrating on.

Oh, he had it figured down to a gnat's hair, all right, and his finger started squeezing the trigger. He was smiling now, actually smiling, and he was probably seeing himself cutting quite a figure among the pilgrims and dance-hall girls; and people would probably buy his drinks for him just to get him to tell how it felt to kill a man like Tall Cameron. Bucky was going to be somebody after this. He was going to get himself a rep utation as a gunman, and nobody had to know that he had got it the easy way. All he had to do was pull the trigger.

I could see those thoughts going around in Bucky's mind as he started the squeeze. I had time to move about six inches before the hammer fell—and that wasn't time enough or far enough.

It's funny how your mind works at times like that, being aware of a lot of things but not actually seeing anything in particular. For instance, I knew that Marta would be watching it all and smiling in that detached way of hers, although I couldn't see her. And Kreyler would be too busy with the kid to notice what was going on until it was too late. It was just me and Bucky.

By that time I had lunged forward and was crouching like a wolf ready to spring. But Bucky wasn't worried. He was seeing me lowered away into shallow ditch with somebody throwing dirt in my face. And then the gun went off and the explosion went crashing around the room, and I was wondering why I didn't feel anything, why I didn't go down.

But I didn't wonder long. I crashed into Bucky and he went limp like a bag of grain slit open with a sharp knife, and that was when I realized that Bucky was dead. He was dead before I hit him. I didn't know how or why, and this wasn't the time to ask questions. I threw him aside and wheeled on Kreyler, who was clawing for his gun.

He never got his gun out, though.

There was another explosion and Kreyler took two quick steps forward and one step back, like the pride of the ball getting warmed up for a do-si-do or a skip-to-my-Lou. His eyes were faintly bewildered and pained, as if somebody had just played a rather nasty practical joke on him. Then he started falling like a tree in a forest. He crashed to the floor, and he could have been a side of beef for all the fuss he made after that.

Along about then was when I noticed Bama for the first time.

He had that old .36-caliber Leech and Rigdon clutched in both hands, and a curl of white smoke was coming from the muzzle and making a hook near the ceiling, like a question mark over Bama's head. We must have all stood there for a minute or more and nobody did anything or said anything, and Bucky and Kreyler got deader and deader there on the floor. I hadn't seen Bama get out of bed, and I guess Bucky and Kreyler hadn't either. But he had managed it somehow. He had hobbled on one leg to the door, just as the party was getting into full swing.

I said, "Thanks, Bama. I guess that's a favor I owe you."

He didn't say anything for a minute. His wound had come open and blood was pouring down his leg again, but he didn't seem to notice. Then he leaned against the doorframe and panted. I caught him before he fell and got my shoulder under him and dragged him to the bed.

"Marta!" I yelled. She appeared in the doorway, and from the way she looked, I guess she expected to get belted all over the room. "Get some whisky," I said. "I don't care where or how, just get it."

Things were moving too fast for Marta, I guess. The situation had changed so often that she wasn't quite sure whose side to be on. She just stood there.

"Look," I said. "Do you want to go to Mexico with me or don't you?"

Her head bobbed. She wanted to go where that silver went. She knew that.

"Then get out of here and get the whisky!"

She got out, and I got the bandage back on Bama's leg and stopped the bleeding.

"My God, I thought I was finished," I said. "I guess I forgot that a man's never finished as long as he has friends around."

Bama didn't say anything. He lay there with his eyes closed, and maybe he was remembering that just a few minutes ago I was ready to run out on him. More than likely, though, he was thinking about that whisky that Marta was going to bring.

I went in the other room and the kid was just picking himself off the floor and trying to get the blood out of his eyes. I've seen men lose their seats in the van of a stampede and not look much worse than Johnny Rayburn did at that moment. But I took him over to the washstand and threw a couple of dippers of water in his face and he didn't look so bad. His nose was swollen, maybe broken, and his mouth was split and puffed, but there was nothing wrong with him that time wouldn't cure. I poured out some more water for him, and then I went outside.

I found Bucky's and Kreyler's horses by the side of the house, and that was going to save me a trip back to the livery barn. I didn't see anything or hear anything out of the way. Those thick adobe walls had probably absorbed most of the noise of Bama's shooting.

I went back in and the kid was drying off his face and looking a lot better. Papacito was crumpled up in one corner of the room like next week's washing. I went in where Bama was.

"How's your leg?"

He opened his eyes and shrugged.

"Are you going to be able to ride?"

"Ride where?"

"To Mexico, where do you think? You sure can't stay here. You've just killed a United States marshal."

Bama studied that over quietly, turning it over in his mind and looking at it from all sides. Finally he said, "No, I think I'll just stay here, Tall Cameron. I don't feel much like running any more."

I could see that he was getting all wound up to make a long speech, but about that time Marta came in with two tall bottles of clear tequila. I uncorked one of them and put it in his hands.

"Here, you're going to need this."

He lay there, holding the bottle up and looking at it, and finally he put it aside. "No," he said, "I don't think I want it."

That jarred me.

"What the hell's wrong with you, anyway?" Then I raised him up and put the bottle to his mouth and poured. It went up his nose and over his chin and down the front of his shirt, but some of it went in his mouth too. He coughed and choked, but I kept pouring until almost a quarter of the bottle was gone.

"This isn't just whisky, it's medicine. Drink it."

I went back in the other room and lifted the old man off the floor and put him in a chair. "Don't forget what I said about the silver, old man," I told him. "If you want your worthless daughter back, don't forget."

He couldn't understand my language, but he knew what I was talking about.

Chapter 12

We rode out of the moonlit town that night and into the dark hills, with Kreyler and Bucky lashed behind our saddles like blanket rolls. About a mile out of town we found a dry wash with a bed of soft sand, and the kid and I dug a long ditch with our hands, and that was where we buried the Marshal and his pal. We covered our trail as well as we could and we scattered brush and leaves over the grave. I figured nobody would find them for a few days. Maybe a month, if we were lucky. Marta and Bama watched from a little knoll while we finished the job; then we got on our horses and rode again toward the south.

Three Mile Cave, it turned out, wasn't a cave at all, but a kind of box canyon eating its way back into the side of a hill. The entrance was just barely wide enough for a horse and rider to get through, but after a little way it widened out to maybe twenty yards in the widest place. There was a little grass for the horses, but there wasn't any water. Well, I could do without water for a day, and so could the others. Bama wouldn't miss it at all as long as the tequila held out.

So that was where we stayed, and it didn't turn out to be so bad after all. The next day I got my rifle and went out and beat the brush until I scared out a couple of swamp rabbits, and we ate them for supper that night.

The next day Bama's leg began to act up. It began to swell until we had to loosen the bandage around it, and the flesh around the bullet hole had a red, angry look. By the middle of the afternoon little red fingers began crawling away from the wound and down the leg, and I knew what that meant.

But I didn't know what to do about blood poison. And Marta didn't either. All we could do was sit there and watch the fever spread and keep him hopped up on tequila.

But he ran out that night. I heard the empty bottle when it hit the ground and I went over to where he was.

"It's beginning to stink," he said. "In a couple of days it'll turn black and smell like all the cesspools in the world come together." He laughed abruptly. "This is a hell of a way to die, Tall Cameron. But then, I guess there isn't any good way to die, is there?"

"What are you talking about?" I said. "The old man will be here tomorrow with the silver and we'll buy you the best doctor in Mexico."

But I don't think he heard me. "There was a lot of blood poison during the war," he said. "I've seen men rub blisters on their heels and in a few days there would be a surgeon amputating the whole damn leg. I was in a field hospital after the battle of Chickamauga—did I tell you about that?"

"No, I don't think so."

He seemed to forget about the hospital. I rolled a cigarette for him and put it in his mouth. "I've been thinking about the war," he said as I held the match. "I wonder if anything was decided by it. There's a theory that wars are inevitable because the natural blood lust in a man demands them. What do you think about that?"

"I don't know anything about wars."

"But you know about killing. It's the same thing."

"It's not the same thing. Do you want to know how I got a reputation as a gunman? It all started one day in a little town in Texas. A drunk Davis policeman pushed me off the plank walk. A little thing like that. Well, I hit him and that raised a big racket, but Pa managed to get things quieted down, and we thought it would blow over. But then another guy hit a cavalryman, and that made two of us, and the Yankees figured they'd have to do something about it. The first thing I knew, the bluebellies were wanting to put me on the work gang, so I had to light out. The federals came out to our ranch and wanted to know where I was, and when Pa wouldn't tell them they tried to beat it out of him. They killed him."

I hadn't thought that I could ever talk about it without getting crazy with anger, but all that happened a long time ago. It was almost like telling a story about somebody else, some person that I only slightly knew.

"That was the way it started," I said. "I came back home and killed the bluebelly. Then it seemed like everywhere I went people were hunting me. They never learned, goddamn them—they would just make me kill them."

It was quiet for a minute. And Bama was right about one thing—I began to smell it.

"I went back once," I said, "to that place in Texas. It was a crazy thing to do, I guess, but there was a girl there and it seemed like I just had to see her. But I shouldn't have done it. I had teamed up with a famous gunman, Pappy Garret, and got myself a reputation, and things weren't the same any more. She was afraid of me. If I had touched her I think she would have fainted. Anyway, she was going to marry somebody else. I guess I'll never go back again."

I had never told those things to anybody else. I don't know why I told them to Bama, unless maybe it was to get his mind off his leg.

"I wonder," Bama said, "what would have happened if you hadn't run away."

"I would have put in two years on the work gang."

"Would that have been so bad?"

I knew that he was talking about Johnny Rayburn, not me. I got up and went to my own bunk.

It was about two o'clock in the afternoon, and our tongues were beginning to get too big for our mouths, when Marta's old man finally showed up. Around noon I went up on the bluff that formed the south wall of our cave, and there he was, him and his two burros, about three miles away and looking like three bugs crawling up the side of a mountain. He had the silver, all right; I could tell that by the heavy way the burros moved. There was nobody with him, and nobody following him.

"Here he comes," I shouted down to the others. "Johnny, you gather up the horses." Then I went down and we all waited in the mouth of the cave.

The old man was puffing and blowing and the burros were all lathered up as they pulled in. Marta swung onto Papacito's neck and they both began to jabber away in Spanish. I went around punching the big leather pack bags, and they all seemed solid and heavy enough, so I guessed that all the silver was there. Marta had found a canteen somewhere and was swigging from the neck when I came up and took it out of her hands.

"No!" she yelled. "For Marta!"

"It's for all of us," I said.

The kid was coming up with the horses, so I gave him a drink, then I poured a little in my hand and let the horses wet their muzzles. "Get the horses stripped down," I said, "and throw away everything but the saddles and guns. You can start getting those pack bags split up and we'll divide the load between us."

Bama was sitting with his back against a rock as I came up with the canteen. "Have a drink of this," I said.

He turned the canteen up and gulped. His leg didn't look any better. The flesh around the wound was beginning to turn a dark purple, like a deep bruise, and he had that wild look that fever puts in a man's eyes.

When I got the canteen there was about a mouthful of water and some dregs in it. I emptied it and hung it over my shoulder.

"Do you feel like riding?"

He shrugged. He should have been in bed. He should have had a good doctor and a roomful of nurses, and maybe a few preachers to say some prayers. But he was going to ride, because there was nothing else to do.

"How far are we from the border?" I said.

"Only a few miles," he said, "if we go straight south. But we can't go that way. Federal marshals and Mexican soldiers patrol that country. We'll have to ride into the mountains and take one of those canyons that the smuggler trains use."

"How far will it be that way?"

"Fifty miles, maybe. It's pretty rough country, but you have to go the long way around with the load we've got. We wouldn't be much good if it came to a horse race."

Bama was right, as usual. All right, we would go the long way around. Fifty miles wasn't so far. Not for the rest of us, but for Bama it was going to be a long, long trip. Of course, I could lighten our load by leaving Bama behind. It would make things a lot easier for me, and chances were Bama would never last the trip anyway.

But I didn't have the stomach for it. I said, "I'll have the kid bring your horse around and we'll put you in the saddle."

There was one more way to lighten our load, but I was going to wait until the last minute to do it. I went up to the mouth of the cave and helped get the silver loaded. A lot of it we got in the saddle bags, and the rest of it we had to lash on behind the saddles. It was a clumsy way to do it, and the horses could hardly walk, much less run, but I couldn't think of anything better. When we got to Marta's horse I said, "Throw the saddle off of this one."

The kid didn't ask any questions this time. We stripped the horse and loaded the rest of the silver in those pack bags.

I found Marta and her old man just outside the cave having another one of their arguments. Papacito was all blown up with anger and Marta was stamping her foot and spitting. I thought I could guess what the argument was about.

I said, "Shut up for a minute and ask the old man how they're taking it back in Ocotillo."

I guess the sight of me reminded Marta of the silver, and she forgot all about the old man and flashed a smile at me. She turned and spat out the question. The old man answered sullenly, angrily. I had almost forgotten how much he hated me.

"Papacito say much anger in Ocotillo." She cranked her hand by her ear to show how the men felt about losing their silver. Well, to hell with them. Maybe the next time they wouldn't run off when there was a job to be done.

"Ask him if he saw any cavalry," I said. She asked him and shook her head.

Then the kid and Bama rode up, leading my big black and Marta's animal, which we had turned into a pack horse. She didn't get it at first. She just looked surprised, like somebody had pulled the chair from under her. But when I swung up on the black she got it. She started screaming and screeching and clawing, trying to pull me out of the saddle.

"Get out of here," I said to the kid. "Take Bama up in the hills and I'll catch you there." And all the time the girl was yelling her head off and cursing me, I guess, in Spanish. I gave her a kick and sent her reeling against the old man, and Bama and the kid began squeezing their way out of the cave. Before I could get my own horse through, Marta was clawing at me again. I yelled, "Take her, old man! Get her away from me. That's what you want, isn't it?"

That was what he wanted, but he didn't know how to go about it. He tried to pull her away but she wouldn't budge. The first thing I knew, she had snatched a pistol out of my holster and was shoving the muzzle in my face. "No leave Marta!" she yelled. "No leave Marta!" And all the time she was wrestling the hammer back with both hands.

It was no time to play the gentleman. I rammed the steel to my horse and he jumped and knocked the girl rolling in the dust. But she was up like a cat. She ran to the mouth of the cave and stood in front of it, yelling all the time. She pointed that pistol at me again, but by that time I had my black horse right on top of her. The pistol exploded, but she wasn't a very good shot with a thousand pounds of horseflesh pounding down on her like a runaway locomotive. The bullet must have hit a rock somewhere, because I heard the disappointed whine as it shot up toward a million miles of sky. And that was all for Marta.

We went right over her and blasted through the opening, and the only reason she wasn't killed was because horses, unlike people, are naturally neat animals, and they won't put a hoof down where it's likely to get messed up if they can help it. I looked back once and saw that she wasn't really hurt. The old man was standing outside the cave clutching those wooden beads around his neck, and I suppose he was offering a prayer of thanks because I hadn't run off with that wildcat daughter of his. Or, come to think of it, maybe he was just cursing. I know that's what I would have been doing if I had been in his place and had been stuck with a girl like that.

So that was the last I saw of Marta. There she was lying full length in the dust, beating the ground with her fists and shredding the air with screams like a madman tearing a rotten shirt. Good-by, Marta. The black horse fogged it down a slight grade and we headed for the higher hills where Bama and Johnny Rayburn were waiting. After a while I couldn't hear her screams any more.

We didn't travel far that day—about ten miles, maybe, and by that time Bama had taken all the jolting around he could stand. So we unbitted and unpacked in a gully where some water oozed out of a broken rock. The kid helped me get Bama stretched out in the shade, and then I went down and filled the canteen and gave him some water. That was about all I could do.

The trip hadn't done Bama's leg any good. It was getting blacker—almost to the knee now—and the inflamed underflesh reached down beyond that. His face was bloated and spotted with fever, but he cooled off some after we got some water down him, and after a while he went to sleep.

"He ought to have a doctor," the kid said.

"Sure," I said. "Why don't you just ride over the hill and find one?"

His face warmed, but he had his teeth in the idea and he wouldn't turn loose.

"There's a doctor in Tucson."

"There's also a company of cavalry and bevy of U.S. marshals. Besides, it's a three-day ride, and Bama hasn't got that long to go."

"You mean he's going to die?"

He said it as if the idea were new to him. He sounded scared.

Of course he's going to die, I thought. But I didn't say it. I said. "When we get across the border I'll get him a doctor."

"Do they have doctors in Mexico?"

"Well, hell, yes, they have doctors everywhere." But I wasn't so sure about that. Come to think of it, I'd never seen a Mexican doctor. I'd never even heard of one. But then, Bama wasn't going to last that long anyway, and it didn't really make any difference if they had any doctors or not.

Around sundown I went out with my rifle, but there were no rabbits up there in the mountains. We didn't have any supper that night. We built a little fire and sat there looking at it and wishing we had something to cook, but that was as far as it went.

"Do you think Bama will be able to ride tomorrow?" the kid asked.

"He'll have to ride whether he's able or not. We can't just sit here and wait for them to come after us. You don't think that girl's going to waste any time getting her story to the marshal's office, do you?"

That gave him something to think about. Up until now he had just been coming along for the ride. I guess he had never figured on winding up like this, being chased out of the country and being hunted by half the lawmen in Arizona.

I watched him closely, because now was the time to find out if he had the guts it took to face it out. I had taken it for granted that he was the kind of kid that could be some help to me. It came as a shock when I realized that maybe I had guessed wrong.

We sat there for a long time, not saying anything. He knew what he was in for if he stuck with me. If he wanted to get out of it, all he had to do was ride off toward Texas and that would be the end of us.

The stars were very clean and cold and superior that night. The kid lay back and watched them, and maybe he was thinking that those very same stars were shining on that wild piece of Texas brush country that he called home—a place that he might never see again.

It all depended on what he decided. If he wanted to know about guns and how to cut aces from the middle, I was the one who could teach him. If he wanted something else ... Well, that was up to him.

And still we sat. An orange slice of moon came up behind the hills and a coyote came out and barked at it. A slight wind came up and rattled the parched grass. I listened to the thousand little night sounds, and to Bama's labored breathing, and finally the kid got up.

"Well," he said, "if we're going to travel tomorrow I guess I'd better get some sleep."

It took me a few minutes to realize that it was all over. He had thought it over in that slow, deliberate way of his, and he had decided to stay. He had built himself a hero to follow. And I was it.

We traveled about twenty miles the next day before Bama's leg stopped us again. He suddenly dumped out of the saddle and hit the ground, and my first feeling was relief. No sorrow. No regret, or feeling of loss. Only relief, because Bama was finally dead and now we could push across the border.

But I was wrong about Bama. At that moment he was as close to death as a man can get, but he wouldn't die. He lay there clutching like a drowning man at that razor-thin piece of life and he wouldn't let go. For a moment I hated him. He was going to die anyway, so why didn't he do it now while it would do us some good? Why did he have to hold on with that death grip and pull us down with him? I just sat there on my horse, watching, waiting. Die, goddamn you! But he wouldn't turn loose.

"He's bad," Johnny said. "Real bad."

The kid was already out of the saddle, wiping the dust off Bama's flushed face.

Well, that was that. I couldn't just ride off and leave him, so I helped get him back on his horse and we held him in the saddle for a hundred yards or so until we came to a washed-out place in the side of a hill. That was where we laid him out. Then I sent the kid out to look for water.

"Bama."

He didn't say anything. His face got as white as tallow, and it seemed that he would go for minutes at a time without breathing. At last he began to shake, and I knew the chills had started.

The kid came back with the water, but we didn't need it now. We stripped the horses and piled the saddle blankets on top of Bama. We lugged the silver into the wash and staked the horses out. Then we settled down to wait.

Night came finally, and there was no change that I could see. My stomach growled and knotted and ached, and I tried filling it up with water, but that didn't help.

I said, "Get some sleep, kid. When you wake up in the morning it'll be all over."

But it wasn't. Bama was shaking when I went to sleep and he was still shaking when I woke up. When the sun came up I took my rifle out again and this time I came back with two rabbits.

We skinned them and cooked them like the other time. Me and the kid finished them off because Bama couldn't eat. He couldn't do anything except lie there and shake.

The day dragged on somehow, and to pass the time I got to figuring on our chances of getting out of this. I counted up and discovered that about fifty-six hours had gone by since we left Marta and Papacito at Three Mile Cave. Three days gone and we hadn't traveled more than thirty miles at the outside. Three days. Marta could have got the word all the way to Tucson in that length of time. More than likely a detachment of cavalry was already headed south. Under forced march they would be right in our front yard by this time tomorrow.

The future wasn't exactly bright. I made my mind up once to pull out of there, but when the time came to do it I didn't have the guts for it. For one thing, I wasn't at all sure that the kid would be willing to leave Bama and come with me. And, too, I kept remembering Kreyler and Bucky. It was Bama's time that we were living on now.

The next morning Bama began freezing with chills one minute and burning with fever the next. He kept us busy piling blankets on him and then taking them off and putting wet rags on his head. Along toward noon he went to sleep again. The kid walked out in the sun and stood there breathing in deep gulps of clean air. For a moment I thought he was going to be sick.

"Isn't there anything we can do?" he said. "Anything at all?"

"We're doing everything we can."

"But he's going to die, don't you see that?"

There didn't seem to be anything to say after that, so the kid went over and sat on a rock and held his head in his hands. All this was new to him. He had never seen a friend of his die like this before.

I found a rock for myself and sat down, wondering about the cavalry. What if they had already picked up our trail? Well, it was too late to worry about it now. We'd have to shoot it out with them, and if there weren't too many of them maybe we'd have a chance after all. The kid would be a help. He was good enough with a rifle, he had already proved that in the smuggler raid. And thinking of that made me feel better. We'd fight our way out of it somehow, just the two of us.

I don't know just when it was that those thoughts turned on me, but suddenly I found myself thinking, And then what?

There would be more cavalry, and more U.S. marshals, and you couldn't go on killing them forever. Where was it going to end?

It doesn't happen often, but once or twice in a lifetime a man takes a look at himself and sees himself as he really is, and I guess that was what I did then. I knew where it would end. In a deadwood saloon with a bullet in my back, the way the end had come to Hickok. Over a dice table, the way it had come to Hardin. Or on a lonesome Texas hilltop, where Pappy Garret's career had ended. Not even Pappy had been able to go on forever.

And what about the kid? What about that girl of his, and that little cocklebur ranch that he was so set on?

That, I suppose, was the way my mind was running when the kid spoke. I didn't hear what he said, and it wasn't important anyway, because I was thinking of something else. Then he spoke again and I stood up and said:

"I wish to hell you'd stop whining." My voice was hard and full of anger, and the kid looked as if I had just hit him across the face with a pistol barrel. He didn't understand what I was mad at. And he wasn't alone. Neither did I.

"There's one thing you'd better understand," I said. "If you're not willing to take the hard bumps when they come, then we'd better split up here and now."

That outburst kind of knocked the wind out of him, I guess, because he just sat there with his mouth open. He groped around for words, but this was a situation that he had never even thought about and he couldn't find any words to fit it. I said, "You've done nothing but complain. Not that I expect much out of you, because I haven't had time to teach you anything. But guts come natural, and if you haven't got them you're no good to me or anybody else."

He closed his mouth finally and stared at me with bugging eyes.

He said hoarsely, "I didn't mean to complain. If I was doing it I didn't know it."

"You didn't know it," I said. "You don't know anything, and that's the whole trouble."

Something had gone wrong, but he couldn't understand it. He stood up and wiped his face and shifted from one foot to the other. "Well," he said, "I know I'm pretty green. But I can learn—you said so yourself."

"Maybe I was wrong. I've been wrong before."

He shuffled around some more, putting his hands in his pockets and taking them out. He walked around in a little circle, still not able to understand what had happened. "Maybe," he said, "I got things all mixed up. I thought all along that you were glad to have me ride with you. I thought we were going to be—well, partners. Something like that."

"You thought we were going to be partners," I said dryly, and his face turned beet-red. Then he stopped his marching around and really looked at me for the first time.

"I guess I was jumping at conclusions," he said after a long pause. "I had kind of a crazy idea that you liked me."

"I like you well enough, but that doesn't mean that I want to take you to raise."

He took it all right until then. But now he started to burn. His face started to cloud up and his mouth clamped down to a grim line.

"If I was being so much trouble," he said tightly, "why did you let me ride this far with you?"

"I do crazy things sometimes. I guess everybody does."

At last he began to get it.

"Are you trying to tell me that you don't want me around any more?" he said. "Is that it?"

I said, "That's it."

And that tore it open. He hadn't believed that a crazy thing like this could happen, for no reason at all. But it finally sank in. For a long moment he just stood there staring at me like a backwoods nester looking at a circus freak.

Then he turned and walked stiffly to the wash. He came back with his saddle over his shoulder and headed down to where the horses were grazing.

It was all over. And the whole thing was almost as much a mystery to me as it was to the kid. I needed him. He was my life insurance. And now he was going.

I stood there on a knoll watching him cinch up, wondering how I was going to fight off a detachment of cavalry by myself. After a while he got the saddle on to suit him and he rode up to where I was.

"Well," he said, "I guess this is good-by, Mr. Cameron. No hard feelings."

"No hard feelings," I said. "Part of that silver is still yours."

"I don't want the silver," he said.

He started to pull away and I happened to think of something else. "Where do you aim to go, kid?"

"Back to Texas," he said without turning around.

Back to the work gang. Back to that wind-swept, thorn-daggered land where strong men broke their hearts scrabbling around for a kind of living. Back home.

"Well, good-by, kid."

But he didn't hear me. He rode straight over a rise and dipped out of sight. And that was the last I saw of him. It was hard to believe that just a few minutes ago both of us had been sitting here waiting for the end. Now there were just me and Bama—and, the crazy thing about it was that I wasn't sorry.

I stood there for a long time trying to understand why I had deliberately sent him away. He was sure to wind up on the work gang—but then, there were worse things than a work gang. Maybe that was the answer. I waited until I was sure that he was well in the hills, and then I went back to the wash.

"Bama."

The fever had gone from his face and left it weak and flabby, like the face of a very old man. I felt that my face must look something like that. He opened his eyes and I got the canteen and dribbled water between his lips.

"How do you feel?"

He moved his shoulders just a little in the barest hint of a shrug.

"Your fever's gone," I said. "You're going to be all right in a day or two."

But I wasn't fooling anybody. The sickening smell of rotten flesh still hung heavily over the wash. Bama worked his mouth a few times, licking his cracked lips.

"Why don't you go?" he said. "You and the kid. You can still make it if you go now."

"The kid's not here," I said.

He fumbled that around in his mind.

"Where is he?"

"Headed for Texas," I said. I was suddenly tired of thinking about it and talking about it. "What difference does it make? He's old enough to have a mind of his own." I got up and paced the wash. "He can go clear to hell as far as I'm concerned."

Bama didn't say anything. He just lay there with those wide, staring eyes watching me as I marched up and down.

"Well, what are you looking at?"

But he only gave that whisper of a shrug again. "Did you tell him to go?"

"Sure, I told him to go. I was goddamn sick and tired of looking at his stupid face."

Bama closed his eyes again, as if the conversation had worn him out. He lay there for a minute, half-smiling, or grimacing in pain. I couldn't tell which.

"Have you got a cigarette?"

I built a cigarette out of the last of my makings, put it in his mouth, and fired it.

"I guess I never knew you, Tall Cameron," he said. "Several times I thought I did, but about that time you always did the unexpected."

"What is that supposed to mean?"

"Nothing. Not a thing." He dragged on the cigarette, burning it quickly to his lips, and then he spat it out. "You've got to get out of here," he said. "Take the horses and silver and try to make it to the border. There's no sense in your staying here. Nothing is going to help me now."

"Nothing's going to help you if you don't shut up. Now, try to get some sleep."

He lay there for a while with his eyes closed and I thought that he had gone to sleep. Then he said, "I wonder if she ever married."

"What the hell are you talking about?"

But that was all he said. And pretty soon he went to sleep again.

I squatted down in the wash and listened to his breathing, coming strong for a while and then almost stopping completely. He was a crazy sort of galoot and I had never understood him any more than he had understood me. I had hated him and liked him in spells. There was no foolishness about him. He saw himself as he really was—not just rarely, like most people, but all the time. Except maybe when he was drunk.

I unholstered my off-hand gun—Marta had the other one—and wiped it clean with my shirttail. Then I punched out the cartridges and wiped them clean and put them back in the cylinder. I couldn't help wondering about the cavalry. They must be somewhere in the neighborhood by now. Marta must have told them the direction we had headed.

I climbed out of the wash and got my rifle and began cleaning it off the way I had the pistol. I went down and got the horses and picketed them there in the draw where they would be out of sight. Once again the thought crossed my mind that I ought to get out of there. But it just wasn't in me to let Bama die by himself. He had lived by himself. That seemed to be enough.

It was then, I guess, that I first heard it. Or I thought I did. Maybe I just felt it. I listened hard and there was nothing but the sound of wind. But that feeling was there.

I saddled the black horse, and holstered the rifle, then I rode as quietly as I could up to a hogback ridge just east of our wash. When I got near the crest I crawled the rest of the way to the top and looked over. Sure enough, there they were, the United States Cavalry.

There were eight of them about four or five hundred yards down the slope, and they had got together for a pow-wow, trying to decide which way to go, I guess. The lieutenant was pointing toward the ridge, and the sergeant was pointing to the south; and then they both dismounted and put their noses to the ground, looking for sign.

The wind must have blown most of the sign away, because they still looked pretty undecided when they climbed back on their horses. Then they did what I was afraid they were going to do. They spread out to scour the whole area. I got the lieutenant in the sights of my rifle once, but about that time the wind changed, and by the time I made the changes in sighting he had ridden around the side of a hill. Well, it was just as well. I would only have brought the other seven troopers down on me. The best thing to do was to go back to the wash, where I had a good line of defense, and make my stand there.

So that was what I did. I got that black horse in the draw and wrapped his forelegs and made him lie down. I picked out a place about a dozen yards from Bama. And there I stood, waiting for them to find me and come after me.

It seemed like a long time, but I guess it wasn't. I stood there and looked at the hills to the west and wondered what was behind them. It never occurred to me that I could get on my horse and find out, while the cavalry was still scattered out. I heard a sound behind me then and I thought Bama had waked up and was wondering what was going on.

"Bama."

No sound.

"Bama, are you awake?"

Still no sound, except that of the wind coming down the canyon. I left my position and went over to where he was. "It looks like we've got a fight on our hands," I said. "I just spotted some cavalry over behind the ridge. They're spread out now, but I guess one of them will find us before long."

He didn't say anything. He lay there with his eyes wide open, staring up at the sky. I knelt beside him and took his pulse. There was no beat, not even a flutter. His chest was quiet. He was perfectly still. After a while it dawned on me that Bama was dead.

I don't know what I did next. I think I got up and fumbled around for the makings of a cigarette, and finally I remembered that Bama had used the last of the tobacco. I must have stood there for quite a while, and I had a queer, uncomfortable feeling that Bama had died just as a personal favor to me. A thought kept nudging the back of my brain, warning me to get out of there. There was no reason to stay any longer. Bama was dead. You can't help a dead man.

But I was in no particular hurry. I wondered if I ought to try to dig a grave for him. But I didn't have anything to work with, and anyway, the cavalry would dig him right up again when they found him. Finally I took off my neckerchief and spread it over his face.

Well, so long, Bama. This isn't much of a send-off, but it's the best I can do.

Then I noticed that pile of silver. It wasn't going to help me, or Johnny Rayburn, or Bama, or anybody else. The kid didn't want it, Bama couldn't use it now, and I sure couldn't take it with me if I meant to outrun the cavalry. Poetic justice, I think they call it. The funny thing about it was that I didn't care.

I got my horse out of the draw and stripped everything off him except the saddle and rifle. I walked over to Bama again, still feeling that there was something I ought to do. If I knew any prayers, Bama, I thought, I'd say one for you. But I didn't know any. There's the Lord's Prayer, I thought. Everybody knows that. But when I started on it I got bogged down in the first line and had to stop. I was wasting precious time, but still I had a feeling that somebody ought to say a few words over him, and I sure couldn't depend on the cavalry to do it. So finally I said:

"Well, rest in hell, Bama. Amen."

Then I got on my horse and rode west.

It surprised me, I guess, as much as it did the troopers, when I got away with it. I rode out of the draw and into the hills, with the soldiers beating the brush all around. Once I got a few miles away, I was safe—for a day or two, anyway. That silver was going to keep the cavalry busy for a while, when they finally found it, and by the time they got around to thinking about me I would be somewhere else.

There was no use heading for Mexico, though. Without money Mexico was no good. Maybe I could head north, where everybody was too busy fighting Indians to pay any attention to me. Maybe I'd try to get to Wyoming or someplace like that.

But that was a long way off, and I was just beginning to realize how sick and tired I was of running. And maybe that explains the crazy thing I did that same night.

A thing like that builds up in your mind, I suppose, and grows and grows without your knowing it. Then at last it breaks as clear as a summer day, and you know what you have to do.

I still remember that night sometimes, pitch-black and the chill of the mountains coming down. But still I had to keep running. My horse almost went over the edge of the bluff before I saw the emptiness looming in front of us. He took a step forward and skittered, and I heard rocks and gravel begin to fall away into a black nothingness. My stomach curled up like a prodded sow bug and I tried to get braced for the sickening plunge.

But that horse had more sense than I had. He reared and wheeled and his forefeet slammed solid earth. We were safe then, but it was a close thing and it took something out of me. I climbed out of the saddle and wiped the sweat off my face. I was scared. Pretty soon I stopped being scared and got mad.

Nobody but a damn fool would try to cross country like this at night—and maybe that's just what I was, a damn fool. And finally I guess I got it through my head that it was time to do something about it.

What I did was to take my pistol and throw it as hard as I could over the bluff, and I listened and listened and after what seemed an hour I heard it hit. Then I scooped the .44 ammunition out of my saddlebags and heaved it into the darkness. And after it was all over I stood there panting as if I had just come through a long spell of sickness.

Maybe it was a fool thing, throwing my pistol away like that, as though by a single act I could throw off everything that was bad. But that pistol was a part of me. And I didn't want it any more. A doctor cuts off a leg when it's rotten. It was the same thing. It was with me, anyway. I felt naked without it, but I wasn't sorry it was gone.

The rifle I kept in the saddle holster. A rifle is a defensive weapon, a tool for getting food. It isn't the same as a pistol and it can't get to be a part of you the way a pistol can.

I stood for a long time in the darkness, thinking about it. I half expected to start cursing myself for an idiot as soon as the heat wore off. But I didn't. Without that gun I would never have killed the first man. I'd never have been on the run. Maybe I would have had that ranch in Texas like Johnny Rayburn would have someday. Maybe...

But it was too late for a lot of things. Maybe too late for anything. For all I knew, the cavalry was just a hop and a skip behind me, and the important thing was to keep running.

Keep running. It didn't have the same sound that it once had. The feeling of urgency wasn't there any more. I got back in the saddle and the black horse started marching off into the darkness, just as if there were a place out there somewhere that he knew about—a place where we could stop and rest and live like a man and a horse are supposed to live. It was a crazy idea. We kept traveling.

THE END

Clifton Adams Bibliography
(1919-1971)

Crime:

Whom Gods Destroy (1953)

Death's Sweet Song (1955)

As by Jonathan Gant

Never Say No to a Killer (1956)

The Long Vendetta (1963)

As by Nick Hudson

The Very Wicked (1960)

Westerns:

The Desperado (1950)

A Noose for the Desperado (1951)

The Colonel's Lady (1952)

Two-Gun Law (1954)

Gambling Man (1955)

Law of the Trigger (1956)

Outlaw's Son (1957)

Killer in Town (1959)

Stranger in Town (1960)

The Legend of Lonnie Hall (1960)

Day of the Gun (1962)

Reckless Men (1962)

The Moonlight War (1963)

Hogan's Way (1963)

The Dangerous Days of Kiowa Jones (1963)

Doomsday Creek (1964)

The Hottest Fourth of July in the History of Hangtree County (1964)

The Grabhorn Bounty (1965)

Shorty (1966)

A Partnership With Death (1967)

The Most Dangerous Profession (1967)

Dude Sheriff (1969)

Tragg's Choice (1969)

The Last Days of Wolf Garnett (1970)

Biscuit-Shooter (1971)

Rogue Cowboy (1971)

The Badge and Harry Cole (1972; as Lawman's Badge, UK, 1973)

Concannon (1972)

Hard Times and Arnie Smith (1972)

Once an Outlaw (1973)

The Hard Time Bunch (1973)

Hassle and the Medicine Man (1973)

As by Matt Kinkaid

Hardcase (1953)

The Race of Giants (1956)

As by Clay Randall

Six-Gun Boss (1952)

When Oil Ran Red (1953)

Boomer (1957)

The Oceola Kid (1963)

Hardcase for Hire (1963)

Amos Flagg—Lawman (1964)*

Amos Flagg—High Gun (1965)*

Amos Flagg Rides Out (1967)*

Amos Flagg—Bushwacked (1967)*

Amos Flagg Has His Day (1968; reprinted as The Killing of Billy Jowett, 1973)*

Amos Flagg—Showdown (1969)*

Amos Flagg series

Classic hardboiled fiction from the King of the Paperbacks...

Harry Whittington

A Night for Screaming / Any Woman He Wanted
$19.95 978-1-933586-08-3
"[*A Night for Screaming*] is pure Harry. The damned thing is almost on fire, it reads so fast." — Ed Gorman, *Gormania*

To Find Cora / Like Mink Like Murder / Body and Passion
$23.95 978-1-933586-25-0
"Harry Whittington was the king of plot and pace, and he could write anything well. He's 100 percent perfect entertainment." — Joe R. Lansdale

Rapture Alley / Winter Girl / Strictly for the Boys
$23.95 978-1-933586-36-6
"Whittington was an innovator, often turning archetypical characters and plots on their head, and finding wild new ways to tell stories from unusual angles." — Cullen Gallagher, *Pulp Serenade*

A Haven for the Damned
$9.99 978-1-933586-75-5
"A wild, savage romp and pure Whittington: raw noir that has the feel of a Jim Thompson novel crossed with a Russ Meyer film." — Brian Greene, *The Life Sentence*. Black Gat #1.

Trouble Rides Tall / Cross the Red Creek / Desert Stake-Out
$21.95 978-1-944520-11-3
"If these three Whittington novels are the only westerns crime fiction fans ever read, they will have experienced some of the best the genre has to offer." — Alan Cranis, *Bookgasm*

"Harry Whittington delivers every time." — Bill Crider

STARK HOUSE

Stark House Press, 1315 H Street, Eureka, CA 95501
griffinskye3@sbcglobal.net / www.StarkHousePress.com
Available from your local bookstore, or order direct or via our website.